SEASIDE MERGERS BOOK ONE

Terms of Inheritance

ADORABOL
HUCKLEBY-ORDAZ

Paperback ISBN: 979-8-9873688-0-0
E-Book ISBN: 979-8-987-3688-1-7

Theme Song

"Let it Be Mine" – Brett Young

To my third-grade field trip at the library and that first book about a princess in a boarding school. You opened a door that can never be closed.

Chapter One

CLEMENTINE

Blue lights surrounded me, even though the room was dark. Muffled sounds both engulfed and buried me in the hustle of the moment. People spoke to me but I didn't listen. I didn't even pretend to listen. Not like I used to. Not when the only thing I could think, to hope was, *I'm free.*

Hope was something I hadn't clung to in a long, long while. Freedom. That was something I'd never thought I'd see the possibility of again. But as I sat there, huddled up in the carpeted corner of my husband's bedroom surrounded by lights and cops and noises, I dared that hope.

My husband was dead.

My captor. My tormentor. My demon. He was gone. And I could suddenly breathe again. Ragged, labored, uneven breaths, but breath nonetheless.

I never thought, never *dreamed* of this happening in a hundred years. Not in a million. But it was true, he was gone. In the most sudden way possible, he was gone and done with. A man so big in my eyes, so daunting, that he'd stolen the very breath from my lungs and the very hope from my soul.

"Clementine."

My name registered in my ears like a shot to the head. I jerked upon hearing it, rearing violently back to the present. To reality.

I was sitting on the floor of my husband's room in his Seaside estate in nothing but a nightgown. And that husband, monster that he was, was lying dead in his bed. The bed I had been making my way to on-time and ready like I always did. Like I'd always been ordered to do. But this time was different.

Usually, even though Ron was old and evil and mean, when I arrived at his door at exactly midnight, he was ready for me.

Waiting for me.

I would expect nothing less for his favorite obedient pet.

This time, when I knocked on his door the allotted two times I had learned were the most agreeable to him, I didn't hear the grumble of his weathered voice telling me to come in. I waited, then contemplated leaving after I knocked again. Two delicate wraps, just as he liked, but still he hadn't answered. Even though I assumed he could have fallen asleep, a rare occurrence but not impossible, assuming had gotten me in trouble before.

So instead, I turned the gold foil knob leading to my least favorite room in the entire house. When I did, I stepped in and was assaulted by a foul smell I had never smelled before. Coppery, thick, and pungent. I wanted to gag, and to leave.

But prior conditioning forced me to step further into the room.

Long, dark curtains spilled from the tops of the floor-to-ceiling windows. Windows which were open and pouring in moonlight from the sea facing landscape beyond. It was hard to see the beach in the darkness of midnight, but I heard the rolling waves clearly. We were that close. They seemed to crash and land much more violently than usual.

They seemed to be warning me.

The room was big. Big enough that the rest of the furniture, all dark mahogany and old ancestral wood, was pushed up against the walls, not visible in the night dark shadows of the room. The bed was the only thing visible in the moonlight.

The bed, and what was *on* the bed.

Ronaldo José Fernandez lay in the middle. Centered, because God forbid he makes room for anyone else by his side, even when he was expecting them. Naked, because he was a man of habit and had been expecting his pet to show up when called. And dead. From the looks of his blue lips, wide-open eyes, and mess of a face, he'd either choked to death or... Or something else.

When I realized Ron wasn't playing games—and that yes, that really was blood and vomit leaking out of his mouth and onto his chest—I couldn't tell you what emotions went through me exactly. There was fear, shock, and maybe even elation.

But there was also something else.

Something that caused me to move even further into the room to inspect. I had only taken two soft steps forward before lifting onto my pale painted toes to peer down at him. And there he lay, so dead, I didn't even need to move closer to confirm. *I knew.*

My eyes caught on the windows. More specifically, the openness of the windows and how Ron, my husband, was *dead.* It was possible from the looks of him that he'd choked or had a stroke or suffered some other thing that a man in his mid-seventies could so easily suffer. But Ron was in good health. So, it was also possible that someone had come in through the window and killed him somehow.

And for all I knew, they could be here waiting around to kill me too.

3

Panic started to creep in.

Fast, *so fast*, I fled the scene. I hadn't wanted to get caught up in any suspicion. I hardly had any prints around the room, save for the bed, and I wouldn't be adding any more tonight.

Down the long tan hallway, I reached my room quickly and grabbed my phone from a drawer beside my bed. It was charged but turned off. I found little use for phones these days, not being allowed to contact anyone anyway. But, once the small thing powered up, one of the few contacts that hadn't been blocked from me glared bright in my eyes.

With shaking fingers, I dialed it.

"911, what's your emergency?" A too cheery voice chirped through the receiver.

"Hello?" My voice came out scratchy and underused. I didn't talk much anymore and not just because I didn't use my phone. Aside from saying, "Yes Ron," and "Please Ron," I was not required to say anything that couldn't be conveyed by a nod or gesture. So, when I spoke into the phone, I spoke as if I hadn't used my voice in years rather than the five or six months between visits from Ron's friends where I was usually required to play the dutiful wife. "Hello. I think there's someone in my house."

"Ma'am, do you think you're in immediate danger?" she asked, her cheeriness disappearing.

"Yes."

"Is anyone injured?"

"Yes," I said. I looked around my room, my closed window coming into view and then my open door. Moving quickly, I used maybe a little too much force to shut it, clicking the latch of the lock shut. "My husband is dead."

All business now, the woman said, "What's your address ma'am?"

I gave her what little information I knew. I told her the address of Ron's estate, located off the smooth edges of the middle coast Rhode Island slice of beach he owned. I gave her my report on how I'd found him, laying in a mess of his own fluids, and I gave her the truth about what I knew of the potential intruder.

Does anyone else have access to the house? She'd asked. And I told her another truth. *Everyone has access to come in, I'm just not allowed out.*

In telling her everything she needed to know, I hoped she could pay me a service in return. Because it wasn't until I had told another person that my demon was dead, that I finally felt a sliver of hope. "Are you able to contact someone for me?"

That's how I found myself huddled into the corner of my husband's bedroom. Cops had populated the entire circular drive of the pale stone estate. They had needed to dispatch *four teams* just to cover the house, not to mention the investigative bureau sent in to question me.

They found nothing in the—not one, but *three*—searches around the house and grounds. And they questioned me for so long I felt my voice practice itself back to life, only to wear back to nothing by the time they were done. The scene had been marked, prints had been taken, and I had been ruled out as a suspect. Or at least a *primary* suspect.

Hearing my name being called for maybe the umpteenth time in the span of a few hours, I immediately prepared to launch into my story once more.

Until I realized the person, whoever they were, had called me by my name. Not *Mrs. Fernandez* as the detectives insisted on calling me and not *Tiney*[1], like the people I was waiting for would call me.

"Clementine?" The voice called out to me again. I recognized this time that it was deep and close.

I jerked, but my back was already against the wall so I had nowhere else to go. Instead, I pulled my legs up to my chest. *All* the way to my chest, not caring if whatever I had (or hadn't) pulled on underneath the nightgown was on display.

---

[1] Tiney: /tie-nee/

5

I tried to see, but I couldn't see past thoughts of blood and cages and the fact that the lock to my cell was just within my reach. It was a terrifying and invigorating feeling that consumed me whole. There was roaring in my ears and a heavy throbbing in my throat. My gut felt like liquid and acid, and my hands were sweating cold. Cold as I was, I was sweating everywhere. My forehead, my neck, even my arms and back.

"Clementine." The low, calm lull tingled in my ears again and I jerked my head in that direction, still unseeing. "Come here."

That sound. That voice. It wasn't the voice of my brothers, or my father. It wasn't the voice of the detectives or even the police deputies who had been running around all night. Morning? Whatever.

This voice was new and somehow...

I blinked.

And I blinked again.

One more time. This time long and hard and slow. I *needed* to see. I couldn't afford to be blind anymore. When I opened my eyes, I saw dark, dark eyes looking back at me. Deep and black and pensive.

"Did you hear me?" the deep voice, that I now associated with a blurry pink mouth and those deep dark eyes, asked me. When he spoke again, it was slower, as if he were repeating himself. "Clementine, you have just been released. They have no more questions for you. Let's go downstairs."

I hardly think I breathed as he continued to stare at me, his eyes roving over my face. I made no move to get up. He made no move toward me. "Will you come with me?"

I shook my head slowly. *I needed to be smart.*

"Your brothers are here," he said slowly but matter-of-factly. As if he *knew* that would mean something to me. Who was he? And how did he know me? I let my eyes leave his and roam over his person, cataloging what stood in front of me.

A large man. Tall, lean, and muscular from the looks of his forearms. He was crouched before me, his arms resting on his knees. Deep olive skin stretched over his features. Short, dark hair spiked in multiple different directions, full and healthy and obviously tousled from sleep and maybe a nervous hand. Stubble graced his jawline, a jawline that was sharp, chiseled, and handsome. And those eyes. What were those eyes trying to do to me? Staring right at me with such intensity that, if I had been capable of it at the time, I'd start to squirm under their scrutiny.

He squatted back on his haunches a few feet from me. A respectable amount of distance. The gesture was small, minuscule even, but I appreciated it.

That respect was what finally allowed me to move my head in a nodding motion.

"Will you come with me to see your brothers?" he asked again, and I continued to nod. A short breath left him and he gave a curt nod before placing his hands onto his knees and pushing himself up.

And up, and up.

Scrambling, I got myself to my feet before he could offer his help. Before he could touch me.

And I kept scrambling. Lurching myself in front of him and scuttling a good distance away as I stalked out of the now suffocating room. In the hall, the noise of the scene immediately fell away, and so did this overwhelming buzz of anxiety.

Still, panic remained over me. The sense of no control and no vision of the future was daunting, but just being out of that room was…nice.

I let out a long breath.

"Do you have a robe?" That voice asked from behind me. Was it being rude or not? I couldn't tell. It was short and to the point, but still…

I looked over my shoulder, minutely pleased to see that he was still trailing me from far behind. He was tall. *I* was tall, and he towered over me, so he was *tall*. Which meant he could have caught up to me, but he didn't. He'd given me my space. I appreciated that. So maybe that's why, instead of glaring, I simply shook my head and continued down the hall.

7

"Alright. Your brothers are downstairs. I'll give you all a minute," he stated, then walked away.

The night gown I chose must have really been short, or scandalous, because as soon as I made my way down the long half-moon staircase and into the large open kitchen, the boys (my brothers) stripped off their jackets and hoodies and thrusted them at me, telling me to cover up.

I did, figuring it was easier to comply than to insist I wasn't cold. I took a seat in a low chair around the little breakfast nook tucked into the side of the kitchen. I knew they didn't miss the way I'd shied away from touching them, hugging them. But they didn't comment.

Clint, the oldest Ferguson and the most...*Ferguson* of us all— straight-forward, haughty, and dull—leaned against the countertops near the sink. His long, thin arms, naturally a milky dark brown color, lay folded loosely across his middle. His textured hair faded and wavy. He stood eying me, a prominent frown etched on his face. He was always frowning, so I didn't delude myself into thinking it was because of me.

Connor, big as he was, stood tucked into a far corner of the room. Silent and stone faced. Who knew what he was thinking. Who ever knew?

And Clay.

Clay, Clay, Clay.

I could have shaken my head at the sight of him. Tall, broad, chiseled, and *mean*. He stood in the dead center of the room, directly in line with me, his feet spread shoulder width apart, his arms crossed high over his chest. He stood there and stared me down.

Clay looked the least like the rest of us. Despite our mixed heritage of black and Hispanic, the boys and I had always looked more black than anything, taking after my mother in color. I was the darkest and

8

Clay, who took largely after our Mexican papa, was the lightest. He had an almost golden hue to his skin, as it shined in the light of the kitchen, tattooed ink popping off spots along his arms. The only features that tied him directly to us were his curly hair and his trademark Ferguson eyes. Eyes that cut into me as he glared.

He spoke first. "Did you do it?"

My gaze flickered up to his, unsurprised by his question. A flash of deep blackish red against pale skin flared through my mind, sightless unseeing eyes still showing terror and surprise. A shiver racked me and I crossed my long arms around my torso, shaking my head.

"You're skinny." That was Clinton, still unmoved from his spot at the sink. Still beaming me through slitted eyes. I shrugged. "*Too skinny,*" he elaborated coldly. I shrugged again.

"Why call us, Tiney?" Brash as Clay was to ask why I called my own brothers after the possible murder of my husband, I found the corner of my mouth twitching. But my shoulders still dropped. How could I even explain this?

"Who else could I call?"

"After five years?" He pressed, those arms going tighter around himself. "Five years in the dark, Tiney."

I swallowed but somehow it still left my throat dry. Looking left, I ran my eyes over the dark living area that was connected to the kitchen. Sleek furniture filled the room, paintings lined the walls, and whatever other details that made a home filled in the spaces between. Looking right, I found the rest of the kitchen, now occupied by Fergusons. It held the stainless-steel refrigerator, various mahogany cabinets and cupboards, and a dedicated area for coffees and tea.

The space was clear of police officers, of detectives, of strange men who didn't seem to belong to either group and...of him. So, I slowly brought myself to my feet and picked up the phone I had brought with me "just in case". I twisted my palm up and offered the small device over to Clay.

Without uncrossing his arms, he slid his gaze down to it and back up to my eyes. Confusion shone through his hard expression. I offered my hands up higher, nudging the device further toward him.

"Are you planning on speaking more than once every five minutes?" Clint, now beside me, clipped. I shrugged, still holding the phone up to Clay.

Suspiciously, he swiped it from me and turned it in his hands. I moved to return to my seat while the boys moved forward to crowd Clay's shoulders. I didn't need to watch to know what they'd find.

No contacts, save for Ron, the hair stylist, and the doctor whom I saw frequently because, *'what was wrong with me to not be pregnant after so long'*, right? If they tried to dial in their numbers manually, the phone would ring but their own phones would not. If they tried to save their numbers and unblock their caller IDs, the new contact would disappear outright. If they tried to dial a number Ron hadn't prepared for, something brand new, an alarm would start to blare from the receiver, letting Ron know I was trying to run.

He let 911 stay accessible for both selfish and sadistic reasons. If I called the police and tried to weasel myself out from under his grasp, he knew enough people that anything incriminating that was reported could be brushed under the rug. Also, Ron had no illusions that he was getting any younger. If something were to happen to him, much like it had tonight, someone would need to call for help. And if Ron had lived tonight and later found out that it hadn't been me to call for help… Not good.

Clay must have tried at least a few of these options because that long loud siren-like noise blared out the bottom of the phone. This earned me a glaring look from my brothers, even Connor, as they held it away from themselves and poked at it to make it stop. It wouldn't stop, not until I went upstairs to his office and opened that damn bottom drawer in his desk.

I didn't have the energy to do that. Instead, I said, "Just turn it off."

They did, their heads appearing to be on a chain link as they peered down at the device and then slowly back up at me with warring expressions.

Clint was analytical, eyes tracking over every detail, ears perked to every noise.

Clay was temperamental, always quick to act with his emotions first, his sense only catching up retroactively.

And Connor was wary. The slowest to trust but the most unwavering in his loyalty once he does.

Just like they had always been. But something had changed between them. Something in their dynamic, in the way they let Clay speak while they just flanked him. It confused me. Clint had always easily fit into the mold of oldest child and successor. Always taking charge and taking care. Had he stepped away from that?

The thought brought my eyes to him. He was already watching me, his gaze traveling slowly over my person. Over my face, my arms, my legs, my feet; eyes sharp, suspicious, and judgmental. He held my gaze for one, two, three long seconds before he let them flick down to his younger brother and said one word. *Demanded* it.

"*Clay.*"

"What the hell does this mean, Tiney?" Clay asked me, voice growing agitated as he finally got the blaring to seize.

My eyes still laid on Clinton, impressed. He hadn't stepped away from anything. He'd just delegated. I could have smiled, could have appreciated him for all his growth, if only it didn't remind me that I hadn't been there to see it for years.

"Tiney?" Clay snapped impatiently.

I looked at him.

And looked and looked.

I saw a muscle in his jaw begin to tick, irritation showing under the surface of his sour face. But I could do this all day. Even before Ron, I could. Clint must have been the only one to remember this, because he

11

interjected, playing peacemaker.

"Tine, tell us." His voice didn't get softer by any degree, but something about his tone caught me up. Something in his voice revealed it was less of the demand and more of a...plea. They wanted to know what had happened to me?

Now, they wanted to know who they had sold me to?

Well, they wanted to know too damn late. I let that show in my voice as I answered. "No contact with anyone except Ronaldo, a fertility specialist, and whatever groomer he's hired for the week. No wandering outside unless with him. No physical activities that might 'hurt me'. No other activities that Ronaldo found unfit. No visitors, no outings, no nothing. Nothing but *screwing* him. Every morning and every night and sometimes during the day when he's had a little too much to drink. No thinking for myself, no breathing too much of my own air, no silly little books or propaganda to plant silly ideas into my brain. Nothing. At all. But him. Him and this house."

"Jesus." This was Clinton again who was stalking away from the boys and beginning to pace.

Clay had gone stony and a little paler, my phone growing smaller in his hand as he curled his fist around it. His eyes were distant, far away, most likely mentally beating something, or someone, up. With Clint pacing, like he hadn't ever thought me falling off the face of the earth for five whole years meant a cause for concern, and with Clay concocting another reason to hit something, it could only be Connor's quiet eyes I felt on me.

He moved toward me, and my eyes flashed. My shoulders reared reflexively, causing him to halt and our eyes to lock. Slowly, he raised his hands up, showing me his palms. Surrendering.

"He touch you?" He growled. My face must have portrayed something like smartass sarcasm because he let his eyes flick over me again, his hands falling to his sides. "*Fists*, Tiney. Did he hit you?"

I shook my head. A look passed between him and my other brothers that portrayed something I must have missed in our earlier conversation. Some discussion they must have been having without me. *About me.* I watched carefully, sweat pricking the back of my neck.

I felt…I didn't know how I felt.

It was good to see my brothers. To see their faces, more grown up into men than I thought they could be. Their frames large and imposing and healthy. But it was also hard to think of anything past my current situation. I could still see blue lights in my periphery. I'm pretty sure if I wasn't holding my hands together on my lap, they would have been shaking. And I knew in the pit of my stomach, it was fear I was feeling.

Finally, I caved and asked, "What is it?"

Clint stepped forward, one hand going to his hip and the other rubbing at the back of his head.

"We can't take you, Tine. There's no direct breach of contract," he said, regret dripping from his every word.

I felt sick. I shot to my feet but my body didn't agree with the motion. My knees gave out, and I faltered, my hip landing against the hard surface of the table. I slapped a hand down to steady myself, bowing my head.

The contract. The damn contract. The piece of fucking paper that signed my life, my youth, and my freedom away. Even after I told my family I had been kept as a glorified *sex pet* for the last five years, the contract was still intact.

But what the hell did that mean when the bastard was dead?

Dark eyes flashed in my mind and I felt my body move before I even wrapped my mind around it. I whipped around, my head spinning but not caring. I looked to my brothers, who all looked as if they had their tails tucked between their legs, or as much as my prideful brothers could. My head fell into the cradle of my hands.

Five years of solitary confinement, one night of trauma, and a lifetime of being treated as a bargaining chip and somehow, someway, I was still under obligation of a contract. I could've screamed. If I could

13

find my voice, I *would've* screamed. But all sound caught in my throat as it started to throb and my breaths began to thicken.

I had to think.

They wouldn't just leave me here at the scene of his death, would they? They couldn't. Realization was like a freight train as it crashed through me. I looked at each of them standing in front of me, but I let my eyes settle on Clay. He would tell me like it is, no bullshit.

"Who is he?" I croaked out as a vision of eyes so onyx black that they resembled granite flashed in my mind. Somehow, my body knew something my mind didn't yet, because it started to shake. Rejecting this reality with everything I was.

"His name is Oaxaca Fernandez[2]," Clay spoke, staring me down. "He's his grandson."

Well, fuck me.

---

[2] Oaxaca: /waa-haa-kuh/

14

Chapter Two

OX

Goddamn my abuelo. Goddamn him and his goddamn contracts, and his goddamn greed. Truthfully, just fuck that guy.

That might sound like harsh judgment for a man I'd known well my entire life. A man who had just been found heavily compromised on his deathbed, but trust me, it wasn't. It *so* wasn't. If people knew how he taught me how to ride a bike, no one would ever call *me* cold again.

And if they knew the true way he conducted business… Let's just say this empire we sat on wouldn't seem so carefree and cushy to the rest of the world anymore.

My grandfather did business in any way that got the job done. Mergers, hostile takeovers, underhanded alliances, and sometimes— *primarily during a psychotic break and a three-quarter life crisis*—in marriages.

He was old school. An immigrant from Mexico with zero money in his pocket but dreams in his heart. He came to America through Texas, but almost immediately started to miss the sea having grown up fishing in the Gulf with his family. While most of his counterparts were going west, he saw potential to the east, and that's where he led his family. One brother, two sisters, and his pregnant wife, Rita.

Slowly but surely, he found his way. And what a way he made for us. *All* of us. He'd built this family from *underneath* the bottom of the barrel, yet somehow—through hard work, grit, and getting to know the right people—made it to the top. Soon, his small businesses became larger businesses, and then those garnered more businesses. And many, *many* more.

Over the years, Abuelo's[3] businesses swept past and ate up most of the other agencies in the area. The only true competition in the whole northeastern region rested high on the upper side of the shore. A family called the Fergusons, who hailed originally from New York but had branches all over the United States. A family who had their ties so deeply rooted into the business world that not even the radical attempts to dismantle them had ever worked. Abuelo knew where he stood with them, so instead of making an enemy of the Fergusons, he made allies. That alliance has carried over generations, making the upstart Fernandez's and the seasoned Fergusons the last two powerful forces in the east.

Now, after a life of hard sacrifice, networking, and a bit of luck, Ronaldo Fernandez's children and *their* children were sitting high in one-hundred story skyscrapers running Fernandez corporations for energy, general goods, and technology. He was cunning, and he was a grinder. But most of all, he was obsessive.

That obsessive nature is probably what I had to thank to be sitting

---

[3] Abuelo: /uh-bway-low/

down at my own dining room table at six in the morning, having gotten
no sleep and unexpectedly having to cancel all my meetings for the day.
Across from me sat a tall, skinny, beautiful, *terrified* girl. A girl who
had been my abuelo's wife. I tried not to eye her, but she still had that
damn nightgown on. The one that barely covered any part of her and I
knew for a fact she didn't have anything under.

Clementine Ferguson.

She was the only daughter to the Ferguson heiress, Marsha. For
Marsha, being a woman in charge of such a huge corporation for the
first time in history, she was always fighting to assert her competence.
But the Fergusons had grown as large as they could on United States
soil. Sure, they could've branched out on their own, especially because
her new husband and oldest son had finally been granted dual
citizenship, but Marsha was an only child and her mother was still alive
and grieving her father's death. If she didn't want to leave her only
family all alone while in another country, she'd have to make a choice.
Either move from their home to upstart their international debut, or
merge with a partner. A partner who already had profitable roots in
Mexico and Central America. The Fernandez's.

Abuelo had been all too happy to agree to a merger in respects to his
lasting friendship with the late Marshall Ferguson. The only thing he
wanted in return was Clementine, who was only four years younger than
my twenty-nine years. Meaning, she was about nineteen going on
twenty at the time of her marriage to him. Even younger when the
agreement was initiated.

I shook my head.

It unsettled me. The thought of her with my abuelo, the thought of
what she had been on her way to do in his room, the thought that an
otherwise healthy man had died in his bed and we were yet to truly know
why *really* unsettled me. But what unsettled me the most was that this
girl had yet to shed a single tear.

Not in agony, not in mourning, not in fear. Not in *anything*. She was

17

numb to it all, or at least it appeared that way.

Truthfully, the look she portrayed seemed dead and empty. The only true emotion I read from her was trepidation. So much anxious energy radiating in deep dark waves off her shoulders, through her eyes, in her every jerky movement she made.

I hadn't wanted to scare her by bringing her home with me, but we'd been in that house long enough. *I* had been in the house for more than long enough and it was only a few hours. She'd been there for five years, and who knew how many times she'd ever gotten out.

"Do you speak?" I asked as the minutes ticked by, me staring at her like she was a skittish animal, while she focused on the floor wordlessly.

Slowly, she brought those big hazel brown eyes I had noticed even in the dark of Abuelo's room up to my own. She watched me, unblinking, and unmoving. Her dark skin looked dull, and her honey features were tired.

I felt for her, I did.

Having been traded by your own family for money and power couldn't have been an easy thing to swallow. Having been bartered away twice because of the same contract… *Ouch*.

And it was because I felt for her that I asked. I wanted to know what she needed right then. How I could help. As the oldest grandchild, it was my responsibility to do…to do fucking everything, frankly. And as of five hours prior, this beautiful broken thing had become one of those responsibilities.

"Do. You. Speak?" I asked again, my molars grinding. I was getting a headache.

Slowly, almost imperceptibly, she nodded. Just once, and so excruciatingly stiff, if she was metal, her gears would be grinding.

Her answer glared loud and clear. Yes, she spoke, but she wouldn't speak to *me*.

And what could I do? Force her? No, I wouldn't do that. But I also wasn't about to keep sitting here with her in this weird, loaded silence.

18

So, I stood abruptly. Possibly too abruptly, judging by the way she flinched. Her shoulders jerked away from me and her neck cocked back further, giving herself a full view of my body towering over hers.

In case I tried anything, I realized.

Shaking my head, I turned my back to her and started walking. For some reason, her fear tasted bitter in my mouth. I had done everything I could to shake the stigma of Abuelo's reign from my own name. I was strict, and I was firm, but tried to never be cruel. My father wasn't cruel, and he resented his father for being as such. I took after him in the sense that I never wanted to be like that. Still, people often took the fact I didn't moon in conversation or air my personal business for the world to see, for the assumption that I was cold. Distant. Cruel. When really, the cruelest ones could be just as charismatic on the surface.

Slipping a glance over my shoulder, I could see she was in the same spot. Not having moved even to look after me as I exited. That bitter taste hit the back of my throat again and I wanted to spit to get it out. Instead, I spit my words.

"Follow, Clementine."

Obediently, she rose to her almost full height and began padding softly after me. She would have probably been a whole inch taller if she would unhunch her shoulders and stand up straight. In front of her, she played with her fingers, wringing them thoroughly as she moved. Curly brown hair trailed after her on her back.

Her long legs ate up the space between us quickly and I was surprised to find she creeped closer than the allotted ten feet she'd been keeping between us. Earlier, she'd even had her brother, Clay Ferguson, the one with the mouth, drive her to my house instead of just coming with me. Now she neared a measly five feet, catching me off guard.

I didn't reach out to her or even turn back to her as I stalked through the long hallways feeling somewhat awkward. When buying the house, I had gone large, but nowhere near as large as the mausoleum of a house she'd been living in with Abuelo. It somehow made the space seem more intimate.

My walls were white, my accents mostly beige or some variation of tan, and the decor the interior designer had chosen was a mix between *Italian gardens* and *sandy grassland beach*. I'd always liked it compared to my elder's dark tastes, and now I felt grateful, if only for the fact that I knew this place would not remind her of the one she'd just come from. The one she'd been locked up in for so long.

Silently, we padded up the stairs and down the halls to the largest room second to my own. It swept along the back side of the house, opening up with long floor-to-ceiling windows that showed the expanse of the garden below. It was soft in that it was furnished in white linens, furniture, and curtains. The natural accents and decorative leaves scattered about the room in vases, and frames were laced with a scent I couldn't put a name to, but I liked it. The bed was large but not massive and underneath it sat a plush shaggy rug.

It was a girl's room through and through. I mainly had sisters and knew any visitors would mostly consist of those little wenches, so I'd instructed the decorator to design it accordingly. It seemed to match this soft woman well too.

I didn't enter the room. Only pushing the door open and stepping aside. She didn't enter either, which may have pulled a tired sigh from my lips. I hadn't meant to let it slip, but I was exhausted. And I had much more to deal with today than a skittish, quiet widow.

"Go and get some rest. I will be out for most of the day, but I left my contact information on the counter downstairs in case you need to reach me. Most of my staff speak Spanish and English, so converse with them as you like. Considering our recent situation, I have men stationed out front, out back, in the gardens and down the drive. We don't know what happened yet, but until we do, you'll be protected here." I paused and let myself eye her.

She stood under me by a few inches which made her taller than most women, as I was around six-two. I knew her family was mixed. Black and Mexican, and she'd inherited the deepest, richest, dark features of both cultures. Those eyes though, I wasn't sure where she'd gotten them from as they shone brighter and more beautiful than any I'd ever seen. She was gorgeous, and she was half dressed. *Vulnerable.*

Pursing my lips, I stopped myself from commenting on her nightgown again. She hadn't liked it when I'd done it the first time, but seeing her exposed like that, I couldn't help but add, "There will also be two more men stationed outside your door. Lock it. Don't come out unless you've found something...*warm* to wear."

I left her then. Holding my breath as I blazed down the hall, down the steps, across the foyer and out the door.

"Listos?" My mother asked from across the room, her head drooping noticeably in exhaustion.

She was sitting on the other side of my large top floor office at *Fernandez Inc.* While my parents occupied the overstuffed black couch in the lounge area, my brother and sisters were scattered like the vagrants they were.

Mateo[4], closest to me in age by a few years, sat nearest in one of the leather chairs across from my desk. Ceci, short for Celestia[5], sat at his side, tapping away at her phone like she'd done from the second she'd walked in. My other two sisters, Melissa and Alta were sitting somewhere off in a corner staring each other down, like they'd done all their lives.

We had piled into the large office hours ago to debrief and organize the arrangements for Abuelo's funeral. Now, everyone had just about had enough of it. *Just* about. But with all the Fernandez businesses being signed over to me—a grandchild Abuelo had made known he thought

---

[4] Mateo: /Mah-tay-oh
[5] Celestia: /suh-les-tee-a/

was soft, incapable of upholding the family legacy, and always found room to criticize—my entire family had this weird hum of anxiety and anticipation about them. No one trusted him, not even in death.

With another whooshing sigh, I turned to everyone from the spot I had been pacing a hole into behind my desk. "Well, I think we're done here."

I saw my dad's dark brown eyes tracking me as he held his cheek in his hand. His elbow rested on the armrest and his other hand had reached across the space to clutch my mother's hand in her lap. My mother stared at a corner of the room in some sort of haze. The woman had launched herself into "take care and plan" mode the moment she heard what the situation was. In the fifteen hours it had been since I informed them of what happened, a statement had been made, a funeral service had been planned, and documents of succession had been signed. Even though the body had been and probably would be tied up in an investigation for months, she had made it work.

"When will we read the will?" It was my brother, Mateo, who finally asked it. I had seen him trading glances with our other siblings across the room. Exchanging some weird sort of telepathic communication, I guess everyone understood except the eldest sibling.

I tried not to let it irritate me. The fact they had clearly talked about this without me. They had all decided *something* I had no idea about and I was never *going* to know about because that's just how things were. What did people always say? The eldest child is like the third parent. Well, it couldn't have been truer in this sense. I had been outcasted from these brats a long, long time ago, and instead of the sibling hangouts and inside jokes, I just got variations of *'Ox can you do this?'* and *'Ox can we get that?'*

Despite all that, the fact of the matter was, no one wanted the businesses but me. Not even my father, who had worked for and retired from *Fernandez Inc*, wanted to step his foot back in for even a second. The business was draining, daunting, and altogether life sucking. But it was our legacy, *my* legacy. And I had been taught as much since the moment I was able to listen. As *not* eldest children, my brother and sisters weren't trained from the time they could speak that the family business would be their life. Instead, they had gotten into other hobbies. Hobbies which turned into passions, then into budding careers.

Looking around the room, even I could tell that these stony faces were just a ploy. They were all shitting their pants because no one, and I mean *no one*, wanted to take my spot. Not even Ceci, who I had yet to see take much of an interest in anything in her twenty-one years on earth.

"The solicitor will read it after the funeral, Mátti," I said, my voice holding a chastising tone. He glanced up at me and I shot quick darting eyes toward where our parents were sitting, trying to send a *'what the fuck'* message. "We can worry about that later, though. Let's make sure Apá and Amá get some rest now."

Alta, the empath, shot up from her seat at the *'I must beat my sister at everything'* table and rushed over to our parents. "Lo siento tanto Apá," she apologized. Looking up to me, she asked, "Should we all go have a quiet dinner somewhere? I doubt Amá wants to make anything."

"I can make something!" Melissa offered... Like a three-year-old. Alta shot her a dirty look.

"No. I'll have something sent for you. *All* of you stay at Amá and Apá's tonight. And be *good*."

"Where will you be?" Mateo asked. Thank you, someone, for caring.

"I have some...*things* I need to take care of," I said, hoping I was being discreet. It wasn't likely, seeing that every head in the room turned to me. Every pair of eyes scrutinizing. Apá spoke first.

"La esposa de tu abuelo?" His eyes seemed to widen as he understood. My mother's narrowed and everyone else seemed to suck in a breath.

Yes. Our grandfather's wife.

The topic of Clementine Ferguson was one that seemed to be

expertly avoided in my immediate family. From the time Abuelo had shown an interest, to their nuptials, we had all avoided the odd arrangement like the plague. No one understood why Abuelo had wanted her so badly; so bad in fact, that he'd basically married a whole family of men into the business that would lead to a series of mergers and collaborations which could not be avoided.

In some ways, ways of business mostly, it had worked out for the best. The whole northeastern region was run by two major conglomerates, *Fernandez Inc.* and *Ferguson Enterprises.* With an alliance secured some half a decade ago with the marriage, the two families had moved on to accumulate all their outlier business competitors. Essentially, our two families, made one by Abuelo and the Ferguson's Union, were unstoppable.

But that was just the thing. The family part of the union had come up majorly lacking. Aside from their wedding day, that had come off more like the sentencing of a prisoner, we had never seen the girl Ferguson. Even as Abuelo attended family functions, stayed active on the company's board, and continued to court the Ferguson men on various ventures, the wife had never been brought around again.

No one understood it, and with Abuelo being the kind of man you didn't question, no one cared to try.

"Oh, you mean that gold digger?" Ceci fluttered a hand dismissively.

"Celestia Rose!" Amá chided. "Basta!"

Ceci shrugged and rolled her eyes. Mátti nearly snorted. "More like the prized horse. Abuelo kept her locked up like she'd run away. Actually, she probably would if he gave her the chance. Do you remember her face at the wedding?"

"I don't," Ceci said matter-of-factly, obviously not caring either. "And the fact of the matter is, forced or not she still showed up, she still married the money, and she's still here. *Gold. Digger.* Just calling it like I see it."

"The fact of the matter," I inserted, my volume raising, irritation present, "is that she was present. She was the one who found him, and she can't leave yet because of their…contract. She can't go home, Ceci. She's alone."

"You left her there alone, Mijo?" Amá rose from her seat, exhaustion evaporated. "Qué haces, Mijo. Por qué?"

"What am I doing?" I asked, irritation rising higher. "I have no clue, Amá. Do you?"

She worried her lip and started wringing her hands. She glanced a pleading look in my father's direction and he looked away. He had never warmed up to the reality of his father marrying a girl younger than some of his children.

Tsking in sharp disapproval, she turned back to me. "Mijo, maybe we should invite her to eat with us. Or we should all go there."

I shook my head before she'd even asked. "No."

"No? Por que, no?" She argued, hands on her hips.

"*No*, Amá," I repeated. She stared me down, waiting for something. A reason I suppose. "She's skittish. She barely wanted to come with me, I doubt she'll want to be around a big group right now."

Not to mention, I had no idea what to do with her and I wasn't sure if I wanted my family to see that level of incompetence just yet. She would hardly even look my way let alone speak to me, so I could hardly imagine her in a room with Ceci. *God.*

The mental image of a bloodbath, Celestia on top with her signature smirk plastered across her face cemented my decision. I shook my head once more. "No, it won't work."

Amá pursed her lips and leveled me with a stare. After a long scrutinizing moment, I let out a deep sigh and squared my shoulders with the woman.

"Que, Ma?" I asked, knowing she had questions and just wanting to get this over with so we could get the hell out of this miserable room.

"Is she okay?" she asked.

"No."

"Is she upset?"

"Not about Abuelo, I don't think." Ceci scoffed and Mátti snickered. I shot yet another ugly look their way. "But upset, yes. She won't talk much."

Liar, she won't talk to *you* at all.

"Is she… Did he...?" She trailed off and somehow, I knew what she was getting at. Only I had been old enough to remember the way Abuelo treated his first wife after Abuela Rita had died. It was *ugly*. And it didn't end well. He would go on to have many more wives that he'd treat in many other ways of malintent. Clementine had been his final, and we suspected, his favorite. Poor girl.

I shook my head, understanding her meaning. "No sé, Amá. Nothing physical, from the looks of it, but I have no idea if he—*what's* been done."

She nodded, her eyes going solemn, suddenly looking drained and far away. "Okay, okay. Talk to her Oaxaca, don't just ignore her like you do."

"I do not—"

"You do, Mijo." She interrupted. "You are too young to be acting like such a grumpy old man, you know."

More snickering. I swallowed, suppressing a *'grumpy old man'* grumble. She spoke again but louder, not at me, even though her eyes stayed on mine. "But I understand how your degenerate, lazy brother and sisters drive you loco. I don't blame you. I really don't. I'm sorry I made such lousy company for you."

A collective groan of snickering, scoffs, and "whatever's" filled the room, which had my mouth twitching upward and a soft chuckle escaping my chest. As much as these sorry little idiots sucked, especially at times like these, they were *my* sorry little idiots and I loved them.

"Te amo," Amá mouthed to me with a smile that didn't reach up very far. "And thank you."

I reached forward and palmed her shoulder, giving it a squeeze before turning back toward the room. With hands sliding into my pockets, I set my shoulders.

"Alright. You heard her, degenerates." I couldn't help but smirk as they all scowled. But to their credit, my siblings all started to rise and file toward the exit before I even said to, all lined up in order—Mátti, Lis, Alta, and Ceci taking up the rear. "Everybody out."

Chapter Three

OX

The house was dark when I arrived home.

Strange.

I usually had staff working around my property when I came back from work, or at least when I came back from work on time. Maria cooked on weekdays while her daughter Sylvie cleaned. Not to mention the landscaping, dry cleaning, security, and other services that made their rounds throughout the home every day. That morning I had called Sylvie and asked her to tell her mom not to come in. I'd pay her and the rest of my staff for the week, but I specifically asked Sylvie to keep anything she might hear away from the older woman, afraid that if she found out the current situation, she'd start to dote on me and my family, which was appreciated but unnecessary. She was a grandmother to her own large family and didn't need our complicated issues distracting her. I also had a feeling she would try to barge her way into Clementine Ferguson's affections if she had the chance to.

The kitchen light was the only light on, however, there was a smell lingering. Something like chicken broth and celery. When I skirted my eyes across the lightly colored room, they caught on a stone pot sitting idle on the stove. It was covered and there was a note stuck to the top of it. I strode over to the pot and snatched the pink sticky note up between my index and middle fingers.

Don't you know I watch the news boy? Call if you need anything.

I left extras in the fridge.

-Maria

I blinked, and somehow, I was unsurprised. Moving to the fridge, I reached back to dig my cell out of my pocket. Sure enough, right there on the screen there was a response from Sylvie. Probably something about how she couldn't control her mother. I slipped it back into my pocket instead of reading it. Opening the stainless-steel door, it swung backward to reveal rows and rows of dishes and pans, lined with foil and tops and labeled with Maria's signature sticky notes. This did pull a reluctant smile from my lips.

I very well should have known.

Letting the fridge door swing closed, I moved over to the stove again, turned the knob on the eye closest to the back and pushed the pot to the warm heat. I had a feeling it was soup. Lifting the lid and seeing the clear yellow liquid and floating vegetables, I felt a surge of contentment. I loved chicken soup.

I felt my gaze wander over to the open space where the kitchen and living room met. The stairs dark and shadowed in that direction.

I hoped someone else liked soup too. I doubted she'd eaten anything yet. It honestly didn't look as if she'd eaten anything at all, judging by how undisturbed the area was. But then again, Maria or Sylvie could have cleaned…

My gaze trailed up, losing focus as it moved toward the top of the stairs and got lost in the darkness. A sigh caught in my throat, lingering there because I thought if I let it out, I might talk myself out of going up there. So, holding it, I made myself walk toward the second floor.

The hallway was just as dark as the rest of the house. So much so that I barely registered the two men that were still standing outside of the tall door near the end of the hall. Their backs to it, hands folded neatly and obediently behind themselves. When I flicked on the light, they winced from the sudden brightness. It made me wonder how long they had been there like that, standing in the dark.

Nearing them, I looked from one short-haired, serious faced man to the other. "Has she left the room?"

One slight shake of their heads.

"Have you checked to see if she's still in there?" I stepped even closer. A single curt nod.

"And she is?" Another nod. I sighed. I had paid them not to talk much, but mainly it was for her benefit. I needed a status report, and I damn sure knew I wasn't going to get one from her. "Okay, thanks. You can go join the rest of the stations outside."

I listened to make sure they were completely gone before squaring my shoulders with the door in front of me. With a big breath, I slid the rest of the way up to the door and leaned in with my shoulder so close, it almost rested against the wooden frame. Listening carefully, I heard absolutely nothing on the other side. I fought the urge to sigh again. Was she sleeping? No, she had probably slept all day if she hadn't left the room. Was she okay? There was a bathroom in there, sure, but what about food and water?

That thought got me knocking on the door at last.

With the softest *tap, tap, tap,* I could muster, I knocked, and I waited.

And waited.

And waited.

Tap, tap, tap. I knocked again and got nothing. This time I did let myself grumble. And sigh. And clear my throat.

Tap, tap, tap.

"Clementine." No answer. Not even the sound of a shuffling body. *Tap, tap, tap.* "Clem, are you in there?"

As I waited, I listened to the sounds of the house. Leaning further in, I damn near had my ear pressed against the flat surface of the door.

Tap, tap, tap. "Clementine?"

Still nothing. I sighed and felt my shoulders slump. I was tired. So fucking tired, and this was one of the last things I had to check off my list before I could finally rest. It was also the most sensitive.

I let my hand run through the styled black mass on top of my head. I was going to take a shower anyway, who cared if it got a little messed up. Raising my hand to tap again, I hesitated. She wasn't going to answer. She wouldn't even talk when I was standing right in front of her. There was no way she was going to shout through the doorway. No way in hell.

"Clementine." I breathed low, collecting myself. I was almost done. I could do this. "I just need to make sure you're alright. If you won't answer the door, I'll have to open it. I won't come in as long as you're okay. I'll just peek."

I waited and waited some more. Maybe I even waited about a minute longer than necessary before giving the door another absent *tap.*

"Alright. I'm coming in now."

Just as I was reaching toward the handle, I heard it. In response to my constant tapping was a loud, solid, *knock, knock, knock* from the other side of the door. I sat on my heels for a second, genuinely surprised. Something formed in my stomach. Something hard and soft all at once. Because she had responded.

Knock, knock, knock.

She knocked again. More soundly, more confidently. Somehow this gave me peace, if only the smallest bit of it.

"Are you okay?" I asked.

Knock, knock, knock.

"Have you eaten?" Stupid question, as the two brutes I had just dismissed stated she hadn't left the room. She didn't answer. "Are you hungry?"

No answer.

I wanted to tell her that she should eat. That she should leave the room and not stay holed up in there. But who was I to tell her anything? I wasn't her family; I didn't even know her. I was simply here to make sure she stayed alive until we found out what else to do with her. If she didn't feel like eating or sleeping or walking or even *breathing*, who was I to judge that?

"There is soup downstairs in a pot on the stove. Chicken noodle. I'll leave it out for a while. If you're hungry, you are welcome to go down and get some." No answer. "I plan on having dinner and going to bed. If you need me, I'm down the hall."

Knock.

I guess that was it then. "Alright. Good night, Clementine."

I didn't turn to head back down the stairs until I heard her solid response of three more steady knocks.

Later that night, I wouldn't be able to get to sleep until I pulled a small bowl down from the cupboard, filled it up with warm soup, and set it on a tray with crackers, bread, and a cup of warm lemon tea. I felt guilty until finally walking up to her door again and setting the loaded tray down on the floor in front of it. Against the wall, I scribbled a short note onto one of the sticky pads Maria liked to leave around and then slipped it underneath the door.

Finally, with that done, I could turn toward my own room, walk the short distance there, and fall asleep knowing one thing.

At least I tried.

Chapter Four

CLEMENTINE

No matter how I thought about it, the day ahead of me seemed daunting. Too daunting for me to handle on my own. And I knew I wouldn't have to. Between my brothers, who I had seen in the last three days more than I had in the last five years, and the tall man whom I now temporarily lived with, I knew I wouldn't be left to fend for myself.

But I was still nervous and sick to my stomach and dreading this.

Pacing around the room that had been my new prison cell for the last few days, I let my mind wander to the tall man in question. The one who came by my door every morning and every night with a quiet *tap, tap, tap* that I was beginning to realize meant so many things.

Sometimes it seemed to mean, *'How are you doing'?* Sometimes, *'Are you okay'*, and often simply *'I'm here'* or *'I'm leaving'*.

The first night he came to my door and tried to talk to me, I had been curled up in the corner of the room, in the big bamboo chair where I had been all day. I didn't dare move from the spot, trapped by my own thoughts, my body trembling with possibility. In that spot in the corner, I had dared to let myself hope.

Why?

I didn't totally know why. Something about the way he'd led me around his home earlier, showing me where things were and what different rooms were used for had given me the impression that this house wasn't the same as Ron's. Even though he was his grandson and I was to stay with him until we found out what else was to be done with me, I wasn't going to be locked up. *He* wasn't going to lock me up. So maybe after this was all settled and done with, I wouldn't have to be the Fernandez pet any longer.

The possibility had been enough to send me into a hopeful daze. At the same time, it had made my body feel like lead, and I hadn't wanted to move from that spot all day. Paralyzed with possibility.

Until the *tap, tap, tap* sound had jolted me out of my trance and brought my attention to the door on the other side of the room.

Even if I felt hopeful, I still wasn't ready for him to come in. He would ask questions, make demands, stand too close. I was sure of it.

But he didn't do any of that. He'd sounded frustrated for a while when I wouldn't answer him, and he'd threatened to come in on the grounds of making sure I was okay, but when I decided to stand and pad my bare feet across the carpeted floors and return his tap with a knock, that had been enough.

I was surprised and relieved that, small as it was, it had been enough for him. And it continued to be enough as every morning while I lay awake in bed, I heard the *tap, tap, tap* of his greeting and got up to answer with a knock of my own.

I'm okay. I'm still here. I won't leave yet, is what I hoped I was conveying with those knocks.

Just like that first night, he continued to leave a small tray outside my door of what I assumed was whatever he was eating plus a cup of tea. And just like that night, every time I would take the tea and leave the rest.

I still had that small sticky note he'd slipped underneath the frame of the door the first time he'd brought me food. It was stuck on the wall next to my favorite corner chair. If I had a pen, I would underline it. Place a star next to it. Maybe even go as far as draw a smile there. The note was simple, short, and to the point. But the message was loud and resounding and monumental.

The funeral is in three days.

- O

Now, three days later, there I was. Dressed in mourning black, wedding ring still burning my finger, and my last name still tied to that man. But there I was, so close to freedom. Steps away from salvation. Minutes away from the rest of my life.

This was the most excited I'd been in a long, long time.

That fact was probably the one and only reason why, when I heard the first two taps of a familiar greeting, I was to the door and swinging it open before he could even deliver the third one.

There, in his own striking blacks, was the man of the house. Tall, fit, slim, and stone faced. His complexion bright in the natural light of the hallway. His hand big as it hung half raised in the air, poised to knock. With a slick clearing of his throat, he let that hand raise to his collar and tugged.

"You're ready," he noted in a deep, cautious voice. If he was surprised to see me at the door waiting and alert, he only let it show momentarily before masking it in that stoic manner he kept.

He reminded me of Clint in a way, always serious. Always grim. But then he did things like bring me food and deliver my brothers straight to my door whenever they came to visit, that made me think there was something under that layer. Something I hadn't had a glimpse of in a long time. *Consideration.*

He must have seen my eyes bouncing, looking for said brothers because he tugged at his collar once more and eased out, "You're with me today. They aren't here."

My eyes stopped bouncing and landed on his. Deep, dark, unmoving as he watched me. "You'll see them at the service, but for appearance's sake, you'll stick close to the Fernandez family for the day."

I said nothing. Only swallowing down the stinging feeling that was starting up in my throat. Stay close to the Fernandez family? I had barely even met them. Why would I—*how* would I get through the whole day sticking close to them?

"My family is annoying, but they're easy to maneuver." He went on, like he was reading from a script. "If you want comfort, stick close to Amá who will always be close to Apá. And maybe Alta, who wouldn't hurt a fly. If you want to be judged, Melissa. If you want to laugh, Mateo. And if you want trouble, try your hand with Ceci but fair warning, you might lose it."

My face scrunched, my forehead probably wrinkling with it. I couldn't help the surprise his dry rehash of his family gave me. He came off almost as cold and as distant as his grandfather. But He wasn't.

There was just something about him that was still warm under all that monotone business-like control.

That thought had me thinking of something else. He had left himself out of the synopsis. Whether it was because he didn't count himself as part of the family or he didn't believe he was someone I would want to hang around, I wasn't sure. But he had left himself out of it. Which made me wonder.

Slowly, so he wouldn't think I was attacking him or anything, I raised my hand and pointed a finger. Leaning forward only slightly. I reached an arm out and let that finger cross between us and land in the center of his chest.

And I waited.

I waited until he understood. Even though it took him studying my arm, my hand, and then my finger, he raised his head to study my face with a grim question written clearly across his. Eventually, he understood.

"Me?" he asked. I nodded my head once, letting my hand drop to my side. He let out a short breath of a laugh, the corner of his mouth pulling upward just slightly. "Stick with me anyway. I'm your backup."

The burning in my throat dulled and something in my stomach seemed to pull. Stick with him. Stick with the grandson. He said he had my back. And didn't he? In four days—if we counted that first morning from hell—he hadn't touched me, hadn't yelled at me, he had hardly seen me.

Instead, he brought me food, brought me tea, brought my brothers. He gave me a comfortable room, sent someone to grab changes of clothes for me so I wouldn't have to go back to that house, and he had stationed men outside my door. Good men, who popped their heads in once or twice a day, but otherwise left me alone.

Stick with me anyway.

That seemed easy enough.

I'm your back up.

Suddenly, maybe stupidly, I believed him.

The rest of the day passed in levels of my headache. When the grandson finally coaxed me out of my room and led me from the bright halls of his home to the wide manicured driveway where his car was parked, my head started to lightly ache in anticipation for the day's events. I was nervous to be outside, to be around his family, to be around *my* family. To be filmed and scrutinized and judged and spoken to. I was nervous to have to pretend to be some beacon of matronly grief that I simply wasn't. I was self-aware enough to know that I came off more like a wounded animal than a grieving widow. And I was afraid others would pick up on it too.

The funeral service was intimate, just like the grandson had promised. There were close friends and family and a small group of media there to cover the service. It was held at a large Roman inspired Catholic Church on the far end of town. It was gargantuan in all its pale stone glory. Vibrant blue slabs of intricate stained glass lined the dome shaped windows, and the city scape of inner Seaside surrounded us. I didn't go into the city often, so being around the sudden hustle and bustle of it gave my headache another painful layer.

We had to enter the church through the back to avoid the tons of press workers who were not invited but showed up anyway. The knowledge of people trying to nosey their way into the affair, people who the Fernandez or Ferguson families had no control over and were able to write whatever kind of story they pleased, gave my headache a more throbbing pulse.

Inside the church, during the short, clipped service, I noticed the Ferguson and Fernandez families had been split up. Fernandez's on the right, Fergusons on the left. I'd had to sit on the Fernandez side. Smushed snuggly between the grandson and who I assumed was his mom, judging by the softly weathered look of her skin and the presumptuous, but soft, palm of support she laid on my knee.

I didn't dare to look around at the other Fernandez children, not wanting to take the chance of my eyes landing on the "judgmental" one or God forbid the one that he'd simply said was trouble. Just because I didn't look didn't mean they didn't take their sweet time staring at me. Or *glaring* at me. Or giving me pity eyes. Or smirking in my direction. Or rolling big brown irises away from me.

I noticed them studying me in my periphery, clearly sizing me up. Waiting for me to say something or slip up or, I don't know, breathe wrong maybe?

Whatever their scrutiny was about, it sent my head to outright pounding. So much so that, by the time the speaking was over and it was time to stand, blood rushed to and from my head so fast that the room started spinning.

Left and right my body slumped as I fought to keep my equilibrium. I felt my shoulders bumper car both sets of shoulders beside me as I bounced against them. I gripped the back of the pew in front of me to hold myself up. Only, there was no pew in front of me and I was suddenly stumbling forward. *Barreling* really, straight for the ground. My arms swung weakly in front of me, gasps sounding around the room.

And...

There was a hand, large and warm at the scruff of my neck—on my dress really—yanking me upward and standing me up straight. Around me, I heard snickers, whispers, laughs, and scoffs. Somewhere to my far right there was a low feminine snort followed up by,

"Look out below, Ox. Someone's got bad sea legs." More snickering.

A male snicker. A feminine hiss. A huff. And then the brush of someone leaning close to my neck. "Understandable, since you're more suited for digging."

What the—? Digging? Like *gold digging*?

I was going to be sick. I fought myself and my balance as I tried hard not to lean into the grandson and also not to fall. Unfortunately, my vision was blacking out, and I was losing the battle. The already rough grip on my nape seemed to tighten, and I swallowed a whimper as my eyes opened and met the grandson's straight on.

I gawked at his expression. His face was so determined, so serious. I wanted to cower away from it. But those eyes cut behind him and he hissed several words in Spanish to whoever occupied that row. Though I spoke little, I understood every word he said to them—thanks to my dad, who spoke Spanish frequently to my brothers and I when we were younger.

"Celestia, say another word and we'll see how good your sea legs are when I send you to Mexico to fish with Tio Angel for the summer. *Again.*" He hissed over his shoulder. He wasn't finished.

"Mátti, Lis. You're going with her if you keep fucking laughing."

"What about Alta?" Someone whined behind me.

"Oye!" he, and maybe someone else beside me hissed at them in return. Then he leaned a shoulder deep into their pew and spat in a low angry voice, "This is your abuelo's goddamn funeral. Act like it."

He straightened up, his height seeming to double. The other presences around me seemed to shrink away and on my other side, the parents said nothing.

Damn.

The grandson had put his foot down, I guess. And what a foot it was to get them all in line so quickly.

I'm your backup. The memory of those words shot through me like fire, warming me from my cheeks to my toes. I guess he wasn't lying.

My eyes flickered upward to my side to find said backup, looking straight at me. The same grim expression I assumed he used on his siblings; he was using on me too. I winced away from it, suddenly scared for my pride, or my dignity? Possibly both.

"So, you're a liar, then?" he asked.

Um...what?

I felt myself physically flinch as I leaned back to get a better look at his face. Hopefully, whatever face I was giving him showed just how *'what the fuck'* I was feeling. Because seriously, what?

But I didn't have enough time to dissect it fully, because we were moving again, shuffling out of the pews and filing into lines going God knows where. I felt my head starting to swim and my vision began to blur again.

With a yank to my elbow, I was being pulled upright. This time, a long muscular arm ran the length of my own. This was the only part of our bodies that touched and since I was currently in a state of keeling over, I guess I was okay with it.

Breath hit my ear, hot and angry. I flinched hard this time, startled by his approach. "You told me you've been eating."

His voice was deep and accusatory. Not far off the menacing tone he'd used with the others. When I didn't answer, he kept going. "You. *Lied*."

Technically, I hadn't. When he asked me if I had finally gotten something to eat, I had knocked three consecutive times because that seemed to be the proper sequence to put his questioning at ease. Each time he'd left food, I'd left it neatly on the tray and taken the cup of tea. Later, I'd return the cup to the tray, empty. He was usually gone by the time I finished the tea, and who knows who had been disposing of all the untouched food after that...

So, did I lie? No. Was he still angry? Hell yes. Especially when he seemed to read my apprehension to his accusation on my face. Color spotted him and I sensed his frustration was getting the better of his usual coolness. He moved, reaching down at something as we filed out of the church. From his pocket, he pulled out something that crumbled and crackled noisily in his hand.

He extended it toward me and, like a mind-controlled robot, I opened my hand and waited. His fingers grazed my palm for just a second, leaving a tingle and...candy? I peered down to see a singularly wrapped sweet mint. It was large and pastel green, wrapped in clear plastic.

"In your mouth, Clementine," he instructed dryly.

The wrapping paper crunched between my fingers as I slowly unwrapped the candy and brought it up to my mouth. As soon as it hit my tongue, it started melting. The sugar hitting where it was supposed to almost instantly. I nearly sagged in relief.

"Jesus," he spat. "You'll have them thinking I didn't feed you."

I gave him a frown. *Them who exactly?*

"Your brothers, Clementine," he clarified. I noticed he'd let go of me, and I was no longer swooning. Again, the comfortable distance between us had been restored, and I felt another pang of appreciation for that trait in him even though most of his other traits were cold and harsh. "The loud one might scare everyone else, but I have a feeling the big one's a tiger brother."

He was right. While Clay, who could only be the so-called loud one he was referring to, was rowdy and in your face and would probably hide a body for me—after killing said body. Connor, the biggest, quietest, and shyest, of my brothers always had our backs to the bitter, bitter end. Back when I was first married off, he'd threatened to sell all his shares of the company, expose our parent's offshore funds and bring to light all the shady "fixer" types on my family's payroll. If he would have done that, he probably would have been disowned, especially being the youngest son. I had only talked him out of it by making him believe I was going willingly.

So, the grandson was right to assume that, against Connor, he'd be nothing more than a twig in the way of the man scaling a tree.

The look I gave him must have said everything I was thinking, because right then, on the way to bury my demons, he gave me a full faced grin, a small chuckle escaping him. I peered up at the sound. It was nice. The handsome face making the sound was also nice.

That thought had me quickly looking away.

Behind us, someone grumbled, "Ox gets to laugh, but we don't?" A series of hisses quickly shut them up.

Ox. They called him, Ox.

42

Chapter Five

CLEMENTINE

The Fernandez family home was massive. There must have been something hereditary about showing off in this family, because the large Tuscan style home that stood on miles of its own land and could probably house each of the five grown children they had, maybe even more, reminded me of Ronaldo. Maybe it was the warm deep colors of the house or the fact that it was just as large as my last pretty cage, but pulling up to it made my stomach drop.

We were pulling into the long double-wide driveway to have lunch. It wasn't going to be a large gathering. This time just the Fergusons, Fernandez's, and whoever else was close enough to already have the family's home address. Everyone else had been left at the church.

I had wanted to go straight home. Not home to Ox's, but home with my brothers. I knew we still had to read the will, and the reason the Fernandez's had organized such a private, intimate lunch in the first place was so they could sneak off and do just that on special request. By then, I was past the point of hopeful. Ron was dead. What more control could he have over me?

In the time it took to drive just out of the city to the Fernandez family estate, I finally figured out why I had been so excited to get this day over and done with. It was anticipation for when I would finally feel this five-year-old weight of responsibility lifted from my shoulders.

Even though I had been there in his room and the finality of that scene was indisputable, there was something more eternal about saying goodbye. There was something so final about a funeral, so definite that it couldn't be disputed. With a burial came release, came closure, came the end. *Finally*.

But Ron's body wasn't at his funeral. Ron's story was probably long from being fully over and with that came the other half of weight he'd left behind.

That being, my husband was dead, and I was a widow. Yet I still felt the same.

Leaving the church, I had expected to feel differently. Sure, it felt good when my brothers hugged me hello. It felt bad when my mother and father barely looked my way. It felt *new* when the grandson, Ox, smiled at me.

All those feelings were more feelings than I had felt in a long time. But that was it. That was the extent of it, good and bad and it was frustrating because I had expected to feel *more*. To feel like I used to before Ron. Instead, I was still numb, my senses deadened to the emotions around me and the realization that there wasn't such a simple fix made me feel queasy all over again.

I wasn't the only one.

Three times someone had asked the pretty girl with the round flushed face if she was feeling alright. The siblings took turns telling her she looked pale or feverish or just plain bad as we headed down the church steps together. The "bad" comment had come from the one I learned to be Ceci and despite my better judgment—and the fact that she'd called me a gold digger not ten whole minutes before—I still found it amusing. That was until I noticed Round Face starting to go down. She was stopped only by the broad back of the most uncourteous Ferguson.

Clay had grunted at her like she was some kind of ugly thing on his shoe, and it had taken him several moments to move just enough to flick her off of him. *"Flick"* because he literally used one singular finger to push her body aside. I thought she would fall again, but quick as ever, the man who had been by my side for most the day cursed and lunged to grab her under the arm. I winced. Not because of his rough handling, but because she had looked like a rag doll in his grip. All limp and panting and weak and I had no illusions that I had looked any better.

The two of us were deposited in the backseat of the eldest son's car, given more candy and water, and told to sit tight in the cool air while the capable adults handled the rest.

God, I was so embarrassing.

The only salvation of my mood had been that, as the door shut and I pressed my head against the cool window, I caught a glimpse of my brothers standing together as they talked to the Fernandez's. Clay noticed me staring, catching my eyes even through the dark window tint, and he'd sneered, lip curling and everything.

This brought a deep giggle from the bottom of wherever I'd stored them for so long. Making me laugh like I used to with them, with my family.

"Your voice is pretty," the sick girl beside me whispered. Then she reached across the middle seat and snatched my hand up in her own, squeezing it tightly in her icy grip. "Just like you."

So, this was Alta, the one who wouldn't hurt a fly.

I didn't look over at her. I had already noted her round face and dark hair. Her skin was slightly paler than her family's, and she had a sweet voice to match her sweet attitude. Instead of looking over at her, I squeezed her hand back.

I must have dozed off because I hardly remembered the drive until we turned onto a long road surrounded by wide open space and a deep voice rumbled across the quiet cab.

"We're almost there," Ox said in a soft, almost leering voice that would have made me feel uncomfortable if it wasn't for the girl next to me. That tender worry I heard had to be for her.

The family's estate managers and staff greeted guests upon arrival. According to Ox's briefing in the car, there were drinks and fruit and bread and cheese, along with tortillas and spiced cucumbers and grilled meat and salsas. Before we left the car Ox turned around and pointed at us sternly. "Eat something. Both of you, before you actually pass out."

"Okay," Alta said easily to her brother, exiting the car. I moved to follow her but was stopped by a hand around my wrist. Large and warm and new.

Chin over my shoulder, I looked at him and was met with pure black. His eyes, his hair, his clothes. *Black.*

"Will you eat?" he asked me.

I nodded.

"Are you lying to me?"

I shook my head.

His mouth went into a grim hard line, like he knew I was full of it. Sighing, he squeezed my flesh slightly before releasing me. Had he given up on me? I exited the car before I could find out.

I didn't want to lie. Everything sounded delicious, but as we headed up the sandy driveway, my stomach churned and retreated as it had been doing for a while now. I knew I was hungry, but I had no desire to actually eat anything.

The choice was taken away from me, however.

Not five steps in the doorway with Alta by my side, I was rounded on. Clay—who had gotten his hair lined up and cut since the last time I saw him, his longish curly strands staying neatly—stood before us in a slim black suit, stopping me dead in my tracks. Alta stopped too, if only because she was startled by the suddenness of his movements.

Others dodged and moved around us, not looking twice because a second look would mean questioning Clay. You didn't want to do that.

"What do you want to eat, Tiney?" he asked, tone sharp.

I gaped. And then I shook my head, casting a not-so-subtle glance at my side where the Fernandez still lingered dazedly. I wasn't planning on staying quiet forever but… But I still didn't know what to say to these people.

And even if I did, out of anyone, Ox deserved my thanks first and most of all. For getting me out of that room—that *house*, when he did. For doing something when he could, instead of waiting for someone else to do it.

Clay, with all of his finesse, turned his shoulders on the girl, and crossed his arms over his chest. Leaning forward he snapped. Right away, he snapped. I suppressed a groan and an eye roll.

"Hey! Earth to Atlas. Yo, anybody home?" He waved a hand in front of her face and when she jolted, her hazelnut gaze flickering up to him, he smiled. In a canine sort of way. "There ya go, sweetheart. Now that you're back from outer space, beat it. I gotta talk to my sister."

Again, I gaped. What a complete asshole. Alta was in total agreement with me because she blinked and turned red with what I assumed was anger. Clay sat back on his heels and looked at her, his eyes flicking over her face, down her front and then back up to her eyes. And then he scrunched up his nose.

"You might want a sandwich or something too while you're at it. You look a little…low on calories."

I turned to him angrily. It was one thing to be grouchy, but this girl was sweet. Did he have to be mean to *everyone*? When he caught my gaze, not surprisingly, he just shrugged. So, with as steady as a hand I could muster, I reached over and grabbed the girl's forearm, giving her a gentle squeeze.

Sweet but short, she gave me a fleeting smile over her shoulder and walked off.

I cleared my throat, and Clay looked at me. "Her name is Alta."

"Yeah? And—so what? You guys are best friends after almost passing out together?" he asked.

"No," I said. "But at least get her name right if you're going to be an asshole otherwise."

"And what do you care? You're not even talking to them," he said. I grumbled and looked away, irritation crawling up the back of my neck. I cared at least a little because—because I don't know why, but it seemed like I should.

"What's up your ass, Tiney?" he asked in the same way you'd ask someone what the weather would be that day. I looked at him, hard. He didn't budge.

"Guess," I finally said, sweetly. Too sweetly.

"I know," he said, and he reached forward to grab onto my shoulder, yanking me to his side and starting us along the path across the wide-open foyer. "You're hangry. You need to eat something."

The churning feeling came back.

"Clay, I don't feel like eating right now. We just got here."

"Tough shit, sweetheart," he barked. I groaned.

He truly meant tough shit, because as soon as we entered the main room of the house, he steered us straight for the food. Bypassing all the pretty paintings, stone benches, and abstractly shaped vases—not to mention curious glances along the way.

I knew he wouldn't leave me alone until he watched me ingest *something*. Reaching forward, I picked up a few slices of cheese and started nibbling on the corner of one before glancing up to catch his eyes.

Happy? My gaze asked him. He wasn't. But there were people around also trying to grab food, so he shook his head and let me steer us away from the table.

"What? You sick or something?" he asked after watching me barely nibble through half the slice before taking a break. I shook my head.

"Pregnant?"

"Clay, no!"

He grunted. "I just had to watch your ass dangle from that guy's fingers in the church and you expect me to believe you're alright?"

One nod is all I gave. He sighed loudly.

"Fine. Be that way with me if you want, Tiney, but I'm sending Clint over to deal with your ass next. I'm tapping out." Well, *that* made me feel shitty. So shitty in fact that I let my mouth run off unfiltered, something I never did.

"Oh, like you did when you let mom and dad sell me off?" That too sweet tone was back and vicious.

He sucked in a breath, side eyed me like I'd just slapped him across the face and let it out shakily. Nodding a few times, he reached up and over, laying a palm on the top of my hair.

"I'm sorry, Tine," he croaked. "Just go sit down somewhere and relax. The *royal family* told us this lunch was for the rest of the guests, but they've arranged for that bastard's solicitor to come as soon as possible so they can get this shit over and done with. It sounds like they want as little to do with it as you and me."

He ran his hand back, pushing hair away from my face, "Just a few more hours and we're out. Okay?"

I looked at him, my heart clenching and unclenching as I nodded.

"Okay."

Chapter Six

OX

"What in the fuck is this?"

I slammed down the thick stack of papers, bound together by a massive binding clip. The document was dense, but the words were clear.

Marriage.

I was to be married. More precisely, I was to be married to my grandfather's widow within three days of his funeral. It said so right there, not only in the immense span of paperwork that was their initial marriage contract, but also in the unofficial copy of Abuelo's will which had been read by his solicitor, by me, by each Ferguson boy, and by my parents. Now it was being passed around by everyone again like it was some sort of football. It had been passed around so much already that the solicitor provided us with another less rumpled copy and a deadline to which we accept or deny the terms before he left for the day.

"In the event that Ronaldo José Fernandez demises before his young wife Clementine Margarite Ferguson sires an heir to unite their extended families, Ronaldo's first grandson Oaxaca Manuel Fernandez is to marry and conceive with his widow if he has not yet married at the time of Ronaldo's death." My younger brother read aloud with a surprisingly straight countenance as he sat in one of the armchairs on the far end of my parents' drawing room. My parents sat on the two-person couch nestled against the large back window. My sisters were not present, having tired out less than an hour into the luncheon. But we had company. A thrice party company that upheld the name Ferguson.

"If Clementine Ferguson does not uphold these wishes, all assets, wealth, and property gained in the marriage will be forfeited. If Oaxaca does not uphold these wishes, all corporate positions, status, and jurisdiction in any Fernandez enterprise will be forfeited and unredeemable. The only exception to these conditions is in the event of either party's death."

I pinched the bridge of my nose and finally stopped pacing the center of the room. My other hand went to my hip, and I tried hard to take some sort of measurable breath. Through my teeth, I said, "Thank you, Mátti, for reading that to the room. *Again.*"

My brother made a face at me, but kindly set the copy of the document he'd been reading on the card table in front of him. He knew when it was time to shut up, and now was one of those times.

I turned to my parents.

My dad's gaze had been tracking me for a while as he held his cheek in his hand and waited. He'd had a grim look on his face all day, I knew it wasn't only because of all of this.

As bad as Abuelo was, he was his father, and he was now gone. I wanted to get this over and done with so he could have some peace. Or at least as much peace as anyone could when their father had died unexpectedly in their sleep and you had to act like everything was fine to uphold public appearances.

God, I wanted everyone out of this house. I wanted every loose end tied, and I wanted to take control of the situation. I hated seeing people I cared about upset. I hated leaving problems unsolved. But most of all, I hated *being* the problem. Now, because of Abuelo's will, I had become part of it. Me and the unfortunate Clementine Ferguson who was contractually obligated along with myself to stay locked in the cage of my grandfather's creation. Damn.

"Do you have objections to marrying?" My father finally asked.

"No."

"Is the girl an ogre?" He continued, knowing damn well she wasn't.

"No." I didn't spare a glance up at her brothers, even as we talked about their sister so plainly.

"Then what are your objections to marrying? From what I can tell, there are no divorce clauses."

"You *know* why there's no divorce clause," I grumbled.

"Why?" The loud, rude Ferguson piped up from across the room. It seemed, unless it was a matter of settling the final decision, he was the only one that ever spoke. And most of the time it was in demands.

I let my gaze flick up to him, not bothering to mask the sheer irritation I knew was visible in it. He was the rude one, after all. I had watched as he'd basically dragged his sister around the room trying to force-feed her. Followed by scowling and pissing off every single person he'd come across afterward. Yeah. He wouldn't care what my face looked like.

"The Fernandez's don't divorce," I said, my voice sounding matter of fact because in truth, it was a fact.

Not only was it bad for business for a multi-billion-dollar conglomerate to have divorce settlements flying around willy-nilly, it was against our views as a family, or so it was said. However...

"I seem to recall a certain old ass man having about three failed marriages before this...thing started with my sister," Clay Ferguson accused.

"Yes, well, that was an exception. Abuelo went through trauma with Abuela Rita's passing." I spoke carefully. "He was acquitted of some questionable choices from that time."

"The way I see it..." Clay started. He had been leaning against the far wall in the corner of the room, his brothers sitting or standing around him. With his legs crossed over one another and his arms folded loosely across his middle, he gave the illusion that he was nonchalant or indifferent. But as he began to unfold himself, his body going to his full height, he got big. Right then I knew, *I knew*, he was going to say something bad. I may have even seen Apá flinch in preparation. "My sister—my too skinny, too skittish, afraid of everything, twenty-five-year-old goddamn sister—has been through some shit with that bastard too. Not to mention finding him with his stomach all over his chest while he paid a visit to God... All due respect, and all."

If Apá hadn't flinched before, he definitely flinched after that.

"Clay, you're done," a calm but aggravated voice demanded. Clinton, the taller, older, milder brother. The one that reminded me too much of myself and too little at the same time. He rose from his seat and pointed at it rigidly, staring Clay down until he reluctantly started moving toward the chair.

"That's my fucking grandfather, who we just buried today. *His* father. Show some respect." I barely gritted through my teeth without crossing the room and going chest to chest like some caveman wannabe. It wasn't protectiveness for my grandfather that brought me to this point, but for the family sitting there in the room with me.

"I said all due respect."

I glared, and Clinton shot a look over his shoulder.

"We understand this is your family and we're here to pay our respects, of course. But this is our sister he's trying to protect, in his own way," Clinton said calmly. Maybe too calmly. As he crossed the room, he'd unbuttoned the one button on his suit jacket and let it fall open mechanically and fluidly all at the same time. I fought the urge to wrinkle my face. Somehow, I may have preferred Clay over Clinton, even though the older brother was much more efficient at the business and negotiations side of this. "We do apologize, but he does have a point."

I inclined my chin—the only movement I made to insist they keep going.

Clinton walked forward, putting himself just outside the circle of his brothers. They didn't exactly flank him, but they did lean forward with his movements. Protectively. Instinctually. A well-oiled machine. "It's obvious to us that Tine—*Clementine*, hasn't been treated well. She won't tell us everything, but a blind man can see that she's off. Contract or no, that's not what we agreed to when the marriage was arranged."

I blew out a breath, my head tipping back just a little as I remembered her sitting at my dining room table just staring. Her eyes weren't wide or rattled or seeking, they were just dead. Thinking of her face at that moment, I couldn't help but agree. So, I nodded one singular time. Then I let out a croak, not caring if my frustration showed. "Did you guys even read this contract before signing her over?"

This got me an *'are you stupid'* sort of look from the brothers. "I believe we had about as much say in business affairs when we were twenty to twenty-four as you must have in your family's business. Otherwise, we wouldn't have signed our sister over to your, may he rest in peace, *seventy-year-old* grandfather in the first place. *All due respect.*"

Clay snickered in the background at his brother using his line.

These fuckers—

"They're right, Ox." It was Apá who spoke. Which had my head whirling around to see him. He was still there, in his chair, looking tired and ready to be over with it.

"They're what?" I couldn't help but ask.

"They're right, Mijo. If you have no objections, and there's no divorce clause, and this is an unwanted marriage on everyone's part, then why are we fighting an uphill battle?" he said. "We're all in business together. We've got too much money in this to back out now. It would be counterproductive to keep something that only a dead man wanted, just for the hell of it—"

"My sister is not a *'something'*," Clay piped up from somewhere we could no longer see. Clinton had gotten closer, blocking the other two men and joining the big boy circle.

Apá continued. "We have a contract and a will to uphold. But we also have lawyers. More contracts can be made. A well-timed divorce can be arranged and everyone can wash their hands of it. We don't have to keep her for longer than necessary."

"You can't just wash your hands of a marriage, Ronny." This was my mom who was hissing as low as she could to my father, not wanting to argue in front of guests. "Our first son, our baby. You would just sign him away?"

"He'll be alright." My dad also failed at whispering. And I didn't know if I agreed with my mom or my dad, but I knew I was starting to feel sick to my stomach and of this goddamn conversation.

Clinton must have felt the same, as he stood so still with one hand on his hip and the other pinching at the bridge of his nose. "How long then? She's already wasted five years. She's young now but won't be forever and she deserves a life after all of this."

I didn't disagree. Her face flashed in my head again and the memory of seeing her nibble on small snacks to placate her brother nipped at me. *Still not eating.* She *did* deserve more than this. She deserved not to be so…broken.

"Three years." My father was in a deal making mood, it seemed. He stood and now we were in an honest to God pow wow, the three of us forming a distanced huddle as we faced each other in various stances of hands-on hips, fidgety movements, and scowling faces. "It'll be enough time for outsiders to get used to something so unorthodox. It'll give Clementine enough time to heal from what she's gone through this past week—" It wasn't only the Fergusons who scoffed at the wording. This past half decade was more like it. The slip earned me a scowl from both my parents. Apá continued. "—And it will be more than enough time for it to be believable that the marriage has run its course."

There was a curse from somewhere in the background and a dramatic "Dios Mio" from Amá. Then, unsurprisingly, the loud one spoke again. "This is pretty fucked up, you know that?"

"This is business, son."

"Hey! I'm getting sick and fucking tired of you referring to my goddamn sister as a thing, or as business, or whatever the fuck else. If I hear it again, I—"

"What you're not going to fucking do is threaten my dad in his own goddamn house," I snapped before even thinking twice.

"Yeah? And what the hell are you gonna do about it?" He was getting up, or at least trying to, before a large hand clamped down onto his shoulder, shoving him back into his seat.

"Clay!" The oldest Ferguson let out a mix between a groan and a command. Tipping a chin over his shoulder, he shot daggers at his brother. "They signed a contract, man. Will you just let me handle it?"

One. Two. Three beats of silence, before a deflated, irritated breath filled the air.

"They should've signed your stiff ass over instead," he grumbled as he fell back into his seat completely.

I swallowed a snort. I did like him. I did.

"Niños, por favor?" Apá's patience was really dwindling if he was Spanglishing around guests. "I'm sorry it had to come to all this. I really am, I feel for your sister. We didn't do enough in that situation. We are trying to do more now.

"You boys are all men now. Men who know what an agreement means, especially when it complicates so much business between us, yes?"

Grumbles.

One grumble was burley and commanding. It took a second longer to realize that it was the silent giant, finally speaking. And all he muttered was a low rumbling, "Clint?"

Whatever the hell *that* meant, Clinton Ferguson must have understood it, because he did that glance over his shoulder thing once more before turning his head back to Apá and I. A thoughtful look on his face.

"And..." He paused, grumbled a little to himself, and then reset. "And what about us?"

"What about you?" Apá asked.

"Well, that night, when Clem had the authorities get a hold of us, It... That was the first we'd heard from her in years," Clinton explained.

I felt my pulse in my throat. The throat that was closing up in, what was this? Anger? I swallowed the thickness of it as best as I could, blinking away the ire as I tried to listen. To focus.

But, *years*?

"We thought she was done with us a long time ago and when she called after so long... We just thought it was because of the situation. That she was freaked out by everything that happened that night. But when we got there, she showed us her phone. It's jailbroken with some pretty advanced stuff. No calls in or out. Only two numbers. Ron and 911. No messaging, no anything..."

I coughed. My gaze going to my father, *wild*.

"Her wallet too. All her former credit cards were closed when she first married and we thought she'd just opened new ones in the Fernandez name. But her things were empty. I didn't even find an ID."

I sucked in a breath and then coughed it out. I had seen it. I had noticed the bare walls of Abuelo's house. The cold distance between his and her rooms. Everything else that had seemed strange and out of place and wrong in that house. I hadn't put it all into perspective, but I should have.

I mean, the girl wouldn't even talk to anyone except for her brothers. Judging by the way they were constantly crouching over her like wolves protecting their pack, whatever she was saying couldn't be good.

I heard myself curse rather than saying it intentionally. Because *fuck. Fuck, fuck, fuck*, Abuelo, what the hell?

"We had no idea." The words dropped from Apá's mouth solemnly. "I'm sorry."

"Look, Oaxaca is a good man. He won't hurt her. She will have whatever she wants whenever she wants it. And she will be a part of our family. *Really* part of it this time." His voice had taken on a more sincere tone. "Plus, I've got daughters. I'm sure they would love to spend time with her. I'm sure they would all get along just fine."

A loud snort came from the other side of the room. Clay again. "Yeah, no offense boss, but your daughters wouldn't know nice if it hit 'em in the ass."

A snicker from Mateo, who I'd forgotten was even in the room. "Alta's nice."

A snicker from me. God, were we a family of animals with bad temperaments?

"Congratulations, one of five of you idiots is decent. Do you want an award?" Clay chastised.

I curled my lip.

"The point," Clinton swiped a hand at his brother to stop. "The point isn't that she needs a new family. We just want to make sure she's allowed to see the family she's already got. We weren't given the luxury of being a part of the negotiation process of her last wedding. If this has to happen again, we need to know that it isn't going to be like last time."

This was it. This was my fate. To be married off at my dead abuelo's will with no say and no way out. There was no choice. Because it was either this or give up the family business. Throw away my dad's, and my own, life's work and for what? A few years of a contractual agreement?

No.

I wouldn't throw away something so massive for pride. And I would never ruin my family for my own benefit. I'd never made a single decision without my parents, my brother, or my sisters in mind. If protecting them meant saying '*I do*' to someone, arranged or otherwise, I could do it. I *would* do it. It was as good as done. And as I stood up straighter, withholding a big sigh, I told them as much.

"Ferguson, get me your terms. I don't care what they are, as long as they pertain to her, I can almost guarantee it'll be done. She can reopen whatever old cards and accounts she wants, but as a Fernandez widow and now wife once again, she'll have access to her own lines of credit as well as monthly deposits made to her personal checking, savings, and investment accounts."

Okay… I guess I was doing this. I was rattling things off like I was doing this, so I must be agreeing to it. And if I was surprised by the things I was saying, I must have been doing a great job at hiding it, because the surprise radiating off of everyone else's features was even more prominent.

"You can see her whenever, whyever, and however you like and vice versa. Just inform me or someone close to me so that I know what's going on."

"And your relationship?" Clinton asked.

I stared, wondering just what kind of relationship he possibly thought I could've built with his sister in three days. All of which she holed up in one room and didn't leave.

Someone cleared their throat from behind me and again I was reminded of my little brother, being so good for a change. "I think he means—"

"He means, are you gonna screw our sister?" said the only person in the room who would dare say it.

My eyes jumped from one dark and handsome face to another. They were all serious faces. It must have been the deciding factor, because they stood and closed in on the circle, filing in at their older brother's sides and staring me down for any traces of bad intentions.

"This will be a marriage of contract, not of corruption," I replied easily, meaning it. "Your precious sister will be safe from me. Put it in writing if you want."

Long moments passed with no one saying a word. The Fergusons looked at me and then at my parents and brother who had at some point drifted closer. They looked at us for so long and with so much frustration in their glares that for a second I thought they'd refuse and that we were going to have to do this the hard way—Because there was no way this wasn't going to be done.

But after so many long moments of sheer quiet and scrutiny, Clinton Ferguson put his hand out to me and only me and deigned to tip his head down in a silent agreement. I reached forward and shook it, not for the first time, but I can admit for the first time regarding something so sensitive.

And then it was done.

"Clay." Clinton's voice was almost inaudible as he did that glance back thing. "Go get Tine."

Clay didn't hesitate. He turned on his heels, those big shoulders and long limbs turning with him, and he took purposeful steps toward the dwindling gathering outside that room.

Something twisted in my gut. Something new and instinctual and protective and possessive. It had me scrunching up my face and reaching out my hand. It had me slapping that hand on the loud one's shoulder to get his attention.

"Hey. Let me…" I cleared my throat, not liking the sound of hesitation on my tongue. I tried again. "Let me tell her, yeah?"

And after a few raised eyebrows and confused looks, they did.

Chapter Seven

CLEMENTINE

I was hyperventilating.

Why?

Because in my world, and only in my world, did my husband dying mean that I was contractually obligated to marry his grandson or else my entire family's livelihoods and fortunes would be up for forfeit.

Ironically, the news didn't hit me right away. Probably because it was delivered by the grandson in question.

It was him who approached me first. Striding up to me as I sat on a couch in his family's wide open living room. He stopped directly over me, bending at the waist to set something down on the wooden coffee table in front of my knees. I didn't bother checking what it was. I wanted nothing from him, aside from being granted the right to go home with my brothers, so why would I?

Then I smelled whatever the hell was on the table. It was all spice and meat and peppery aromas. It made my eyes flutter, slowly bringing him into focus.

Grave. That is the exact look that was on his face. Grave, and maybe solemn, and definitely resigned. I hadn't seen that look on him before. Determined and serious seemed to be his default setting, but I was yet to see a look so dreaded. Which had my stomach curling into itself.

Dropping to his haunches before me, Ox leaned an elbow onto the coffee table and slid a long-fingered hand behind the object he'd set there. It was a bowl. A bowl of whatever smelled so good, like spices and chiles and home. He was sliding it toward me.

"Clementine, I'd like to do some business with you. Do you think you might be interested?" he asked out of the blue, without context, and with no worry that I might say no.

I lifted a shoulder in a small shrug. I was at least a little interested in what he had to say.

"Good," he said. Those fingers slid the bowl a little further in my direction. "First piece of business, I need you to eat something."

I shook my head on instinct. As I did, the delicious smell of whatever was in that bowl wafted up to me again. I was losing it. Getting lightheaded and feeling faint and I knew if I didn't eat something soon, I would probably pass out. But nothing had been appetizing to me. Nothing had made me want to open my mouth and exert the energy needed to chew until…

My eyes zeroed in on the bowl again. I looked from it to the man in front of me, then back and forth between them again before finally settling on the food once and for all.

I licked my lips.

As if beckoned, the bowl appeared in my lap. Ox set it there so quickly I had to shoot my hands up to catch it by its sides, saving myself from catching it all over my dress.

Once the bowl was settled in my lap, Ox was up and across the room. I watched as he grabbed a wooden chair from a sitting table and carried it back over to me. Setting it down right in front of me, he slid into the seat gracefully. Spreading, like men do, he leaned forward with his elbows on to his knees and a fist going up to cover his mouth.

He watched me the entire time.

So, I watched him the entire time right back.

It didn't faze or deter him. Instead, he just settled in. And when we just stared at each other for more long moments, he finally squinted his eyes into sharp assessing daggers and ordered, "Eat."

Okay.

I picked up the long golden soup spoon. It was warm from sitting in the steam coming off of the reddish-brown liquid. I stirred it around a little even leaning my head forward to sniff. It smelled good, but foreign. Whatever it was, I'd never had it before and I was pretty sure it wasn't one of the food options for the other guests.

As if reading my mind, Ox's eyes moved over my face before they slid in the direction of the food display. After a moment, he looked back at me. "It's not from the concessions. My mother made this last night for my family. It's soup. Try it."

Soup, again. Soup that he'd pulled from his family's own kitchen instead of from the expensive catering order feeding the rest of the guests. Soup I was obediently gathering a spoonful of and bringing up toward my mouth.

With a quick swipe of my tongue, I tasted it, my eyes darting upward to see if I had been caught in the movement.

He'd seen.

He hadn't taken his eyes off of me, of course he would see. But after the taste of the thick broth hit my tongue, I didn't really care. Dipping the spoon back in, I speared off a piece of meat and watched as it fell right apart and onto my spoon. I took a small nibble and again was struck by how good it was.

I could eat this.

So I did. Slowly. Like, *really* slowly. Partly because the soup was hot, but also because Ox just sat there watching me. The *whole* time. It wasn't until I was about halfway through the bowl and was slowing down considerably that he straightened in his chair and leaned back, as if relaxing.

"I want to be honest with you Clementine, always," he started after clearing his throat. *Always*? "The will was read today and you're in it."

This had me looking at him, the spoon in my hand going slack.

Me? In the will?

Long fingers stretched in front of me, scooping up the half-eaten bowl and setting it aside. He was leaning forward again, elbows on knees, hands hanging between his legs. "If I go ahead and tell you what it said, will you promise to try and wait until I'm finished to react?"

I gave a single nod.

The grave look was back as he examined me, his lips pinched in on themselves, his eyes wary. A long, long sigh came out of him and I could feel a faint trace of breath across my skin. He was speaking, or he may have already spoken. I wasn't sure, because after the first five words my ears started to buzz.

"We are to be married. You and I. The gist of the condition is that we marry on the account of no heirs having been produced to reinforce the mergers. And if we don't marry, we lose the merger and the businesses along with it."

It was a miracle I didn't throw up right then and there. As soon as I heard those words, I felt the food I'd just eaten lurch in my stomach. I felt my heartbeat start to double in speed. My breath caught in my throat and wouldn't start back up again. My ears rang and I swear the man in front of me started to blur.

Would I faint? I could faint. God, I was going to throw up and then faint into it.

How could this happen? I skirted my blurry eyes around the room in

64

search of my brothers. How could they let this happen? I had just gotten out. Clay had *just* told me he was taking me with him. I had *just* started thinking that maybe I endured all the bad that life could throw at me. That I was done. That I could have a break. And now...

The dark corners of an even darker room flashed in my head, and I swear my body reared back in revolt.

No.

The dread of a certain hour of the night started to creep itself up my spine and sink down into my bones. I felt sick.

No.

The sound of a laugh, humorless and evil, filled my ears over and over again. I whimpered.

God, no!

Something cold bit into my skin. I jumped, startling slightly because, in my hands, Ox had pressed a cold bottle of water. Cool condensation dripped from the bottle into my palms.

"Drink," his calm, deep, patient voice told me. When I didn't move and just stared down at the sweating plastic in my hands, he reached forward with those olive toned fingers and unscrewed the cap for me. Then he ducked his head, his dark eyes finding my lighter ones and said in a softer but still stern voice, "*Drink.*"

Hypnotized by that stare and that voice as much as anyone else would be—and also stunned to hell by the crap show that was my life— I lifted the bottle to my lips and started taking baby sips.

The cool liquid on my tongue and throat soothed me almost instantly. Bringing my mind back down to focus and bringing a strange sort of sad helplessness upon me.

I was getting married... Again.

My face crumpled, but I didn't cry. My nose and throat stung like I was going to, but I gulped down another large mouthful of liquid to keep the tears at bay.

Water wasn't going to be strong enough. Even though I hardly ever drank alcohol, at that moment, water just wasn't going to cut it. My eyes flitted behind me to the tray that had held tall-stemmed glasses full of golden liquid. Someone had set it down on the buffet table hours ago. It was probably warm by now but...

"You haven't touched food in three days. I would advise against the wine," a voice said. My neck slowly turned back around, facing forward. Although he used pretty words like "*advise*" to give me the illusion of choice, I knew what he was really saying was a firm "*no*".

I obeyed. The thought that I had only been a free willing woman for maybe forty-eight hours had my throat burning and my face crumpling all over again.

"I know," he said, his mouth tightening in that grim line again. "I get it. We've been dealt a pretty shitty hand. Me being the oldest in my family and you being the only girl in yours has put us both in a position of...*unavoidable responsibility*."

I blinked in response. This didn't deter him.

"I would love to just tell everyone to fuck off and to stop messing with my life. And I could imagine you feel the same…" He kept trailing off like he was giving me a chance to answer, even though I hadn't once done so. "But I want to keep my company, Clementine. I want to keep my family's legacy, and I want you to do the same."

Silence.

"So, how about we make a deal?"

A deal? With me? I peeked upward to see if Clay or anyone else was around, but Ox blocked my line of sight.

"Clem, I want to make a deal with *you*. Not them. Just you and me," he said firmly.

Me?

He took a deep breath that seemed shaky. The only crack to his otherwise cool demeanor. "In exchange for your hand, I can be your way out of this cycle. We can marry to appease the will, but we can enter our own agreement as well. I want this arrangement to work. Like

I said, I don't want to give up my life's work. But I also have no interest in doing or making you do things you don't want to do. I have no interest in harming you any more than you have already been by my family."

Blink, blink, blink. All I could do was blink.

"So..." He dragged the word out for a while as he took the time to survey my unchanged face. "So, I'm asking you what you need to make this something you'll agree to."

Blink.

"I'll give you whatever you want."

Blink.

"Will you really never talk to me?" He sighed. It was soft, but it still showed testimony to his frustration. Determined as ever, he pushed on. "What do I need to promise for you to agree to do this with me?"

With him? Promise? This was a contractual agreement. A decision that had been made *for* me before I was old enough to make them. Didn't he know that I barely had to agree to anything? Why was he even asking? I *had* to do it. I had no other choice. But...

But he was giving me one anyway. He was putting this on me, and finally making this a decision that could be made on my terms.

I could decide.

I gulped at the realization and at the opportunity. I could decide? He was saying so, wasn't he? But... What should I do? What *could* I do? This was all so new and sudden and...Exciting.

"It's fine if you can't pin down what you want immediately, this is all happening suddenly. We can flesh out the details later. *Together.* Right now, I just need a yes or no."

I set down the water bottle I'd been clutching for dear life. The cool bottle pressed against my leg and cold seeped through my dress. Cautiously, I leaned forward, my hand making it to the very edge of a tall, muscular knee. I knocked his limb twice.

Because what? What was he talking about? My head hurt and my stomach churned and my throat burned.

67

He looked down at my hand for the longest time and then his slow gaze moved up to me again and I could have sworn something burned hot in that gaze.

"Contrary to all our previous 'conversations', I don't speak Morse code, Clementine," he grumbled, his frame leaning backward in his chair. His knee bobbed slightly, which caused my fist to bob with it.

My eyes bugged at him. *Rude.* But fair. Even so, I still couldn't seem to swallow enough to clear my throat. I couldn't make enough room for the words to come out. So, I knocked on his knee again. Hoping, *praying* that I was getting the message across. *What are you talking about?*

Another grumble. Another sigh.

"I'll put it like this. I need you to be my wife. I'm willing to offer you money, property, connections, possessions, whatever you want in exchange for it." He adjusted again, taking my fist with him. I waited patiently, not caring in the least that I was touching him. That I was so close. I just watched his eyes as he watched me, eyes fluttering around my form like he was examining a cut of meat to pick up at the store. "Or if it's fresh air, space or time with your family you want, I can arrange for that too. I'm willing to give almost anything for these three years."

My eyes popped to his. Questioning. *Three years?*

"Three years. That's it, Clementine. There's no rule against divorce in the will. We just need to make it believable and make it legal and then we can make it whatever the two of us want it to be," he said. "I won't touch you. I won't harm you. I won't control you. I might hardly even see you with my schedule. We will be glorified roommates who respect each other's time and boundaries. And hopefully, eventually, we can start to be friends."

And there it was. I guess he was serious. We were obviously *obligated* to marry, but he was still giving me a choice in the matter. A choice to make something out of this shitty situation. He didn't need to do that, any of it, but he did.

So, with the same knotted stomach, sweating palms and burning throat, I rose to my feet. Not missing a beat Ox rose to his too, towering over me in an elegant stance. Reaching between us, I extended my hand and waited.

He took that hand in his, those eyes steady on my face. His big palm was warm, and it swallowed up my narrow one in its grasp. With a firm shake, an agreement was made.

Now, after the conversation I thought I half dreamed up, I sat in the nearly all black kitchen of my older brother's penthouse condo, stacking papers into a manila folder and sealing it shut. It was the final run through of our contract. Not the contract my brothers and the Fernandez lawyers had drawn up. The contract that Ox Fernandez himself had sat with me in the very same kitchen and helped me outline to the letter. Just like he'd promised.

And I was hyperventilating.

Because in just a little over twelve hours, I was going to get married. Again.

Chapter Eight

OX

I stood in the back garden of my responsibly sized home with a frown on my face. I could see her. Everyone could see her. She was right fucking there, standing in the backyard garden. Leaning on her brother, Clay, who I was surprised to learn was her favorite. *Hyperventilating.*

Chewing the inside of my cheek, I narrowed my eyes. I would have gone down there myself and demanded her to just breathe goddammit, if it weren't for the fact that I was standing in my garden on a Sunday morning in front of my immediate family at the end of an aisle. My wedding aisle. Because I was getting married.

And the bride was hyperventilating. *Dammit.*

I was irritated. Looking out among the "guests" didn't help much either. Since the guest list itself consisted of my siblings, my parents, and the couple of cousins I didn't completely want to maim—plus Clementine's very small guest list of just her three brothers—the ratio of people who would and wouldn't give me shit about this was not in my favor. As if confirming the fact, I caught the faces of my siblings all grouped together in a mocking huddle.

Mateo had his cheeks puffed up as he spurted out short silent laughs. Alta was alternating between shooting me pitying looks and glancing backward to see if the scene at the other end of the aisle had changed at all. Lis was also alternating looks between rolling her eyes at Alta and checking her watch. Ceci was sitting there, leaning back in her seat and staring straight at me. *Sneering.* Sneering and mouthing taunts like "*gold digger*", "*sell out*", and "*what the fuck, Ox*". And above all this, they were leaning into each other, whispering back and forth. Talking about me, I guessed. Irritating me, I knew.

I was tempted to let out a whistle to get their attention. They'd know what it meant. *Shut up.* But my dad beat me to it, the sound coming out loud and clear. Echoing slightly around the green manicured garden. The Fernandez idiots straightened up.

So did the bride, I noticed, as my eyes bounced back down the stone path we had deemed an aisle for the occasion. It looked like it had taken some force from Clay to get her going, judging by the vice grip he had on her shoulder, but it was finally happening. All dressed up in a gown that flowed loosely around her, so pale pink it almost looked white and with her dark curly hair in loose waves around her gaunt shoulders. She was finally, *finally,* making her way toward the altar.

Thank God.

She held no flowers, wore no veil, and looked about as far from a blushing bride as someone could get. With noticeably shaking fingers, she gripped her brother's sleeve and took ragged, uneven breaths with every step she took toward me. Tongue in cheek, I fought the urge to screw my nose at the scene.

What the hell was she so afraid of? Was she not aware that the arm she was stuck so firmly to was attached to a loud-mouthed idiot with no regard for others' feelings or emotions? How could I be comparable to him?

So annoying. So irritating.

Was she really afraid of me? Me, who had hardly even spoken to her, instead mewing at her like she was a horse that would scare easily. Me, who had taken care to stay at least three paces away from her at all times so as not to make her uncomfortable. Me, who had offered most of the terms for our marriage negotiations freely, even when they did not exactly benefit me, because *she* couldn't be bothered to come up with any on her own. Me, who had for all intents and purposes treated her like she was my lord and savior instead of my fucking charge.

So, *so annoying.* And *irritating.* And *spoiled.* And yet...

The pair of siblings made it down the aisle. The music quieted and Clay slowed, preparing to hand her off to me with a look that could slay gods. That's when her skittering nervous eyes finally fluttered to mine and my heart skipped.

I realized it then. That *I* was the asshole here. I knew it right then. Because in her eyes, the only thing I saw was trauma. And it was like seeing those eyes was the compass I needed to finally see the other parts of her she was screaming at me to find.

It wasn't just her hands that were shaking. It was her entire body. Clay hadn't been holding onto her shoulders like that just to support her down the aisle. He was holding her *together.*

Something I should have been doing instead of cursing the very air she breathed. *Fuck.*

Stepping down off the dais, I met them before they could reach me. I scowled momentarily at Clay's ugly mug, but my attention was singular. Looking down at the shivering little creature before me, I brought my hands up between us and turned my palms to face the sky.

"Clem." My voice was low, but it still made her jolt. Leaning forward, I lowered it even more. "Can I walk you up?"

"Aren't you supposed to ask me—" Clay's words were cut off by a hiss of pain, but the only movement I saw was the slight flutter of Clem's soft pink dress. Did she step on him? *Hopefully.*

She shot a quick glance her brother's way, and he leaned sideways, plopping a kiss onto the side of her head. It lingered ever so slightly and I thought I heard a mumbling of, "I'm sorry, Tiney," before he pulled away.

Next thing I knew, her hands were in my upturned ones and he was on his way to his seat.

A shiver racked through her and I closed my fingers around hers. Three big steps and we were both stationed up on the pretty white dais, a floral arch before us, and a Catholic priest who we'd bribed to officiate outside of the church on such short notice. Alta and Amá had to work with what they could. I doubted Clem even cared. As we faced the altar and the priest, it seemed like her eyes were in another solar system.

The music began to quiet down completely, and I leaned my shoulder down into hers, careful not to bump it and scare her. "What's wrong?"

She shook her head, her long hair brushing against my wrist, which was flush against hers as we both held onto each other's hands. Leaning back, I took in what I could see of her face. Yeah, nope. She was not okay.

"Clementine, *what's wrong?*" I insisted.

Her eyes racked to mine and then quickly up to the wedding arrangements.

And then she did it. She said something. Something so low and so broken up by stuttering, chattering teeth that I missed it.

Fuck.

With a slight tilt to my head, I took in the profile of her scared to death expression and I swallowed. Leaning back down, I got closer to her ear, letting our shoulders just graze each other this time. "Do you want to face me instead?"

Those big brown eyes swung up to mine and her head was nodding before I even met them. So, I did what any man would do. I gave the woman what she wanted.

Turning us, I brought her forgotten hand back into my upturned one and gave an encouraging squeeze. When there was a noticeably awkward pause that caused more than a couple people to clear their throats, I slid my gaze to the priest and barked, "Start."

For the next few minutes, we ran through the correct prose and hymns of a perfect wedding speech. He knew not to make it long, but with every hitched breath and twitch of her hand Clem made it seem longer. She stared right at me, clutching my hands like they were life rafts in the middle of the ocean.

"*Breathe*," I mouthed to her. She sucked in a greedy almost gasp through her mouth and held it there. After three seconds, I gave her hands a little shake. Then I made a quiet show of blowing a breath out of my lungs. She mirrored it.

Okay. I guess we were doing this together.

After a few synchronized deep breaths, she started to quiet her hitching and shaking, still giving one or two here and there. The whole time, her eyes stared up at me. I could do nothing but give her my strongest stare in return, hoping it conveyed what I was trying to say to her.

I've got you.

"Oaxaca Manuel Fernandez, do you take Clementine to be your lawful wedded wife? To have and to hold from this day forward, for better, for worse, for richer, for poorer, in sickness and in health as long as you both shall live?"

"I do," I said immediately.

"Clementine Margarite Ferguson, do you take…"

My breath hitched slightly in my throat as the priest started addressing Clem, who was essentially mute in public and with anyone other than her brothers. I swallowed. How had I not thought about this? Maybe I could just tell the priest that she needed to write her answer down. I doubted a nod would suffice as a legal agreement, but maybe…

"I do." It took me three extra seconds to realize that it was her speaking. *Her* voice, sweet as her name promised. That shy undertone present and perfect. Her eyes still on me.

I blinked and then I blinked again. And then—like I couldn't help it—I smiled. A surprised but pleased smile that couldn't have stopped even if I tried. She didn't smile back, only fluttering her eyes before letting them drop to my shoes.

"I now pronounce you man and wife. You may now kiss," the forgotten priest was saying.

With slow, trackable movements, I brought her left hand up toward my face. The one that now wore a four-carat tennis style diamond band around it. With caution, I placed a short, dry, closed-mouth kiss on the very top of her hand and set it back to her side. As I was straightening up and passing by her shoulder, close enough to her ear that I could speak only to her, I felt the need to reassure her. I had stupidly noticed way too late how much she was struggling just to make it down the aisle. I wanted to put her at ease somehow. To make it better.

Angling my mouth so that my words were for her ears and her ears only, I murmured, "Well done, Clementine," before setting myself back upright.

It was later, when we were sitting out under the shade of the long stone pergola, that Clementine spoke to me again.

After the wedding ceremony, Alta and Amá had a small brunch arranged. Small meaning a full spread of fruit, veggies, waffles, churros, eggs, breakfast meats (American and Mexican) and drinks. The meal had been quiet for all of a few minutes before the shenanigans started.

Almost immediately Lis and Alta started at each other's throats, Lis starting it mostly. Amá was too busy fussing around everyone's plates and her arrangements to break up any arguments. Mátti sat by the silent giant trying to get him to answer in more than head nods and grunts while simultaneously trying to shove as much food in his mouth as humanly possible. Apá and Clinton sat at the far end of the table talking seriously about something sounding suspiciously like the acquisition strategy we'd been working on for months. I trained my ears as much as possible on that conversation, but Amá caught me and scolded me for ignoring my bride. And for the love of God, it must have been some kind of sick joke that Clay Ferguson and my sister Ceci sat side by side one another. Because the entire time they did, they both took turns giving each other looks of disbelief and horror when one of them said something. Literally anything. It must have been noticeable too, because beside me, after maybe a good forty minutes, and what I noticed was about three mimosas later, there was a giggle. Light and feminine and *cute*.

I leaned back in my chair, crossing my ankle over my knee and slid a look to the woman at my side. While I'd been worrying about her little episode during the ceremony, I hadn't had a chance to truly take her in. Not her soft fitting gown that showed pinker under the shade than it did in the sunlight. Or how she was wearing makeup for the first time since I'd met her. Jewelry too. She was normally bare of all adornments and had her hair done consistently in a long simple braid that showed off curly textured hair even while bound up. Today it was straightened and re-curled into waves that fell even longer along her back.

Alcohol must have loosened her up, because instead of sitting ramrod straight with her mouth pressed in a straight line and her hands twisting in her lap like she had been when we first sat, she was sitting slightly pushed away from the table, her body leaning forward as her elbows supported her against it. She had a soft smile on her lips. Hardly even noticeable if it weren't for the crinkle of amusement present in her eyes as she watched over the party.

She turned her head, hair swinging across her back, and she looked at me. And her soft, soft smile fell.

I frowned.

Leaning her head forward, she rested a cheek on her hands and let her gaze flicker over me.

"You're mad," she said.

I could only hope I didn't flinch at the sound of her voice. If I did, I had no clue. Because hearing it again was like both fire and ice racing through my veins. Hearing her speaking to me when she spoke to so few inflated my fragile male ego just a smidge. It made me feel special and responsible for it somehow. Responsible for her, for keeping her and that voice she guarded so closely protected. But it also felt like a punch to the stomach at the same time.

"You're speaking to me for the first time and that's what you decided to say?"

A blink of a smile pulled at the right corner of her mouth. Then it was gone. "No. The first thing I told you was that I was scared. Then I said, 'I do' and now I'm saying that I happen to notice you're angry."

"Hmm."

She wasn't wrong. I hadn't been able to hear the very first thing she'd said to me, and now I wasn't exactly pleased that she was admitting those first words consisted of *"I'm"* and *"scared"*. I bit my cheek to refrain from scolding her, as I had a tendency to do with people.

"Will you tell me why?" she asked quietly. Sweetly. Damn, I was going to need fucking portion control on that voice. Every time I heard it, it made my stomach lurch and caught me by surprise.

"I'm not angry. Just a little irritated," I admitted.

"Why?"

"It's not a big de—"

"If it's not a big deal, then just tell me why." She blinked and added, "Please?"

I looked at her from the side of my eyes for a moment. A resigned sigh slipped out and I shook my head a little. "I don't like that you were afraid of me."

Her mouth worried into a frown in response.

"I thought we had an agreement, Clementine."

"We do," she said, her eyebrows furrowing together.

"And I was clear about what this is, yes?" I asked. Her big eyes stared up at me for just a second too long. I narrowed mine. "*Yes*?"

Her only response was an unconvincing head nod, so I spoke again. "No romance, no controlling, no doing things we don't want to do. We outlined all of it."

"I know," she croaked, that sweet voice going hoarse.

"Then am I just that scary?" I asked. I couldn't *believe* I asked, because who was I? Someone who needed validation from the random woman he was forced to marry? No. That wasn't like me. But I do admit it would have been nice to know that after all the effort I was putting in to treat her delicately, that at the very least she wouldn't be fucking terrified of me.

I must have grumbled because her shoulders hunched dejectedly and her wringing hands were back in full force in the cradle of her lap. I immediately regretted what I said.

"I'm sorry," she said on a whispered breath. The sound was so sad and disheartened that I hated myself in that moment for making her sound like that.

"Don't—" I started to say before frustration clogged my throat. Dammit. I tipped my head back, letting my eyes scan the green vines along the pergola before closing them. I counted to three, collecting myself. "Don't apologize for me being grumpy over something. I almost always am. *I'm sorry*."

Silence.

"Are you having a good time?" I tried, hoping this conversation was salvageable or that I could at least bring the lightness back to the set of her shoulders.

I didn't. Instead, she turned those shoulders back square to the table and murmured, "Mhmm."

Damn. I was fucking this up.

The thought was on repeat in my head as we sat in that weird silence for long minutes, both wanting to say something but not knowing how. Finally, when I had nearly given up on her speaking to me again and was thinking about going over and setting the record straight with my teasing siblings, I heard her clear her throat delicately.

I looked at her and she was already looking at me, those soft eyes burning me where I sat. It looked like she was trying to tell me something through that gaze. Something she couldn't say in words alone. I swallowed.

"I wasn't afraid of you, Ox," she said, her voice a mix between quiet reassurance and gruff emotion. "I'm really grateful for what you've done. I just... I'm just sick of being auctioned off like chattel. Marrying Ron wasn't the first time they used me like this, but it was the worst."

Any and all words I might have thought to say stuck in my throat. I couldn't respond. I couldn't possibly get them past the big stupid knot that had formed from the center of my chest to the hollow of my neck. She reached over and placed a thin hand over my forearm and squeezed.

"I'm sorry I made you feel that way. It was never you; it was me. It's *always* me."

And then she got up and walked away.

Later that night, when everyone left and the party had been cleaned up, I laid awake in my bed. I was just down the hall from Clementine, who had decided to stay here with me for the night before heading to her brother's place while I was away on business for the next couple of weeks.

I was beyond surprised she was here. As part of my formal negotiations with her, I had offered to rent out a condo or buy her a house so she wouldn't be forced to live with me. Her answer to that had been that she'd just stay with her brothers instead. So, after the wedding, when everyone in my family had hopped into their cars and peeled off, her brothers lingered. I imagine they were worried this would turn out like the last time she'd married a Fernandez and they would never see her again. I couldn't blame them. They *all* had trauma surrounding the marriage.

"Tiney, you coming with me?" Clay had asked.

She shook her head, her face looking tired as she stopped right next to me in the wide-open landing of the doorway. We all looked at her.

"You know I'm leaving tomorrow morning, right?" I asked quietly. She nodded. We all continued staring.

"I'll come tomorrow," she offered finally. "For now, I should get used to my new home."

The threats I received from all three brothers after that declaration were colorful to say the least. I had to assure them that I would neither corrupt nor ax murder their sister, even though she had already been staying with me for the better part of a week anyway. In the end, she actually stayed. We all knew how much more comfortable she would be staying with her brother, yet, *she stayed*. And I had no idea why.

At least when she was staying with Clay for the days leading up to the wedding, she ventured around his place. Here, she just stayed in her room. A room that she promptly retired to as soon as her brothers left for the evening. A room that seemed to be haunting me, because it was the only light still on in the house even as late-night hours turned to early morning ones. I didn't know if she was awake or had just fallen asleep with the light on, but having her here now, as my wife, was messing with me.

Turning over so I couldn't see the light shining out of her window, I sighed into my pillow and closed my eyes. If I just thought about all the contracts I had to read on the plane I was waking up for in just a few hours, I would for sure start drifting to—

Knock, knock, knock.

I jolted out of my tenuous dozing and jerked my head over my shoulder. Was I dreaming or—

Knock, knock, knock.

Okay, definitely not dreaming. Grunting slightly, I pulled myself out of my bed and started crossing the room.

"Clem?" I called out.

She didn't answer and as I neared the door, I saw the shadow of her feet passing back and forth on her side of it. She was pacing? It was midnight, and she was pacing. I reached the door and immediately flung it open, spreading my arms in the doorway and leaning forward against the frames, looking for her.

It was hard to miss her honestly as she padded away from me in a short midnight blue nightgown that frankly was so short it covered nothing, instead just showing most of her ass in a matching thong. When I opened the door, she jolted and turned quickly to scurry back to me. The front of her gown wasn't much of an improvement. It was lined with black lace and dipped down past her cleavage in a sharp "V" shape. I swallowed something in my throat and brought my eyes up to hers purposefully.

"Is everything alright?" I asked. While I was watching her eyes, she was staring at my throat, refusing to make contact. Her expression seemed off. "Clem, is something wrong?"

No answer. Why was I still surprised that she wouldn't fucking answer? Did she ever?

Ducking down just slightly, I used a knuckle to tip her face by her chin. She let me. And as she brought her eyes back up to mine, I thought I saw a trace of that fear I'd seen earlier in the day. At the altar.

My throat constricted and I felt that same rush of irritation prickle at my neck. She was the one to come to me and now I was scaring her again. *Great.*

"Clem? What are you doing here?" I clipped.

I watched as her eyes went from me down to herself and then somewhere behind my shoulder. I turned to see what she was gazing at with that distant dead look in her eyes, but I saw nothing out of the ordinary in my room.

Looking back down at her, I tried—tried so hard—to gentle my voice. It must have come out harsh anyway, because she flinched as I said, "What?"

Her eyes widened, and she looked down at herself again, this time more pointedly. I set back on my heels and looked at her through a narrowed gaze. What the fuck was she trying to say?

She just stood there. Albeit looking gorgeous with her hair strewn about her shoulders in a messy but sexy sort of way, and her tiny gown hugging her in good, good places. But the gown looked familiar in a way that made me uncomfortable. I'd seen her in something way too similar to the night I'd found her in Abuelo's room… In Abuelo's room where she had been on her way to *see* him right around this time of night.

Goddamn.

Clearing my throat pointedly this time, I didn't even try to be soft. I pulled my hand away from her so quickly, you'd think it had been burned. "Do you know the purpose of a contract, Clementine?"

She nodded.

"Then why do you continue to expect things that aren't in ours?" I gritted out.

She began worrying her lip with her teeth and brought her hands up between us to start wringing the fingers there. She dared a look up at me, "Ron, he liked—"

"Stop." I held up a hand in a stop motion, rubbing the other along my forehead as I squeezed my eyes shut. I didn't want to picture it. When I opened my eyes, she was pacing again, this time closer to me and, Jesus, did she *know* what a robe was? "Clementine, come here and face forward."

Obediently, she did. And she looked up at me with big, terrified eyes. I sighed, feeling the knot in my chest grow.

"Listen to me, alright? I'm going to make this as clear as possible, since a written agreement doesn't seem to be doing the trick." I wish I could later blame the hour of the night or the circumstances on how rude I was being, but truthfully, I just let my irritation get the better of me. "I am not having sex with you. Not tonight, not any night. *Ever.* This is not a real marriage. This is a means to an end. If you're confused about the contract, read it again."

I swallowed that knot down as far as I could, even as it fought to make its way back up my throat. She was staring at me. Just fucking staring. With big brown eyes that looked a little wet. That scared expression on her face, *still.*

She opened her mouth to say something. Something too sweet or docile or good, I'm sure. So I cut her off, not wanting to hear her voice again. "Do you understand?"

She nodded one time, her expression becoming sad, her shoulders hunching in on themselves. Big deal, I was used to that expression from everyone else. *Everyone.*

She could get in line.

"Go to sleep then," I said. "I'll see you soon."

I didn't *slam* the door in her face. I didn't. But when it seemed like she wasn't going to answer, or move, I shut the door and went back to bed.

Chapter Nine

CLEMENTINE

I would not see him soon. In fact, it would be three full weeks until I saw him again. And truly, that was fine.

It hit me harder than I thought it would. The wedding, the vows, the flowers, the cake, and all the forced merriment that came with marrying someone I didn't really know. Contract or no contract, I'd done it before and it had wound up being a nightmare. My every move watched, my every decision made for me, and my every mistake punished. So…

Seeing Ox standing on the dais, underneath the altar had brought up bad feelings for me. Bad memory after bad memory, and I freaked out a little. Did it mean I had forgotten every single good intention he made known to me? Not exactly.

But then he got angry with me. Already, he was angry and when men got angry, plans tended to change. Did I think Ox would be cruel like Ron and punish me for not being every single thing he ever wanted me to be? No... *Maybe,* no? But did I think he was still capable of the near God complex most men seemed to have, not to mention *rich* men? *Definitely.*

I saw how he handled himself. He made *demands*, he didn't ask, and he just expected them to be met. So, while I was already awake at that hour of the night I never, ever, got any sleep, I went to go see—*just to see*—if he was a man of his word.

He was. *Of course,* he was. I knew he would be. Somewhere deep down, I knew. I just—I guess I just didn't understand it. I didn't understand where so much of that good was coming from in him. So I tried to uncover the bad, and naturally, I found some. He had some Ron in him, after all. That condescending, know-it-all, my way or the highway air that I managed to bring out of him in full force while standing outside his bedroom door. And while I appreciated his respect for our contract, he didn't have to be so *rude* about it.

The tone he used was far from the soft deep purr I was getting used to from him. The roughness of his voice had left me feeling itchy. And irritated. And a little bit threatened. Like if I upset him more, he'd keep talking to me like that. That didn't sit well with me.

It didn't sit on my mind for long, though. Not long after I woke up the next day, hours after Oaxaca had already left, there was a knock on the door.

It wasn't a quiet *tap, tap, tap* either. Instead, about four consecutive bangs followed by the ringing of the doorbell sounded throughout the house. When I rushed to pull myself out of my room and to the front door, I was greeted by navy blue.

"Seaside Police. Are you Mrs. Fernandez?" The police officer, tall and bulky in the doorway and flanked by two smaller officers, demanded.

I closed my cardigan around myself and crossed my arms over my chest. Then I nodded, because I was. Mrs. Ronaldo Fernandez, Mrs. Oaxaca Fernandez, one and the same.

"We have a few important questions for you ma'am. Can we come in?" The officer asked.

I nodded again and stepped aside, letting the three, four, and five large men file into the clean house with dirty boots and multiple weapons.

Okay.

I told the damn near police brigade they brought to simply *"ask a few questions"* to settle in anywhere and watched as they chose to stand. I found my arms crossing over my body even tighter as I asked, "Would you like any water or tea?"

Those were the only two things I knew were in the house. Water I could find easily enough, but the tea I would probably have to search for.

Thankfully, the one I assumed was in charge since he was the only one answering said, "No, Mrs. Fernandez. We just came to talk."

Instantly, I wished Clay or Clint or even Connor were there with me. I wished for someone to step in front of me and handle this. I knew what they were here for. What they wanted to ask me. And I didn't want to do it.

I walked to the large loveseat on the far end of the living room and slowly descended into it. This was the first time I was ever sitting in the living space at all and I wish it wasn't. I wish I could find some comfort in the soft cushions of the furniture, but I couldn't. Not with the five stooges standing there watching me like I would run at any moment.

Momentarily, I thought of Ox. The way he took command of *everything*. From the hair on his head to the final detail of our sham wedding, he had it all under control. Ox had been there when I'd found Ron. He was the first; I remembered. Arriving almost as soon as the authorities did. And he had protected me then. Backing the officers away from me, standing in front of me when I was indecent, and answering any question I expressly did not need to answer myself. Ox had handled it then and I bet if he was here, he would handle these guys too.

A long, deep sigh slipped out of my throat as I thought briefly of the look he'd given me before he closed the door in my face the night before. Even then, after I'd upset him last night, I somehow knew he would still take care of this for me.

That broke my heart a little. Because I had a feeling he was going through a lot himself. He was probably just as scared as I was, and here I was waiting on him to do all the work. Him and my brothers. And wasn't that unfair of me? To expect to be protected without doing any protecting in return.

"Mrs. Fernandez?" The officer called.

"Yes?" I answered immediately. I could do this.

"Where were you the night your late husband died?" he asked, no warm-up questions to precede his interrogation.

I stammered a little at his directness, but ultimately, I said, "In our house."

"But not in your bed?" he asked, a pen materializing from behind his ear and a pad flipping open off his belt.

"No, I was in my bed. Ron and I had separate rooms," I corrected. He cast a glance up at me and then at one of his men, but otherwise didn't comment.

"And you entered his room at—", he flipped a page backward in his notepad, "—12:07 that morning? Why?"

I flicked my eyes up from where I had been staring at their boots, wondering if they were going to stain the pretty clean floors. I glared at them, all seeming unfeeling and insensitive. I swallowed hard.

"He was my husband. I was…*visiting*." They didn't nod or show any form of understanding. They just waited for me to explain. I didn't want to. "Like I did *every night*."

"Visiting why, Mrs. Fernandez. How?" He probed.

"I—Ron and I…" I stumbled hard on the words, no grace or finesse. And these assholes, they just waited.

I wanted to curl into myself. To disintegrate. To literally die before I had to tell them I was going into that room to be used as a sex toy for maybe about the thousandth time by a man three times my age. I also didn't want to tell them I preferred to wait until I had my big brothers here for further questioning. And, God forbid, I try to reschedule so I could have my *new* husband, who was also my old husband's grandson, here to handle everything for me.

It sounded ridiculous.

This crushing weight started to hammer down on my shoulders. The familiar feeling of hopelessness was like a crutch for me at this point. I used it often to get away from having to feel this kind of embarrassment and shame. Because who the hell cared what everyone else thought about your life when you didn't even have control over the life you lived in the first place?

"Mrs. Fernandez?" The voice of the officer had gotten distant in the roaring of blood in my ears.

"Ron scheduled sex for him and I. Always in his room, always at midnight. When he didn't answer the door, as was our routine, I got worried and let myself in." I hoped they could hear me because I really didn't want to say it again. I thought I had already told them all of this, but I guess not. "When I got into the room, it was already too late."

"Did you wait to call the police? Or did you call right away?" They asked.

"I called immediately. I had to leave the room to grab my phone." I paused. "I didn't want to go back in until the police got there. So, I waited in my room afterward."

"Do you know of anyone who would want to hurt Ronaldo?" he asked, scribbling diligently in his pad, the others following suit. "Or anyone with the reason to do so?"

"No." *I don't really know much of anyone at all*, I wanted to say.

"Not your family?"

"No."

"Your brothers?"

"*No.*"

"Not even his grandson, Oaxaca Fernandez? Whose house we're in now." Another officer piped up from closest to the door. I wish he'd just turn around and walk through it.

"I didn't know Ox before this, so I wouldn't know their history. But I know him now and I would say no. Not *even* him." I moved my eyes not to the officer who'd spoken up but to the door beside him, hoping they would all take the hint and leave.

"Isn't he your soon-to-be husband?" The same officer asked, stepping forward from his post.

This time I did look at him and stared. He was a tall blonde man, with pretty boy features and a know-it-all smirk. I hated him. I hated him instantly. He looked like the kind of guy who would get rough with me just because. And maybe that's why I didn't mind getting smart with him. Not in defense of myself, no one cared what happened to me anyway. And not in defense of Ox, who could easily take care of himself. It was simply because I didn't like him.

"He is my husband," I said simply. "As of yesterday."

The eyebrows on the men shot to the ceiling and they all grumbled uncomfortably, pulling at their collars and shifting their stances. I may or may not have smirked internally.

"And you don't know him?" Smartass went on.

"Not well, no. Just like my first marriage, this one was arranged. By my late husband. If you have questions on why, you can probably ask his solicitor. But I have no clue." *Other than that Ron was a sadist.*

"Your *late husband* arranged your marriage to *his* grandson following his death?" he asked. I sighed and nodded. He grumbled under his breath. "Fucking rich people, man."

"So the grandson had no interest in you, that's clear, but what about in the businesses?" Another officer murmured from the far left, his glasses clad nose stuck down into his notepad. I grimaced only slightly at his wording, because wasn't it the truth? Ox and his family had known I was there in Ron's clutches the entire time. They only started to care when they had to.

Still, the reminder that I was nothing but another obligation to this family and my own brought my attitude out.

"I don't know," I answered him curtly. I wasn't going to talk about Oaxaca when he wasn't here to defend himself.

"You don't know?" The rude officer asked.

"*I don't know*," I repeated, slower.

"How do you not know?" he asked, his voice raising. "Isn't your family involved in the business too? Aren't you all co-owners?"

I stayed quiet and I kept my eyes pinned to the floor in front of me. Someone mumbled something to him, trying to get him to stop. I wanted to thank that someone. Only briefly, because a second later Rude-ass was gritting his teeth and throwing an exaggerated hand through his hair.

"So, you're out here bouncing around these guys like a pinball and all you happen to know is what time to show up and get—"

"Hey!" A raspy voice shot through the room from the direction of the kitchen. "Pinche cabrónes! Get the hell out of here!"

The herd of police officers promptly began shuffling out of the way, dodging something at their feet as they lifted the big booted things up toward themselves. As they moved out of the way, I saw a small, dark-haired, olive-skinned woman come into view. Her hair was the color of dark chocolate, tied back and secured with a vibrant red scarf in the middle. She wore black stretchy pants and a big long-sleeved t-shirt. Around her was an apron that secured from the waist down. And her feet were slippered.

Had she been in the house this whole time? Who was she?

"Ma'am, this is a closed questioning," one of the officers tried.

"Questioning my ass," she said, punctuating the statement with a lunging motion toward the men. I then realized she was sweeping at their feet with a broom. "If you don't get your nosey asses out of this house right now, it won't even matter that you're here asking her questions without probable cause. Or a warrant. Or an arrest. Ox will have your asses anyway, for coming in when he's not here."

"Excuse me ma'am, what are you doing here? This is a private investigation. This woman's husband was found dead last week. Maybe even murdered," the rude one added in. *Like he really needed to say it out loud.*

I winced, but watched as the girl raised the broom, poised for another attack. I could only sit and watch as the scene unfolded, too stunned to do anything else. Too numb to even try.

And the police officers... The officers grudgingly shuffled toward the oak wooded front doors, almost as if she was right in her accusations. The leading officer's parting words sounded a lot like, "We'll be in contact, Mrs. Fernandez," right before the door slammed in their faces.

Without missing a single beat, the woman turned to face me. She discarded the broom against a nearby wall and then ventured closer, her hands hovering around her hips. When she was close enough to be in full view, but still far enough to be cautious, I let my eyes graze over her beautiful form once more before landing on pretty brown irises.

"Thank you." I dipped my chin in an appreciative nod.

She shrugged a shoulder up toward her ear and swayed awkwardly on her feet. "Ah, don't worry about it. They were assholes."

"Cops always are." I don't know why I said this, only, I'd heard my brothers say it before. As soon as I did, the girl's lips parted in a wide grin. She nodded like she agreed.

Chuckling softly, she said, "Well alright then. Ox said you're an innocent, but I might have to keep an eye on you."

Hmm? Did she say Ox? Ox had talked to this woman about me? Ox knew her? And he had called me innocent?

This is not a real marriage. Ox's words came back into my head. Under my skin. Burning there like a brand. *I am not having sex with you. Not tonight, not any night. Ever.*

It wasn't like I wanted to have sex with him, or be in a real marriage with him, or even for him to particularly like me just…It was just that words like that hurt, even to the people who you think were already broken. Everything had the possibility of breaking further.

But why was that popping into my head now? It couldn't be that I was curious if he already had someone he wanted to marry before being forced to marry me. Nope. No way. But if he *had*, could it have been this woman?

As if my staring eyes said the words out loud, the girl took a breath in and nodded her head. Then, with the will and determination of someone who had hyped themself up for something, she squared her shoulders with mine and charged directly in my direction, hand extended. "My name is Sylvie. It's good to finally meet you. My mom and I take care of the house for Ox. She cooks, I clean."

She reached me and stuck her hand between us. Not wanting to be rude, I rose to my feet and shook it quickly before recrossing my arms around myself. I paced away from her and toward the kitchen. I had wanted some breakfast earlier, but my stomach was suddenly feeling unsettled. Tea instead then.

"It's nice to meet you," I said with a sideways smile. "I'm sorry I didn't know who you were, Ox didn't tell me you'd be here."

She followed me into the kitchen, detouring slightly to grab her broom. "I wasn't going to be at first, but Ox texted me because he was worried. So I swung by."

This had my eyes lifting to her and looking at her again. Pretty face, pretty hair, cute body under those work clothes, and a cultural match for Ox. And he'd texted her. Casually? That was…*interesting.*

"Hmm," I said, my frown probably evident in my voice. Fortunately, my back was turned to her as I rummaged through the cabinets. "You're Clementine, right?" she asked, almost shyly. I gave a barely committal noise, losing more interest in conversing with every second that passed. "Well, what are you looking for, Clementine?"

"A mug. And maybe some tea, if you could point me in the right direction." I tried to hide my embarrassment as I faced her.

She just smiled and sauntered purposefully over to the far cabinet beside the fridge, pulling down one of the soft edged square mugs Ox liked to use. Then rummaging through a drawer, she pulled out a long, clear rectangular box, then shut the drawer with her hip. Watching her, I couldn't help but notice how well she knew the house. Even though her mom was the one who cooked, apparently, she knew the kitchen so well. She moved toward me, laying her findings on the counter beside me before backing away again.

The clear box was some kind of organizer, stocked with a decent variety of tea flavors. I scanned it quickly and raised my head to look at Sylvie again. I was being rude, all because of some police officers and a stupid comment Ox had made when he was angry. So what if he *did* know this girl in more than just a boss-employee kind of way? That was none of my business. What *was* my business was the way I was treating someone who'd saved me from those invasive, degrading questions not too long ago.

"Thank you, Sylvie," I said and gave her as much of a smile as I could muster. I opened the box and started fingering through the teas, wondering which one Ox had selected for me those first few times. "For more than just the tea. I really appreciate you getting rid of them."

"No problem, really," she said. I saw her shift out of the corner of my eye. "I wasn't kidding about him being pissed they were here while he's gone. He's not going to like that."

I couldn't help the weak smile and laugh that came out of me, "I don't think he can control *everything*, no matter how bad he wants to."

This brought a smirk to her lips. "Innocent? No way. Ox doesn't know what he's in for if you're starting to see through his brand of bull already."

My smile dropped as I thought about this woman who had Ox's number and used it more like a friend than an employee, and that maybe she didn't know about Ox and I's agreement. And I didn't know if I wanted her to know.

So, I didn't say anything, instead I looked around for the kettle I swore I'd seen previously. Again, I was wrong, as Sylvie bent down underneath a cabinet by her knees, pulled out the kettle, and handed it to me. I smiled my thanks and hoped I was hiding my embarrassment well.

"Ox said you liked tea, so I just assumed you knew where everything was. I'm sorry." She gave me a sheepish smile.

I shook my head, "Don't be. It's my fault for not knowing my way around this place. Ox made the tea when I was staying here before."

"Ah," is all she said. Nodding her head politely but looking me over with more than just a couple of questions in her gaze. I pretended I didn't see it as I thumbed through the tea options again, still unable to decide. I saw movement beside me and felt a presence close by. One long milky arm reached into the container and plucked up a pretty white tea bag with pink flowers skirting across it. Twisting the packet in her fingers, she handed it to me. "If you want the tea he made you, this is probably it. Jamaica[6]."

I couldn't help it, I looked over at her—all red-cheeked and big-eyed—and the tiniest, tiniest ball of *something* formed in my throat.

"His favorite?" I asked her quietly.

She nodded. "His favorite."

I nodded back. Taking the tea bag and giving her a weak smile, if not a grimace. "Okay."

And then I made the tea. It only took a small swallow to determine

---

[6] Jamaica: /Ha-MY-kuh/ - Hibiscus flower

that, yep, she was right. This was the tea he had made me and according to his cleaning-friend-possibly-mistress, it was his favorite. She knew him well. And I didn't know him at all.

I was just a living, breathing obligation he was checking off list requirements to 'handle'. He was doing what was expected of him. It was stupid of me to want him here for even a second to help me. Yes, he would have done it but not because he wanted to, because he *had* to. He was the perfect eldest child. Ron's grandchild.

God. What was wrong with me?

"You don't have to worry about Ox, you know?" She said as she continued to survey me. "He always keeps his word, and he always does the right thing. Always."

This is not a real marriage. This is a means to an end. Those words struck me deep in my stomach, making me feel sick.

Other words sprang into my head, chasing the last nasty set. *You're out here bouncing around these guys like a pinball and all you happen to know is what time to show up and get...*

I coughed into my tea. He was right, wasn't he? Officer Rude-ass. The rest of them, too. All of those police officers had their own opinions of things. He wasn't the only one. And truthfully, the police were probably the least nasty people I had to worry about. People weren't stupid. Word would get out that I was being used, yet again, as the instrument at the Fernandez family's disposal. I might be treated like a wife, but we all knew what I really was.

I was a tool. Hadn't I told Ox as much at our wedding brunch? I had *always* been a tool, to use when convenient or horny or bored, and as long as I was kept shiny and new in someone's toolbox, no one would ever know that I had fundamental flaws.

So, with my tea in my hand, I smiled at Sylvie. I told her it was nice to meet her and I would see her again soon. Then, I turned my ass around and went back up to my box.

Where I fucking belonged.

Chapter Ten

OX

It only took about thirty seconds of being settled into the back leather seats of the rented chauffeur's sedan as I was enroute home from the airport for my phone to ring. I purposely waited until I got to the car to turn it back on, knowing someone would be trying to get a hold of me and not wanting to deal with it as I lugged my large suitcase across the runway and through the busy airport.

While I had never flown commercial and probably never would, in order to get to the cars, the private airway passages connected through the commercial terminals. I could have paid extra to have special securities for the car guy to pick me up right beside Nebula, our familial jet, but I had working legs and I'd wanted to blow off a little steam before diving back into the craziness of my life.

Also, I was back early. Well, technically I was back late, a week later than my original plans actually, but it could have been two weeks later if I hadn't worked like a dog and negotiated my ass off. Why? I was still trying to figure that part out.

Before, when my brand-new wife had come to my door in the middle of the night and insinuated *things*, I hadn't wanted to be in that house another minute. Leaving the country couldn't have been more well-timed. Being in Mexico (where I only visited twice a year) I often got jam-packed with business meetings and distant family visits and appearances. So, for once, the grueling schedule was welcomed.

But that had only been when I was fresh off being upset, and surprised, and just altogether overwhelmed. I had just been pushed into marrying a stranger after all. Pushed into accepting outrageous terms of inheritance that would alter the course of my life. And to add icing on the cake, I was pushed into a stereotype in my new wife's mind of what she thought Fernandez men were like. What she thought *I* was like.

That had pushed me too far. Who was she to judge me like that? To put me in a box with Abuelo just because we were related. She didn't know me, so she had no right to act like she knew what I was thinking. I'd done what I was supposed to. I'd married the girl. I'd done more than marry her. I made sure she was taken care of. I worked out a comfortable agreement with her, giving her my word that I wasn't going to hurt her like he did. That I wasn't *like* him.

And she still chose to believe otherwise.

So, I ran away.

However, not long after I was gone, guilt started to creep in. While I always had to fight against being seen in the same dark shadow of my grandfather, she had also been fighting. Fighting real memories of her first marriage to him. A man almost three times her age who had some sort of sick fascination with her while she was forced to pretend she liked it. She had to act as if it was her choice to be used and abused like it was nothing, or else face the consequences of her own family. And right when she thought she might be free of that nightmare, she was being forced to do it all over again.

So maybe I *had* taken my own frustrations out on her a little that night. And in hindsight, looking at her situation versus mine, I felt bad.

Updates from Sylvie and Maria had done little to relieve that guilt. Their ever so frequent, "still in her room" and "hasn't come out today" messages were concerning. But her brothers were around, they had to be taking care of her, right? I sure hoped so.

But as my phone flashed bright blue almost as soon as my toes touched U.S. soil and I saw it was the loud Ferguson's name running across the screen, I lost some of that hope.

Tapping the green icon, I brought the black box up to my ear and repressed a sigh. "Yeah?"

"Yo, what the fuck have you done to my sister?" He was speaking before I'd even opened my mouth, our greetings crashing into each other.

"Hello, Clay, how are you?" I said steadily, just to be a jackass.

"Guess, Fernandez. I'm pissed," he said, shuffling something in the background. "You said no funny business with my sister, yeah? You signed on it."

"Yes. We were all there," I grumbled, especially unimpressed by his attitude today. Even as his words caused a sudden flutter to flip around in my stomach. "What's the problem?"

"The problem is that nobody has seen or heard from her since your weird ass wedding. No one's answering the door, she doesn't have a goddamn phone, and you're not answering yours!" Every word he spoke got louder and louder. I had to pull the phone away from my ear by the end.

"That sounds like a problem between you and your sister, Ferguson," I said as I glanced out the window. We had just pulled away from the airport and were merging onto the highway. Approximately twenty-five minutes away from home.

"No. It's a me and you problem if you're the one in charge of her shit," he said. "Why haven't you answered? I've been calling you for weeks."

"I was in Mexico. I just got back."

"Oh," he grumbled, annoyingly but understandingly. "What's up with that? I thought the whole Brady Bunch usually makes that trip?"

"In light of recent events, it was just me this time," I gritted.

"You home?" I heard the jangle of keys somewhere on his end.

"I'm not. Not yet. I just landed not too long ago."

"Why haven't I been able to reach Tiney? You forget to get her a new phone?" he asked. "Or did you lock her up or something?"

"No, God—no Clay!" I said, exasperated. "Why do they always send you to talk to me?"

"Cause I'm your favorite, pretty boy. You just don't know it yet," he said and despite myself, I sputtered a laugh. "Where the fuck is she, Ox?"

"I don't know, I haven't spoken to her," I croaked out with a good amount of reluctance. I felt so stupid when I said it out loud. *I don't know where my wife is. I was too busy throwing a pity party to care.* "I got her the phone. It should already be pre-programmed with important numbers. Yours, mine, your brothers, my family. She probably just hasn't turned it on yet."

Silence. The brother I almost exclusively referred to as *'the loud one'* in my head, was silent. And then he made a low hum, asking hesitantly, "You haven't tried calling?"

Why did it feel like a sock to the gut to hear that hesitance in his voice? As if it wasn't his business to ask. As if it was *my* business what went on in *my* marriage.

Damn. This *was* stupid. I was being stupid.

I watched the exits begin to wind downward as we cruised along the highway. Twenty-one minutes left.

"No."

"You get in a fight already?"

"No."

"Did you make my sister cry?"

I sighed and laid my head against the window. Nineteen minutes. "You went by the house and no one answered?"

"Affirmative, Sherlock."

"And she hasn't tried to reach out to you *at all?*" I asked, honestly surprised because I thought she'd for sure want to see her brothers once I'd left. She told me herself she was staying with them so she wouldn't be alone. What happened to that?

"Do I have to repeat myself completely? Yes, Ox! Yes, yes, and more fucking yes. Tiney is AWOL. No one has seen or heard from her since you know what and it's been long enough and I'm getting worried. You always get me on the phone and me in your face because I'm the only one who's gonna ask you straight up how it is. Fuck the contract, man. Where's my sister?" He blew up, obviously frustrated. We were now around sixteen minutes away from home and I had been on the phone with Clay Ferguson for way too long.

"You know, it's kind of cute when you worry like this?" I joked, poking the bear. *Hard.* He made a sound that confirmed it and I choked on an amused chortle. "Kidding. Mostly. Listen, I'm almost home. Just let me get there and I'll handle it, okay?"

"I can be there in twenty—"

"Let me see what's going on first," I said, my voice losing any sort of humor. Some kind of protective instinct rose in my chest and spread throughout my body. "Let me just get there and see her and as soon as I know she's okay, I'll text you. Once we get everything else sorted out, I'll tell her to call you ASAP."

He said nothing.

"Approved, your fucking majesty?" I asked, my bear poking stick out again.

A grumble sounded and then the sound of keys clanging in the background. "Yeah, yeah."

The phone clicked as the chuckle rolled out of my mouth.

Around fourteen minutes later, the driver pulled into the rounded half-moon of my front drive. I hated having drivers who weren't my regular guy, Rictor, knowing my address. But he was on vacation with his wife and four kids for another week and worked hard enough as it was. He could use the time off and I could fend for myself until he was back.

Promptly exiting the car and paying the man a two hundred percent tip to not drag my name, address, and every word I'd uttered during the car ride through the tabloids, I moved up toward the front doors of my English country style home with purpose.

Inside the front door, I left my bag, wallet, and keys by the landing and charged into the main living areas. It was afternoon on a Wednesday and every light in the house was off. I had dialed back the security on the main floors since the official investigation had started and the police were ruling out hitmen—but mainly because Sylvie and Maria had begged me to get "those distracting men" out of their workspace. There were still men who rotated the gardens, the gates and the rest of the outdoor spaces, just to make sure no one was out there skulking around.

But even so, Sylvie and Maria were supposed to be back up to their full-time schedules. They should be here every other day, cooking and cleaning and adding life to the bland colorlessness of the home, like they so often did. Laughing and whispering and sometimes arguing when they thought I wasn't around or listening. I had scheduled them back on when I was away for Clementine's sake, thinking maybe she'd like the company of some women for a change. Or some company at all. But looking around, it seemed like the house had been in this state for a while. Not unclean, but untouched. It looked like *everyone* had been out of town, not just me.

Flicking on the lights as I passed the kitchen, the living room, and the long hallway that led to the foyer with the stairs, I looked from side to side seeing if I could catch a glimpse of someone hanging around in a corner or curled up in a chair somewhere. No luck.

I climbed the stairs and before I knew it, my legs had carried me right in front of a familiar door. A door I had left food, and drinks, and notes at on more than one occasion. A door I should have visited that night, just to offer an olive branch, but didn't. I shook my head and raised my hand, knocking three times with my usual soft tapping so I wouldn't startle her.

When I heard silence for more than a couple of minutes, I gave it another shot. *Tap, tap, tap.* "Clem? Are you in there?"

No words came from the other side of the door. I even leaned my head forward, straining my ears to listen inward, but I only heard rustling sounds and maybe, *maybe* a soft groan. I tapped again, hoping to get her attention. And, because it had worked once before, I added, "Clementine, I'm coming in, okay?"

I waited a few beats, just listening to the closed door, but heard no other sounds. A frown tugged at my lips as I twisted the handle and cracked the door open just slightly. Then I waited for her to react. When no reaction came, I cracked the door open even further and poked my head in just far enough that one eye could blink around and survey the room.

It was dark, the curtains drawn shut allowing only muted amounts of light to shine through. This made the frown I wore deepen and I pushed the door open further, wondering with a small pang of panic if she was even still here. Until I noticed the tangled heaping ball of sheets near the top corner of the bed. I don't know how I'd missed her before, all rolled up like a tumbleweed.

With a sigh, I wandered further in and looked down at the ball. It was breathing softly but deeply, meaning she was asleep. Peering at my black watch (a present from my siblings "to match my black soul") I saw that it was one in the afternoon. She should not be asleep. God only knew what the hell she was supposed to be doing, but it wasn't sleeping.

I slipped my cell out of the back pocket of my jeans. I'd skipped the suit this time and instead wore simple jeans and a long sleeve t-shirt for travel. Scrolling past my lock screen, I brought up my text messages.

> **Me:** Found her. She's sleeping. No locks, no bars. Would you like a picture?

> **Clay:** Fuck off.

> **Clay:** Tell her to get her ass up. It's daylight out!

> **Me:** On it, Majesty.

Slipping the phone back into my pocket, I took a deep breath, squared my shoulders, and rounded the side of the bed nearest to the ball of sheets. Easing down to the edge of the cushy mattress, I leaned my body forward enough to reach her, but sat far enough not to crowd her.

I reached into the ball, thinking I was going for a shoulder. It only took a second of my fingers connecting to know it wasn't her upper body I had grabbed onto. I had gotten a handful of ankle. Small and delicate and attached to long, slight feet. I wrapped my hand around the skinny limb and gave it a gentle squeeze, the soft, smooth skin there distracting me momentarily. Preoccupied with the feeling of her gripped in my hand, I didn't even notice when those deep breaths from earlier became shallower.

"What are you doing?" A soft sleepy voice asked.

Hand around ankle, I froze. Where was her head? Turning slightly, I angled myself in the correct direction of her upper body. "I'm trying to wake you up. Do you know what time it is?"

Making soft sleepy noises, she moved, twisting in her cocoon to look at herself and the clock. Or at least I figured that's what she was doing. I still couldn't see her upper body. It was still all wrapped up like a caterpillar before it became a butterfly. As she moved, so did my hand, sliding down her ankle to her foot. When she turned back, making an *"I don't know"* kind of sound, the hand slid back toward her calf again. I squeezed the flesh there once before letting go, making myself stand and take a few steps away from the bed, hand tingling by my side.

"Get up. It's too late for you to be laying around in bed." She whined as her response and I raised my eyebrows, not that she could even see them. "Clementine, *get out of bed.*"

She whined a little more pointedly this time, like a toddler throwing a tantrum. My eyebrows jumped up even higher, but I watched in amusement as she sat up in bed, her lower body visible but her entire torso and head wrapped in a hive of covers and blankets.

"Clem," I sputtered out in a chuckle. "It's one in the afternoon."

"You already mentioned that," she said, finally speaking real people words.

"And you're still in bed," I pointed out.

She hummed her acknowledgement.

"Sleeping."

Arms shot out of the blanket cocoon. Dark fingers wiggled and rose to yank the blankets from around her face. The soft white and cream fabrics fell around her shoulders and landed at her elbows. I sucked in a breath at the sight of her tired looking features. Tired and grim. Damn, maybe I should have been checking in on her.

She surprised me by addressing me clearly and directly, her voice harder than I'd yet to hear it before.

"Oaxaca," She started. My eyebrows stayed up near my hairline, despite my attempts at a poker face. "Do you always repeat yourself so much?"

"Not usually. Most people listen the first time."

"You're bothering me."

"You're still asleep."

"You're still pointing out the obvious."

A low hum escaped, and I was surprisingly fighting a smile. Narrowing my eyes, I wondered, "Is this supposed to be you in a bad mood?"

She elbowed the covers down further and they fell past her hips and pooled on the mattress around her. It was then I realized what she was wearing.

Every inch of her torso from collarbone to wrists were covered. Long white sleeves and a baggy button down made up the top of her cute *sensible* pajamas. They were a soft, muslin fabric, and were decorated with little gray polka dots. Seeing them made a smile spread across my face. I turned away from her before she could see it, moving over to the far dresser and leaning my hip against it.

"You got the pajamas," I said.

"Clearly," she muttered, using her hand to push stray curls away from her face. "I'm surprised it didn't come with a *robe*."

"Testy, Clementine." I tsked, shaking my head and looking at her face fully. She was grimacing, her nose scrunched, her eyebrows pulled in tight, and her shoulders slumped. I felt my chest pang with worry. "What's wrong?"

"Nothing's wrong."

"You're holed up in here in the middle of the afternoon sleeping. *Something* is wrong." She shot a look at me. I crossed my arms over my chest. "Why haven't you activated your phone?"

"I may have," she protested softly. I looked down my shoulder and spotted the small brown box I noticed on my way into the room earlier. Still sealed and shoved toward the back of the dresser, disregarded.

"Are you going to lie to my face or will you just tell me what's wrong?" I asked, moving my gaze to her again. "I'll give you fair warning, though, one path is easier than the other."

"Are you threatening me?"

"I'm not. I'm promising you that one way or another I'm going to get what I want and right now I want you to tell me what's wrong with you."

"Where to start." She chuckled without humor.

If my eyes could narrow any further without completely closing, they would. "Clementine?"

I watched as her shoulders slumped and her face crumbled into that stone mask of sorrow and *nothing*. "I just... I haven't felt like talking."

"Only sleeping?" I asked and it most definitely sounded judgmental.

Her face crumpled in a way that had nothing to do with sorrow and was more like a pout. "You don't have to be mean."

"You are the one who's being difficult," I pointed out.

Her only response was her body shifting downward in a dejected slump. Seeing it produced a tickle in my chest that felt a lot like regret. Damn, I was "*Oxing*" this whole situation up. Judging and scolding like I always did.

Clearing my throat, I tried again. "What I'm trying to say is that I just want to know what's bothering you. I'm worried."

She popped an eye up in my direction, roaming it over my person skeptically. "Worried?"

"Yes, worried." Pushing off the dresser's edge, I crossed the distance to her bed. Beside her, I lowered myself to the edge, not wanting to intrude but wanting to see her face. "I've been gone for weeks and I come back and you haven't been outside your room. *Again*. You haven't used your phone once and you've been ransacking the tea box like there's no other consumable products in the house; don't think I haven't noticed."

Her mouth quirked, and she looked away as a laugh left her in a soft puff. A slow triumphant grin spread across my face and I leaned my shoulders forward, hoping to catch her eyes. "I'm surprised something so small could consume that much liquid. Did you find the tea box yourself?"

"Sylvie showed me."

"You two met?" I asked, surprised. It looked like Sylvie hadn't been here in weeks.

"We did."

"And?"

"And what?" Her eyes narrowed and she assessed me, like she was waiting for something.

"And how was that for you? Did you talk?"

"We did."

"Did you like her?"

"She's very nice."

"Could you two be friends?"

She gave me that look again and then turned her head away from me, a pouty expression taking over her features. "I don't need any friends."

Looking at that expression, I couldn't help but wonder about her. She was so mild about everything, it was hard to tell what she was really thinking. Yet, I was noticing her tells anyway. The way she was turning away from me told me how closed off she was trying to be. Yet, she was talking to me. Holding a conversation with me. Being *real* with me. That was a level of openness she hadn't had before we'd gotten married.

Maybe that small opening of herself was why I suddenly felt the greedy need for more. She couldn't keep doing this to herself. Whatever was eating at her, she couldn't just let it destroy her without fighting.

And she no longer would, if I had anything to do with it.

Rising to my feet, I took purposeful steps back across the room. Snatching up the box with her new phone off the dresser, I tucked it underneath my arm before turning and giving her an assessing look.

She was stuck. Stuck in this room by herself. Stuck into this family against her will. Stuck in this life that she'd hardly ever had any control over and now that she did, she didn't know what to do with it.

"Get up," I borderline growled. I know this because she startled slightly, her shoulders and neck rearing back and her eyes assessing me closely. I didn't adjust my tone. "And get dressed."

"Why?"

"You're leaving this room," I said as I realized that's the only thing I wanted. Her out of this room. Out of bed. "Actually, you're leaving this house."

"To go where?" she asked incredulously.

"Anywhere you want." She stared back at me like I was insane. I stared at her for a second before another half growl came out. "You don't have anywhere you want to go?"

"No," she said, looking at me like I was the crazy one.

"Nothing you've been wanting to do?"

"*No*," she insisted.

"Okay," I said, rubbing my hands along my pants and gazing around the room as I tried to think fast.

My eyes caught on a bundle of tall brown grasses collected in a vase in the corner. The girls had found them out on the beachy part of the shore one day and they each had a hand-picked bundle in a vase in their room. This was Lis's room, so hers were the most even and symmetrical of them all. It was a good memory of everyone getting along. We'd walked the beach trails and sifted through the sand and just talked. Maybe the warm sand and sounds of the ocean would have the same effect on Clem.

"We're going on a walk." I decided. "I'll show you around the trails and the neighborhood so you can get to know your surroundings."

"You don't need to—"

"I do," I said firmly.

"Meet me downstairs in twenty."

"You really don't have to, Ox."

"I really do."

"Why?"

"As your husband, it's my job."

That pout came back to engulf her face. I decided right then I didn't like seeing it there. "You're not my husband, you're my contract, *remember?*"

Okay, maybe I deserved that for being a dick outside of my door that night. But still, I would not back down. I would not just sit back and let her slip away into herself. What kind of husband would I be, real or otherwise, if I did that?

"Clem, *come out with me.*" One step outside of this room, this house, this fog is all I wanted from her. I could help her. I could take that step alongside her. I was good at helping, at managing. That's what I did. If she would just let me try, I could *help*. "Please?"

There was that look again. The one where she burned me with her irises. The one where she picked me apart with a stare alone. No expression, just the sting of her gaze as she examined all I was made of.

"Okay," she said finally, in the soft voice I recognized as hers. She was done being grumpy, I guess.

"Okay." I turned to leave right away, not wanting to give her another moment to protest.

A feeling of immense warmth spread from my forehead to my toes as I walked out of her room and shut the door behind me. I didn't know if it was contentment for getting conversation out of her or pride for getting her to agree to an outing.

Whatever was causing this tingling feeling to crawl throughout my body, I knew it was all Clementine.

Chapter Eleven

CLEMENTINE

Oaxaca Fernandez may have the longest and leanest limbs I'd ever seen. I knew this because I had been walking behind said tall, lean man for twenty minutes, watching as his appealing frame strode two steps ahead of me with strong, purposeful steps. I didn't know what possessed him to decide we go on a walk along one of the sandy beach trails. At first I was skeptical, but after we'd walked the initial minutes to the edge of the boardwalk entrance where my brand-new running shoes started to pick up sand, I started feeling grateful for the impromptu outing.

The sun was out, but the breeze was cool the closer we were to the water. That meant I was pretty comfortable in my long gray athletic pullover and ankle length black leggings. Before we left the house, I pulled my hair up into a tight bun on the top of my head and tucked my brand-new activated cell phone into the tight side pocket of my leggings.

When Ox had taken it from my room, I thought he'd given up on me using it altogether. But when we met up at the front door, me clad in someone else's workout clothes and him clad in his usual all black—the only color I'd seen him in so far—he held the small device in my direction with an unyielding look on his face.

"Here," he said. And when I looked from him to the phone and back to him, he'd sighed and taken my hand, placing the cool box into my palm. "I know you don't want to, but take it. I need to know where you are, what you're doing, *if you're safe*. So, I need you to carry it. Deal?"

How could I argue with that? I couldn't, so instead I wrapped my fingers around the phone and slipped it directly into the pocket of my pants, not even bothering to look at it before saying, "Deal."

His eyes cataloged my movements. But he only pursed his lips ever so slightly before turning his shoulders and grunting out, "Let's go."

And go we did.

Now, as I watched him trudge ahead, periodically pointing out irregularities in the path or glancing back at me to make sure I was still there, I felt the urge to use the gift he'd given to me.

My fingers twitched at my side and I fisted them to stop myself from grabbing it. In front of me, Ox paused, stiffening slightly. Inclining his head, he looked right and then left before he turned his shoulders halfway to look back at me. "Do you hear that?"

"What?"

"It's like a dog crying. Maybe a cat." He took a few powerful steps forward, his posture urgent, his gaze searching.

I felt my heart do something funny as I padded after him. Before we even got to the end of the boardwalk, though, I saw and heard him breathing a sigh of relief. The view of the beach had opened up, unveiling a pretty blue sky and the even bluer water of the Atlantic. The beach was private, so the sands were clean and free of debris, the waves gentle this time of year. The sounds of the ocean were smooth and calming as the water lulled around itself. Down the long stretch of yellowish white sand, a small family huddled. A man and a woman standing side by side, looking out over the scene of two small children waddling as they chased an even smaller puppy around.

"Oh." Ox breathed, seeming genuinely relieved. "Just a few pups."

My lips pulled involuntarily at this man, the same one who'd told his sister he'd send her to Mexico to fish as punishment, using the word "pups". Not to mention him referring to *all* of them that way, even the kids. And he was still *grumbling* as he said it. So contradictory.

What would he have done if they weren't okay? Save them? Did this man know how to do anything besides take action? From what I could tell, the answer was no.

My fingers twitched again, and this time I let them. My chest was doing this warm tingly thing and I figured the only way to get it to stop was to give it what it wanted. I pulled the cell phone out and quickly opened up the camera app.

Ox was still looking out at the family, so part of his profile was in view. Crinkles formed at the corners of his eyes as his mouth pulled in that closed mouth grimace-smile he did. Clear tan skin and reddened lips filled out the rest of his face, his nose angular and severe. That only took up a small part of the screen. The rest of it was taken up by his black T-shirt clad back, all broad and lightly muscled. Long arms hanging at his sides and black athletic shorts which fit just right over his shapely lower half filled the rest of the frame.

He looked good, but he always looked good. That's not why I wanted a picture. I was taking this photo because, at that moment, sharp edges and all—he looked distinctly like himself. Stern but gentle.

"Are you getting tired? Because we can, oh—" he cut himself off as he turned to glance back at me. Before he could turn around completely, I quickly snapped the photo and pivoted the phone so that the camera was facing the beach. "Am I in the way?"

"No!" I basically sang to avoid choking on my embarrassment. I pretended like I was taking photos of the beach before promptly pocketing the phone again. Later, I would change his contact photo to the one I'd taken. The only contact that would have a photo, I realized with a surprising glow of approval.

A few quick steps and I was catching up to him, hoping to fall into his rhythm as we entered the sandier part of the beach trail. Noticing this, he slowed his gait, and we lined up perfectly as we walked along the back edge of the shore. My muscles were working pretty hard to keep up, even with Ox's slower pace and I couldn't help but think about how good it felt.

Tired legs, breathless lungs, the sound of nature. They were all things I hadn't experienced in a long time. Even if I could, the experience would have been tainted within the hellish haze of the last five years. But now it was like I was reliving these stimulants for the first time, and it surprisingly felt nice. Refreshing. Something else that was surprisingly nice was having Ox by my side while doing it.

There was something about this Ox, this side of him that I was seeing for the first time. A walking, breathing puzzlement of stubborn determination, bitter impatience, and calm, caring resolve that was so damn confusing. But also reassuring. It was good to know that I wasn't the only person flailing under the pressure of who I am and who I have to be. Ox was doing a much better job at all of it, sure, but regardless I was starting to see that I wasn't alone.

"Catching up on messages?" Ox asked when we settled into a companionable pace.

"Oh no, I don't have many."

"No?" he asked a little too casually. "None from your brothers?"

I pressed my mouth together and glanced up at him. Air blew out of my nostrils and somehow sounded accusatory. "So that's what's up with all of this? You were sent on '*Tiney Patrol*'?"

Ox looked down his shoulder at me for a hard, scrutinizing second.

I didn't look back, not wanting my traitorous emotions to show on my face. So what if Clay or Clint had put him up to this? It's not like the alternative meant anything anyway, just that he was tired of me stinking up his guest room and drinking all his tea.

His *favorite,* if that Sylvie knew what she was talking about.

"Whatever you're thinking right now, I'm sure it's incorrect, *Tiney,*" he said with a bit of a mocking tone toward my lifelong nickname.

I scrunched my nose, but my mouth wobbled out a smile. "I don't think I like you calling me that."

He mimicked my face perfectly, down to the scrunched nose, then huffed a short laugh. "I don't think so either."

Peeking a look his way, I tried to gauge if that had come off as harsh. It wasn't that I didn't want a nickname from him, it was just that *that* nickname had always been ours. Mine and my brothers'. Not even my parents called me that growing up. Just my three idiots who I both amused and annoyed daily. Who took care of me and took up for me and were always there for me.

Up until they weren't.

Ever the intuitive, Ox picked up on my change of demeanor and must have put two and two together. In a movement I wouldn't have ever expected from him, he took a large sidestep and shoulder checked me with enough force to knock me sideways. When I actually began to stumble, he set a calm hand outward and caught me by the shoulder to straighten me out.

"Why won't you answer your brothers?" he asked this with a pretty serious face for a man who just bumper-carred the shit out of me.

Surprised, I sputtered without thinking, "I don't want to bother them."

"Bullshit," he said, sounding like Clay. "Tell me the real reason or I'll do it again."

When I stayed quiet for thirty seconds too long, Ox's shoulder and hip came barreling at me like he promised. The impact was mostly gentle, but he'd used his long knee to take out the weak spot at the back of mine, causing me to sink. He made no move to catch me this time and I went sinking butt first into the sand, landing with an impressive, "Umph."

Scowling, I remembered. This guy had three sisters. He knew exactly what kind of torture would be most effective, and sand in tight clothing was definitely on that list. An unwanted vision of him doing the same thing to his sisters came to me and my stomach suddenly soured at the thought that he'd just treated me like a sibling. Something about it didn't sit right with me.

"Mercy?" he asked.

"Is that really all the torture you have in you?" I laughed. "If it is, I'm disappointed, Mr. *'I get what I want when I want it and that's a promise'*."

He grinned at my mocking but offered me a hand. As he pulled me up, he said, "It doesn't feel right twisting your arm for information. You're too sweet to torture."

This effectively stopped whatever words I had been preparing to say in my throat. I swallowed audibly to clear it up. Not noticing at all, Ox leaned down and began brushing sand away from my thighs with deft fingers. The touch was intimate, but not sensually. More in a doting familial kind of way. It had me freezing in front of him as he worked.

"Clem?" he asked, still swiping at my legs. "Answer, or you're going back in the sand. I don't mind doing this twice."

More touching? I gulped. Then I remembered my butt had also landed in the sand. With burning skin, I rushed to swipe particles off the area before Mr. Unaffected could get his hands back there first.

"My brothers... They don't really need me like they used to," I started. Ox took his last few swipes, then stepped backward to inspect his work. Satisfied everything was perfect, he turned his gaze up to my eyes expectantly, waiting for me to continue. "They used to ask me for things all the time. It was always, 'Tiney do this or that'. And now I feel like all I ever do is stress them out."

"What kind of stuff?" he asked.

I peeked over at him, trying to gauge if he was actually interested or if he was just trying to understand what my problem was. To my surprise he seemed patient. We'd been walking for quite a while but the beach trail showed no sign of ending and he showed no signs of wanting to be anywhere else. So, we kept going.

"Okay... For example, I can cook maybe three good dishes. I bake a lot better than I cook but none of them are very big into sweets. Back then though, they would still ask me to come over and cook for them constantly, even knowing they'd get one of the same three edible meals or have to stomach a pretty bad one." I quietly watched his reaction to see what he was going to say. When he just nodded his head and continued our walk, I went on. "Or they used to take me out shopping when really, they just wanted opinions on their own clothes. They used to ask for my help with Christmas decorations or we'd argue over what kind of drinks to keep at their places for guests. And I mean, we still fought and got on each other's nerves all the time, but it was different. I know that stuff seems little and not all that important, but they used to, you know, *need me*. And now they don't."

"So it's about feeling needed?" He gave me a quick sideways glance.

"Yeah."

"I like sweet things," he said out of nowhere. I choked on nothing. Hadn't he just called *me* sweet? Was he saying? ...*No*. But I wasn't exactly sure of that as he flicked his eyes down and up over me before connecting his gaze to mine. He licked his lips and eyed me for one second too long, then cleared his throat and glanced away. "If you want someone to bake for, I'll eat it."

I shook my head, not even able to begin addressing that. "It's not just about *feeling* needed, it's about being essential. Or useful, or helpful, or anything really. Right now, I'm just this thing that they suddenly have to take care of again, and I've been gone for so long, it's hardly like I'm even still their sister anymore. Not really."

"Clem, I can tell you right now that you are still their sister and you are still just as important to them as I assume you've always been. Exhaustingly so." He saw me give him a weird side eye and held onto my gaze for an extra second before continuing. "But it *has* been a while, like you said. They probably just don't know how to approach you."

"They're my brothers, they don't need to know how. You just do it, you know?" But in their case, they had failed at it for five long years. How did I expect it to change now?

He nodded. His hands were in his pockets now, and he had slowed to an almost lulling pace. I wasn't complaining. I was starting to feel a burn in my thighs from all the movement. "Do you want my honest opinion?"

"Sure."

One long moment passed. Then he stopped, turned his shoulders to me, and used his long hand to gently halt me. I schooled my thoughts away from the feeling of his hand gripping my shoulder and instead focused on what he wasn't doing. He wasn't shying away from me or hiding behind stuffy orders like he usually did. He was studying me openly, still stern, but... not. Looking down on me, he wore the same serious expression he frequented, but there was something soft about the edges now. Something more relaxed.

"The train goes both ways, Clem. They've been yanked around emotionally these last few weeks and from what I'm understanding, a lot longer than that. *Just like you*, they've had a life they knew pulled from under their feet. *Twice*. Give them some time to adjust, let them come back into the role of being your brothers in their own way. And at the very least, answer your phone and let them know you're okay."

My gut churned with the guilty feeling of being a complete asshole. Reaching into my pocket, I pulled out the phone and opened up the main screen. Calls, messages, voice messages, and video calls flooded my folders in immeasurable amounts. Seeing this rooted the guilt down that much further.

I nibbled my bottom lip, swallowing roughly and peeking up at him. He was looking down on me with that burning stare, waiting for me to admit that he was exactly right. But I let my eyes flutter back down to my fingers as they locked the phone and put it away.

He *was* right. *So* right, but I still felt sick when I let myself think about the years without them. When I had been truly helpless and they had left me fully without help.

I tried to push the thoughts out of my mind, but the vision of that red bubble and the number on the screen wouldn't disappear. They loved me, I knew that. And they were trying; I should try too.

"Clementine?"

"Do you want to know *my* honest opinion?" I asked, without looking up at him.

"Always," he answered, his voice going softer.

I gave him a closed-mouth smile that was all sarcasm. "I never want your honest opinion ever again."

He looked at my face, taking in the pout that I'm sure followed up that statement. And then a slow smile spread across his own face before...he laughed. His chin went up slightly, exposing his long tan neck. His shoulders bobbed as he emitted deep rumbling sounds. The sight made me smile with no reservations and it warmed something inside me, bringing me the smallest sliver of pride that I, boring timid useless Clementine, had made this stoic man smile. *Laugh* even.

Using one of my shoulders, I bumped him too. It landed near the top of his chest. "Stop that. You're a know-it-all and you know it."

He chuckled some more, but nodded. "I know."

"You do, huh? Are you willing to share a little wisdom?" I was smiling, laughing softly too, but my heart was shriveling again, feeling dried out and empty like it always did. "I could definitely stand to know a few more things."

A long moment passed where we didn't say anything. I wasn't

looking at Ox, but I wasn't *not* looking at him either. I was just thinking. About how I could be better. How, if I could just be a little better, I could have a place in this world. A real place here.

"You know you can ask me for the things you need, Clementine."

I blinked him into view and saw that he wasn't looking at me. He had turned his body toward the water, watching the waves from so far away. I used the opportunity to take him in fully. So tall, so strong, so capable. He wasn't shy; he didn't hesitate; he was all do, do, do. From the second I'd met him I hadn't seen him *not* doing something. He was a handler. And I could admit that the knowledge brought me comfort. When the cops had come, I had instantly wanted him there because I knew he'd handle it for me.

That was who he was.

"Don't you already have enough people asking you to take care of things for them?" I asked, feeling loose in the tongue I guess or maybe I just really wanted to know what he'd say. Would he get overwhelmed like me when people wanted too much of him? Would he feel suffocated? Would he get angry?

But a soft smile touched his lips as he glanced down at me and then away. "Not really. Only my family asks me for things. And now your brothers I guess, but that's more because they don't want to ask too much of you. They're waiting for you to heal."

All these allowances for others, and not one for himself? It was like he didn't count himself as a person. Like he didn't think he was worth more than the support he gave. All of a sudden that '*can do, will do*' attitude I admired in him seemed sort of sad.

I didn't like it. My dry, splintered heart softened again at this man who held so much responsibility to others, to me even, without expecting anything in return. And this weird burning feeling started to overtake me. I didn't like it at all. So, I shoved it down as deep as possible.

"I've noticed you sort of run them. You're like a soccer mom."

A little snort escaped him. "I know you don't know my mom well, but never say that around her. She'll take huge offense to one of her headaches getting the credit for her mothering."

"Noted," I said with a smile.

"And as for the other headaches." He sighed with his whole body, but when I looked up to see his face, his smile had grown bigger. "I'm more like a naggy old man to them."

"They love you." I offered.

"You've met them how many times exactly?" he asked, dismissal and disbelief in his tone.

"I can tell," I said, not giving him a chance to discount it. He didn't answer and didn't look at me. Instead, he just shook his head and shrugged. Something forceful shot through me and in another breath, I turned toward him and grabbed his forearm. He looked at me then, his eyebrows knit in question. "*They love you,* Ox. You don't show up like they have for people you don't care about."

He scrutinized me for a moment, before the softest noise left him. "No?"

The look he gave me, the voice he was using, they both somehow placed visions in my head. Visions of Ox standing over me helping me to my wobbly feet that first night in Ron's house. Of him catching me in the church and hauling me up before I fainted. Of him at the funeral lunch, kneeling before me and offering to make an agreement with me just to give me some sense of control.

Memories that, in one lens, told a certain story, but in the lens of my unique circumstances meant nothing. Although Ox had shown up for me in the same way I was describing, there were also signatures and money and familial expectations between us. Obligations didn't count, and I knew what I was in this situation. *An obligation.*

He was right about my brothers and I was right about his siblings, but when it came to the two of us, things were different. Still, I couldn't help but feel like he was trying to say something with that stare.

But so what?

Whatever that something was, meant nothing. His stare meant nothing. Him barging into my room to check on me, or making me smile, or bringing me tea, or knocking me into the sand just to clean me off with his own hands—they all meant nothing. Not when he was just doing the things he was *supposed to* do. And if I let myself believe otherwise, I'd be opening the door to more pain. I knew better than that.

I stepped away from him, shaking off that look. Knowing now to avoid the things that lead to the same pain I'd experienced when my family, *my whole world*, had turned their backs on me out of obligation, I found it easy to shake my head with absolute confidence and say, "No."

Later that night, after we'd walked home, Ox had gone into his office to work for hours. I had fallen asleep on the couch just to be woken up by the smell of delicious food being heated up. We'd shared a meal together in an almost complete but companionable silence. Finally, we said goodnight to each other and went our separate ways, me with a cup of tea in my hands and him with a tall glass of water.

Much later, I walked into my bathroom to take a shower. Savoring the feeling of the warm spray over my sore muscles so much that I stayed in there for what felt like hours. By the time I dragged myself out, I had gone a little lightheaded.

When I exited the ensuite bath, foggy steam swirling around me, I thought the pretty orange shape on the far dresser could have been a tired hallucination.

But the next morning when I woke up, clear headed and well rested, it was still there. In the light of the day I could see the object better. It was a small box, about as tall as a snack container.

I hopped out of bed quickly, my back and legs feeling far too stiff to have only been on a long walk, and walked right up to the dresser.

I stopped breathing. And then I sighed out a ragged breath, before smiling.

On my dresser, was the prettiest orange box, with dark rust and gold swirling designs lining the edges. On the top, it read:

Hecho en México

Té de Clementina. Surtido de Té, Negros, Verde, y Especiadio.

It was an assortment of tea from Mexico. Tea that had my name on it. Tea that was so pretty and smelled so good, like Californian orange farms, that it was impossible to think it was purchased with anything other than the recipient in mind. Anything other than *me* in mind.

My chest ached, causing me to choke out a sound that was in between a coo and a laugh. Ox had gotten me a gift on his trip abroad. Something he knew I would like and appreciate. Something that was unique for me.

I picked up the box and a little orange sticky note fell from one of its sides. On it, a harsh dark scroll read:

Clem,

Ask me for anything. Take me for all I'm worth. Turns out, it's a lot.

-Ox

I laughed *loudly*, because, what an arrogant ass. But really, I knew he wasn't. He was Ox. He was serious and straight to the point but also funny and he clearly thought about others. He was *surprising*.

I clutched the note to my chest, that ache there intensifying and the only thing I could bring myself to think in response to the feeling was:

Oh. Hell.

Chapter Twelve

OX

I hated my cousin Manuel. We were born in the same year, went to the same schools, and we even shared a name. But despite all the glaring reasons we should probably get along, I still completely hated him. And I was stuck in a private hotel bar with him until further notice.

It was a week after my walk on the beach with Clem and, before this meeting, I had been feeling pretty good. The walk had been a surprisingly successful wager to have come up with on the spot. On it she had opened up, laughed, smiled, frowned and for days now I had been reeling off the fact that she had talked to me. Not just answering my questions or telling me what I wanted to hear, but Clem had really talked to me for maybe the first time.

I'm sorry... It was never you... It was me. It's always me. The words she spoke to me at our wedding table came into my mind and I winced. Okay, maybe it wasn't the very first time she'd talked to me, but it was the first time that had felt *right*.

"Oaxaca? Would you like to join us here on Earth?" Manuel said from beside me. I looked to him, taking in his familiar frame, dark hair and dark eyes, a Fernandez man through and through. *Irritating.* "Oh wait. If whatever you're thinking about is *that* good, I want in on it. I bet it's that sexy hand-me-down bi—"

"Watch it Manny," I growled before he could finish.

"*Whaaat?*" He said in a chuckling laugh. "What? I can't talk about your fake wife? Like you actually give a shit."

"My wife is very real and I very much give a shit. Let something like that leave your mouth again where she's concerned and I'll make sure you're sorry she even crossed your mind."

Silence.

Well shit. I didn't know where *that* came from, but I sure as shit wouldn't take a word of it back. Manny knew how to pinch all the wrong nerves in me and he was being especially exceptional at the job tonight. Leaning forward, I set my glass of whiskey neat down on the hard wood of the table. The motion brought Venny, another cousin of mine, and Mátti into view. They both sat back, staring at me with stunned looks in their eyes.

Rolling my own eyes, I picked the glass right back up and threw the rest of the whiskey down my throat. These guys were annoying, but they weren't wrong. Manny was being an asshole, but I was acting out of character for something or someone that would have never cracked a dent into my surface before. And I didn't really know why.

It's always me.

Damn. Had she been that obvious? Before Mexico, had she really been so desperately obvious about her struggles? And had I really been so caught up in myself that I didn't notice them? No wonder she was struggling with adjusting back to her old life, I had just left her out to dry. But that still didn't explain everything. I doubted one mean comment from me was the reason she hid from her brothers for three weeks.

Before the wedding, she had been all about her brothers. Wanting to see them and talk to them and only wanting to be around them. But the minute we'd gotten married, she changed. She insisted that it was for their benefit but from my perspective, something inside of her was defaulting to the smallest possible version of herself. Whether it was an attempt not to be seen or a coping mechanism for what happened to her following her first arranged marriage, I didn't fully know. But it was almost like she was trying to discard herself before someone else could discard her first.

Dammit, Abuelo. I wasn't going to do that to her. I wasn't going to be like him. Taking things just because I wanted them and discarding them when they didn't interest me. Keeping things just to be stingy and greedy and to feel power. Caging Clementine Ferguson... *Fernandez* was just about the last thing I wanted to do. And I assumed it was the last thing she wanted either, even if she was defaulting to it as some kind of survival instinct.

That's probably why, the day after our walk, I'd come into her room bright and early to wake her up.

It was to my surprise that she was already up, sitting on the bed in her loose pajamas and thumbing at the box of tea I had set on her dresser the night before. The box had caught my eye when going through the markets in Mexico because of the color. The bright orange seemed so brash to me at first, I had almost turned away from it. But then I saw the name on the tea box and Clem's face at our wedding flashed in my mind. Her face and her words.

It's always me, she had said. And I wanted to show her that no, it wasn't her. It was Abuelo. It was my abuelo that had done this to her, but it was her own efforts that could undo it.

"Thank you for the tea," she'd said in her sugary voice. I could only reply with a nod before telling her to get dressed, swiftly leaving the room.

I wasn't really used to being thanked so sincerely. Everyone else just expected me to do things like that because it's what I've always done. So, hearing it from her caused a hockey puck sized knot to appear in my throat. It stung, but it also felt good. It made me want to make her feel good in return.

I wouldn't do it though. It wasn't my place to make sure she felt good. It was my place to make sure she *was* good. Good equaled well taken care of and accounted for. Making sure that her hurting was healing and she could move on after all of this was over. The Fernandez's owed her that much.

So, after she'd gotten dressed and came downstairs to share a small cup of coffee and toast with me, I'd loaded her up into my car and drove her to what I thought would be the easiest brother's house. I knew Connor would be home because I had done some recon with Clay beforehand to put my plan into motion.

It backfired immediately. I realized this when she'd come home later dejected and drained, made herself a cup of tea (not mine), and headed straight up to her room without comment. I knocked on her door later, when it was obvious that she'd be skipping dinner, to see what was wrong. She explained that Connor grilled her the whole time about the last five years and asked for detailed retellings of what she'd been doing and why she'd let things get so bad.

Further reconnaissance revealed that Connor was not the easiest brother, he was, in fact, the hardest. On top of being the most no nonsense of them all, he was apparently very in tune with his emotions, and expected everyone else to be as well. That description of him in hindsight explained the drained and hopeless expression Clem had worn upon her return.

The slump didn't last long however, because after a day or two of wallowing in her depression bubble, Clay called and asked her to make him dinner at his place. (A decision that may or may not have been made because of me texting him: *Your sister wants to make you dinner. Invite her over.*) And thank God for that decision, because she had come back from dinner at Clay's with a smile on her face and leftovers boxed into elegant glass stowaway containers. When I'd asked her how it went, she was quiet like usual, but the happy sort of quiet.

She told me she made him one of her three specialties and he'd suffered through baking cookies with her. After they were done, he had eaten two, and they'd given the rest to the doorman to take home to his kids.

"Save me a couple next time, okay?" I asked, and she had given me a funny look before nodding softly and giving me that full smile of hers. "Okay."

As our lives intertwined, I saw more of her. Mainly just glimpses around the house. Sometimes in the hallway going to and from her room, where she was almost always holding a mug. Full if she was headed in and empty if she was headed out. Sometimes I caught her in the kitchen poking around Maria's leftovers or on the couch dozing off with a half-drunk cup in her hand. I even peeked my head into her door to ask her if she wanted to walk in the evenings.

When I did this, I usually noticed the orange box on her bedside table closest to where she slept, still untouched and unopened. I told myself not to be disappointed she hadn't used it yet, or that she hadn't taken me up on another walk. I knew she was sore, judging by the way she gingerly waddled up and down the steps and how she sat with as little bending as humanly possible for a few days after our first one. She would say yes again one of these days, I knew she would. I would just keep asking until that day came.

"Ox," a voice cut through my thoughts. I glanced up to see Mátti leaning forward on his knees as he spoke to me in hushed tones. Venny and Manuel were talking about something in their own sidebar. "You good? You are seriously spacing out today."

Sighing, my eyes drifted downward to where I had set my phone face down on the table. I had resisted the urge to turn it off earlier when I received call after call from an increasingly familiar number. Detective Munson from the Seaside Police was now a frequent caller.

Grinding my molars together, I tried to tamp down the urge to throw the phone at someone. Preferably Manuel, but anyone would do.

The fact that the local police refused to give up the possibility that Abuelo's death resulted from some sort of foul play was wearing a hole in my resolve. At first, I was grateful they were leaving no stones unturned. But now, after having laid to rest a family member with no body and seeing my family suffer as a result, I was ready to have the situation over and done with.

Not to mention, they kept pressing on the topic of Clementine. They found it odd she wasn't there to witness the stroke turned heart attack, or to call the ambulance sooner. The fact she has no remorse for her dead husband and went and married his grandson just days after seemed to be raising suspicions too.

If they only knew.

For a short while, maybe some days after I'd first taken Clem in, I thought of the possibility that she could have hurt Abuelo. She had nothing else to lose and everything to gain from the situation. A stroke like Abuelo's could be manufactured by poison or toxins, and the police weren't just investigating for the hell of it. They knew *something*. But as the days turned over and the reality of her state became apparent, it was obvious to me that she wasn't responsible. She was hardly functioning herself, I doubted she was the mastermind behind some unsolvable murder.

But the police kept pushing. They kept insisting to see her, speak with her, and to get her side of the story. They wanted to interrogate her. They wanted more details, and the more I said no, the more they seemed to want in.

I wouldn't give it to them. It wasn't good for my family and it wasn't good for Clementine. She had just started coming out of her room at the very least. Eating a little more each day. *And talking.* It would be thoughtless of me to throw her to the wolves and let them rip apart the small progress she'd made.

No. I'd protect her like I protected my family.

I reached forward and picked up my phone, opening the messaging app. The previous message from hours earlier was still on the screen where I'd left it.

Detective Munson: Can we set up a meeting?

With a deep breath in and out, I typed a reply and pressed "send" before I could think twice.

Me: Wednesday. 3pm.

Pocketing the phone in my jacket, I looked up at Mátti and paused. He wasn't all that much younger than me, but what he lacked in boyish features he made up for in charm. He was all smiles all the time. Happy, jokey, all-around fun to be around. He never took anything too seriously because he never had to. I always had things covered for him, and on the rare occasion I didn't (an occasion we had yet to encounter) I knew he was good for it. He looked back at me with careful concern in his eyes. Then waggled his eyebrows stupidly, and I cracked a smile.

I wanted to protect *this* at all costs. I would not let some mall cops playing secret service get in the way of that. So, I let that small smile become a big one and I laughed.

"I'm fine. Just thinking," I answered finally, willing my voice to go light.

"About?" He cooed.

"About…" I paused, trying to think of something and failing. My eyes wandered around the room, taking in the dark of the walls, the expensive leather furniture, and wooden fixtures. This was a place most of the men in my family frequented. It was member only and they valued discretion. It was a safe place away from the office to get some of our more private contracts done. I brought my eyes back to Mátti and gave him a knowing look. "About how glad I am this is finally over."

"You mean that you finally secured your throne?" Manuel jumped in, his voice loud as he cut his way into our conversation. "Efficient as always, Ox. You wasted no time sealing us in our little playpens forever while you get full access to the big house."

Cutting my eyes to Venny I asked, "How many has he had?"

Venny shrugged and put his hands up as if to say he's out of it. Mátti, however, was also not a fan of Manny's shit and shook his head incredulously. "What are you even talking about, Manny? For the last time, *it's a W - I - L - L*. None of us had any say in it."

He forgot to mention that will or no will, Manny wouldn't be first, second, or third to inherit anything. Technically, they were *our* abuelo's companies. Although Ronaldo's brothers' and sisters' children, and their children called him "Abuelo" too, and were given positions in his multitude of companies as a courtesy, he still had no inherent right to any of the physical, intellectual, or other property of my grandfather's. He was just a nephew.

If I really wanted to be mean, I could point out to Manuel that he was essentially worth nothing.

But I was *gracious*.

So instead, I said, "You've been given better accommodation in the same *'playpens'* you've always had. And Manny, try to remember that nothing is forever. Things can always change."

"Like your marital status?" He grumbled into another sip of his drink.

"Jesus, Manny, did you want her or something?" Mátti asked, sitting back in his chair and shaking his head. I cut him a glowering look.

"It would sweeten this shit deal, I know that much," Manny said. "I wouldn't mind inheriting *that*."

The word "that" was emphasized with the lewd squeezing of both hands mid-air. I wanted to punch him right then and there.

"You wouldn't be good together," I rushed out with a clear of my throat. Three heads whipped to me simultaneously. "What?"

"And you are?" Venny asked with a laugh.

This irked me. He was one of the few cousins who had been at the wedding, which meant he'd seen Clem and I together. The thought that he didn't think we worked well together, as partners only of course, bothered me.

"You don't think I am?" Heads shook. "Why not?"

"What does it matter? You already got her anyway. You win." Manny huffed.

We all ignored him. Venny was the one to speak up first, scratching at the back of his neck like he was nervous to say what he was thinking. "She seems a little skittish, Ox. That's the kind of girl that needs a ton of patience and you...aren't."

When I was quiet, he felt the need to continue. "Patient. *At all.*"

I grimaced, my eyes flicking to Mátti to see if he agreed. His silence said that he did.

"She's amenable to me," I said, not wanting to admit to these assholes that, yes she was sometimes difficult, but nothing that was too much for me to handle. At least not yet.

"Yeah?" Mátti challenged with a smile. He leaned forward and raised his eyebrows. "Is she talking to you yet?"

I frowned. How did Mátti know she hadn't been talking to me? And why did it feel like we were placing bets on Clem? "I don't see how that's any of your fucking business."

Mátti sat back as he laughed, clapping his hands animatedly.

"You're only in it for the pussy and the money, anyway. Better that she shuts the fuck up and pops out that baby as soon as possible," Manny, who really needed a muzzle, added.

We all groaned. I shot Mátti a quick look before digging into my pocket and pulling out five big bills. Only our immediate family knew about operation divorce as soon as possible and the agreement I'd signed with Clem. The cousins, precious as they were, would cause unnecessary drama about it and we wanted this to be as clean as possible.

Mateo rose too, dropping his own share on the table and shoving his hands into his pockets. "On that note," he looked at me and raised his eyebrows. "You ready?"

"I'm ready," I agreed.

It was Friday night, and Friday nights and Sunday mornings for the Fernandez's meant family meals. Over the years, the frequency of them had ebbed and flowed, but it felt imperative lately that we spent as much time as a family as possible.

Apá would be happy with the news that all nondisclosures, employment tenures, and transfers of equity had been signed and shipped off to the lawyers. Not much had made him happy these days, but I assumed the next step in gaining closure was to tie up loose ends.

"We're out. See ya when we see ya." Mátti called over our shoulders as we turned toward the door to leave. I gave a quick two finger wave to the pair as we exited. We made it through the bar, to the elevators, and down to the lobby of the hotel the bar was located in. It took one more set of elevators to get to the underground parking garage where Mateo had parked his ridiculous bright blue sports car.

Once inside, I immediately pulled out my phone. I first checked my messages and saw nothing. Next, I opened my emails and knocked out three new correspondences that had popped into my inbox since I'd last checked. Everything else seemed to be unimportant or something I could have Urse, my assistant, check on in the morning.

I was just about to open up an amended contract I was sure was perfect but wanted to double check, when I noticed we hadn't moved.

Looking up and over I caught Mátti assessing me like he was the one waiting on something.

Closing my phone and setting it down in my lap, I turned slightly toward him. "What?"

"What was all that?" he asked, his voice sounding dazed and disbelieving.

"All what?"

"All that macho man *'I'll kill you if you talk about my woman'* stuff." I wrinkled my nose. "Macho man? Really?"

"Deflecting!" he called out, pointing a finger at me. I grabbed the finger and squeezed until he whimpered and pleaded mercy. Then he mumbled, "Violent deflecting."

He was lucky I only squeezed and didn't bend. "I'm not deflecting. I just don't know what to say to that. What's the big deal? You think I'm just going to let him talk shit about someone who's not here to defend themself?"

"Something tells me you would have reacted like that even if she *was* here." He was right. I would have. But that was beside the point. And his slow smile said he knew it, too. "That's not all. You got all sulky when Venny said you two weren't a good match."

"Because we're already matched! What's the point in saying we aren't good now?" I protested.

"But it's not *real*, so what's the big deal if you aren't?" He protested right back.

"It isn't a big deal, okay? I just don't appreciate being treated like I'm this temperamental hot head who can't be trusted with some girl's emotions. I'm not. I'm just busy. If I appear impatient, it's because I've got one hundred other things to do than wait around for someone to make a decision they should have made before they wasted my time.

"If I'm cold, so what? She's an adult, I'm an adult. We can both figure out how to tolerate each other for three goddamn years. And even if we can't, I don't see how it's anyone else's business but ours what goes on within a marriage we were *both* forced to enter.

"Don't act like I'm some fire breathing demon who's going to corrupt her soul. She's fine. I'm making sure of it. So, you all can just sit back and mind your own goddamn business." When I finished my little tirade, I crossed my arms over my chest. Like a toddler.

Mátti stared openmouthed at me for an entire minute before the corners of his mouth pulled upward into a grin and he turned in his seat. Snapping his seat belt in place, he put the car in gear and pulled out of the parking space. We drove for a couple of minutes before Mátti shook his head and grinned even harder.

"You're gonna eat her alive."

Amá was in the kitchen when we arrived home. The girls were here somewhere too, probably all congregated in one room watching videos online or fighting over who was wearing who's clothing this time. Apá was squirreled away in the living room on his favorite extra-large love chair with the remote in his hand and soccer on the TV. Mátti went straight for our dad, plopping down on the large sectional beside Apá's chair and asking who was on. They immediately fell into easy conversation, and I craned my neck as I made my way to the kitchen to see my mom, hoping to catch the expression on my dad's face. I couldn't tell from where I was, but it seemed as if he was relaxed. I noted the cold, sweating beer sitting on top of a coaster on the side table next to him and breathed a sigh of relief. Even if he wasn't relaxed, he would be soon if he was having beer tonight.

Good.

Inside the kitchen, I found my mom with her head damn near in the oven as she bent over to grab something from the very back. As soon as my body seemed to cross the threshold, she was calling out to me. "Oaxaca, Mijo, could you grab the rajas from the fridge and add them to the pan? I'm running behind."

Without missing a step, I moved over to the fridge and grabbed the first bowl I saw. An Aztec printed mixing bowl full of colorful tomatoes, peppers, and onions. I had already been rolling my sleeves up on the way in, knowing she would need assistance with something. How she knew it was me without even looking? She'd call it her motherly intuition, but in reality, I was the only one who helped her. At first it was because I was the only one old enough to do it, and later because it had become our thing.

"Amá, Por qué está tu cabeza en el horno?" I asked her with a chastising cluck of my tongue.

"Cállate, Mijo. Ayúdame." She hissed at me to shut up and do what she asked. I did, hoping she'd at least get her head out of the oven if she wasn't going to tell me why it was in there.

My wish was granted just as I was dropping the vegetables into the already hot pan. Not only had Amá removed herself, and a dish full of tortillas from the oven, but she had turned toward me in a rush of movement only to halt like something had run right into her.

I startled as she startled and we both looked at each other like we were crazy.

"What?" I asked at her stricken expression.

"Dónde está?" she asked, looking left and looking right then to the doorway of the kitchen into the living room. Setting my own dish down, I picked up a couple of discarded dishtowels and walked over to her. Plucking the warm dish from her hands, I walked it over to an empty potsticker on the counter and set it there. A quick scan of the counter produced the lid and I plucked that up too, plopping it down on the pan to keep the tortillas warm.

"Where is what, Amá?" I asked, discarding the towels and picking up a wooden spoon to stir the veggies. They sizzled and popped as they caramelized under the heat. In front of the veggie pan, I noticed Amá's big red ceramic pot that she usually made stews in. I glanced over my shoulder and pointed at the pot with my spoon. "Albóndigas?"

Sopa de Albóndigas was a meatball and vegetable soup my mom

used to make us whenever we were sick. I never got sick, or at least when I was sick, I never got to play hooky like the rest of my siblings. So whenever I got to have Albóndigas I would get so excited, because finally it was my turn for something special. The feeling hadn't weakened apparently, judging by my excitement at seeing the stewing pot.

But my mom was shaking her head and moving around the kitchen looking under and around things like she was insane. "No, no. It's Menudu, Mijo."

I looked at her again, my eyebrows knitting together in confusion. "Otra vez?"

Again?

Menudu was another soup. One that she only made for holidays and grievances. It was strange she was making it again when we'd had it not too long ago. Especially because it was generally poorly received among our family. I didn't really care one way or another, and Mateo was the same. The girls, on the other hand, didn't care much to eat animal parts that no one else wanted, though I supposed Melissa pretended to tolerate more than she actually did.

"Si. Apá likes it and so did Clementina," she said. My eyebrows touched my hairline. She went on. "Where is she? With the girls?"

"Clementine?" I asked, giving her a look I hope portrayed *'what the hell are you talking about crazy lady'* respectfully.

"Si, Oaxaca! Do not act dumb with me!" And they said *I* was impatient?

"She's not here, Amá," I said, aware that it came out weirdly. Almost like I could have said, *'Why would she be?'*

She hissed sharply, her shoulders rearing back in a physical recoil. And then she was all over me, advancing on me in seconds and swiping the wooden spoon from my hand just to wag it in my face threateningly.

"And why is my daughter-in-law not here? You didn't ask her to come eat? Are you starving her? I didn't raise you like that, Mijo!" she said.

"I don't know what you two are talking about, but that sounds like Ox, Mami. Whatever it is, he did it." Ceci strutted in from the other side of the room, two sisters flanking her sides.

"No, Amá!" I said, swiping the spoon back from her and setting it aside. I glared a look over at the little pip-squeak and mouthed a colorful expletive her way. Her response was to cackle as she threw her head back and reached for the fridge. Amá huddled over and popped her hand away, telling her she'd spoil dinner and to go sit down somewhere. I crossed my arms and leaned my hip against the stove, looking down my shoulder to check the veggies.

They only needed a few more minutes tops. When I looked up, I found the waiting eyes of four women watching me. Ceci sitting on a stool at the island, her chin in her hands. Melissa sitting next to her with her hands clasped in front of her on the countertop. Alta stacking some of the table placements near the edge of the counter and my mom standing in the center of the room facing me with her arms crossed over her chest.

"God, *what*?" I groaned, unsuccessful in my attempts to suppress it.

"You really didn't invite her?" she asked.

"I didn't know the invitation was open," I said.

"Aye, Mijo. How can you be so heartless? She is your wife." My mom whined as she placed her hand to her forehead like I was the worst son in the world.

"Technically," Ceci grumbled. Melissa reached over and thumped Ceci's temple, causing her to screech dramatically. "Ow! Why'd you do that?"

"Respect, Ceci. Try it sometime," Lis said before turning her gaze back to me. "And speaking of…"

"You too?" I ask, my voice coming out way calmer than my heart felt in my chest. Had I truly done something wrong here? Was leaving Clem out of a family gathering like this the first step in me becoming just like Abuelo? I swallowed the sudden dryness in my throat and when it didn't go away, I walked over to the fridge and pulled out a bottle of water from the bottom carriage. My mom moved over to the stove to pick up where I left off.

"It's just dinner, Ox," Melissa said, and I noticed she sounded tired. Looking at her, though, she looked as she always did. Neat, clean, and proper. "But if you're here, who is she having dinner with?"

Dammit. Since when did Melissa make so much sense? I looked at her again, her low dark bun and big square glasses making her extra formal today.

"She's all alone, Oaxaca?" My mother might as well have screamed she was so loud. "What is wrong with this boy? I thought I raised a good boy. But apparently, I was wrong."

"Oh my— *I'm sorry*, Amá. Next time, okay?" I said, trying to tamp down her dramatics. This brought another raging gasp from her mouth.

"Next time? No! You call her and invite her now!" I looked at her like she was crazy, and she didn't like that. Raising the spoon again in a silent threat, she said through her teeth, "*Now*, Oaxaca."

Looking around at each face in the room, I sighed and dug into my pocket for my phone. "She doesn't drive. It'll be more trouble than it's worth."

"You can go get her." Amá offered casually.

"That'll take an hour at the least."

"That's okay. We have time." She shrugged like it wasn't already pushing eight at night.

"Dinner is ready." I pointed out.

Her head snapped up and the spoon snapped out. "Dinner is ready when the family is here to eat it, Oaxaca. Your wife is not here, so we do not eat. You can explain to your hungry brother and sisters why they can't have food tonight if you fail to do it."

She had the nerve to shrug again. Like she wasn't being wholly unreasonable and offhanded at the same time. Grumbling, I clicked on the screen of my cell and found Clementine's name in the messaging app. I had checked it earlier and no messages came from her. That was still the case now and she almost never carried her phone around, so if I texted her, she probably wouldn't get it.

Sighing, I only gave myself a few seconds to contemplate calling her before I was tapping the call button beside her name. The phone rang three times before the receiver picked up and the questioning tone of my wife filled my ears.

"Hello?" she greeted directly into my ear. I imagined her holding the phone with two hands, her bottom one cupping the bottom of the phone like a bowl. I had seen her speak to her brothers a couple of times like that and found it endearing, if not a little strange. "Ox?"

"Hi," I said in my normal business-like tone. I heard the sharp intake of a breath and nothing else. For a beat I thought she would say something, but when she didn't, I found myself clearing my throat.

"Is everything okay?" she asked in a whispery voice. I couldn't help but notice (aside from the fact that she was whispering) that she sounded worried.

"Yeah, of course," I said, inching over to the far corner of the kitchen to give myself some privacy. Gentling my voice, I asked, "Is everything okay with you? Why are you whispering?"

"Oh—I'm sorry, you just sounded, I don't know, like something had happened."

"No, Clem, everything's fine," I said and something that had tightened in my chest loosened when I heard her breathe a sigh of relief. "What are you doing?"

"About to meet up with the guys. They're all off work now, so they invited me out."

"Have you guys eaten?" I asked, sort of hoping they had so I didn't have to invite her *and* all three of her brothers to my family dinner.

"No, we were going to order something and maybe watch movies," she said. I hummed, nodding. Apprehension had filled me. Not because

139

I was shy to ask her over, but by asking I was cutting into the family time those four were needing. "Ox?"

I looked over my shoulder, wondering if there was any chance my mom wasn't watching, and I could get away with telling her Clem was too busy to join dinner. Unsurprisingly, every eye in the kitchen was on me, watching me like I was their favorite TV show. Turning back, I swallowed my sigh so Clem wouldn't think it was for her.

"If you guys haven't ordered yet, my mom invited you to dinner at her house. She usually makes a feast on weekends." I spoke just loud enough that Amá would hear the invitation.

"When?" she asked.

"Right now. We're almost ready to set the table."

I walked in a little half circle as I talked to her, my mind on the fact that four Fergusons might be crashing our family dinner soon. While the sudden change in plans put me a little on edge, I was feeling sort of relieved to be hearing Clementine's voice for the first time that day. A voice that sounded a little off even after she had stopped whispering. Something about that voice had my mother's invitation turning into my own, and against my previous objections, I began to insist.

"The three stooges are welcome too. Come eat, Clem."

"Would we have to bring anything?" she asked, that nervous hitch appearing in her voice.

"Just you is enough."

There was a pause on the other side of the line before she breathed close to the phone in her husky whispering voice again. Tingles shot through my arms and legs (and other regions), as the sensation felt like she was breathing right into my ear. "Let me ask, okay?"

"Mhmm," I grunted, sliding a hand into my pocket and hoping to adjust myself without being noticed.

There was distant mumbling in the background. Deep grumbling which may have put me on edge if I didn't know she was with her brothers and in a few seconds, she was back on the phone with an exhaling breath.

"Clint says we can be there in twenty minutes. Is that alright?" she asked.

"Perfect," I replied.

After saying goodbye and hanging up the phone, I turned to my audience and gave them an *'are you kidding me look'* because what they were doing wasn't even considered eavesdropping. They were blatantly watching my conversation with her. I shook my head. "She'll be here in twenty."

Twenty minutes later, I was opening the door for my unexpected house guests and ushering them in. As soon as I laid eyes on the only person I truly had been waiting to see, it was confirmed. That tired, worn-out quality her voice had held over the phone was transferred into her face. Her eyes even looked like they might be red rimmed.

Grunting a quick hello at her brothers and telling them where they could go wash up and sit for dinner, I turned to Clementine before she could follow. In the middle of the foyer, we weren't exactly alone, but tons of space separated us from the living room, dining room, and kitchen entrances. If someone was listening, they were trying to.

Stopping in front of her, I looked her over with no interruptions. I'd already noted the tired, sunken, and possibly tear ridden state of her face. Her hair was done in that sensible curling braid again and she wore a loose white sweater and loose black pants that flowed around her legs like a skirt. She liked to mix up her clothes, I'd noticed, and it was decidedly cute to see her current look. Swimming in yards of fabric so elegantly and pretty. But what was not cute was the worrisome look on her face.

"Hey," I said, trying to catch her gaze as she pinballed it around the room. Finally, it settled on me and she seemed to smile genuinely, if not weakly.

"Hi." She hiked up something on her shoulder and I noticed a midsized tote bag she had there for the first time. It looked full, with shapes protruding out its sides.

I reached for it and slipped it off her shoulder while asking, "What's this?"

"Just something for your parents, for inviting us. Clint had it already so…" she shrugged and I peeked into the bag to see two bottles of wine and a six-pack of beer. Nodding, I closed the bag and swung my eyes back to her.

"I'll take them to the fridge."

"No!" She shot her hands forward, one landing on the bag and the other landing on my forearm. My skin tingled under the soft touch of her hand. Quickly, she adjusted so they were both resting on the bag, stilling me from moving away. I raised an eyebrow at her. "I wanted to give them to your mom."

I couldn't explain the small tenderness that snaked into my heart at her wanting to thank my mom. Opening the bag again, I reached down and pulled out the six-pack, handing it to her.

"Amá's just happy you're here. Take this to my dad instead." When she just stared at me, I reached forward, grabbed her hand and wrapped it around the handle of the six-pack. "Trust me. She's always watching. Two birds, one six-pack."

She nodded weakly, and I frowned, thinking for sure I would at least get a smile out of her. But nothing.

"You okay?" I asked, not knowing what to say since I figured *'you look like shit'* wouldn't have been an appropriate approach.

"Yeah. Just tired." She answered. I felt my mouth twist to the side, hopefully hiding my deepening frown. She peeked up at me and leaned forward, lowering her voice conspiratorially. *"And hungry.* It's Clint's turn to choose take out and he's *so* bad at it. I was going to have to fake an upset stomach before you saved me. Gracias, Oaxaca."

She turned, held up the six-pack as if to say thank you again, and then sauntered off into the living room where she was greeted by a surprised sounding Apá and the insistent urges for her to sit and watch whatever was on TV with him.

The twist in my mouth remained as I tried to fight the pleased smile trying to break free. I don't know if it was the sound of her speaking Spanish or of her thanking me *again* that had the muscles in my face jumping up in an attempt to grin.

I needed to get back to the kitchen before someone caught me staring like an idiot. Only, as I turned, my gaze was met by four bodies lined up consecutively. Each of them carried a dish in their hands and they looked as if they were headed to the dining room, only, they could have taken about three other routes to get there.

They were just eavesdropping. *Shamelessly.*

When I executed a dirty look in their direction, they all snickered and continued on their way as I headed for the kitchen.

It was Mateo who stalled slightly, looking over his shoulder with one of his mischievous glances. "Color me shocked, I think I stand corrected."

And dammit, I didn't know what the hell he meant by that.

Chapter Thirteen

CLEMENTINE

I ate a cow stomach. I had eaten cow stomach happily and heartily until the moment I realized it was cow stomach. The reason for my blunder?

Oaxaca Fernandez.

I had arrived at the Fernandez home hungry and exhausted both emotionally and physically. Earlier that day I had gotten a call from the police station asking if I could come down to their city location for follow up questioning. I'd immediately been put on edge by the change in location, but they'd assured me that this was no interrogation and they just didn't want any more distractions as they hadn't gotten through all the questions the first time we met.

I knew I should have asked one of my brothers or Ox to go with me this time, but I'd wanted to do something on my own. Even if that something was a meeting that I absolutely dreaded.

So, I'd gotten myself ready, lied to Sylvie and Maria about where I was going, and called myself a car.

The police asked all the obvious questions, most of them being the same ones they'd asked already before, just in a different, more cunning way. Hoping to trip me up, I assumed. I gave them the same answers as before, granted with a little more attitude than usual. But they had brought that loudmouth officer back, probably because they knew he got under my skin. And he had been just as insufferable as the first time. Asking invasive, judgmental, nonsensical questions.

It was exhausting to say the least. So when Ox called and invited me to dinner, I was nervous at first but warmed up to the idea of a home cooked meal pretty quickly. I felt kind of bad that I was forcing my brothers to spend their Friday night with my inherited in-laws. They were getting food out of the deal and would be free to do whatever they wanted later since I'd probably go home with Ox.

After Ox's call, seeing him suddenly became the only thing I wanted to do. My big day of taking care of things on my own had left me wanting to curl up *metaphorically* under the protective arm of this new Ox I was getting to know. Plus, I had barely seen him in the week past save for when he was carting me off to my brothers' places. It had been a bummer that the last few days, when I was finally feeling up for another walk, he hadn't been around to ask.

When he met me and my brothers at the front door of his parents' house and welcomed us inside, I felt an unexpected rush of comfort at his presence. And when he'd slipped my bag off my shoulder and asked if I was alright, I'd wanted to spill my guts to him right then and there. After our walk on the beach that day, I'd started feeling the urge to tell him things. Like how my day had been or how Maria had let me cook with her the other day or how I'd finally been able to make Clint laugh after so, so long. I found myself wanting to know how he'd react to the

145

little moments of my day, but I knew I shouldn't. Because, in reality, he probably wouldn't care.

So instead of telling him about my mental exhaustion courtesy of Officer Asshole, I smiled as best I could and told him how hungry I was. He bought it and we'd continued on through the night sharing an all-around pleasant, if not a little awkward, dinner with his family.

It was when I was filling my small bowl up with a second helping of grilled vegetables that Ox's mother, Martina, called toward me from across the table. "Clementina, have some soup, Mija."

"What kind?" I asked, stalling my movements toward the vegetables and giving a curious glance toward the big stew pot in the center of the table.

"Menudo," Clint's voice said from far down my right side. "Dad's favorite, remember Tine?"

Both Connor and Clay snickered, and I scrunched my nose against my better judgment.

They were snickering because they knew my exact thoughts on the traditional soup made up almost entirely of beef stomach. It was the only thing my dad ever cooked himself, swearing it put him back in his grandmother's kitchen in Mexico. He'd sold the boys on it, but he had never once gotten me to try it.

I sat back down and turned to Martina with what I hoped was a genuinely grateful look. "Lo siento Señora Martina. No me gusta."

She nodded but gave me a funny look. When I sat my bowl back down on the table in front of me, Ox swiped it and rose to his feet. Leaning forward, he uncapped the lid on the pot and spooned in a small portion of the stew before returning it to the pot. Setting the bowl down in front of me, he gave me an expectant look. I leaned away from it in a not-so-subtle gesture for *'hell no'*.

"Clementine," he said in that deadpan way of his. "You've had this before. Here, smell."

He held the bowl out in my direction, and flicking a glance up at his eyes, I hesitated. Facing me he whispered, *"Don't be such a baby. It's good."*

This was the same whispering tone he used to talk only to me at our wedding when he was trying to get me to breathe deeply. I had trusted him then, so I might as well humor him now.

Simply to appease him, I leaned forward and took a sniff. The faintly familiar aroma of spices and meat hit my nose, and I furrowed a confused look at him. Leaning in further, I sniffed again, and then I set my shoulders back to look at him fully as the realization set in.

I *had* eaten this. After the funeral service at the luncheon, Ox had fed me his mom's home cooking. I had eaten this infamous beef stew my family had teased me about forever unknowingly. And it was good.

One look at my expression and Ox knew that I knew, and his reaction was to throw his head back and laugh.

Three eavesdropping parties set their forks down and gawked. Clint was covering his mouth in amazement and Clay was grinning ear to ear. Connor was smiling too, shaking his head slightly.

"You got her to eat it?" Clay asked Ox, giving him a look of surprise. "Damn boys, I guess our man Ox here wins the bet."

"Bet?" I asked, turning to my brothers in shock.

"Yep," he said as he reached forward and flicked my nose. "You think we asked Dad to make it so much because we *wanted* it every week?"

My mind decided to recall memories of each boy, even Connor, actively trying to get me to eat the damn soup. Following me around with spoonfuls or trying to convince me to drink it instead. None of them had ever succeeded and when I'd grown into my teenage years, and things started getting weird between me and my parents, they'd stopped.

"I'm impressed. Abuela's threats of no dinner couldn't even sway her back then," Clint said, leaning backward. The boys agreed.

I swallowed, my heart lurching painfully at the mention of our abuela. Yet another part of my past that had been left behind, forgotten. It still made me sad. I turned back to Ox, ready to tell him about my sadistic brothers and their antics, but his eyes were up past my head, looking to one of them in a questioning way. When he noticed me looking, he gave me a small smile before pushing the bowl in my direction.

"Eat," he'd said. "You'll like it."

I did.

The reason I was still thinking about this over a week later was because of the constant cow spam I had been getting from my brothers ever since. First, a gift had shown up for me at the door the next day with cow printed pajama pants in it. Then, when Clint had driven me home from his house, I'd noticed a cute little cow plushie in the passenger seat, all strapped in and everything. And now, floating high above me and anchored by my bedside table were a bundle of cow shaped balloons. Their cute cartoon faces smiled down at me widely. I giggled and then snorted when I noticed the elegant white place card that simply said, *Con.*

Connor, of all people, was in on it too. Those losers. *My losers.* As hard as it could be at times, like when they talked about mom and dad so casually as if I hadn't been cut off from them, I was still glad to have them back.

Today my heart felt good. After having a good laugh at Connor's surprise, Ox knocked on my door and told me that he'd be home for the weekend. He invited me to have my tea out in the kitchen while he had breakfast if I wanted.

After only fussing with my hair for a short moment (*just* to make sure it wasn't a rat's nest) and checking in the mirror briefly (*just to make sure* I didn't have any drool stains), I took him up on the offer.

I had my usual breakfast of black tea and toast while he had his normal (to me, since I'd only shared this particular meal with him a couple of times) breakfast of coffee, eggs, chorizo, and spinach.

It was a pleasant and mostly quiet meal. We exchanged a few words about the weather or about our respective drinks. Mine was more of his special tea from Mexico, and I offered him a sip which he declined. His was imported coffee gifted to him from his mom. When he offered me a sip in return, just to be nice, I was intrigued by the sound of it. The coffee was bitter on my tongue and I puckered my mouth at it before shoving it back his way. Ox liked his coffee nearly black, apparently, only a bit of cream splashed in there to cut through the harsh brew. My reaction made him smile though, so I didn't consider the bad sip of coffee a total loss if that was the result.

The only downside to the morning was that he still hadn't offered to walk with me out on the beach again. I had somehow missed the opportunity when I'd been too sore to function. But that's okay, because the morning was otherwise pretty good.

After getting myself dressed and peeking a head out the window, I decided to take myself on that walk. I could do it by myself. It would be good for me. The late summer weather was mild against my skin and the beach winds were just as soothing as they were the first few times I'd been out there. Walking alone wasn't quite the same, but it was still nice to get out and move around.

I took a couple pictures of the horizon and of pretty shells I found along the shore. Using my phone's fitness app, I tracked my progress as I moved and racked up a full hour of walking the beach before I headed back to the house.

As I walked through the garden and around the front to the door, I realized there was something up there. I froze. Leaning my entire torso forward, I tried to get a better look from afar. The figure was moving in anxious motions along the front stoop. The pattern they followed went: pace to the left, pace to the right, charge the door, stop, breath, bang, yell.

"Ox! Goddammit you stubborn ass, please? Please help?" It was a woman's voice, that much was clear. And she was asking for help? I found my steps drifting forward just slightly as I reached up to my tiptoes trying to see who it could be. I didn't even think Ox knew any women other than his sisters... And Sylvie.

That last thought was grumbly and wreaked of envy and I had to school myself from that kind of accusatory thinking. It wasn't my place to question who he knew.

Light coppery hair swung behind the small woman as she tossed her head back and groaned. And then I think I heard her growl. Watching her as she straightened up again and raised her fist to the door, her profile flashed and I realized I recognized her.

It was Ceci.

The feeling that came over me was weird. In the same instance, I was overcome with both relief and dread. It was just Ceci. Not some random stranger, or worse, some woman who was not a stranger at all. If it hadn't been for her uncharacteristically light hair compared to the rest of her family, I probably would have noticed her sooner.

But then it hit me. Ceci was at Ox's front door, banging her fists against it and begging for help. Was she hurt? Had something happened?

"Ox? Ox!" she called again as she banged. "Ox, please? I fucked up, okay?" She let her fist slide down the door and drop to her side, hanging her head. Shaking it. "I really fucked up. I'm sorry."

Okay. This was weird.

Speed walking the rest of the way up to the front door, I called out, "Celestia?"

It was when I said her full name that I realized I'd never addressed her directly before. That's probably why she didn't make any indication that she heard me, instead banging on the door again and calling out with as much vigor as she had before.

"Ox!"

Either Ox had stepped out or his ears were clogged not to be hearing all her banging and shouting. I hustled up to the door and stopped right behind her. Reaching a hand out, I tried to grab her shoulder but she whipped around and swatted my hand away with splitting force. I let out a yelp and yanked my hand back to cradle against my chest. "Celestia!"

She turned to face me, a glowing rage on her face. A face that was pale and red all at the same time. She had dark, dark circles underneath her eyes and it looked like her lip was bleeding.

Forgetting about my hand, I stepped forward again and reached for her. "Oh my gosh!"

She stepped back, dodging me this time instead of attacking. Narrowing her eyes at me, her mouth turned up in a sneer as she looked me up and down. "Let me in."

"What happened?" I asked, alarm in my voice. I cast my eyes down her little body, scanning for any more signs of harm. There were a few bruises along her arms and it looked like some of her fingertips might be bleeding. What the hell? Had she gotten in an accident? Had someone done this to her? I felt my throat clog and my head wash with memories of how bad people could be and how much harm someone bigger than you could bring simply because they wanted to. I took another step forward, caging her in against the front door. "Celestia, *what happened*?"

She yanked her chin to the side and averted her gaze. "Where's Ox?"

"He must be out. Have you tried his cell?" I asked, my hand reaching into my pocket and grabbing the singular key I'd carried with me. I rushed for the door, pushing past Ceci who barely moved to give me any space. When I couldn't get the key in the lock right away, she leaned forward, her chest grazing my shoulder, and she let out a ragged breath. I looked down my shoulder at her to find her eyes closing while she took deep measured breaths. Working the key into the lock finally, I pushed the door open and quickly slid an arm underneath her shoulder.

And she let me. Which was *not* a good sign.

"Celestia—"

151

"Ceci," she snapped, correcting me.

"*Ceci*," I said. "Are you hurt anywhere else?"

"I'm not hurt. I just need to talk to Ox."

I scoffed, my nerves frying as I stood there not knowing what was going on and not knowing what to do. Walking her into the living room and setting her down on the couch, I turned swiftly toward the open kitchen and called out, "Maria, Sylvie?"

It was the weekend. They were usually off work, but not always. So, I tried anyway, assuming they would know what to do more than I did. *And they would know how to deal with Ceci too.* But naturally there was no answer to my calls.

I shuffled quickly through the house, doing a quick search for Ox. His study was empty, his bedroom was empty (his bathroom too). His cars were still parked in the garage which was strange but not totally uncommon. Sometimes he got rides with his brother or parents when they went somewhere together. Plus, his driver was back from being out of town and could have driven him someplace too. The only other place he hung out besides his office was the back garden, and he would have heard Ceci screaming at the door if he was out there.

He wasn't here.

Rushing back to the living room, I found her slumped against the arm of the couch, her cheek plastered to the hand resting there and her eyes closed as she breathed calculatedly.

She was decidedly *not okay*, and Ox wasn't here to help either of us. We were going to have to figure it out on our own.

"Ceci," I said again, my voice doing this thing I'd never heard it do before—becoming all deep and assertive. "*Celestia, listen*. We're going to get you cleaned up and then we can call Ox and see if he can come home right now."

"Call him now," she demanded in a groan.

"I'll call him when you tell me what happened. He'll ask."

She opened her eyes and gave me a glare that said, '*are you completely insane*'? Only, she had to be the completely insane one if she thought I was calling Oaxaca Fernandez and telling him his sister was sitting on his couch hurting without knowing what the hell else to say. So, I looked at her with my *'serious Clem face'* and crossed my arms.

I knew I couldn't beat her in a staring contest, but I was persistent enough to keep my word on not calling her brother until I knew what was going on. *And if she was okay.* She just continued staring me down, proving she'd inherited the same steel determination gene as Ox at birth. After an entire minute, I sighed.

"Celes—"

"*Ceci*," she insisted through gritted teeth.

I curled my lips into my mouth and took a slow breath. Dropping my hands to my sides, I thought to myself, *screw it.* This was as good of an occasion as any.

I charged out of the living room and into the open kitchen. I still hardly knew where anything was located, so I rummaged through every cabinet, swinging doors open and not bothering to close them after, until I came across what I was looking for.

Liquor.

"What are you—" Ceci started but stopped when she saw me grab a handle of the first thing I saw and unscrew the cap to take a swig directly from the bottle. She snorted. "Oh shit, you're unhinged."

"No," I said as I rounded the corner of the island and walked the twenty or so feet back to her. I extended the bottle toward her and huffed. "You're just that hard to deal with."

She snickered, then grinned. She had a busted lip and bruised skin, and she had the nerve to grin. "Ooo, my turn?"

I sloshed the bottle a little and extended it further, my patience and my nerves fracturing further. "Yes, here."

She didn't hesitate to bring it to her lips. Taking three shot sized gulps, it looked like she was gearing up for a fourth before I lunged forward and snatched it from her. She followed the retreating bottle with her arms out in front of her, her hands making *'gimme'* motions.

"No," I said, clutching the bottle to my chest and glaring my best Clay look at her. "Now we can either go upstairs to the nice big bathroom and get you cleaned up, or I can drag your little ass to the kitchen sink and we can do it there."

She gave me a stupefied look and I shook my head. "What?"

She chuckled, "You said *ass*."

"You've never heard the word ass before?"

"Not from *you*. You sound like your brother." Pausing, she shook her head. "No, you sound like *my brother*."

Tsking, I moved to set the bottle down and went over to the couch to help her up. She could walk just fine on her own, but she wasn't moving otherwise. With her arm slung around the back of my waist and her weight leaning into me, I looked down at her as we started to move toward the pathway to the stairs.

My head shook of its own volition and my voice was so low I didn't know if I was talking to her or myself. "I don't know how you thought this was a good idea. He's going to *flip*."

She snatched the discarded bottle off the table and then obediently let me guide her up the stairs. We made it to my bathroom and after setting her down on the closed toilet seat, I rushed over to the marble standing bathtub and started running it.

"What the hell are you doing? I'm not five! Turn the shower on!" she complained.

I gave her a look over my shoulder, "I can't help you if you're in the shower."

"You don't need to help! You're not touching me while I'm *naked*." She shoved off the toilet seat and stumbled over to the shower instead. Turning it on as hot as it would go, she started stripping. She was inside before I even had a chance to argue.

Sighing, I turned the bath water off and slumped over to the toilet seat, sinking down and picking up the bottle she left there.

"Tell me what happened, Ceci. Maybe I can help," I said, hoping the alcohol had dulled her *'fight, fight, and more fight'* senses.

She was quiet for a long, long time before she sighed and the motions of her cleaning herself started to make sounds. "I fucked up."

"You said that already," I said. "What happened?"

"I…" she paused and then blurted out in a rush. "I got robbed!"

Shooting up to my feet, I immediately felt sick to my stomach. "You what? By who? Were you mugged? Have you called the police? We should call—"

The glass door of the shower, which had fogged from the steam, opened and Ceci popped her head around it. "If you're gonna help, you *cannot* freak out more than I'm freaking out."

Slowly, I sat back down and pressed my lips between my teeth. My mind was racing a mile a minute but in order to help her I needed to listen. She had been out front murmuring about how *she* fucked up after all. There must be an explanation.

Satisfied that I was done freaking out, she returned to her shower. "I've been—I *was* seeing this guy for the last few months. I met him out at one of those townie bars down shore. I thought he didn't know who I was."

This was…different. Not anything like I thought she was going to say.

"The whole time we were together he never really showed signs of knowing anything about me or my family. So I thought I was in the clear."

"But?"

She sighed, cut the water off, and opened the shower door. She had grabbed a towel from the inside hook and wrapped it around herself. She was dripping wet and beautiful as she stood there staring at me, her face contorted in anger.

Feeling a pang of sympathy for her, I extended her the bottle again.

She took it as she shook her head.

"But this past week he ghosted me. I went to his place and no one answered for days. I finally got someone to let me in and..." looking at me, she shook her head and took another long swig. "And he was gone."

"Shoot," I said.

"*Shit.*" She corrected, leaning her back against the damp wall of the shower.

"And *then* I get a call from my bank wanting to verify a recent "substantial transfer".

"Fuck," I hissed.

"Correct," she agreed, setting the bottle down on the stone of the shower floor below her and raking a hand through her wet hair. "There's no way that was a coincidence. Anyway, I hunted him down. He wasn't far. He was staying at one of his loser friend's places, who apparently was the one to tell him about me in the first place. They were both in on it together."

I felt my whole body stiffen. I was looking at her now, but she wasn't looking at me. Instead, she stared at the head of the shower, her mind someplace far off.

"And they hurt you, Ceci?" My voice must have been weird because her head snapped toward me, her eyebrows pulling together in a very Ox-like expression.

"No!" she almost snorted.

"No?" I croaked disbelievingly, my eyes moving to her obviously hurt body.

"No," she said again. Turning toward me, she popped a hip out and rested her hand there. "I went over there to beat the shit out of them."

I guffawed. That's the only explanation I had for the spurting noise that left me. "You beat up two men?"

"Me and my bat." She confirmed with a curt nod.

"And you're okay?"

"I got a little banged up, but not as much as their faces. And all their stuff. And their cars," she said, but her body seemed to slump a little bit, even with all her gusto.

"Then what's wrong?" I asked, confused times two, now that she was apparently okay with assaulting people. "Are you heartbroken?"

She scoffed, "No."

Looking at her, I realized that she was probably telling the truth. Not once had she shed a single solitary tear. Nothing but pure anger radiated off of her.

"No, I'm fucking embarrassed and Ox is going to be so mad."

"He'll understand."

"He won't.

"How much money did they take?"

"Just two," she said. But the way she turned her head away from me was weird.

I narrowed my eyes. "Big or small?"

She looked at me, and it seemed as if she was assessing me for the first time and was surprised that I wasn't a total idiot. Hanging her head, she mumbled, "Big."

I sucked in a sharp breath. *Two million dollars.* I took it back. Ox would be furious. It would be a miracle if he didn't string her up by her feet when he found out. *If* he found out.

"Can't you call the bank?" I asked.

"I missed the verification call. The money's in the middle and it'll probably be in their accounts on Monday. But the problem isn't really getting it back." She let out a sigh that was decidedly defeated. "The problem is my brother."

"Ox?"

"Yes, him!" she whined. "He's specifically warned me to tell him about the people I meet so he can do his stupid little big brother detective thing. And I guess now I know why."

"And in order to get it back, you have to tell him all...*that*." I nodded, finally understanding the gravity of it all. Ox was going to kill her, plain and simple. She was going to be fishing in Mexico after all.

She whined into her hands as if she was coming to the same conclusion.

"He won't cut you any slack? I mean, you were robbed by your boyfriend."

She shook her head, one of her feet kicking at nothing on the tile. "I'm not Alta. He won't believe that I got taken advantage of."

"Ceci, you *did* get taken advantage of."

"Yes, because I fucked up," she said and as she looked up at me, it was as if she was angry all over again. "And it's not the first time. He's going to be *so* mad."

I sighed and racked my brain for something helpful to say. On one hand, she was fine. She obviously hadn't gotten hurt too badly and, in the end, there was a way to get her money back quickly with a fraud claim and a little confessional with her brother. But on the other hand…

I looked at her crumpled form in the standing shower. She'd slid down the wall and was holding her head in one of her hands, her face screwed up in in angry downturn as she whispered, "I just fucking fucked up."

As if the memory was sent straight into my mind, I thought about the other week in Connor's house, where he sat me down and grilled me for hours on every choice I'd ever made. I thought about how bad it hurt coming from him because he, of all my brothers, had always had so much trust in me, and I had disappointed him. And I felt for Ceci.

She was okay, yeah. But she was still standing in my bathroom naked, betrayed by a lover, and staring down a (let's face it) ox of a brother in the mouth. She was going to get ripped a new one.

Unless I helped her.

Getting up, I left the bathroom only to come back a few minutes later with some random clothes I'd found in my dressers. When she didn't stir, I walked over to the shower and poked my finger at her naked shoulder.

"Come on, Ceci. Time to get out," I said.

"Just let me die here." She moaned dramatically and I rolled my eyes.

"You aren't going to die. And, if you let me clean up your cuts, you won't have to tell Ox either."

This got her peeking an eye up at me. "Because you'll do it for me?"

"No, you little brat," I said with a smile that I genuinely felt. She was kind of cute in an *'I'll take you for all you're worth'* kind of way. "Because I'll get it back for you. Now c'mon."

She stood as I tugged on her arm, but she looked at me through a narrowed gaze, an obvious disbelieving expression on her face.

"How are you going to do that?" she asked.

"Fraud."

It was her turn to guffaw.

After she finally agreed, I left the clothes on the counter and closed the door halfway as I returned to my room.

Pacing the length of it, I bit my lip, thinking. I had to tell Ox *something*. What if we ended up needing his help after all? And who even knew where he was, he'd be coming home at some point and he'd walk into a shit storm if I didn't feel the situation out ahead of time.

Working up my courage, I pulled my phone out and pressed the call button on one of my only contacts.

Ox didn't answer the first time. Or the second. On the third try, I was debating even trying a fourth when I heard the deep tone of his voice.

"Ox!" I had been pacing the entire time I waited for him to answer and when the receiver clicked on, I halted, my voice breathless as I got him on the line.

"Clem? Is everything alright?" he asked in a clipped, serious tone. I could tell by his voice that he'd noticed the urgency in mine.

"No, we're in a little bit of trouble," I said, glancing back at the door that held Ceci. "And she's asking for you. Where are you? Wasn't today supposed to be an off day?"

"It was, I walked down to the store with Sylvie. She needed a reload on a few supplies, then I got called into the office. Just for a few hours. Can you tell me what's going on? Who is asking for me?" he asked, his frustration and confusion seeping through to his voice.

Something in my stomach fluttered in a sickening kind of way. And I felt my body whip around, God only knows toward what. I cleared my throat but the tingling there didn't go away, so I cleared it again. "This morning? You walked with Sylvie this morning?"

"Yes, Clementine," he said, and his impatient tone felt like a sharp pinch in my heart for the first time ever. "Can you tell me what's going on? I'm in a meeting and I don't think I can get out right away… But if it's urgent—"

"Just come home when you can, Oaxaca. She's here. She's safe, but she came here for you, not me. I gotta go, okay?" I said and then I did something mean. I hung up on him.

Later, I could tell him I was too busy with Ceci for proper phone etiquette. But really, I didn't like the sharp feelings I was experiencing after speaking with him. Something that felt a lot like jealousy and hurt was clouding over me and I wanted it to stop immediately.

My phone may have buzzed a few extra times, but I couldn't confirm nor deny it because I left it on the bed in my room, far away from Ceci and I in the bathroom.

When I reentered the bathroom and found Ceci sitting primly on the toilet seat we kept trading, I went straight to the sink and started washing my hands. Beside me, she sat swimming in my clothes, looking almost cartoonish in my too long (brand new) cow pajama pants and oversized white thermal pullover.

I was totally prepared for an uphill battle, getting this done before Ox found out. I had yet to see Ceci be agreeable to just about anything since I'd known her. To my surprise though, when she looked at me the first thing she did was grin.

I scoffed. "You're drunk!"

"I'm tipsy," she said. No slur. But she was raising the still not empty bottle to her face again, well on her way to being drunk sooner rather than later.

Shaking my head, I went back to washing my hands, getting the suds all the way up to my elbows. I could feel her watching me from my side. "What are you doing?"

Stopping mid-lather, I turned to her with my hands up in the air like a surgeon. "Getting sterile."

"Jesus, you're a *nerd*," she said. But I could see something on her mouth. It definitely wasn't a smile, but it wasn't a frown either. It made me smile as I leaned forward and rinsed the exaggerated suds off my arms and hands.

Searching underneath the wooden cabinets, I wasn't surprised to find the large white first aid kit right away. I'd snooped a bit when I first arrived here, just in case I needed to find something to defend myself with. Or maybe an alternative way out. I knew the first aid kit was well stocked and fully loaded with more than what we needed for Ceci's scrapes.

Settling down in front of her, I leaned in at the waist and started dabbing the soaked cotton ball, to her lip. She didn't react to the sting. Instead, she blinked up at me and asked, "So what's the plan, Ferguson?"

I glanced down at her and noticed that her eyes were amber. I guess she had gotten all the recessive genes in the family. Her appearance was so different from her brothers and sisters. "How much of his personal information do you have?"

"The usual."

"Did you take anything when *you* mugged *him*?" I asked.

She smirked. "Computer, some bullshit games he liked, let his cat run away. Nothing good. No safes if that's what you're asking."

Purposely glossing over my concerns for the cat comment, I nodded. Finishing with her lip, I smeared a small dot of cream on it before crouching down to take hold of one of her hands. "The computer is more than enough."

"He changed all his information. I already checked."

"That doesn't matter." I shrugged as I worked at her fingertips. What did she do to them anyway? Claw their skin off? "We have the device and the IP address. I'll unload his backups and change some things around. Then after, we should probably burn the evidence."

"Burn?" Her eyes bugged out of her head as she sputtered out a laugh. "You know how to do that? Like hack him or something?"

I shrugged.

She nodded and we fell quiet for a while. It was when I'd cleaned up all her fingertips (convinced she'd gotten dragged or something) and was wrapping the last band aid around her pinky that she asked me in a very quiet, very non-Ceci like voice, "How did you learn how to do that stuff?"

"What?" I asked, casting her a quick glance. "Wrap a band aid?"

"No, the other stuff," she said, face completely serious.

I gave her a long look as I sat back on my heels. She was looking at me too like she was genuinely seeing a different person than she'd seen before. I knew my face had screwed up and I stood to hide the grating feeling of embarrassment and shame rushing through me.

"I knew some things before…you know," I said, hoping I didn't sound defensive.

"Before you decided you'd marry rich and never work again?" she asked, but her voice didn't have the same bite it used to.

I turned my shoulders, looking her straight in the eye. Not blinking, not backing down this time. "Before it was decided for me."

Me and the Fernandez that hated me the most had a lot of fun committing a crime that afternoon.

After she was successfully doctored up, we split up to collect everything we needed. From her car, which was a surprisingly cute baby blue SUV, she collected the asshole's computer and game consoles she'd stolen from him. From Ox's office, I snatched the tablet I noticed never moved from the far window bench, and the laptop he kept perfectly in line in the middle of his desk as well as a legal pad and a pen.

We met back downstairs and huddled at the coffee table in the center of the living room. Ceci had gotten down before me and had taken it upon herself to grab more alcohol from the pantry and supply us with a bottle of wine each. I just shook my head as I cracked open all three devices and watched as the screens booted up.

Realizing I would have no idea what Ox's password was, I turned the keyboard toward Ceci and waited.

"Oh." She was finishing a swig from her bottle but set it down to lean toward the keyboard. "It's always the same date. July twenty-ninth."

"Why?" I watched as she typed in the numbers and the computer accepted them immediately. "What's it mean?"

"It's the first time all seven of us went to Mexico together. Ox was twelve and I was four. They say I was rotten, and he had to carry me everywhere. He loves family shit like that."

I smiled, picturing a preteen Ox carrying around his fat baby sister. "I can see it."

"Me as a baby?" she asked, leaning over me to unlock the two other devices.

Bumping her shoulder with mine, I said, "You being *rotten*."

She grimaced, and we settled in to work quietly until we cracked into the good stuff.

It took me a couple of tries to remember the cross-referencing and decoding software my brother used to experiment with when he was younger. I was never into any of this stuff personally, but Connor went gaga over it, which meant I picked up a few things in passing.

This process, I was piecing together sporadically from the time someone hacked my computer and I got locked out of all my accounts. Email, bank, shopping websites, all my information had been changed, and I didn't know any of my cloud security passwords to force reset them. I had racked my brain worriedly for days on how I would tell my parent's. But—within hours of him finding out—Connor was able to find all my passwords, access my accounts, and figure out where the hackers were located. Let's just say, Clay took care of the rest.

Ceci and I weren't going to do all of *that*—just use a few of the tools Connor had unknowingly left behind.

It took me twenty minutes to copy over the code and gain access to his locked disk where he'd saved multiple backups. We used the broken-up laptop as the guinea pig so whatever activity we did on it would be traced right back to that asshole. The other devices were used to look up things we didn't know, jot down important information we might need later and brainstorm our next move.

It took a little while, but the minute we found the asshole's information it was like the unlocking of two caged animals. The first thing we did was try logging the information we found into his bank. It worked instantly, confirming that no, he hadn't gotten the money yet. But he did have *just* enough in his account for us to play around with.

Ceci turned her head to look at me and I mimicked the motion. Her eyes were a question, *'what do we do now'*?

"We are now," I paused as I leaned forward and read from the cracked up screen, "Peter Knoll. We do whatever we want."

So, we did what any girls with money to blow would do. We went shopping.

We tested the waters by ordering something small, an icky used blow-up doll that was definitely getting used for more than just decoration, and had it sent to his address. It was invigorating and terrifying all at the same time. I could tell Ceci thought so too, because when we hit "order now" that first time we both sucked in an audible breath and leaned away from the laptop like it was going to blow up. When nothing happened for a few minutes, we looked at each other and smiled, her wickedly and me triumphantly, and then we sprang into action.

The goal was to get the account frozen for fraud review before the transfer from Ceci's account stuck. We took the goal very seriously.

Ceci bought five hundred dollars worth of merchandise off of some weird insect website that had me looking at her like she was insane. I bought five hundred dollars worth of toiletries and had them delivered to a woman's shelter which had Ceci looking at me like she wanted to slap me. We both agreed on a donation to a charity for minority women (a shock on my part because up until this point I had truly believed that Ceci had no soul). The rest we spent brainstorming ideas and buying the first things that came to mind. It only helped that we were both steadily working on our wine bottles and definitely starting to feel the buzz.

At some point during the charade, we stood up and carried the broken laptop around like it was an infant baby and the bottles of wine around like they were its twins. The alcohol induced "brainstorming" went a little something like:

Me: "We can send him baby clothes, so he thinks he's going to be a dad."

Ceci: "Yes!"

Ceci: "Let's buy one of those shit-on-fire-grams and send it to his front door."

Me: "Yes!"

Me: "Let's get a stack of porn magazines high enough that everyone who passes can clearly see them."

Ceci: "Yes!"

Ceci and I both after looking at each other with wide eyes and communicating in some kind of strange telepathic drunk girl stare down:

"Dildos!"

We bounced around the living room and kitchen, drinking and laughing as we absolutely destroyed this man's bank account. I changed all the important contact verification information to something we could access, and I verified every purchase the bank's electronic meter skeptically asked about. We were downright partying (in an illegal fraud-theft kind of way).

It's only when Ceci and I were debating two things: one, whether or not we should open more alcohol, and two, whether or not we should purchase live animals to leave at his doorstep (Ceci saying yes because goats are hardly animals to begin with and me hardly even having a tangible response to her nonsense) did we hear the sounds of the front door opening.

Ceci was bent down low, digging through Ox's pantries again and I was leaning over the counter with the jacked-up laptop in front of me setting everything I needed up to report the "fraudulent activity" on Peter Knoll's account.

"Clem?" Ox's deep voice bounced off the high ceilings, sounding urgent and strained. "Clementine, I'm here. Come down."

Ceci and I stared at each other wide-eyed. We didn't need drunk girl telepathy to figure out what each other was thinking. *We are so dead.*

In a burst of movement, Ceci started barreling across the room toward the two devices we'd snatched from Ox's study. She closed out our browsing history and shut them down before scooping them up and spinning around in a circle, looking for a place to put them.

"Under the couch!" I stage-whisper-screamed at her. She heard it and dove to her knees to delicately slide the expensive devices under the furniture.

At the same time, I moved through the kitchen, high and low, shutting all the cabinets we'd splayed open.

"I saw Ceci's car in the drive. Is she here?" His voice was getting closer and rumbling more agitatedly if it was even possible.

Ceci and I shared a look and I banged at the keyboard to get it to hurry up. I still needed to wipe the disk memory clean and then we needed to do *something* with it. I had just been exaggerating when I told Ceci we should burn it, but after all the fingerprints and drunk girl DNA that we'd left on it, maybe it wasn't such a bad idea.

The drive though, the drive definitely needed to be wiped clean.

"Ferguson! He's coming!" Ceci rushed up to my side, looking at me expectantly before looking down at the laptop. "What's taking so long?"

"It's *loading*."

"Can't it load *faster*?"

"Oh, let me just ask it!" I said sarcastically.

"Go do something about Ox, and I'll hide it somewhere," she said. I gave her that same '*are you completely insane*' look she'd given me earlier.

"You go do something. He's your brother!"

"He's your husband!"

"Not according to you, you little brat!" To emphasize my point, I bumped her away with my hip.

"I'll make you fucking regret that!"

"I can hear you both. What's going on?" Ox put the word boom in booming, his voice bouncing off the walls as he approached. We could hear his dress shoes on the wood floors now. He was *right there*, just one more turn of a corner.

Ceci and I stared at each other with wide, wide eyes and just as Ox materialized in the wide space leading from the foyer to the middle of the living, dining, kitchen area, I bent down and set the loading laptop on the floor under us. When I popped up, my head swam and my drunk girl equilibrium began to fail. Ceci clamped a hand on my shoulder, pulling me upright before placing both hands on the countertop and clasping them together "innocently".

In front of us, Ox tracked the movements with hunter's eyes. They went from me popping up from the floor to Ceci's hand snatching me upright, to Ceci herself standing in his kitchen in my pajamas, to the obvious disarray his house was in. We'd tried our best to clean up, but it still looked like a tornado had run through the room. Bottles of wine lay on their sides on the floor, the middle island, and the coffee table. Had we really drank that much? Well, Ceci had at least.

Those stupid games we hadn't even needed sat on the island bar stools, not inherently suspicious, but still out of place. And Ceci had brought in the damn bat! At some point when she'd been at her drunkest, she brought it in to show off how she'd "taken care of" those assholes who stole her money. Now it was just lying on the floor like a beacon of our guiltiness.

"What the hell is going on?" he asked, his voice not calm, but controlled.

Suddenly, my shin was in pain after receiving a hard kick to it. I whimpered and leaned down to grab at it. Then I pinched her side on the way back up. She yelped, and surprisingly, she sounded like a girl. Like a *girly girl*. It made me snort.

"Ladies?" Ox interrupted, his words grinding out through his teeth. And then his eyes caught something, causing him to step a little bit closer. His voice turned shocked and a little frazzled. "Ceci, what happened to your lip?"

Ceci shot a look at me that mirrored my own thoughts: *Fuck.*

But I spoke up first. "W-we got into a fight!"

His eyes went from me to Ceci, down to her bandaged fingertips, back up to my untouched body, and finally back to Ceci's eyes. "And you lost?"

Okay, rude. He didn't have to sound so disbelieving that I could ever win a fight against Ceci. But Ceci also looked like she thought I was insane, even as she nodded her head in agreement. It was quiet for a while as we all engaged in a three-person stare down (Ox was winning, of course). The only reason the intense moment broke, was because someone else burst through the space carrying a few grocery bags in way too tailored of a suit for it to look natural.

"Just set them on the table then you can go Rictor, thank you," Ox said without looking back.

Rictor was the name of his driver I had yet to meet. The man who stood behind us, unloading paper grocery bags onto the dining table looked like he could double as a driver and a bodyguard. He was all broad muscles, deep skin, and hard lines.

But this wasn't why his sudden appearance had me narrowing my eyes. The bags he was holding did, the bags that Ox had gotten from the store on his little trip this morning. That's what got my attention.

Ox was dressed in his usual black slim fitting suit, his hair perfectly pushed back from his face, and his perma-scowl rightfully in place.

All this, with the sight of those bags being set on the counter brought a souring to my stomach. When exactly had he changed out of his leisurely athletic clothes and into that suit? How far had he gotten on his walk before his driver had to pick him up? When had he parted with Sylvie?

"Okay," Ox addressed us again, unbuttoning the button on his suit jacket and shoving a hand in his pocket. Slowly, he started to walk toward us, a leveling look on his face.

Nervously, Ceci piped up, "If I may—"

"You may not." Ox cut her off. "This is not a courtroom; you don't get to make objections. You two are *going* to stop with the lying, right now. And you're going to tell me what's going on here. Something obviously happened. If you just tell me, I promise I'll help."

He punctuated this with his hands spreading wide on the island across from us, propping his body up as he stared us down. My eyes had gotten stuck on the bags behind him, though. Rictor had left, but my eyes just kept lingering there.

"We don't need your help anymore," I said, my voice nonchalant, my eyes still on the bags.

The silence that filled the room was deafening. Ox's gaze whipped to me—his eyes wild with something. I didn't know what, because I hadn't looked at them yet, only seeing him through my periphery. Even Ceci was surprised, judging by the frantic pinch I got at my hip bone. I stomped on her foot to get her to stop.

"You called me at work and asked for my help." He spoke slowly. "I rushed over here to give it to you."

"Rushed? It's been—"

"An hour and fifteen minutes," he answered first, cutting me off. "Twenty minutes to finish my meeting. Twenty minutes to reschedule the rest of my day. Ten minutes for Rictor to get back and pick me up earlier than expected. And twenty-five minutes to make it here from the city in Saturday afternoon traffic."

I swallowed hearing his detailed account. Ever efficient and ever so smug. For some reason, I didn't want him to win this time. "Your day was supposed to be open. If it had been, like you'd said it would, you could have saved twenty minutes."

Ceci's eyes did a bug-like thing and went wider than I'd ever seen them as she turned to look at me. I ignored her too. Ox's gaze narrowed on my face. "Clementine, what's wrong?"

"We handled it." I shrugged, my eyes glancing briefly at him and back away, past his shoulders again.

"No. What's wrong *with you*?" he asked. As I stood there, I knew his eyes were glued on me, but I couldn't get myself to look at him. He just kept on staring me down, trying to will me to do so anyway.

Ceci's voice cut in between us, causing me to look at her as she slowly started backing away from her spot at the island.

"Okay!" she said a little too cheerily. Yanking a thumb over her shoulder she continued, "I'm just gonna…" She trailed off, not even bothering to finish her sentence as she rushed away from us, opposite of the direction Ox was standing.

Passing by my shoulder she whispered, "Laptop."

Using my foot to kick the open laptop in the direction Ceci went, it slid on the wooden floor, perfectly aligning with her trajectory. She bent quickly to scoop it up and scurried out of the room.

Ox had come around to my side of the island and was standing right there next to me where Ceci had just been. He was close, so close I could feel the heat he was radiating, probably from the sheer anger coursing through his body. Using both his hands, he turned me by the shoulders to face him. I found a good spot on his neck to stare at while he stared down at my face, studying every inch of it.

"Look at me, Clementine," he said, voice gritting.

"I am."

"You aren't." As if to prove this, he took his long finger and placed it on my jaw. With one smooth motion, he moved my face so that it was angled right at his. When I still didn't look, he pinched my chin between his thumb and index finger and forced me to. "*Look.*"

Fine. I'd look. Look at those brown eyes that had lied, that frown that stung my heart, and those lips that had smiled at more than just me today. *Whatever.*

"You told me I needed to come home," he said.

"For Ceci," I clarified.

"For Ceci, yes." He nodded even though I saw a pinch of something else in his features. "And I did. So, what happened?"

"She came over asking for help. You weren't here, so I handled it for you." I stared at him hard, my irritation grinding at the back of my mind. "Is that allowed?"

"Don't patronize, Clementine."

"*Never,*" I said in a perfectly patronizing tone.

He glared, but his finger extended and moved along my jaw blatantly stroking the skin there. Raising his thumb upward, he smoothed his thumb over the corner of my mouth where my frown lines usually were. "Tell me what's wrong. Why are you mad?"

He was obviously angry at being left in the dark, but his tone was also oddly resigned. Like he'd hung up his fighting gloves and was ready to fix the problem in front of him. *Me.*

My body had an adverse reaction to this. That twisting in my stomach spread throughout my entire chest, making me want to wretch. I did not like these sensations and I tried to pull away, but Ox's gentle yet firm hands were keeping me rooted in place.

"Tell me, Clem. What did I do?" He had gentled his voice to his soft *'Clementine'* octave. The way he usually spoke to me. It was then I realized that it was different from how he spoke to anyone else. Soft, patient, steady.

He stroked a hand up and down my arm and moved his other one so that he was cupping the entire half of my face. His fingertips landed at the nape of my neck and felt *good.* I had to fight not to close my eyes and groan as they rubbed the sensitive skin back there. "Tell me what I did so I can fix it."

I shook, my body coming to life at his touch, melting in ways I don't think I ever have before. In some ways, I needed this. To feel the gentle way he handled me. To hear the voice of the Ox I was getting to know and not the Oaxaca Fernandez that everyone else did. But in another way, I needed reassurances. Reassurances that I shouldn't be finding in him. Ones that my heart wasn't ready for but was seeking anyway.

"Nothing's wrong, Ox. I fixed it, okay?" My voice had melted into this weak plea for him to let it go. It was pathetic the way he could thaw me. The feeling of being utterly helpless against his touch and voice was new and I wanted to get away from it as quickly as I could.

Ox's gaze moved from my eyes to skate around the room again before landing back on me. "You fixed it?"

I nodded.

"Ceci is okay?"

"Yes."

"I don't like secrets, Clementine." His voice gritted, his grip tightening just slightly.

"It's not a secret, it was just a girl thing. About a boy," I said, and it wasn't a complete lie. But I still felt bad.

He must have sensed this because he stayed quiet for a beat, his lips sucking inward as he studied me again. But he just nodded his head slowly before letting it bow down close to my face.

For several long seconds, he lingered there. Our faces were so close, our bodies inches away from each other, our breath mingling in the same air. My body tingled in response to his nearness—every nerve firing and every peak standing on end. But I was still buzzing with this unknown irritation. It was palpable, noticeable. I thought he would comment on it, never one to beat around the bush. But after a long moment, he just let me go.

With a good amount of distance reestablished between us, I felt like I could breathe again. Ox looked a little resigned though, and a lot irritated.

"I need to speak to both of you about the state of my house," he started. He looked at me for a long second and then away. "But as for your 'girl's day', it can stay between the two of you. For now."

It was only when I had run up to my room, where I found Ceci curled up in my bed with the laptop still loading in front of her and my pretty tea box in her hands, that I was finally able to feel it. The cool sense of relief.

Because from the second Ox had walked in, I'd been burning all over.

Chapter Fourteen

OX

I laid into my little sister—and apparently my sister's new best friend—for over an hour. They'd trashed the house, they drank their skinny ass weight in wine, and they were hiding something from me.

The latter is what irked me the most. I hated secrets. My siblings always kept secrets from their big bad brother until they came needing something from him. Seeing Clementine do the same set my nerves on edge. But she had done it for my sister, and that fact at least calmed me enough to see reason. Which is why, in the end, I was the one who cleaned the house.

The lecture I delivered only ended so early because the two girls had fallen asleep right there on the couch, their heads huddled close together, their limbs tucked underneath themselves like they were cold.

Shaking my head, I just grabbed a couple blankets and covered them.

As I leaned close to Clementine, I frowned, remembering how much anger I had seen in her eyes earlier. I frowned even more when I leaned close to Ceci and my eyes locked on her definitely busted lip. No way Clem had done that to her. No offense to Clementine, but Ceci would have ripped her apart if they fought. Plain and simple.

Sometime later in the night, Suspicious One and Suspicious Two woke up in a frantic jumble on the couch.

I was sitting at the table working—wanting to stay close to them but needing to get what I had set out earlier in the day for done— when one blanketed ball rolled clean off the couch. It was smaller, so I assumed it was Ceci and when she shot up and shoved Clementine awake, I stiffened, ready to defend my wife. But Clem emerged from her own blanket and shot what I could only describe as a murderous look at my sister.

Surprised, I settled back into my seat. I guess she could hold her own when it came to Celestia Fernandez. I was impressed.

"Why did you push me?" Ceci growled

"Do you really think I'd push you?" That was Clem, sounding genuinely offended.

"After the way you taunted the bull today, I don't know what you're capable of." Ceci said.

"Mind your own business brat—"

I cleared my throat from my dark corner, not wanting to eavesdrop on the conversation. It was clear something had happened with the two of them and whatever it was, good or bad, it had brought them to some kind of relationship. I *had* to be okay with that, my own feelings about secrecy aside.

At the sound of my voice, they both went ramrod straight, turning around themselves like a cartoon special to find me in the dark. I grinned because I knew they couldn't see me, then offered them dinner if they were hungry. They both declined fervently, Ceci referring to me as her evil overlord and Clementine not referring to me at all. I guess she was still mad.

After a few awkward moments, they seemed to both remember something in unison. Rushing out of the room—blankets still tangled on their limbs—they bickered back and forth about whether or not they should *burn something*, if they were sure something else was *clean*, and what they would do to each other if their scheme hadn't worked.

I had no idea how to put those puzzle pieces together, but the possibilities made my head hurt.

The party didn't stop there. Sometime even later that night they'd gotten a second wind. I knew this because I heard them stumble into the hallway and down the stairs followed up by the symphony of banging pots and pans, clinking glasses and the blare of the TV.

It was later now. Much, much later and I still hadn't finished all my work. I'd retired to my room but brought in my laptop—which was suspiciously sticky—to finish up some final correspondences. I was paragraphs deep into an email on why I thought our supply chain was coming in over budget and what my suggestions were, when I noticed the movement of shadows outside my door.

My stomach jumped at the sight because I instantly knew who it was. The same girl who'd been mad at me earlier and I still had no idea why. The same girl I had told I was in a meeting who then replied that I should "come when I can". The same girl I told I would have the day off before things blew up at the office and I had to change my plans last minute.

Was that it? Was she mad that I had to go into work? Did she really care about that? She'd never cared about me working long hours before. And for some reason, that reasoning didn't seem quite right. It didn't seem like Clem to be upset with me over things I couldn't control. Not after everything else we had both put up with in this situation.

So, what then?

Balancing my laptop on the bed, I cleared my throat and called out, "Clem?"

There was a pause. I watched the shadows on the other side of the door halt, then come closer.

"How'd you know it was me?" Her voice was that sweet and hesitant one, but it also had the slightly frantic quality it got when she was wringing her hands and freaking out.

That had me swinging my legs over the side of the bed and striding to the door immediately. Opening it wide, I was brought face to face with her dark, encompassing beauty. Almost as close as we had been earlier when I'd touched her soft, smooth skin and let my fingers graze across her cheek.

"Because Ceci would never pace out here. She would just come in. What's going on?"

She bit her lip as she looked up at me. Her eyes said more than she was apparently willing to. They bounced around my face, searching for something. Every time they connected with my own eyes they ricocheted off. I could read one silent plea in that look. *Help.*

"What's going on?" I repeated. Slower this time, willing her to just tell me instead of keeping more secrets.

"I can't sleep."

I realized I had been leaning into her because, at her declaration, my shoulders set back. I don't think I was expecting her to say that. And I was definitely not expecting what she said next.

"Can I come in?"

"Sure," I answered hesitantly. I stepped to the side to let her in, not closing the door behind her just in case that made her uncomfortable. She passed by easily and as she did, I caught a whiff of her honey and lemon smelling shampoo. She smelled a little bit like alcohol too and it made me shake my head. The thought had me checking behind her for my little sister. "Where's Ceci?"

"Asleep in my room."

She wandered to the center of my room, her head falling back against her shoulders as she spun around slowly, taking in the details of my space. I suppose because I'm boring and never added more than the necessary furniture, some lamps for lighting, and one full bookshelf opposite my bed, she didn't have to look for very long. When she was finished with her little twirl tour of my room, her shoulders squared, and her eyes landed on me.

I raised my eyebrows in genuine question. "You carried my sister to bed?"

Her nose scrunched, and a sly, playful smile touched her lips. "I dragged her."

A laugh burst out of my mouth. She was being silly, maybe even playful. It was a vast difference from her shaking in anger like she'd been earlier. Seeing her smile return felt relieving. "She could use a good dragging."

She hummed, seeming to agree which pulled another chuckle from me as I edged back around my bed and plopped down in my previous spot. Clementine was showing her dark side. I'd have to thank Ceci later for finally bringing it out of her.

As if she sensed my thoughts, she shook her head. "I just walked her up. She's surprisingly docile when she's tired."

"Docile is not a word I would ever use for Ceci," I said, plucking my reading glasses up from the bedside table and slipping them on. Clem stood in the center of the room, her arms crossed around herself as she nodded silently. I watched her from above the black rims of my glasses, wondering how long she could stay there without asking me for an invitation to sit.

Apparently, it was a long time. I caved before I could find out just how long. "Sit, Clem."

"Okay."

She sounded tired. Wobbling forward on decidedly sluggish legs, I noticed her take a ginger seat on the very corner of my large king-sized bed. As far as humanly possible away from me. Knowing my crowd, I decided not to comment on the matter.

"So, does your being here mean you're done being mad at me?" I asked. I didn't know I was going to ask this, but once it came out of my mouth, it all of a sudden felt right. I wanted to know what was up with earlier.

"I was never mad at you," she said, and I didn't even think she believed her own words.

"Bullshit."

"I wasn't!"

"*Bull. Shit*," I said slower.

"Call it whatever you want, but I wasn't mad." She peeked over at me, and in a quiet voice she added, "*Just a little irritated*."

Touché. Her reference to my little temper tantrum back when we'd gotten married didn't go over my head. I had said the same thing after being pissy the entire first half of brunch, and she hadn't held it against me. We were the same, and if she could let it go, so could I.

"Okay," I said, picking up my laptop from where I'd set it on the bed. Settling back down into the spot, I resumed my typing, swifter this time. Something in me suddenly wanted to be done with work ASAP.

We were both quiet for a while, just the *tap, tap, tap* of my fingers on the keyboard, making the only sound in the room. As I finished up my emails, reports and charts for the night, I couldn't help myself from looking up at her every couple of minutes. Every time I did, she was simply sitting there, her feet tucked under her knees and her hands tucked between her thighs. Her body looked so stiff, but to be honest, her face looked like jelly. Partly satisfied and partly exhausted.

"Clem."

"Hmm?"

"Come get comfortable. I can go sit at my desk."

There I went again, telling her things my conscious mind hadn't yet agreed with my subconscious on.

Whipping her head around to look at me, she grazed her eyes across my entire frame and then sideways, measuring the distance between where I sat and where the other stack of pillows were.

"No. You stay," she said and then she was on her feet.

I thought for a second she would leave but instead she walked to the head of the bed on the opposite side of me, pulling back the corner of the comforter, and sliding underneath. She was still about as far as she could get, with her knees tucked up to her chest and her arms wrapped under them. But she was here, and that surprised the hell out of me.

Letting her head fall down, her cheek resting on top of her bent knees, Clem sighed, and I paused my typing again. I gave her a raised eyebrow as if to say *'what'*? And deep, deep inside me I actually wanted to know her response. Her days had never been a mystery to me before. But in these past couple of weeks as she started to break out of her shell, I was losing track of her. I wasn't entirely sure how much I liked that.

"Today was weird," she finally said as if she was coming to the conclusion at the same time she was voicing it aloud.

"How so?"

"I don't know. I woke up, I had a meal with someone who's not my brother—" She started. I screwed my mouth to the side because *we'd* had meals together before. She flicked a gaze at me that seemed sheepish and longing and weird, before she added, "I went on a walk by myself."

Hmm. She went out there again? It had seemed like she liked our first walk, so I didn't understand why she looked so weird about it now. Even stranger, she seemed to stay quiet for a second too long before fluttering her eyes away from me and sighing. *What was that*?

"And when I came back, there was Ceci," she said, and her eyes went far away.

"I suppose any day spent with Ceci without being taunted and abused is a pretty strange one," I offered, remembering how they'd fallen asleep together head-to-head. It had actually been pretty damn cute, even in my anger.

Clem snorted and laughed at the same time, causing her to make this weird Hyena noise. I cracked a crooked smile. "What?"

"She definitely taunted, threatened, and borderline abused me." She giggled a little and against my will, I thought it was ridiculously cute. When she sobered, her small smile lingered on her face, her eyelids fluttering closed. "But... I sort of felt like I had a sister today."

The weird constricting feeling in my chest was one I distinctly remembered feeling before, when Clementine had gone out of her way to be nice to my mother. But it was being rewritten as she sat there on my bed with her eyes closed sleepily, and her face contented yet somehow also looking sad. She opened her eyes, and when she saw that I'd been looking at her she smiled again.

"Okay. Maybe a shitty little sister. But still a sister. I've only ever been a sister, I've never had one before," she said. Her eyes flickered up to mine and lingered there. No more unsureness, no more nervous glancing, just an honest to goodness stare. "I'm starting to see the appeal."

"Am I ever allowed to know what you two were up to?" I asked, but my voice had gone lighter. There was no reason to keep being upset. Not when my sister was okay and Clementine was here looking so...so in need of someone who wasn't a grumpy, know-it-all nag.

A sleepy smile spread across her face and she shook her head, her eyes staying closed the entire time. "I will take it to my grave."

And there it was. An admission of guilt. I would have to teach her a few things about keeping her poker face. But since she was uninhibited, I wouldn't hold it against her.

"But," she continued, her eyes opening slowly, her stare going intent all of a sudden. I stared back at her. I should really just put my computer away, I wasn't working anymore.

"But?" I coaxed.

"*But* I've got a name, if you want it, Oaxaca." The use of my full name is what pulled me to a mental stop. She was being serious. Was she talking about Ceci again? Someone who had hurt her or something?

I swallowed and made my voice stay steady as I asked, "Who?"

"A bad guy. One who could probably use an overprotective big brother to scare him a little."

I stared at her for the longest time, seeing red and not knowing what to do or say about it. Someone had hurt my little sister. The only one who could fuck with that little shit was us. Someone else had hurt her, and she'd come to me for help. But I'd been gone.

My eyes cleared, revealing Clementine. Clementine who had helped her instead. My chest did that one thing where it tried to squeeze the life out of my heart. I swallowed hard but otherwise didn't try to contain it. I wanted to feel this, if not for me, then for my sister.

"Noted," I said. But after a minute, something flashed through my memory and I felt as if my entire body inflated. With my breath still held in my chest, I asked. "Did he hit my sister?"

Because if that was the case, this was an entirely different story. I wouldn't expect Clem to do anything about that but I sure as hell—My eyes trailed over to Clem, and I stopped.

I didn't expect her to crack a grin. But she did, her eyes open again and her head still in that droopy lull against her knees. I widened my eyes, urging her to say something other than giggle. She laughed some more.

"*She*'s the one who did the hitting. Poor guy," she finally said, her disbelief and total credence of the fact warring with each other, causing her to simply shake her head and chuckle. I knew this because it was the same feeling my family and I got when we witnessed the special way Ceci operated. Another memory from the evening resurfaced and a cool understanding washed over me like a cold bucket of water over my head.

"The bat," I realized.

Clem smiled and nodded. "The bat."

"Jesus," I breathed out, my heart constricting and not in the way Clem made it. Of all my siblings, Ceci would be the one to give me a heart attack. I was sure of it. I covered my face with a palm and shook my head. "Aye, Celestia."

Clem laughed, the sound more tired than before. Opening my eyes, I found her snuggling into herself, wrapping her arms up tighter and adjusting her body so that she was more comfortable. Only, I could see that she was not comfortable at all, and it bothered me.

"Why don't you lay down, Clem," I instructed more than asked. "I've got at least a couple of more hours to work, I'll get you up later if you fall asleep."

"I won't sleep," she said matter-of-factly.

"Lay down then. I won't get under the cover."

"You can."

"Clem, just lay."

"Okay." Shuffling herself down, she laid flat on her back underneath the dark gray covers of my bed. Her hair was down and looking less curly than normal as it fanned out all over the pillows. She squirmed, adjusting herself for a couple of moments. When she got comfortable, I could tell because it seemed as if her entire body released a sigh as she relaxed softly into the cloth around her.

"Ox?"

"Yeah?"

"About what I told you… About Ceci." She paused, waiting to see if I was listening.

"Mhmm?"

"Whatever you do, let's keep it between us, okay?" she asked. Her eyes were open and on me but the rest of her was completely snuggled into the blankets. The hazel orbs looked dreary. "Ox? C'mon, promise. It'll be our first ever secret together in matrimony."

"Is that right?" I was entranced by her sleepy face, watching it outright, even as she watched me back.

"Mhmm. I promise I took care of Ceci. She's okay now. So don't yell at her this time. Our secret, okay Ox?"

My throat constricted and it got hard for me to agree. When it came to my family, I had this sense to just protect, protect, protect. But Clem, who I had been mad at for keeping secrets from me earlier, was offering me a secret of my own. Of *our own*.

"Why can't you sleep?" I finally asked her, finding my voice again.

She shrugged and looked up at the ceiling. "I'm usually up around this time of night."

"You can't sleep at this time often?" She shook her head and bit her lip, casting me a glance and then casting it back up to the ceiling with a sigh. I pressed harder. "Never?"

"No," is all she said for the longest time. I let the declaration linger there for a few moments before deciding once and for all to forfeit my work for the night and close my sticky laptop for good.

"Clementine?"

"Yeah?"

"Try something for me?"

"Okay."

"Close your eyes."

She immediately shut her eyes, all trusting and obedient. I decided right then that I liked it when she was like that. Leaning back, I settled against the pillows, my left arm splaying wide across the space between us, my right forearm resting on my thigh. I wouldn't move closer. For Clem's sake I could suffer at the very edge of the bed if it meant she was comfortable.

"Good, now, tell me three things you like to do."

She opened one eye to look at me and I looked down my shoulder at her too, murmuring, "No peeking."

She closed them again and adjusted her shoulders slightly before breathing out. "Okay…"

But she didn't say anything else.

"Clem."

"Yes?"

"Speak. I don't read minds."

"Okay."

…

…

"Clem?"

"Mhmm."

"You aren't saying anything."

"I don't know what to say!"

I felt something in my chest loosen and suddenly I wanted to touch her. To reassure her. But I could only do so with my words, afraid I would send the wrong message otherwise. "You can say anything you want with me. I won't judge you, I just want to hear you talk."

"Okay," she agreed in a small voice, but still she remained silent.

"Here. I, for example, like math and numbers, I like hanging out in the garden in spring, and… I like the holidays," I said.

"The holidays?" She sounded surprised. "Why?"

"I don't know, the usual stuff. Family, games, food." I slid my eyes over to her and bit back my smile at her totally disbelieving face. "What, is it that hard to believe?"

"No!"

"Liar."

"Okay, yeah maybe! You don't seem like a hold hands around the fire kumbaya sort of man." She admitted.

"I'm not."

"Then why do you like the holidays?"

I paused. I could've told her it was because I loved my family and anytime I spent with them I considered worth it, I *could've*… But this was about *her*. So I went with something she'd appeal to. "Is it wrong of me to say it's because of the dessert?"

She laughed. I liked that sound. "Not wrong, but not any less surprising."

"It's like a non-stop pastry buffet in this family. Cakes, flans,

Buñuelos, candy—"

"Save some for the rest of us, Ox," she giggled again. My grin widened further. "You really like all that stuff?"

"I've got a sweet tooth," I admitted. As I looked over her chocolate brown form, all comfortable in *my* bed with that relaxed, content face on because of something *I* said, and giggling out the sweetest sounds of laughter and *trust*—finally, trusting me—I couldn't help the thought that, yeah, I definitely did have a sweet tooth.

"C'mon, your turn. Three things you like."

"Okay," she said again. "I like *baking* dessert, I like walking the beach, and I sort of like pictures."

Noted. "You mentioned you like baking before. Have you done it since you've been here?"

"No."

"Why not?"

"I guess I never knew what you liked," she said, "I can actually make Buñuelos, they're really easy."

"Oh yeah?" I may have sounded way too excited about this, but the little crispy tortilla fritters were one of my favorites. "Well, be my guest. The kitchen's yours to use, too."

"Okay," she said on a tired sigh.

Okay, I thought, this entire conversation feeling easy. "Now, name three places you want to go someday."

"California, Vermont, France," she answered. Her breaths were starting to slow and her eyes were not threatening to reopen again now that she was settled. I lowered my voice but kept talking.

"Three things you want to try?" I needed paper, I realized. I wanted to write down every single word she said. But I didn't. I couldn't. Not while she was part sleeping and falling deeper with every breath.

"Hmm." She made a thinking sound, but really it was a few full minutes of her just breathing and whimpering under her breath. "Live... Laugh... Love."

I chuckled because it was so cheesy, but then I stopped. The entire time I'd known Clem, she had struggled with those exact things. And according to all the cheesy ads and wall decor, it was supposed to be so easy. Yet she was struggling and fighting for it every day.

I felt like I had a sister today.

She had admitted this to me earlier. It was the same thing, just worded differently.

"Ox?" she asked sleepily.

I cleared my throat and looked over at her again. Her mouth was parted and her little arm had snaked upward to rest behind her head. She wore the same button-down pajamas I ordered her in a rage that first night she came to my door. I realized with dread that, right now it was around that same time of night. Had she been awake every night at this time? Did she ever get back to sleep? A soft whine from her cut me out of my thoughts.

I'd give her an easy one. "Three people you like."

Those pretty lips pulled back in a sleepy almost drunk looking grin. "Clinton, Clayton, and Connor."

I grinned too. *This girl.*

"Three favorite colors."

"Petal Pink, Oaxaca Black, and Tea Box Orange," she said. I looked at her, knowing my eyebrows were knit together so hard they were damn near touching. She still had her eyes closed, panting now, so close to sleep. Oaxaca Black? Tea Box Orange? Those weren't real colors, those were—Another baby whimper escaped as her frown pinched at the corners of her mouth.

"Keep talking, Ox." Her husky voice didn't ask, it demanded.

"It's uh—It's actually Tangerine Orange. Check the label." This is what I thought to say to her? Unbelievable. But I couldn't help it, not when I could suddenly hear my heart beating in my fucking ears. Just because she'd mentioned a few colors? Just because she was basically asking me to talk her to sleep? I'd done tons of other things to put women to sleep, but for some reason this was the one that had my heart beating out of my chest.

"So…practical…always." She panted between long, deep breaths. "I like my tea box. Tea Box Orange."

Well, alright then.

I stayed quiet for several minutes, just listening to the deep even way her breaths had started to come and go. She was almost out, slipping into that dreamland she apparently evaded frequently. I had yet to get underneath the blanket and I doubted I would now that she was there. The last thing I wanted was for her to wake up or roll over in the middle of the night to find me and little me pressed up against her. Nope, I'd be staying on my little sliver of bed the entire time. And I was okay with that.

Clementine shuffled in her spot, burrowing deeper into my blankets. I smiled, remembering before when she'd been just barely sitting on the bed. Yep. This was okay.

I got comfortable too. Leaning my shoulders back against the pillows, extending my black jogger clad legs, and crossing my arms over my chest. I was tired. So I closed my eyes and tried to figure out a way to get myself to sleep with the dim corner lamp still on. I usually turned it off, but there was no way in hell I was moving an inch if it would disturb the sweet sleeping thing beside me. Nuh-uh, you couldn't pay me.

I had just started breathing deeply myself, feeling my limbs going a little heavier and my mind starting to fade into fuzzy slumber when the sound of her voice brought me back.

"Ox. There are four people I like," she said, slurring. I wasn't actually convinced that she wasn't sleep talking.

"Yeah, who?" I asked, humoring her unconscious confession.

"I like my husband a little bit, too."

Yeah. This was *better* than okay.

The next night I knocked on her door around that same time of night. "Clem?"

"Yeah?" She answered right away.

"You up?" I asked even though clearly, she was.

"Always," She answered.

Leaning a shoulder just outside her closed door frame, I fingered the paint there a little bashfully, but willed my voice not to crack at my next words.

"Why don't you come on over? I'll be up for a little while. We can talk again until you...feel like leaving. If you want."

That was sort of a lie. I didn't want her to leave at all. Not when I knew she'd go back to her room and possibly not get any sleep. I had this sick need to know that she was eating, sleeping, and living well, or else I was unwell alongside her. I couldn't exactly say that to her without coming off as overbearing, though.

The door swung open to reveal a familiar looking Clementine. She'd gotten some new pajamas. These were blue and covered in chunky little brown teddy bears. Instead of full-length pants, shorts that showed off her long thin limbs replaced them. In her hand she held a mug that was still steaming, the string of a tea bag hanging out.

"Can I bring my tea?" she asked. I was surprised that was her only stipulation.

"Only a foolish man would deny a cup of tea from Clementine Ferguson."

I held my hand out and made wiggly fingers. She extended the cup out and I took it from her, holding it with all of my fingertips along the top rim. As she exited the room, I first reached behind her and shut her door and then laid a gentle touch to her shoulder to steer her along. Not that my room down the linear hall was hard to find, but just in case she was feeling apprehensive about it.

We settled into my bed much like the night before, her underneath the cover with her cup of tea balanced on her knees and me on the other side of the bed with my thick reading glasses on and my even thicker projection charts in my lap. When she finished her cup and I successfully talked her out of a second one, we settled into our new game of *'Ox fishing for information while Clem got so bored of his voice that she conked out and went to sleep'*. Efficient and effective.

And, goddammit, effortless.

A week of that straight had me realizing that yep, it was *every single* night that Clem had trouble sleeping at that very time and I now had a good feeling the reason why. *Abuelo.* My grandfather was the reason this sweet, funny, beautiful girl couldn't sleep at night.

It was all the more reason I felt obligated to take care of her, to protect her from any more harm, to handle this little thing with the Seaside police officers once and for all.

And for none of it to get back to Clementine.

.

Chapter Fifteen

CLEMENTINE

It was the day after Labor Day, and I was making my way onto the deck of the Fernandez's boat. They never actually went out on Labor Day because supposedly it was always super crowded and made for the worst boating. Apparently, this was some kind of tradition for them. They weren't huge observers of the American slew of veteran, war, and working memorialization, but I guess they drew the line when it came to Labor Day—or, as Ox had put it, it was their consolation for celebrating Mexican Independence Day. Since the Rhode Island waters turned unpredictable after the first week of September, they joined all the rest of us and celebrated the end of Summer like normal people. Sort of.

I was slowly learning that Ox was the master of casually dropping bomb sized chunks of information like they were candy.

For dinners with his parents, he seemed to tell me merely an hour before as if I didn't primarily wear pajamas and leggings and wouldn't need time to get ready. If he had to go out of town, he told me as he was wheeling his bag across the foyer. *When he invited me to his bed...* Yeah, he just outright asked, no warning. As if it wasn't absolutely insane that we had been spending every night of the last few weeks in an odd routine that started with me going to bed as usual, Ox knocking on my door sometime around midnight and simply telling me to grab my tea and come on, and ending with him serenading me to sleep with his magical questions and deep lullaby voice.

So, naturally, when Ox had apparently expected me to be a part of his family's annual boat outing, I hadn't been warned until the day before.

"Are you all set for the boat tomorrow morning?" he'd asked as we made our way down the hall to his room.

"The what?" My feet halted underneath me.

"Labor Day. We take the boat out every year. I told you about it last week, remember?"

I nodded. And then I shook my head. "You didn't tell me I was *going.*"

He'd chuckled but when he noticed I wasn't right behind him he looked over his shoulder. "You're serious?"

"Quite."

"Did you think I would just leave you here?" He furrowed a brow.

"No," I said. "Well maybe. Or just cart me off with my brothers like usual."

"No," he'd said in that Ox finality kind of way. Then he closed the distance between us, placed a wide hand across my shoulder blades, and pushed gently to lead me the rest of the way down the hall. "Tomorrow is Fernandez's only."

"Is it fun?" I'd squeaked, wholly preoccupied with his hand on my body. We didn't touch all that much, but every so often…

"It's hell," he said. "But it's our hell. And you'll make it better for me with all that bad coordination and random Spanish."

"No te gusta?" I asked, not even bothering to fight the coordination dig. It was true. He laughed.

"Me gusta tanto, *Lunita*[7]. Now let's go to bed."

I wasn't sure why Ox had chosen that moment to give me a nickname. Not to mention one that I didn't quite understand, but what I did know is that he was right. As always.

The boat was hell.

Not for all the usual reasons you'd think a boat outing would be hell. It was a three-million-dollar piece of real estate, so the large two-story yacht was cushy to say the least. It was who was on it and what was happening that were the problems.

The hell started before we even stepped foot on the boat. As soon as Ox pulled up to his family's home, I realized they were *that* kind of family. Yep, the kind that took family gatherings to the next level with their togetherness and fun.

I'd shown up with a pan full of Buñuelos that I rushed to make for the family, but mostly because Ox had said he liked them. He hadn't given me ample warning and I had no idea what else to bring—other than beer of course, but I didn't want to be a one-trick pony. Those treats had gotten ambushed and devoured before we even loaded up into the three large town cars we were taking out to the boat house about an hour away. Ox hadn't even gotten to try one and I had saved a specifically perfect looking piece for him.

Maybe it was for the best. I was out of practice with baking and anyway, he had assured me he probably would have missed out on them regardless. Why? Because he was in charge of the cell phones. Yep, cell phones, plural.

---

[7] Lunita: /Loo-nee-tuh/

There was apparently a strict no cell phone rule on family boat days and while that wouldn't usually bother me, in the state of awkwardness I constantly found myself in around his family, something to distract my hands would have been nice.

Since Oaxaca Fernandez was the big business guy who actually needed to work on his phone even on holidays, he automatically got to keep his. And consequently he also got to keep everyone else's while simultaneously guarding their attempts to steal them back. And now that I was *with* him, I was officially on guard duty too.

That morning, as Ox leaned elegantly against the hood of the first car lined up outside of the Fernandez house (and I stood beside him looking not even half as graceful), I watched curiously as he reached into his pocket and pulled out a folded up piece of cloth. He handed it to me and I unraveled it to reveal a midsized dust bag the size of a shoe box. The name on the bag indicated that it had once come with shoes. Probably those fancy dress shoes he wore every day.

"I'll be Good Cop," he said as he straightened and faced forward to the first in a line of his siblings that had materialized suddenly. I had no idea what they were doing and why they had been lining up like kindergarteners at the water fountain.

Until Alta, first in line, held her pretty pink colored phone up in both of her hands as if presenting it to a king.

Oaxaca smiled. "First as always, Al. Go ahead. Plead your case."

Alta straightened up her shoulders and cleared her throat adorably before beginning. "I would like to keep my phone this year because I've been working on this really cool social media project and I'd like to keep track of my stats on deck. I'm also a great photographer and can take family photos of us all."

I felt my eyebrows knit together in utter confusion but when I looked at Ox, he had crossed his arms over his chest and was holding his chin in his hand like he was contemplating her "case".

What?

"Denied. You always complain when we go in the water without you. If you're on your phone, you'll miss out on it again. Phone in bag," Lord Ox said.

Alta looked crushed as a puffy pout overtook her already soft round features. Turning to me she held out her phone. I opened the bag and watched her drop it in there before turning her shoulders toward the cars and stomping off.

"Next!"

Mateo sauntered up next. The big smile he had across his face made the corners of my own mouth twitch. He beamed at his big brother and peeking around I saw that Ox's eyes held affection in them too. And mischief. "So there's this girl—"

"Denied. Phone in bag," Ox said before Mateo had even finished his plea.

Mine and Mátti's mouths both dropped open and a stunned giggle fell from my throat. Mateo, easygoing as ever, didn't argue further as he turned to me, gave me a *'can you believe this guy'* look and dropped his phone in the bag.

Next was Melissa, the mystery of all the Fernandez's. I don't think I'd ever heard her speak. And when she approached Ox at his judging podium, she didn't look like she was about to start. She looked mad and tired and bored with all of this.

This must have been noticeable to more than just me. I realized it when I heard the low, *almost* gentle sound of Ox's voice as he addressed her. "Smile, Lis. You love the boat."

"I've got a lot to do," she said with a sigh.

"Not today you don't. Today is about fun," he said.

"Says the one with the laptop set up in the car."

"That's different." He waved dismissively. "Now, state your argument, Lis. This *is* your tradition we're upholding in the first place."

She gave him a dirty look but seemed to clear her throat inaudibly before saying. "I'm on three board review projects this month and have a deadline for quarter three coming up."

Oh. Business talk.

This had me confused because, from what I understood, none of the other siblings were as involved with the business as Ox was. He'd explained that most of those positions had been spread out across Ron's family which left the other grandkids to pursue things that they wanted. Seeing Melissa apparently so far ingrained in the family business was surprising.

Ox seemed to contemplate this seriously now, unlike his show of fake scrutiny for his other sister. "Send me over the details now and I'll get it taken care of for you."

This got Lis's eyes sparking up. The emotion there was too strange to follow. "Ox, I don't want your lackeys messing up my—"

"*I* will get it taken care of, Melissa. I've got it," he said.

"Really?" she asked, sounding surprised. And so hopeful.

"I said so, didn't I? Send it, and then phone in bag," he said, crossing his arms over his chest again and watching carefully as Melissa executed the motions of sending her work.

As he watched her, I couldn't help my eyes from watching him. As blunt and mechanical as he may be sometimes, the way he treated people was always the same. He was *good* and toward his family, he was the *best*. It warmed a place in my heart but at the same time it hollowed it out.

He'd said that this day was for Fernandez's only. Did that mean the careful way he had been treating me lately was just another way that he put his family before himself? Was it just to keep the peace? And what would happen when I wasn't a Fernandez anymore? Would that care suddenly disappear?

"What'd you do to Ferguson?" Ceci said as she sauntered up to us. She frowned at me and slid daggers in Ox's direction. "She looks just about ready to tear you a new one like that one time *when you were late*."

196

"I was not late—"

"Kidding, kidding," she said, holding her hands up in the most insincere surrender I'd ever seen. She straightened and began pleading her case. "I need my phone because I have a new best bud and he gets touchy when I don't give details."

Both Ox and I's eyebrows shot up before we said, "Denied" in unison.

Ceci's expression turned into a glare, but she moved in front of me and dropped her all black cellphone into the bag. Before she turned away, she grabbed both my hands and leaned in slightly. For a second I thought she was going to swipe the bag away, but instead she started to whisper.

"It worked you know?" The grin on her face was wide.

"Yeah? You got it all back?" I asked, knowing exactly what she was talking about.

"Every cent. They said the receiving account had been shut down for fraud and it was in their best interest to stop the transfer."

I laughed and then smiled. "I figured when you didn't beat down my door with your bat it had gone well."

"It did," she said with a smile I wasn't used to. A *real* smile. "Thank you, Clem."

I swallowed my surprise. She'd said my name. No "gold digger", no "Ferguson". Just a genuine *Thank you*.

"If you two are done?" Ox droned from beside us. It was clear that it was still a bit raw that we wouldn't let him in on our secret, but it was also clear he wouldn't comment on it either. "Let's go."

As me and Ox walked to our designated vehicle, I couldn't help but look over at him and smirk. "*That* was you being 'Good Cop'?"

Right then, Ox tossed a smile over his shoulder that was unlike any of the ones I'd seen before, letting me know that today, he was different. How, I wasn't entirely sure. But the playful, wicked look in his eyes told me that he was an Ox I hadn't seen before.

"I was never one to be all that good," he said and kept on walking.

I rode the whole way in silence as Ox typed away furiously on his laptop like he was trying to set some kind of world record. In reality, he was just trying to finish enough work for both his sister and himself without batting an eye.

God, this man made my chest hurt.

You know what else made my chest hurt? The number of times I was scared by one of Ox's siblings as they tried to steal the bag of phones away throughout our time on the boat. The first thing Ox had done when we got on was charge around like a bossy bull and make sure everything was safe and up to his ridiculous standards. So, in other words, everything needed to be perfect.

This left me open for the vultures. They were like predators swooping in for their daily kill. Even Alta had come up to me and tried to sweet talk a peek at her bubble gum colored device. I would have never thought the job of phone manager would be so hard until I actually had to do it. No wonder Ox basically pawned it off on me.

At first, I couldn't figure out why they even did it. Why go through the trouble of giving up your phone if you were just going to ask for it back every hour? But then I realized it was part of their game.

They were mostly respectful when I had control of the bag. But when Ox had it, they were like kids when their favorite uncle was in town. They dog piled him, tag-teamed him, tried to distract him while someone else swiped the goods, and poor Alta had even tried to tickle him. I say "poor Alta" because she ended up getting tickled instead.

But the real show I hadn't known I'd signed up to see was that foreign look on Ox's face that told me he was having fun too. He was essentially the gatekeeper. He was always "it" in their game of tag. He was Marco while everyone else was Polo. But he didn't care. He was having fun because they all were.

The games didn't stop there. There was a game of Chicken in the deck pool. There was water volleyball there too. Water gun fights up top where the sun chairs were. And there was some kind of slap fight (that only Ceci and Mateo took part in). To top everything off, there was a lengthy scavenger hunt (for the phones) around the boat at the end. Martina and Ronny mostly just watched on. They claimed they were too old to play these rowdy games with their niños, but they followed us around everywhere, taking photos and laughing along with their kids as they all had the best time.

Each activity was full of laughs and blunders and just a good family time. It pumped my heart up multiple sizes, especially because Oaxaca Fernandez partook in every single one of them.

And he was *bad* at some of them.

Ceci almost drowned him when she sat on his shoulders playing Chicken and he continuously got water gun sniped from the top deck by Alta and Mateo during the water gun fight. It didn't help his case that they were all gunning for him, but the fact that they were just proved how much they loved him and how excited they were to have him there participating.

I hated to think this, but I was surprised at how fun he was being. And more so, I was a little disappointed in myself for not being anywhere near as much fun.

Before, I thought we were both the same. Two people so caught up in the trajectory of their lives that they had no more room to fit something like fun into their routine. I knew before that we didn't really fit together in any way that was real, the only thing truly tying us together was a contract. However, I thought at least we were similar in how we were made. We'd do our duty and serve our families and that's who we would be. But after seeing Ox like that, I knew for sure that we didn't fit at all.

And I felt guilty for not being happy for him. He was good. *So good,* in so many ways. And he deserved better than being chained up with me. He could be fun, he could be attentive, he could be protective, he could be sweet, and all I could do was need.

Ox had enough people around that needed so much of him. I could see it so clearly. His siblings needed him in so many diverse ways. His parents would always need him. And me.

I had already started to need him a little bit too. I now needed him to sleep anytime between midnight and two in the morning. And I didn't want to. I didn't want to need him, if only to give him a break from having to take care of all these things.

I also didn't want to need him because what did that say about me? I always needed others to hold myself up. The one time I'd been alone, I'd broken. And now that I was finally beginning to come together again, I could see how pathetic that was.

When the scavenger hunt was over and everyone was returned their cell phones, the siblings all scattered about the large boat. Some went inside to shade themselves from the sun. Others sat up top to bake as much as possible before the season was over. Ox had disappeared somewhere up front, I believe with his tablet in tow. I found a place toward the back of the boat, watching the rumbling backlash the engine shot up as we sailed through the water.

The methodical motion of the waters was soothing. Heat beat down on my shoulders and neck which made me extra toasty, and I realized I hadn't grabbed the hat Ox had told me to grab before we left. He said it was Sylvie's and I had childishly let it slip from my fingers. Fingers that now tingled, probably from the number of times they'd hit the water.

And something was wrong with my head. I felt kind of high. It had been hard to stomach eating lunch earlier as the sun beat directly down on us, so I had foregone it until later. But we were so busy that later had never come. And now the whooshing backlash of the water seemed like it was getting closer to me.

"Woah, woah," the deep voice was behind me, beside me, and in front of me all at once. It was sort of raspy and lazy in a way I had never heard before, and even though I was suddenly sort of seeing stars, I knew it was Oaxaca.

I blinked away from the water and up to the tall, tan as heck brown man in front of me. He had slipped his white cotton T-shirt back over his torso and changed into some tailored navy board shorts. *And* he had his arm wrapped around my waist as he held me close to him.

"Three seconds, Clementine."

" 'Til what?" I asked.

"Until you went swimming with the fish. What were you thinking?" He was scolding as always, but with a voice that was as low as a rumbling murmur, almost as if he was talking to both me and himself.

His cool hand came up toward my face and he pressed it flat against my forehead to check my temperature. When that didn't seem to satisfy him, he reached up and grasped the back of my neck with the same hand. The icy coolness of his touch must have been the result of him holding a beer or some other cold drink. I moaned into the feeling of it.

This startled his eyes down to meet mine. "Clem?"

"How'd you know I was falling?" I asked, and honestly, I sounded drunk.

"Your best friend," he said. "You know, she laughed when she told me? Do you really trust her with your secrets?"

I smiled. It *really* bothered him that he wasn't in on what me and Ceci had done. Since he saved me, again, I made a promise to myself that someday I would tell him. Probably when the sting wouldn't be so sharp. But right then I just laughed and shook my head. It flopped back and forth languidly against his grasp. "She's a wench."

He nodded but was otherwise focused on inspecting me, moving those cool fingers to the other very warm spots of my body. When he pressed into the spot where my shoulders met my neck, I moaned again. His sharp eyes sliced up to mine and he stared at me.

"*Ox*topus," I giggled. That's when I knew I must have been slipped *something*, because, did that really just leave my mouth?

The, *'what the fuck is this girl on'* grin that he gave me confirmed that it surely did.

Slipping around me, Ox grasped onto my shoulders and began to move us. He'd walked us away from the edge of the boat, having turned me in his arms so his chest was to my back and he was steering us by walking behind me.

I couldn't help but to lean into his solidness. I really didn't feel well. My head started to feel like it was inflating like a balloon. Pretty soon it would float right off my head. Ox calmly walked behind me, patiently guiding me along until I felt the distinct sensation of cold shade around us. Someone who'd come up by our side asked Ox if he needed anything and he murmured to them to get a cold rag and a sports drink. But otherwise, that careful attention of his was on me.

"Where are we going?" I asked him.

"We're here," he said. "You're overheating, Clementine. We're going to take it easy in the shade for a while."

"You don't have to," I protested.

Popping my eyes open, I checked to see where we'd gone. Ox had taken me around the front of the boat, but not on the deck where there were stylish lounge chairs and ample sunlight. We were squirreled away in a crevice right underneath the captain's lookout that created a block of shade sized big enough for one. Or two if you smushed together.

I watched as Ox bent into a crouch and dusted the space off with deft hands. Then he turned, still crouched, and reached both arms out to me, waving his hands in a *'come here'* motion. I swallowed and blinked slowly, my head still swimming. "Ox, you don't have to stay with me."

"But I do. Husband and wife, remember?" he said. Oh, *right.*

He reached forward, killing the space between us and pulling me toward him by the waist. Turning me around, him crouching and me standing with my butt literally in his face, he then tucked an arm around my torso to pull me flush against his body. We both sank into the space smoothly. His chest held me upright and his groin pressed into my backside as I sat in between his spread legs.

I wish I could say I was stiff and uncomfortable against him, this man I've only known for a few months now, but I was too dizzy to be so on guard. Instead, I melted into my spot—that was basically in his lap—as soon as my body was coaxed to. I hadn't noticed before just how unstable I'd been out on the back of the boat, but now that I was grounded, I believed that there was a possibility I actually could have ended up in the water.

Sighing, I closed my eyes and tried to count, hoping that maybe I could count away the spinning in my brain. But when I opened them again, I still felt that sensation of unbalance. I squirmed, fighting to feel okay again, but Ox's hands materialized at my thighs, stilling me. His big arms wrapped around me as a consequence.

Leaning down so that his voice was close to my ear, he said, "Tell me what hurts."

"No hurt. Just dizzy," I answered, not minding at all that he spoke only in demands.

"Did you eat anything today?"

"I ate breakfast with you."

"Anything since?"

"No."

"Aye, Lunita" he said with a shake of his head that I felt more than I saw.

He leaned back, digging his hand into his pocket and I leaned with him, my entire body anchored to his. From his pocket, he pulled something crinkly out and leaned forward again with his arms around my front so that he could work with two hands. I watched as he opened the shiny white paper and peeled a little cream and orange colored candy from inside. "Open up."

I opened my mouth willingly and he placed the candy down on my tongue. I caught the tips of his fingers in passing and could taste the saltiness of them before my mouth exploded with the taste of sweet cream and orange. I chuckled. "What are you, the candy man?"

"I thought I was an '*Oxtopus*'", he teased.

"You are."

"What is that even supposed to be?"

"You act like an Ox, all angry and serious and always charging forward," I started, thinking I sounded completely sane. "But you're always juggling so many things at once. You've got as many hands as an Octopus and they're always busy."

Ox decided he wouldn't respond to this nonsense, or at least I thought he wouldn't when a minute went by and he hadn't stirred, not even a single sound. But then he surprised me by grunting, just like a grumpy old man who'd heard something he didn't like. "Technically, Octopuses don't have hands."

This had me laughing, which then had my head spinning, which then had me wincing. Ox smoothed a hand over the top of my head and I swear the skin there tingled. He leaned forward again and murmured softly. "I'll ask Al to grab you some real food when she comes back with the towel."

"Mhmm," I said, nuzzling into the hand.

"I'm sorry I can't get you any tea. Too warm," he said, I could've sworn his voice was getting softer.

"Boo," I pretended to protest. And he laughed.

Moments later, a breathless Alta appeared with a bowl full of ice water and hand towels. She also held a cold water bottle and a blue sports drink underneath her arm. She had been wearing a pretty little red one-piece suit for most of the day but when I looked at her now, she was covered up by a large hat and a thin, but modest swimsuit covering.

When Alta reached us and her gaze ran over whatever this looked like, interest and surprise sparked through her expression. Quickly, with a little smile on her face, she came forward and handed Ox the supplies, setting the two drinks down beside his legs. Ox cocked his head back, looking up to her as she stood over him, one of his large hands resting on my shoulder like it belonged there.

"You get out of the sun for a bit too, yeah Al?" He said to her, that voice going harder but not as stern and disgruntled as usual.

"Yeah, Ox," she said sweetly. She reached down, gave his head a pat, and scurried away, looking backward only once and giving us a weird knowing smile.

"Alright," he murmured, shifting behind me.

And then the breath left my lungs. All of it, gone. Because Ox's hands were on the back of my neck, but not like before. His hands were on the ties of my black bathing suit peeking out over the scooped neckline of my near sheer cover up. His fingers pulled at the thick knot there, working it unloose.

"Um, Oxtopus?" I asked, my voice this weird shaky thing.

"Yeah?" he asked without missing a beat. He had gotten one round of the knot untied and was working on the other. I felt the cups loosening underneath my boobs and I clamped a hand backward onto my neck to try and stop it. Consequently, my hands landed on top of his. He immediately grabbed hold of me. Wrapping his soft, long fingers around my smaller ones as if on reflex. I shifted, turning my shoulders to look backward. He found my eyes immediately and a calm look is what I found. Giving me an innocent blink, he leaned forward and tapped his chin to my hand, trying to knock it away. Gently he asked, "What?"

"You're untying my swimsuit."

"Yes."

"You're undoing the whole top."

"Clementine, you're stating the obvious." He smirked, and I realized he was making fun of me, mimicking the time I had been grumpy and short with him in my room. I might have scowled, or I might have gaped. His smirk turned into a grin but he untwined our fingers after giving mine a quick little squeeze. I let my hands fall over my half-undone swimsuit ties, instead of fall away. Ox's hands fell onto my shoulders. "I'm just making room for your neck, Clem. A cold rag there will cool you off."

"Can't we do it with my swimsuit still on?" I squeaked.

"It will be on."

"*All* the way on," I clarified.

"There are no secrets between us, remember? Husband and wife."

I turned my shoulders more fully to give him a horrified look and he bellowed a laugh. He was joking. Serious, no nonsense Ox, was choosing to joke around now of all times. I could only sputter.

"Clementine, *it's fine*. I can't even see anything, honest." I just sort of looked at him. He sobered his expression into a close-lipped smile. Noticing I wasn't turning back around, he asked, "What else?"

"I—", I cut off, wondering if I really wanted to say this. "I'll fall out."

"You'll…?" He trailed off, confused, until he wasn't. His eyes went the tiniest bit wider before he schooled his expression. And then he said, as if this wasn't a giant missile to my ego, "I doubt it, Clem."

"Ox!"

"Just hold them!" He laughed.

"Hold them?"

"Yes, wife. Hold them."

"Hold my boobs up while you untie my swimsuit?" I asked, *juuust* to clarify.

This time he furrowed his brow and gave me a real Ox look. And then I saw something devilish and maybe even a little mischievous pass through his expression.

"Want me to hold them for you?" he asked. I gaped and that mischievous look turned into another grin.

Oh. He was having so much fun at my expense. I could play this game too.

Dropping the hand that was laying over my swimsuit ties, I shrugged, schooling my best nonchalant expression onto my face. "Go ahead. What's mine is yours, *husband.*"

His expression dropped and he did this weird swallowing thing as he gave me a *'not funny'* kind of look. I smiled, feeling powerful if only with a stupid joke. Something tickled in my gut at his expression. "What's that saying again? To have and to *hold*."

I could have sworn there was pink peppering Ox's cheekbones. He was full-blown scowling at me now and I declared that my first official win against Oaxaca Fernandez. I chuckled happily to myself at the small victory.

But the warm feeling inside of me quickly got rushed by another twist of my gut. It felt ugly and it had me searching Ox's face for *something*.

He was joking about this stuff so easily and yet... *This is not a real marriage. This is a means to an end.*

I felt my own face heat at the sudden thought of Ox's words from months ago. Why was I thinking of them now? And why did I care?

Seeming to notice my mood change, Ox sobered into a normal expression and looked down at me to study my face. Then he gave my shoulders a squeeze, rubbing his hands down the length of them to my biceps and squeezing those too before rubbing back up. The motion set my skin on fire.

"Only teasing, Clem," he said in that soft but deep way. He looked at my eyes as if asking me something. I blinked a single nod and he mirrored it. "I'm just going to cool you off with the towels. That's it. One for your neck, one for your chest, and one for your forehead."

I gave him a little smile that I wasn't feeling, and then reached behind me to open the back of my swimsuit. It felt too weird having him be the one to untie it. Too intimate.

"Okay." I turned around so he could do what he wanted, scrunching my knees to my chest to hold the front of my swimsuit up.

We were quiet as Ox worked behind me. Reaching into the bowl, he plucked a towel up and used both hands to wring out the excess water. I watched as he folded it up into a long rectangular shape and then his hands disappeared behind me.

I sucked in a sharp breath at the sudden bite of the cold towel on my neck. But then I felt a rush of relief. The warmth there was thwarted immediately and my head, though still a little in the clouds, seemed to clear up some.

"Good?" he asked, barely a murmur as he leaned down again to work on another towel.

"Mhmm." I answered, my eyes shutting and my body seeming to curl forward around my knees.

"No, lay back," Ox ordered. His non-towel hand reached around my shoulder and gently guided my body from around my knees to lean backward into him. My back was flush to his chest *again* as he caged me in with his arms and folded the towel in front of me. He started to bring the new towel down toward me but paused, hovering over my chest. *"Relax*, Clem."

"Okay," I said, but I felt like a board laying stiff against a wall. How could I relax like this? With me against him and him making husband and wife jokes.

"Clem," Ox said in a gentle tone. "It's just me. You know I won't do anything. You sleep in my bed every night now. So relax for me, baby, okay?"

Tingles shot through me like fireworks and a million and one questions raced through my head at once. But then, I realized he was right. I slept next to Ox every night and neither of us had been affected by it. We were building trust and a friendship and that was all.

And that was good enough.

Eventually, I did relax. Leaning more fully against him and settling my heavy eyes shut as I soaked in the cooling sensation of the towel on my neck. The bite of the second towel on my collar bone seemed less refreshing and more like a cold shower. I hissed. Oaxaca laughed.

"Too cold," I murmured.

"Too bad," he murmured back.

One last towel was placed onto my forehead, just as Ox had told me it would be. And just as usual, Ox had been spot on. I felt the rush of coolness sweeping over my body and liquifying the rest of my tension. I was like a melted puddle. Tired, content, and unmovable. I don't think I could have peeled my body away from Ox's if I tried.

Cold, damp hands trailed themselves along my upper arms in long soothing motions. I wondered if he was trying to spread cool water over them or if he was just comforting me. Normally I would say the former, but Ox was being different today. He seemed lighter. Even when he was being Ox, he was being this less high-strung version of himself. Less guarded.

"Fifteen minutes," he said practically into the back of my head. It lay back on his shoulder as I tried to fuse with his body. When I didn't reply, just hummed a little into the air, he didn't comment any further. Instead, just continued his strokes along my skin as we both fell into companionable silence.

Maybe fifteen minutes or maybe fifteen seconds later, Ox removed the towels and started feeding me. Water, sports drinks, little nibbles of fruit. He continued to ask me how I was feeling, and I continued to reply that I was tired. I didn't want to move, not because the little shaded area was amazing or anything. But strangely, I didn't want this weird relaxing feeling of rightness with Ox to go away. Because as soon as we went back to his house and to the normalcy of our contracted life together, it would.

So, I soaked it all in while I could.

Chapter Sixteen

OX

My kitchen was a mess. Well, more precisely, my kitchen had been a mess for what I assumed was every day for the past month. I had just never walked in on it.

Ever since the first time I dropped Clem off with her brothers for sibling bonding time, she'd been coming home with flour or sugar or butter in weird places. And since Ceci had come over that time, I'd started occasionally coming home to the residual scent of vanilla and sugar and eggs. But each time, the kitchen had been spotless, nothing out of order and no food that wasn't supposed to be there in sight.

I doubted Clem was throwing everything she made away after she was done. It seemed way too wasteful for the likes of her. And unless she was making tiny portions, I doubted she was eating it all either. It made me wonder what she was doing with all the sweets she's been apparently making for weeks. Especially since I had never seen or tasted any of them—save for catching a glimpse of the Buñuelos that my family so rudely ate all of. I wondered what the hell she did with everything when she was done.

Now though, as I walked into the open living room that connected to the kitchen, I felt my steps fall short.

Above me, standing up on the kitchen island with her bare feet and dressed in a little brown tank top and little matching shorts that I had *never* seen before, was Clementine. Her hair was a pile on top of her head but had some straggling fly-aways framing her face. Around her were dishes and pans and ingredients and what looked like abandoned pastries on different abandoned place settings. Clem's knees were covered in flour and the rest of her was speckled with little flakes of something edible. Dough maybe? From what I could tell, she had a little on her face too. That face was turned down as she held her hands out far away from her body and did something with the small device there. Her phone.

That's when I looked down.

Directly vertical to the aimed cell phone was the smallest little cake. It was one of those layered tier cakes, but the smallest I had ever seen. The cake itself was a brown color, but the icing was an ivory white. On the top layer were little speckles of what looked like diced up leaves that swirled around a clover of mint placed off center. On the exposed layered side, long vine-like leaves wrapped around it.

It was pretty. It was good. It brought genuine shock out of me. When she said she liked baking, I thought it was sheet cakes and easy-bake cookies. But this little thing looked like it could be someone's wedding cake. Someone small, but someone who would pay good money for it.

My surprise was cut short by the quick flash of Clem's thigh as she adjusted her stance, leaning forward to get a different angle. I could see her back hamstring stretch appealingly and the way her arms were basically over her head like that—

Damn.

"What the hell are you doing?" I asked a little too abruptly, trying to tear myself away from my previous thoughts. Ever since the boat outing with my family, my mind had been wandering to dark lustrous places around Clem.

You want me to hold my boobs up while you untie my swimsuit? She'd asked.

God. Why had she asked it like that? In that split second Clementine had transformed into someone I'd never seen before. This carefree, sarcastic, *flirty* thing that awakened something within me.

Above me, Clem startled and squeaked and slipped around on her flour covered feet on top of the island. My heart could have jumped out of my chest and landed on the floor in that moment. She was going to fall, and I was too far away from her. *Fuck.*

But just as quickly as she lost her balance, she regained it and saved herself from barreling off the side of the countertop and cracking her head open.

Setting my stuff down on one of the bar stools, I speed walked around the side of the island until I was standing underneath her. Reaching a hand up, I gestured for her to come toward me.

"Off," I said, wanting to say much, much more but not wanting to sound pissy. "Immediately, Clementine."

She looked down at me, finding my face and frowning. I frowned right back, staring into her eyes in question. Since when did I get a frown from her when coming home? Not since we'd started this arrangement, it felt like. I didn't think I liked it. "What?"

"Why are you home so early?" she asked.

"Did I break a rule or something?"

"No," she said, but turned around and didn't get off the countertop. "I just didn't want you to come home to such a mess. I'll clean it as soon as I'm done, okay?"

My heart did some acrobatic move where it tried to escape its cage and fall out of my chest as I watched her lean in the exact way that had almost gotten her killed a second ago. I leaned too, bringing my hands up to hover at her shins, in case she slipped again. "I don't like you up there, Clem, get down."

"Ox—" she trailed off as she focused, her voice just doing a shushing thing before she fell into silence again.

I bit my tongue and stopped myself from grabbing her down by force. She may have been giving me a heart attack, but she was also sort of impressing me. Most of the time she was unbothered if something went one way or the other, not really caring how her life played out, just along for the ride. But here she was, being direct and *wanting* something.

I couldn't deny her it.

What I could do was scowl at the fact that, despite trying not to think about how she was wearing the skimpiest thing I'd ever seen her in— except for that night gown that we don't talk about—I couldn't help it. Not while I was stationed right behind her and coincidentally trying not to look up at her ass. Life was sometimes cruel.

Maybe five minutes of Clem taking clumsy steps, scaring me half to death, and then catching herself later, she was straightening. She scrolled through her phone for a few more seconds before breathing a deep sigh of relief and then locking it. She slid it into what had to be the tiniest pocket on the tiniest shorts ever made. Then she turned to me.

And I burst out laughing.

"What?" she asked, confused.

"You're *filthy*," I said. For the first time, I looked at her up close and recognized that she had flour, sugar, and whatever the heck else dusted all over her. Every inch from her feet to her forehead she had something.

She smiled that pretty small smile at me before looking around herself and scrunching her nose. "Everything is. I'm sorry, I thought I'd have it clean before you got home."

"Is this what you normally do?" I asked.

"Lately, yeah."

"Do I finally get to taste something you made?" I asked, my eyes slipping to the miniature wedding cake.

Clem seemed to stiffen as she looked away. "It's not ready yet."

Something washed over me that felt a lot like disappointment, but I pushed it down quickly and stepped up closer to the island. Reaching my arms up to her, I gestured for her again. "Come on. Time to get down."

She nodded and came a few steps toward me. Reaching for her slowly, I wrapped my arms around her thighs and brought her knees down to my chest. On instinct, she let her hands fall to my shoulders, holding onto me as I lifted her from the counter and worked on lowering her feet to the floor. From this position, the only way down was to slip her body down the length of mine. *Slowly.*

It was like slow torture.

But I endured every second of it innocently. Swells and dips and cushion pressed directly onto me. Testing me and my resolve. And I only gulped once when she finally landed in front of me, her front pressed to my front. Her face so close to mine. "What were you doing?"

"Baking," she said

"With your phone?" I asked, not letting her go.

"Photographing what I baked." She clarified. "Before I give it away."

"Is this what you've been doing lately?"

"Yes."

"Who have you been giving them to?" Since it sure as hell wasn't me.

"Your house staff, my brother's employees, Rictor," she said just to list a few.

I may or may not have screwed my face up at the fact that Rictor had gotten to taste before I did. "All those people get some, but not me?"

"Not yet," she said. *Bossy.* I smiled.

"Do I at least get to see the pictures?" I asked, reaching up to wipe butter off of her nose.

She tucked her chin, suddenly looking shy as she mumbled into herself, "If you want."

"Show me," I said, immediately deciding I did indeed want to see them.

Stepping away, I detangled myself from the soft but sticky Clementine and leaned a hip against the island. Clem pulled her phone out of her pocket and swiped it open to the camera settings. Pulling up her camera roll, she swiped far to the left before handing it over to me.

On the screen was a beautiful photo of a small piece of pie. The fluffy moose of it was mostly white but held a greenish tint. It lay on top of a vibrant yellow gooey layer that also lay on a layer of thick crumbling crust. On the very top were little decorative swirls of lime, and shaved around it looked to be orange zest.

"Wow." The word fell from my mouth before I even knew what I thought.

I scrolled to the right and was met with a photo showing a stack of chunky gooey chocolate chip cookies, piled up eight high. The next was of some sort of berry soup topped with a crust that resembled both pie and graham crackers. Another swipe revealed a little bowl full of colorful macaroons.

I looked up at her, because not only did all these desserts look delicious, but the photographs were great too. I kept scrolling and saw pastry after pastry and then I fell on a non-pastry photo of three smiling brothers sitting on a couch, their mouths pulled up in broad grins and their eyes alight with laughter and happiness. Looking at the three of them, I was sure I'd never seen any of their faces look like that before. And I was sure the difference had everything to do with the girl behind the camera. I understood it, because she was charming the hell out of me too.

"You really made all these?" I asked her after I'd scrolled to the end. She nodded, eying me closely. I looked up into her eyes when I said, "They look amazing, Clem. Why do you photograph them like this?"

"So I can remember that I did something, when I start to forget, and it starts to get dark again," she said softly, gazing back at me.

Oh.

I took in the state of the kitchen. "Why are there so many rejects?"

"Because I was trying a new recipe," She chirped up. "Brown Sugar Pecan Spice."

"You make your own recipes?" I asked, impressed and surprised once again. She nodded and I nodded too. Looking at her, I could feel the contented glow that was surrounding her. And for the first time in earnest, I realized that I was attracted to her. To her body, yes—hell yes, but to her radiance as well. She was lighting up my kitchen with her subtle glow and I wanted to suck it all in. I wanted to suck *her* all in. Every time I encountered her lately, it seemed like I wanted more and more.

At the same time it was lighting me up, it was also dimming me down. Because I knew nothing could come of it. Nothing *should* come of it. I'd gotten into this with Clem to help her, not to traumatize her further by suddenly changing my tune.

So, instead of grabbing her by her flour-stained neck and pulling her toward me, I reached a hand up and smoothed hair away from her eyes, crumbling some sugar away. She smiled shyly at me and I smiled a closed lip smile at her before taking a not-so-subtle step away. "I'll help you clean up."

She looked at me weirdly. Glancing from me, down to herself, and to me again. I looked at her too.

And looked and looked. Why was she just standing there? Did she think I meant clean *her* up?

"*The kitchen*, Clementine," I clarified as I turned away from her, suddenly needing to not have her in my line of sight.

Swallowing hard, I grunted as I started peeling off my suit jacket and rolling up my sleeves. This was okay. *I* was okay. Attraction was simple, and maintainable. I didn't have to act on it. I *wouldn't* act on it, because as much as I would like to see all the different sides of Clem—her backside included—I was starting to really like the side I saw now. The slightly feisty, mostly sweet, and continually surprising sides of her she was revealing in layers. And I could tell she liked them too. That it was good for her. I didn't want to change that, to stop her progress.

Right now, it was either her or me. Her recovery or my attraction. Her well-being or my impulses. I could either let her heal or push my own agenda, but I couldn't do both. And I wouldn't try.

Because, when it came down to it, I'd choose her over me every time.

Chapter Seventeen

CLEMENTINE

I wouldn't exactly call my behavior territorial, but others may have.

It was a colder morning in October, which meant the weather would be turning for good soon. It had already started becoming more and more difficult for Ox and I to keep up our now steady routine of walking the beach in the morning before he left for the day. The sand had gotten crunchy and the crashing waves had started bringing in stiff breezes. We wouldn't be able to keep it up much longer.

The realization of this had me feeling a little antsy. With Ox, in every other space, I had come to realize I never knew exactly what to expect from him. He was always his normal determined self. He was always kind, always in charge, and always dependable. But from one instance to another, I could never predict if he'd be the Ox that sometimes touched me and said sweet things, or if he'd be the Ox who simply coexisted with me in more or less companionable politeness. Every day was different, and it was hard to know what to expect from him.

Except on our walks. On our walks, I consistently got an Ox that I could be falling in love with.

Okay, not *actually*. But I did love the side of him who teased me and walked with relaxed shoulders and listened to my smallest, most insignificant thoughts as if they were scientific problems he could solve. Not that he didn't always show me that same kind of respect and consideration, but for some reason on the beach, it felt different. As if we were in our own little bubble where time and space and expectations and reality weren't a factor between the two of us. Like we were just two people, being the people we truly are with each other.

It was one of my favorite times of the day, and sometimes when it didn't come around, I found myself feeling off.

So that's why one morning when I was tying the laces of my running shoes (having sat down on the ground because my long puffy jacket was in the way otherwise) and Ox came into the foyer with a tag along at his side, I blinked like a dumbfounded idiot.

Said tag along was the beautiful raven-haired Sylvie. She was walking with her head down and her eyes cast to the ground, a look I don't think I'd ever seen on her fiery face before. She had her hands stuffed into the pockets of a short puffer jacket (one that didn't make her look like a giant marshmallow unlike myself), and she was under the protective guidance of one Oaxaca Fernandez.

I stood from my spot on the ground, righted myself on my feet and stared blatantly. First at the hand that lay comfortably at Sylvie's back as they walked into the foyer. Then at the workout clothes she wore, different from her usual work attire. And then at Oaxaca himself, who was watching Sylvie like she would fly away.

My gut churned and my face burned.

When Ox saw me standing there staring at them, he seemed to take a readying breath. "Oh good, you're ready."

"What's wrong?" I asked, my eyes coming back down to Sylvie. As they got closer, I saw that Sylvie's face was red and the rest of her features were downcast as well.

Both of them looked at me strangely, Sylvie as if she wanted to crawl into a hole and Ox with a mask of determined steel.

"Sylvie's not feeling great. She needs some air," Ox said. "So, she's going to walk along the beach."

"With us?" I asked, and even I have to admit, I sounded childish.

The weird look Ox gave me confirmed it and the slow way he said, "Yes, Clem. With us." Was like him punctuating it with *'duh'*. I pouted openly.

"Is everything alright?" I asked, my voice weird. Squeaky.

"Everything's fine. I think we all just need a little air," Ox said, and Sylvie nodded. *Weird.*

"Okay." Is all I said, all the wind leaving my earlier sails. Suddenly, I wanted to do anything but go on this walk and watch as Ox doted on her. Asking her questions and strolling slowly by her side.

But I was already dressed and basically out of the front door, it would be weird to back out now. Ox must have sensed my hesitation as I lingered there, stepping on invisible spots on the floor and not saying anything else. Leaning down, he murmured something to Sylvie. She looked up to him before nodding and scurrying past us, charging out the front door. I watched the space she occupied until Ox stepped in front of me and then I watched his shoulder, refusing to look at him.

Ox let out a big sigh but looked at me with light teasing in his gaze. "Lunita, what's wrong?"

"Nothing," I answered quickly. Maybe too quickly because Ox clucked his tongue and shook his head. I turned my head so I wouldn't see his face. What a stupid face it was too. He was too caring for his own good.

He hummed, ducking around to catch my eyes, his eyebrows raised in a sort of shocked expression. He laughed a little more as he said, "What? You can't share the beach just this once?"

I knew I was still pouting, but I didn't care. "I can share the beach."

I trailed off, leaving him to determine what else there was that I couldn't share. He got it, he wasn't stupid. Swallowing, he nodded and then reached out to me. He grabbed at the collar of my jacket, pulling both ends together and zipping it all the way up. Then he reached a hand up and smoothed the top of my hair down.

"You don't have to share me. I'm still all yours, *wife*," he said as he stared right at me.

I averted my eyes, because even though he was being sarcastic and joking around, I burned all over. And then I felt stupid because obviously I was the only one upset about this. *Again.*

"Let's just go," I said as I grumbled past him and out the front door.

And of course, he'd lied to me. The entire time we walked the beach I felt like a third wheel. The two of them talked about whatever the hell they were discussing some ten feet in front of me, while I lagged behind, kicking at sand and finding every excuse in the book to let them get further and further ahead.

The only attention Ox had paid me was when he'd subtly look back to, I don't know, make sure I hadn't floated away from boredom or something. Which was the equivalent of every five seconds.

At one point, he even shouted, "Clem, keep up!"

I lagged even further out of spite.

My bad mood only worsened when I paid my now weekly visit to the police station to give DNA or answer questions or be verbally accosted or whatever other tortures they had in store for me.

Ron's case was going nowhere, and it was clear they were starting to feel pressure. Cracking something high profile like this would be huge for the local Seaside Police, but something had to have been crackable first.

It was only the face of my sweet brothers, who'd picked me up to go shopping for a birthday present for Connor, that lifted my spirits about the day. I hadn't seen all that much of them lately, the end of the business year was sneaking up on them and that had everyone working harder, even Connor on the cyber security side. So instead of hanging out with them, I had been staying home more with Sylvie or with my baking.

I didn't know what I was building this portfolio of recipes and photos for, but I liked the idea of making a master recipe box. One that could be passed along throughout my future family for generations. The fact that I had been thinking about the long term and future families to begin with shocked me, but whenever I thought of this idea, I found myself excited to pass something down. And about having someone to pass it down to.

Someday.

"What's wrong, Tine?" Clint asked me as the three of us roamed the aisle of the computer store. Connor, the brother I had learned my computer sleuthing from, had a whole room in his house dedicated to whatever tech he could get his hands on. It looked like one of those movie security rooms, and it still blew my mind that he knew what to do with all of that stuff.

"Nothing's wrong." I answered, purposely walking diagonally to bump into him. He patted my shoulder lightly but frowned down at my face. Then he looked to Clay, apparently his emotional meter running full already.

"Something's wrong, Tiney. You're about two inches shorter right now. You only slump like that when something's on your mind." Clay said before stopping to pick up something that resembled a black box with buttons up and down the side. He held it up in question to the two of us and both Clint and I shrugged our shoulders. "What? Ox do something to you?"

"Why do you assume it has anything to do with Ox?" I asked immediately. *Defensively.*

They both exchanged a look with each other. Clay disguised his snort with a cough. "It doesn't?"

"No, it doesn't," I said. I crossed my arms over my chest, straightening my shoulders as high as possible.

"Why don't you just let it out, Tiney. I swear you'll feel better when you do." Clay chided. When I said nothing, he continued. "C'mon. We don't care that your husband is your new boyfriend. *We already know*."

"*What*!" I burst out, way too loud to be in this upscale cyber store. Why were we even here, anyway? We had no idea what we were looking for. I hissed so hard I almost bit my tongue. "What are you talking about?"

This time the look they shared was a confused one.

"You and Ox?" Clint said, confused.

"Are not *together*!" I stated. No, damn near screeched. Because *what*?

"But the picture his sister sent. The little one."

"Ceci?" I asked. I didn't know what she did, but I already knew I was going to kill her for it. "What picture? Show me."

The last look they exchanged was the last straw. I narrowed my eyes and held out my hand. "*Show. Me.*"

"And she said nothing was wrong," Clay mumbled under his breath as he dug his phone out of his back pocket and opened it up. A few seconds of tapping and scrolling later and he was handing it over to me.

On the screen was a picture of Ox and I. We were sitting on his family's boat, you could see the nose of it peeking out to the corner of the photo, blue waters surrounding us. And toward the bottom of the screen there we were. In each other's arms.

We were sitting in the same shaded area he'd brought me to when I had overheated. There I was, looking washed out and exhausted as I rested in between his legs. Ox's long limbs were around me, his knees bent on either side of my body, his arms at my sides as his hand rested on my bent knees. I was still leaning back against his chest and we were both leaning back against the side of the boat. *Sleeping.*

I remembered falling asleep, but I didn't remember Ox dozing off *with* me. We sort of slept in the same bed most of the time, but still it seemed different that we'd do it out there in the open for everyone to see. And he hadn't let go of me. Even though I was probably heavy and uncomfortable, he'd let me use him to rest. My chest tightened.

Looking up, I found both my brothers watching me. I pursed my lips to keep my face neutral.

"No, not together," I said. My eyes slid back to the photo for another long moment before I peeked up at them shyly. "But send this to me."

Later that night, when night was turning into morning and I laid in my bed with my eyes peeled back wishing they could close, I opened up the photo and looked at it again.

Something about it soothed me to have something to remember that day by. Yet, something about it put me on edge. Clay's words played on repeat in my mind.

—*Your husband is your new boyfriend…*

I scoffed. My husband couldn't keep his helpful hands off of another woman today. Who cared if he'd nursed me back to health or if he'd fallen asleep with me while doing it? He'd do it for anyone.

I knew he would.

And I should be proud of that.

But I was jealous. And a little bit hurt. Not because he had helped Sylvie, he would help anyone because he was Ox and it was in his nature. But he'd done it on *my* time.

And that made me such an ugly, selfish thing.

Three soft taps cut through my thoughts on the other side of the door. My face screwed up and my gut clenched. I rolled over in bed so I couldn't see the door. I didn't want to be tempted. I didn't want to see him. I just wanted to be alone with whatever this was. Whatever I was feeling.

"Clem?" Ox's voice rang through the door. He waited a few beats before tapping again. "Clem, I'm coming in."

Usually this would send me running, but this time I just snuggled further into my blankets, hoping I'd blend in and he wouldn't see me.

No such luck. Ox came up behind me and stood over the side of the bed. I knew he was standing there. I could feel him hovering, but I refused to turn around to see him. Not when there was so much inside me right now that I couldn't control.

I felt a large, Ox sized hand land on the back of my head. "Little moon girl, I know you're not sleeping."

I tried to make sleeping noises, grumbling and fake snoring. Ox laughed. "God, now I'm *sure* you're awake."

When I said nothing, he rubbed his big palm down my hair once. "You ready for bed?"

"I'm in bed already," I said, not bothering to hide my lucidness anymore. My face, I still hid.

"She speaks," he said, and I felt the bed dip behind me, Ox sitting just on the other side of my back. "*And* she's mad."

"Why does everyone think I'm mad?" I asked.

"Because everyone knows your tells, Clementine." I didn't answer that, and he sighed. "And you haven't spoken to me all day."

Silence.

"Come to bed, Clem."

"I *am* in bed," I repeated, agitation getting a little more noticeable in my voice. I didn't know what was bothering me so much I just wanted to be alone.

"Will you let me see your face?" he asked, his hand moving to smooth away the covers I'd let bunch there. When they got pulled away and I caught his eyes, I felt another pang in my heart.

Not mine. I thought with remorse and longing. *Not real.*

225

"Clem," Ox sighed. "You're that upset?"

"I'm not," I said.

"You're acting like a child." He pointed out.

This was the wrong thing to say. I shot up in bed, surprising myself as well as Ox. But I used the momentum to swing my legs over the bed and raise myself out of it.

I started walking away. I think I was headed toward the bathroom, but my trajectory was thrown completely off when an arm wrapped around my waist and swung me midair in a different direction. I squeaked as I was set back down on the bed with a plop.

"No you don't," Ox said. He crossed the room to my closet and emerged with my sneakers and coat.

"What are you doing—"

"You want to be a brat? Okay." His business Ox voice was rearing its head. Kneeling before me, he slipped my socked foot into the first shoe, using his knee to prop up my foot as he tied my laces. "We'll go for a walk."

"But it's—"

"Barely forty degrees out? Yes," he said, his face tight. "But if this is what it takes to get your ass in that bed with me, then we're going to do it."

I gaped, but I couldn't help the wide smile that spread across my face.

A few days later, I was as sick as a dog.

Chapter Eighteen

OX

I slammed the thick packet of paper that was just sent to my office down on the hard metal table of the police station's "back waiting area". Waiting area my ass. I knew every inch of this goddamn place was wired, watched and recorded. And I welcomed all of it. Because I was through playing these games with them. I was done with entertaining the thought that someone in my family had turned against its head and betrayed him so entirely that it resulted in his death. I was through with them jerking us around and trying to manipulate us into turning on each other for their own agenda.

They had messed with us long enough. Calling and questioning, probing, and prodding. They had intertwined their way into our lives and were trying to pry them open with the finesse of a crowbar cracking open a crate.

And now they were hounding me for information on Clementine. *Again.*

Not to mention, in the last week they had brought Ceci down to the station for questioning, showed up at Alta's apartment to wring details out of her and they had started in on the extremities now too. Bouncing around house to house, workplace to workplace, meeting to meeting with each section of my family. My tíos and tías and cousins all included. This was getting old, quick.

"Fernandez, we weren't expecting you to hand deliver it to us. An email or scan would do," an officer I knew well by now said. He was leaning back in his shabby rolling chair, sipping coffee from a chipped white cup. Officer Dick (the motherfucker who could never seem to keep his mouth shut and had somehow escaped having it shut for him) was in his dick swinging element once again. And Officer Asshole wasn't too far behind him, sitting on the other side of the metal table with a similar cup of caffeine.

"I'm done," I said, placing my hands on my hips and pacing some steps away from the officers. I motioned between us, then around the room. "This is done."

"Hey now," Asshole cooed. This was, of course, not his real name. He was officer Munson, head of the Seaside Police and one of my top headaches. Because aside from him being outwardly cordial and trying to work with me and my family, he was still the shark that was organizing the ongoing interrogation and investigation of Abuelo's death. He was the one with the vision of murder, which made him an asshole. "This could have all been done a while ago if you just cooperated. When are you going to give us the information we need, Fernandez?"

"When the hell are you going to stop harassing me and my family? We aren't pressing any charges and it's been months. We want his body released and for all this to be over," I snapped, already done with this. I had been on edge the whole drive over.

On top of having to deal with a stream of utter incompetence in the office this morning, Clem had stopped answering the phone earlier in the day. It was Maria and Sylvie's day off, so I couldn't ask them where she was, not that she was their biggest fan anyway. But I was worried about her, and now instead of going to find her myself I had to deal with these nosey-ass officers asking me for information regarding Clem since we've been married. A topic that has nothing to do with her and Abuelo or this bullshit investigation.

Needless to say, I was on edge.

"Mr. Fernandez, you have to understand that we wouldn't be pursuing this if there wasn't any prospect of danger," the older officer said, setting his cup of coffee down. He rose and sauntered over to stand in front of me. His graying blonde hair was slicked away from his eyes, and I couldn't tell if it made his face look more or less irritating.

"Yes? And is that why you're asking my younger brother information on me? My sisters? Our cousins? Because you're trying to protect us from danger? Or because you're trying to tear our family apart?" I asked.

"Depends on how you look at it, I guess," Dick had the nerve to say from his seat that he continued to lean in.

The crack in my resolve snapped some more.

Storming over, past the older officer and right up to the metal table, I slammed a hand down onto the hard material. Leaning my full body into it, I pointed a finger right in his face. "If you think for a god-damn second that I don't have your whole branch under my fucking control already, you're idiots. I haven't pulled the plug because I don't want this to get out. But if you keep testing me, my family, and holding my abuelo outside of his peace, I will bring the FBI down on you so hard you'll fucking regret you knew my name."

Silence stretched, followed by audible swallowing from both men in the room. The older officer, Asshole, shot the young one a death stare before turning to me with raised hands. "There's no need for the FBI, Mr. Fernandez. The Seaside Police have got this under control, you can trust that."

"Depends on how you look at it, I guess," I repeated the earlier sentiment.

I swiped up the stack of papers that I had slammed down a few moments before and flipped the front page. "What is Clementine Fernandez's mental state? How has it changed?"

I glared up at them to display my disapproval with the questioning.

"What kind of behaviors has your wife displayed that could be a cause for concern? Examples may include, but are not limited to: at work, at home, in the *bedroom*..." I slid my eyes over the top of the paper just so they could see how fucking livid this made me. No way in hell I was answering something like this. They had to be smoking all the imaginary drugs they *didn't* find because they were such shit investigators.

"We are just being thorough. There are a lot of reasons a young girl like that would marry someone so far from her age." The older officer said. "Her behavior patterns from now to then comparatively can give us perspective on...plausible motive."

"*Plausible motive*," I huffed. I could hardly even say it because it was completely insane.

Hand on my hip, I pinched the bridge of my nose for so long I may have seen stars. When I raised my head again after thinking about these assholes trying so damn hard to get my wife in handcuffs, I knew it was fire I was seeing instead.

"Listen here," I said calmly. As calmly as I could, anyway. "There are and there will never be any charges against that woman. She is good, and she is mine. If you hurt her or continue this campaign to pin something she didn't do onto her back, I will do more than let the FBI steal your 'big high-profile case', I will shut down your branch and make sure you two can never serve in law enforcement another day in your life."

Silence.

Good, I was fucking getting somewhere. Letting the thick packet of similar questions flip shut, I sauntered over to the trash by the door and dropped them there.

"No more conspiring, gentlemen. If you have to talk to one of us, you have to talk to me. The rest of my family won't be cooperating with your bullshit. Not until you have a charge," I said, sliding my hands into my pockets and aiming for the door. I was done with this shit.

Until.

"Your *wife* will," the dick still leaning back muttered as he sat deeper into his chair.

Yeah. I *had* been heading toward the door, but upon mention of Clem I whirled around, the fire igniting in me again. "What?"

The older man was in my line of vision in an instant. Blocking me from seeing the young officer and again, holding up those placating hands. "Nothing, son. We understand your requests. Sorry we crossed the line."

I tossed my head up, chin inclined so I could catch the eyes of that mother fucking slime ball. He held mine like the antagonist that he was. In front of me the older man was now trying to usher me out. I would go. Damn, I would be happy if I could go and never come back. But before I did, I raised another finger in the younger man's direction.

"Lose my wife's name from your vocabulary," I spat.

Storming out of the main police branch's office in the downtown City Hall building, I made my way across the huge main foyer in a rush toward the door. I needed to get some air. I needed to get some air and blow off some steam and find out why the hell Clementine wasn't answering her phone.

Just as I was about to reach the huge double doors that were flanked by security and some kind of metal detecting machines, something in my periphery caught my eye. Something being four tall bodies nestled in the far corner of the City Hall main foyer. One of those bodies was significantly smaller and seemed as if it was being guarded by the rest.

Those bodies were familiar. Familiar as in, my wife and my in-laws were across the room from me.

They were walking in a tight formation. Clem was in the middle, Clay leading the way, and the other two taking up the back, walking close to her feet. From that far away I could see that her shoulders were slumped, her head bowed, and she was clutching the one and only crossbody purse I'd ever seen her wear by the strap like it was her seatbelt on a crazy roller coaster ride.

Something inside of me began to twist, a feeling of dread washing over me. I quickly pivoted on my feet and changed my direction toward them, catching up quickly on their side. The big one was the first to see me and as his gait eased up, so did everyone else's.

It seemed like Clem turned around in slow motion. Her eyes had been on the ground but rose slowly from my feet up my body and then finally landed on my face. The look of absolute dread there sent alarm bells off in my head.

"Hey," I said, looking from Clem's eyes to each of her brothers who were looking pretty wary themselves. I looked back down to my wife. "I've been calling. Everything okay?"

Clem's mouth turned down into a frown. She reached down and pulled out her phone, opening the screen. Her lips pursed at what she saw there, her eyes closed momentarily and then she mouthed a curse.

More alarm bells screamed in my head. Stepping closer, I dropped my voice and searched for her eyes. "Clem?"

She blinked up at me, her gaze roaming my body and then flicking up to my eyes. "What are you doing here?"

I swallowed. I had hoped to have this all sorted before telling her, so she wouldn't worry. But I wouldn't lie to her. So, deciding to say fuck the weirdness and close the rest of the distance between us, I moved forward until I was directly in front of her. Setting my hands on her shoulders, I looked down into those sweet eyes. They looked pained and tired.

Damn, this would stress her out.

"I had an appointment with the police investigators. They still have a few questions for me, but it's nothing you need to worry about. I've got it covered," I told her, and leaned down trying to catch her eyes which had dropped almost as soon as I started speaking. Instead of letting me, she glanced back at each of her brothers until finally her gaze fell on Clay. She held his gaze the longest.

I looked at him too and saw that he looked frustrated, almost angry.

"What's going on?" I asked, my hands squeezing slightly on Clem's flesh. She felt good under my touch, soft. Comforting, even though these looks she was giving me was my main cause of anxiety at that very moment.

"*Tell him*, Clementine," Clay said. I sucked in air.

Clementine, he'd said. Not that horrible nickname he always called her, but Clementine. Clem seemed to flinch at this too, her shoulders hitching and her chin ducking in protection of herself.

My eyes zeroed in on the movements, my mind wrapping around the words. She was keeping something from me. And it sounded like she had been doing it for a while. I would have liked to think that maybe it wasn't as much of a big deal as my twisting gut thought it was, but the looks on everyone's faces said otherwise.

"Oaxaca," she started, and my eyes clamored into hers, my stomach feeling like someone had taken a drill to it. "If I tell you something, do you promise to let me finish and react later?"

I narrowed my eyes. She had learned that from me and I didn't generally use that when what I was going to say would be an easy pill to swallow.

"No," I said. "I don't promise a damn thing. Speak, Clementine."

She seemed to curl even more into herself. And the more she cowered, the more on edge I got. What could be so bad? I wish I could say I gentled my voice but I don't think I could have done that even if I tried. "What is it?"

"It isn't anything bad." She paused. "It's just, you already seem mad and I don't want to make you madder."

Okay. She said it wasn't bad, and although that didn't erase the knot in my stomach, it made me feel at least a little better. So this time, I did gentle my voice successfully.

"Tell me," I said, reaching up and tucking a hair back into her braid. "I promise I'll *process* before I react."

She looked at me warily, took another breath that moved her shoulders up and down, and then spoke. "The police wanted to speak to me too. They've wanted to a lot, actually."

"About...Abuelo?" I asked. Processing, just like I promised I would, but in what seemed like slow motion.

What?

"About Ron, yes," she said with a solitary nod. I hated when she called him that, but I guess that's what he was to her.

I looked down at her for the longest time. Processing, processing, just like she'd asked. And when I had processed enough, my hands jerked away from her like they'd been burned.

"You've been talking to them?" I asked. I watched her nod and my eyes slid over. Far, far over in the direction I'd just come from. "They've been questioning you? All this time?"

I may have stepped in the direction of the police quarters. I may have even taken several deliberate steps that way. To do what? I didn't know. But the fire that had been in my eyes when I'd last been over there was now spreading throughout my entire body. I felt hot, and my skin prickled and my fingertips twitched. I headed straight toward those far-right corner doors with the plaque Seaside Police letters above them.

Quick movement in front of me brought my vision down. Clem had run to catch up with me. Stopping in front of me and bringing her hands to my forearms to stay my movements.

Like a reel, her words played again through my mind.

Ron. Questioning. Police. A lot.

The words spiraled within my brain until they finally made sense. Clementine was here because she had been talking to the police. The police that wanted to convict her of killing my abuelo for no good reason. The same police who had been questioning me about her since the day he died. And this wasn't her first time here either. It wasn't her first or second or maybe even third.

Suddenly, flashes of the same tired look she'd had on her face when I first spotted her, brought itself up in my memory in different instances. When I came home and she apparently had "been there all day", she wore that same look. Sometimes, after her brothers dropped her off, she wore that look. When she came over Amá's for dinner, she wore that goddamn look. How many times had she done this? How much had she lied to me? All those times when she told me she was doing something else, she'd really been here?

And she brought her brothers. She *told* her brothers and left me in the dark. Hell, I wouldn't have been surprised if I was the last to know.

This whole time I thought I had been protecting her by not telling her about the police's skepticism and accusations, she had been fielding it herself. And keeping it from me. What was the fucking game here?

I took a step back from her so quickly that she lost her balance a little. Looking at the little wife I had grown to revere, I felt like I was seeing a new her. One that I hadn't been let in on the joke about. With all her family (*her real family*) standing around her, I felt like an outsider. Even though I had worked so hard to bring her in with open arms.

She trusted them, but she didn't trust me.

I inwardly cursed myself as I shook my head. And she had said, it wasn't '*anything bad*'.

I scoffed.

My mind drifted back to Officer Dick's last words. *"Your wife will"*.

He'd known. He'd been speaking to Clementine not just prior to our meeting but what had to be just minutes before. That smug asshole had been sitting across from her and talking to her and thinking about her and I fucking knew what they thought of her. *I fucking knew it.* She was an easy book, and maybe even more if they could manipulate her, her family, her body… *God damn.*

A tremor shook my entire body, and I felt as if my bones rattled, I was so stiff. My eyes racked up her frame and when they met hers, she knew. I could tell by the way her confused face fell into something else. A look full of remorse and defiance and panic and hurt.

She was hurt? Rich.

Slowly, I brought a hand up to cover my eyes, digging my fingers into them brutally. I couldn't look at her. She wasn't acting innocent, she truly *was* innocent, and it was killing me because at the same time she was guilty. She was a little fucking guilty idiot for ripping my heart out and stomping all over it.

I couldn't breathe. A feeling of relief that she had at least encountered these assholes with nothing bad happening clashed with complete anger that she'd been doing this without telling me in the first place, conflicting my emotions.

"Ox?" A sweet voice asked. "Are you okay?"

"No," I said, not removing my hands from my eyes. I'm pretty sure my voice was calm, but I couldn't hear it past the roaring in my ears. "You mean to tell me that you've been being formally questioned by the police, by yourself, for weeks now?"

"Yes," she said on an outward breath.

"Clementine," I said, letting my hand drop and squaring my shoulders with her. I faced her and only her. "Can you tell me what you were thinking?"

She stood there, not answering. Just being silent Clem. I had once had patience for this Clem, when I thought she wasn't keeping secrets from me. When I had faith that every one of her words, the words she

236

guarded so closely at first, were truthful. But every second that she stood there silent in front of me, I felt my anger bubble up more and more. Taking a step forward, I both raised and lowered my voice, not knowing which one I wanted.

"What the *fuck*, Clem?" I seethed. I could not believe she'd been doing this all this time. I could not believe she hadn't just told me about it in all this time. The anger I felt in my chest bubbled and bubbled until it was rising up my throat. "I'm speaking to you, Clementine. What the fuck were you thinking? Were you even thinking at all?"

"Hey, hey," Clay said from the background. Her other brothers stepped forward alongside him.

I held a hand up to them, but I didn't turn my body away from Clementine. "My wife, my rules. Get the *fuck* out of our conversation."

"Your fucking grave, Ox, if you keep fucking talking to my sister like that," Clay said.

"She's a big girl. She can handle me." The look on her face said otherwise. She looked as if she was barely holding it together. I had already lost it, though. She was winning the composure contest. "Clementine. Explain this to me, *right now*."

"It's just the same," she said, her soft voice wobbling. "I've been talking to the police when they need me to, to help with their investigation."

"Against me?" I asked.

"No, I don't answer questions about you. I never have," she said quickly. Clearly.

Okay. I believed that. But something about the way she said it stuck out to me.

"How long have you been talking to them?"

She looked at me from underneath her eyelashes and then she seemed to duck her head into her shoulders. "Since you left…that time."

I stepped forward. I felt Clementine's personal guard step forward around us. I wanted to lash out at them. Did they really think I was going to hurt her? The reason that I was so mad in the first place was because I'd been trying to protect her from all of this. And I had failed.

"Which time?" I asked slowly.

She tried to peek around me to look at her brothers. I stepped forward again, blocking her line of sight.

She swallowed and then licked her lips. "The first time."

I cursed.

I cursed and cursed and cursed. My hands went to my hips and rested there as I pivoted away from her. Because if I looked at her right then I wasn't sure what I'd do. I looked back at the Ferguson boys, and I knew that they must have known. And they'd kept it a secret, because she asked them to. I looked to the ceiling, because goddammit, mother fuck.

I had dropped the fucking ball.

Then I looked at her. Her hands were clasped in front of her waist, her fingers wringing themselves. Her foot was bouncing nervously, and she kept ticking her neck every so often as if to crack it but it didn't make a sound. She was nervous, she was on edge, but she was staring right at me. That meant she had something to say.

I turned and faced her head on. "What?"

She flinched at the question, probably coming out a little too harshly. I didn't care. Nice Ox had gotten me nowhere with this girl. "Ox. I know you're mad, but it goes both ways. You were talking to the police too. *You* never told me."

"It's different."

"How is it different?"

"You know how it's different, Clementine," I said, giving her a look. One I realized she didn't understand because up until this point, we hadn't had a conversation like this one. *A fight.*

"It's not different, Ox. I did it to help you. Isn't that why you've been trying to handle it all by yourself too?"

"It's different," is all I could say as I shook my head.

"It's not. What's so wrong about someone wanting to help you?"

"You shouldn't have done it."

"Done what? Try to help? Can I not stand by your side or be your partner in this?"

"No!"

"No?" she asked, her own voice doing this scoffing thing, like she didn't believe what I was saying to her.

"*No*," I said more clearly. "I didn't ask for your help. I was handling it on my own."

"You handle *everything* on your own. I thought I could help," she said again.

"You can't," I said almost too quickly. She recoiled, her face screwing slightly. But there was still this look of defiance on her face. This look that showed her thoughts clearly. So I stepped forward, finding her eyes and saying slowly, "*You. Can't. Help. Me.* You can't even help yourself, how the hell are you going to help anyone else, Clem?"

Another recoil. Her voice grew husky, speckled with the definite onslaught of tears. I felt my chest bunch up painfully, but I was too deep in my anger to care. She swallowed and powered through to her words. "I'm sorry, I just wanted you to have a partner in this, that's all. You're always alone and I thought I could help this time. You helped me, so I wanted to help you. That's all."

I shook—*physically shook*—with anger.

"It's so different, Clementine! You could have been taken into custody. You could have been set up. You could have been taken advantage of. God knows what they do to women in this system. Anything could have happened to you. And I would have had no idea. Is that what partners do?" I had lost it and I was going off and with every word I watched Clem get smaller and smaller. "You know what, Clem? You want to know what you can do for me? You can get out of bed for more than a few hours a day. You can take initiative to do *something* on your own. You can stop being so weird around Sylvie, you can talk to

Maria every once in a while, or stop keeping secrets with my fucking sister, or even just leave the house for a goddamn change. You can stop being such a—"

"Ox!" The brothers cut in.

I shut up and raised my hands to my head as I stalked away and back, away and back.

"Such a what?" she asked. Her voice was small, smaller than I'd ever heard it before. Even smaller than when she'd first spoken to me. It made my eyes narrow and for the first time in the last minutes, I could see something other than my own haze of anger. I was hurting Clem. But the part I was still trying to wrap my head around was that, without even knowing it, Clem had hurt me.

Bad.

"What you can do for me, Clementine, is try. Because I'm fucking trying and all you've been is a pain in my ass." I looked at her again and I wasn't as angry. I was tired. There, that's what I was. So damn tired. And the gut punching feeling in my stomach said that I was a little betrayed too. *I thought I had this.* I thought I had *her.* But really it turned out, I had nothing at all.

I turned, trying to remember which way I'd come in from. When I found it, I moved to leave, but turned back to look at her again, my voice just as tired as I was. "You can't stand beside someone by going behind their back, Clem."

Okay.

So, almost as soon as I'd said all that, I regretted it. Especially the part about Clem being a pain in my ass. If anything, my ass had hurt less since Clementine had come around. With her sweet laughs and silly names. Her shy looks and thoughtful nature. She had been a light in this dark tunnel my Abuelo had created. I had even given her a name for it.

But…

But she was insane if she thought I'd be okay with letting my sweet, shy, soft, light bringing wife weather the storm of a police investigation on her own. And maybe I could have handled that a lot, *a lot* better, but I'd *told* her that I hated secrets. My reaction was inevitable.

That didn't stop me from banging my forehead against the steering wheel as I pulled up to a red light. I had already gotten a flood of text messages from the Fergusons that went like:

Clay: You fucking idiot.

Clinton: You could have handled that better.

Connor: Here.

Connor's text was the one that got my attention. Because below the simple message was a video file. My jaw tightened at the sight of it, because no matter what was on it, it couldn't be great.

I waited until I was back at my office, nestled away in the private double underground parking garage to open up my messages again and select the video that Clem's brother had sent me.

The big play button disappeared from the middle of the screen and the scene in front of me immediately took my breath away, before I even knew what was going on. Why? Because the scene in front of me was Clem.

She was sitting down on that big chair in my living room that she always sits in. She looked skinnier and more withdrawn than she has been recently, so it must have been back when she'd first moved in. I watched as she sat there in her long pajamas, that white fuzzy sweater thing she liked to wear wrapping tightly around her. Her head was nodding and her eyes seemed to be following something across the room, like she was talking. Flicking my eyes across the screen, I saw who she was talking to.

The Seaside Police.

Raising the volume on the small phone, I felt as if I was watching with only an inch of space between my face and the screen. I watched as Officer Dick and Officer Asshole lead a whole fucking brigade into my goddamn living room and posted up in front of Clem like she was public enemy number one. Five officers stood before her. Officers who distrusted her and were armed. And Clem just sat there acting cooperatively. She answered their questions, she nodded when she was supposed to, she gave them the information they asked for. Even though she was alone, with no one to lean on and no one to witness this.

And officer Dick was edging closer, leering at her and from what it sounded like, trying to antagonize her.

And you entered his room at—12:07 that morning, why? They had asked her.

She looked *so* nervous. Why? And why was I the only one concerned about it? Everyone else in the room just stared her down, trying to intimidate her into answering.

I was...visiting. She'd said in a small, unsure voice. She sounded uncomfortable. *Like I did every night.*

They didn't leave it at that, though. Instead, they pushed some more. Asking her *why?* And pressing her when she didn't answer. Making her start to squirm in her fucking seat. They were intimidating her in her own fucking house.

I ground my teeth together, already feeling the urge to pull the car back out of the garage and head back to that station for reasons other than apologizing to Clem.

Ron scheduled sex for him and I. Always in his room, always at midnight.... She kept going, but I blacked out. Or was it red? I wasn't sure, all I knew was I couldn't hear and I couldn't see. All I could think was *Damn.* Because I had known the reason why she couldn't sleep was something *like* that, but actually *knowing* suddenly meant something else. And now knowing without her having told me herself, I felt dirty somehow. Like I had cheated her in some way. And I felt sorry.

I ended up having to rewind the video to catch what I'd missed. Which was quite a lot. They continued to question her about things that had already been previously explained. Or about things that were entirely too personal for their "civil" investigation. Questions about *me*. And then Officer Dick—who they should have extracted minutes ago—went and said it.

So, you're out here bouncing around these guys like a pinball and all you happen to know is what time to show up and get—

Moments later, Sylvie flew on the screen and pushed them all out in an impressive show of dramatics. Aside from using a broom, which could be claimed as a weapon against the police, it was flawless. I'd have to talk to her about that. Thank her.

I let a ragged breath leave me, straight from my chest. *—And all you happen to know is what time to show up and get—*

"Fuck!" I clutched the small phone so hard I actually thought for a stupid second that I could bend it. I didn't want to, but I was that fucking angry. With the damn police for being so horrible. With Clem and her fucking brothers for not telling me. But with myself for so much more. For leaving so soon when I knew she could have needed me. For exploding at her in City Hall. For putting that same broken, hurting look onto her face today that had shown up in this video.

I was such an idiot.

I didn't know Ox before... But I know him now and I would say no.

Such a fucking idiot. I had asked her if she talked to the police about me. Of course, she hadn't. *Of course.* I had just been so mad that I lashed out. I jumped to conclusions. And just like at the wedding, I had been mad because of me and I hadn't considered Clem in the situation. Sure, I wanted to protect her and, yes, she definitely should have told me she was talking to the police, but it did neither of us any good if I was making her feel just as low and threatened as those fuckers had. Putting that damn look on her face.

"Fuck," I said again. It came out in a seething whisper. I pulled the message app back up and opened the last chat.

> **Me:** When?

> **Connor:** Day after your wedding.

> **Me:** How?

> **Connor:** She told us weeks later that the police were still contacting her. I accessed the footage after I knew.

> **Me:** You hacked my security cameras?

> **Connor:** Yes.

> **Me:** What else did you see?

> **Connor:** Something to hide?

> **Me:** Jesus, no. I don't care if you watch with popcorn. What else about Clem?

> **Connor:** A few more home visits. Clint made her stop those. Now she only goes there in person, and she only goes with us. She insists on doing it though. On handling it herself.

Thank God I was talking to him over text message, because I'm not sure I would have gotten even remotely this much information from talking to him in person. Both because he was quiet and because I would have already left to go revisit the police. The fact that he'd hacked my home security cameras was far from my mind at the moment, but I'd revisit it later for sure. But for now, I sent him a quick "Thanks" before pulling up another messenger. The one for my assistant.

Usually I asked Ursula to handle more tactful things like double checking expense reports and maintaining my ever changing schedule for the day, or even hiring and firing company employees. But this time I asked her for one thing and one thing only.

Me: Get me the DA's information.

Ursula: Sir?

Me: I'm not going to blow the place up, Urse. Get me a contact, I'll handle the rest.

Ursula: Of course, Ox. Give me twenty.

Good. I exited my car swiftly, but instead of heading in the direction of the main offices, I turned toward the elevators that took occupants of the double underground garage even deeper underground. My job as CEO meant I played a lot of roles. I wore many hats, and I had my hands in anything from project management to marketing to finance to the damn mail. But the kind of work I had to do now had nothing to do with this business and everything to do with my wife.

Before I made it to the elevators, where I would lose all normal forms of wireless connection, I got two messages. One with information from Ursula about the Seaside District Attorney and his chain of command. And the other, another message from Connor Ferguson. Urse's message I made sure to screenshot and file away, just in case I lost it somehow. Connor's, I opened and read as I pressed my personal code into the elevator.

Connor: That was the only video I pulled... But while I was looking for it, I noticed something... What you said earlier is wrong. She *is* trying. She's struggling. But she's trying.

I squeezed my phone hard, wanting to bend it. Wanting to break something, to hurt someone because, goddammit, I *knew* that. I had just been so mad. I was still so mad. And it was so wrong to take it out on Clem. I knew it the minute I saw that look on her face, I just hadn't been able to stop myself.

But I'll be damned if I did it again. This anger that I felt had to go somewhere, and I knew exactly who was going to get the brunt of it.

Officer Asshole and his little sidekick were about to get a name change. Just *Asshole* sounded fine.

Chapter Nineteen

CLEMENTINE

Ox didn't come home after I made him mad. And God, I made him so mad.

The more I'd gotten to know Ox the more I began to realize that when I finally did get around to telling him I had been meeting with the police basically since the moment we'd gotten married, he would be upset. He'd told me up front that he didn't like secrets. But more than that, he always knew everything about everything. Or at least everything about things that mattered to him. I suspected it was because he valued immense control over situations and their outcomes.

Even though I knew he would be mad, I had no idea *how* mad.

I'd noticed over and over again how Oaxaca's family worked to keep him happy, but still it never really occurred to me to wonder why. I realized now that was because I had yet to see him *furious*. He was normally calmer, more controlled, even when he was irritated. But after having him tear into not just me, but my choices, my progress, and everything I had done since we met, I was understanding the general rule of thumb: Don't make Ox upset.

Even so, I had expected him to come home.

Right after the scene at City Hall, I almost entirely shut down. I had never heard Ox yell before. I had never been spoken to by him like that. I had never seen that look on his face. And because of it, I was left shocked and upset and indignant and devastated and maybe a million other emotions all at the same time.

My gut reaction to him being so damn mean was thinking that maybe this was it. Maybe this was the end of our long walks and quiet breakfasts and midnight talks. For an even more devastating moment, I'd let myself worry that maybe this was the moment Ox turned into Ron and started doing every nightmarish thing that I had been fighting to break free from.

That made me feel guilty. So damn guilty, because mean or not, Ox had been there for me in these last months, and he had been the most supportive, constant thing for me in such a long time. He was patient and kind. He took care of me, more than just what our contract outlined, but sort of as a friend. And in turn, he had also taken care of my heart. Hurting him so badly hurt the very heart he took such good care of. The possibility that I could *lose him* after this, was breaking that heart in two.

I only let myself shut down on the car ride home. My brothers constantly tried speaking to me, only to be answered by a dazed, shaking, borderline brain-dead version of myself. I couldn't think past the visions of Ox's face as he looked at me with pure betrayal in his eyes. I couldn't get that look out of my head. So, after I convinced my brothers that I would be okay and they should leave, instead of shutting down even more I did something that wasn't much better. I panicked.

I kept replaying the things Ox said to me in my head. Hurtful words about me not trying or me not being independent. The sad part was, I couldn't help but think that he was right. I wasn't exactly trying as hard as I could be to get myself back out there in the world. I wasn't exactly the most independent person either. I relied on Ox or my brothers or whoever else to cart me around and basically handle everything for me. And I wasn't actively working toward any of that changing.

Now that he had said it, I could see it clearly. Being criticized like that would have hurt either way, but the fact he brought it up at all must mean that he had been feeling this way for a while. Was he at his breaking point? What if he came back and said that he just couldn't do this anymore. That, contract or not, we'd gotten our inheritance and he couldn't work with this arrangement for a second longer.

What if, what if, what if, passed through my mind in a never-ending sprawl of panic.

And what I do when I panic is overcompensate for what I've done wrong and try like hell to make up for it. So, for forty minutes after my brothers dropped me off at home, I racked my brain for something I could do for Oaxaca to make up for the fact that I had fractured his trust in me. And for forty damn minutes I came up short.

This just made me feel worse. Every time I thought of something that might work, I realized it was something Oaxaca had already handled. Cleaning the house, done. Making him dinner, done—even if he wanted to brave my cooking, he wouldn't get to. Buy him a gift? He was a billionaire, he already had everything he needed. The list continued on like that, making me more and more dejected, until something Ox said a little while back popped into my head.

All those people get some, but not me?

There it was! I could bake for him. He'd asked me no less than ten different times if he could try something I made. Each time I said no because I was afraid the one thing I was sort of good at would turn out to be something I wasn't actually good at, at all. And if that was destined to be the case, I was afraid of Ox being the one to realize it first. But now, with this weird fight thing looming between us, it was the perfect time to put those insecurities aside and just go for it.

It was still pretty early in the day and Ox had been making sure the kitchen stayed stocked with baking supplies lately. If I started right away I would have something done by the time he got home. Or I *could*, but there was one more problem.

I had no idea what Ox liked.

He usually asked to taste my desserts without being picky. The fact that he had a sweet tooth was confirmed by how many times he pulled random candies out of his fitted suit pockets. But he had never told me specifically what he actually liked, other than the Buñuelo cookies. And those seemed too simple for an apology like this.

Luckily, I had his mother's number and I wasn't afraid to use it. Okay, I was a little afraid to use it, so instead I texted Ceci first, hoping I wouldn't have to. When it took her five minutes too long to get back to me, I decided that Martina was the best horse to bet on. She answered on the second ring.

Flan.

He liked Flan. I could do flan. Sure, I'd never done it before and I would have to work through it a few times to maneuver a recipe good enough for tasting, but I could do it. Ox had been coming home early lately so we could have dinner together, but he probably wouldn't be doing that today. He was mad at me. He probably didn't want anything to do with me. That was fine. It just gave me more time to work through a recipe.

So, I made flan. For hours. Many, many hours. So many hours that I thought I would still be baking when Ox came home.

The first batch was too custardy and tasted too eggy which meant it wasn't milky enough. The second batch burned and I'm glad of it because it was all around bad anyway. The third batch was almost perfect, but the caramel overcooked and became crystal like. I saved those leftover crystallized chunks for Ox to snack on later.

The last batch was perfect. It only took until a little past nine to get the perfect ratio of cream to caramel, water bath the custard to the perfect texture, and bake it to the exact correct temperature.

I'd scrounged up a small saucer from one of the high cabinets in the back. It was a pretty mosaic red print that made me wonder if he had gotten it from Mexico or if it had been passed down throughout the family. I slid the perfect dome of caramel custard onto the plate and let it cool there completely as I cleaned up around the kitchen.

As I did, my mind wandered to Ox, imagining his reaction to my peace offering. I didn't expect the dessert to make him forget everything that happened, but I hoped it would be a token of my remorse and would let him know that I was sorry. Even if I had been pretty damn shocked to see him at the station too. Even if I was sure that I felt just as hurt to find out that my efforts to keep Ox out of the police investigations had been in vain. Even if this whole thing was a little bit Ox's fault too, I was still sorry. And I wanted him to know that.

But as hours and hours came and went and no Ox showed up, I felt my lightness at accomplishing a recipe I was proud of and my hopefulness that this would mend the gap Ox and I had forged dissipating.

I camped out in the living room, watching the kitchen like a hawk, but still no Ox. I refused to go upstairs, not only because I wanted to catch Ox if he came in, but also because I didn't know where to go when I went up there. I usually slept in bed with him, but how would I get to sleep without him there? I couldn't lull *myself* to sleep with funny, serious, or weird questions. Only Ox could do that.

The midnight hour came and went. So did the one and two 'o' clock hours. Ox had worked super late before—or attended to other things that I never let myself think too hard about—but each time that happened, he would call or text to let me know he would be out late. As far as fake husbands went, he had been perfect so far and I'd ruined it with my piss poor attempts at helping.

Somewhere around the three 'o' clock mark, I felt tears sting the backs of my eyes. I was completely alone in the dark hours of the early morning, but I refused to let them fall. Not for this. This had only been a misunderstanding and I had a plan to work it out. I worked hard on a peace offering and now that we had had time to cool off, we could talk it through. *If he ever showed back up to talk at all.* So I wouldn't let myself get hurt over things Ox couldn't control, like having to work or being under pressure. I would wait until I saw him, and we would work it out.

I fell asleep while putting all my energy into not crying, dreaming of dark sheets and an even darker silhouette coaxing me to sleep.

"Clem?" A throaty voice cut through my slumber.

I jolted upward, my eyes ripping open and clattering around the room in search of him. But it wasn't Ox who called my name. My eyes landed on a curvy woman with a large t-shirt and leggings as her uniform. Sylvie.

My heart both leaped and stuttered at the sight of her. I always felt so conflicted around Sylvie because, despite her being as kind and loyal as they come, I suspected there was some attraction there between Ox and her—or at least coming from her. I hated to think that I was jealous of someone who could have a *real* connection with Ox, or that I was so selfish to want to get in the way of a relationship that could have happened if I hadn't shown up in the picture... But I *was* in the picture and the fact was, her long looks at him while he was turned away, and the fact that she knew everything about him, and especially the fact Ox was just as nice to her as he was to anyone else, bothered me.

But maybe I was just imagining things, and even if I wasn't, I couldn't take it out on her. I could never do that. I wasn't that kind of person. I had been walked over and disregarded and used for most of my life. I didn't want to be that way to anyone else. So even though this conflicting feeling always appeared when Sylvie appeared, I pushed at it and used my big girl manners to treat her exactly how I would like to be treated.

Looking around the living room, I could see that the space was bathed in sunlight from the various windows around the room. Around me was the blanket I had pulled up to my neck last night when I was waiting for Ox and beside me on the side table was a steaming hot cup of tea. I could smell it before I even saw it.

"What are you doing on the couch, mamá?" Sylvie asked and a rush of the good I felt whenever I was around her swam past my heart. She always called me "mamá" or "chica" or something else cute and endearing like that. More reasons that it was hard to hate her and easy to be jealous of her. She was just so…charming.

Pulling myself to a sitting position, I smiled halfheartedly. "Hey, Sylvie. I guess I fell asleep down here. What's the time?"

"It's only nine-thirty. I just didn't want you to get a neck cramp sleeping down here," she said. But she sat down on the couch beside me, leading me to believe that there was more than just her concern for my neck.

I took a second to let my eyes adjust to the light and then I skated them around the room, slower this time. The living room was pretty much in order aside from me sleeping there. I could see from my position on the couch that the foyer leading to the front door was dark, so no one was out there. And across the way, I could see into the kitchen where the breakfast table sat off to the side. There was no Ox sitting there eating eggs or drinking near black coffee. Although I kind of knew there wouldn't be if it was already this late.

I didn't let myself look at the center of the island where I had left the covered piece of flan that I made for him. I wasn't ready to see if he'd taken it yet.

"Where's Ox?" I asked, lowering my eyes to the woman next to me. Her eyes did a weird scrunching thing as she looked me over.

"He hasn't talked to you?" she asked.

If you excluded being berated by him in the middle of a government building then, "No."

Her bottom lip pulled into her mouth and she nibbled it. The nervous motion made me feel nervous.

"What, Sylvie? Is he hurt? He didn't come back last night as far as I know. Did something happen?" I asked, a little more on edge now.

"No, no mamá, he's fine," she said, but she looked at me with something like shame coating her features. I felt myself straighten in alert. "He told me he got back here very late and had to leave almost instantly for an emergency."

"Leave where?" I asked, confused and disappointed.

"Mexico."

I'm sorry, did I say disappointed? I meant, *devastated*.

The last time he'd gone to Mexico he hadn't come back for three weeks. And he hadn't contacted me once while he was away, not that he was talking to me right now anyway. But how does someone just up and leave for Mexico without telling anyone?

My eyes swung to Sylvie, perfect, cute little Sylvie, and I felt that rush of jealousy hit me like a wrecking ball. No, he'd told someone. Maybe even multiple someone's. He just hadn't told *me*.

Swallowing what felt like a mountain of frustration and hurt and pain lodged smack in the middle of my throat, I willed my eyes not to water. "Did he say how long he'd be gone?"

"About a week," she answered with the intuition to keep her voice soft. I didn't know if she knew the details, but she could definitely tell that something was going on. The concern on her face told that much.

She could calm her worries, though. *Nothing* was going on. Apparently, I meant about as much to Oaxaca as gum meant to its wrapper. He would hold me together for as long as he was supposed to but as soon as he could, he would float away in the wind.

With courage and maybe a bit of anger, I lifted my head slightly to see over the expanse of the living room into the kitchen. More specifically, the kitchen island.

And there, of course, was a little piece of flan.

The caramel had started to drip a little, and it looked like the middle might be sinking in from not being stored properly. It was altogether untouched and unappreciated. *Unwanted.*

This sting hurt the most. The sting of the truth. All this time Ox had been playing at caring. Playing at husband. *Playing with me.* He'd been saying and doing the right things because that's what he did. That's who he was. All this time, when I had been starting to *feel* things, he had been checking responsibilities off a list.

Okay.

He'd given me a list too. I remembered it, clear as day. *You want to know what you can do for me...* He had basically yelled it at me before telling me all the things I could do to stop getting on his fucking nerves.

So fine.

Fine.

I was done being a burden. I'm pretty sure that's what he was going to call me during his rant. It wasn't like Ox to call a woman a bitch.

But it turned out, I could be one of those too.

Ox came back a week and a half later. I had no idea he'd be back then, only when Martina invited me to weekend family dinner herself and told me Ox could take me home after, did I realize he would be there.

And he was. Dressed in all black like normal and wearing a scowl that was not to be trifled with. There he finally was. And I didn't say a word to him. Not one. I didn't sit near him, I didn't listen to anything he said, I didn't look over to where I knew he was sitting with his eyes so frequently moving to find me.

The tension was noticeable. I could tell by the way his family passed looks between each other over forced "normal" conversation. I didn't care. I came to this dinner for Martina and so that I could keep fulfilling my list of *'How to Help Oaxaca Fernandez Forget He Had a Wife Forced on Him Almost Five Months Ago'*.

The list fulfilling was going great, actually. The day Sylvie told me Ox had left was the day I decided to use all that money sitting in my bank account. Specifically, to buy a car. A nice black SUV with built in navigation and brown leather seats. Clint had helped me pick it out, making sure it was safe and suitable for a girl who had her license but hadn't driven in years.

This accomplishment would help me fulfill Ox's request that I leave the "goddamn" house. And so would the few classes I'd signed up for. One workout class that switched between Pilates, Yoga and Dance Cardio every other day. One French baking class that met a couple times a week. And a group meeting for struggling spouses.

I wasn't going to do the last one originally. Even though I was mad and hurt and battling so many feelings, it wasn't Ox I wanted to attend the meeting for. It was Ron. I was too afraid to jump into therapy, not ready to be judged and picked apart for the life I'd led up until now. I wanted to see if I could take control of myself *by* myself first. But as I laid awake each midnight with no Ox around to ease my racing thoughts, the torture of that horrible hour kept resurfacing and I realized that all this time I hadn't been dealing with it. With *any* of it. I had just been distracting myself from it.

After dinner Martina was on me like white on rice.

"What's wrong, Mija?" she asked in Spanish. We'd gathered the dishes into piles and taken them into the kitchen, ready to wash. Only, Ox was already at the sink, poised to wash dishes like he always was. Eager to give his mom a break after cooking dinner. My eyes traveled to him warily at the sound of her question. There was no way he couldn't hear us. Martina picked up on this and turned to her son. "Sácate, Oaxaca. *Out.*"

Ox paused his washing and looked back at us. He let his eyes skate over me, gunning for my face. I averted my eyes. In my periphery, I saw that he lingered for one, two, three seconds before calmly turning off the water, drying his hands, and walking out.

All I told her was that he hadn't told me he was leaving and I was worried. I suspected she knew it was more than that, but she didn't push me. Instead, she told me about their plans for Thanksgiving while we washed the dishes together.

Later, when I left by myself, I got a text from Ox as I was driving home. I asked the car to read the message aloud as I needed all my focus ahead for my unskilled trip back.

> **Ox:** Where are you?

> **Me (at a red light):** Almost home.

> **Ox:** How?

> **Me (parking in the driveway):** New car.

That's all I said to him that night. Even when he came to my door and knocked lightly as he tended to do, I didn't answer. I couldn't. How could I just fall back into things with him like they were normal? None of this was normal, it never had been. It was time I started to see that.

The next morning was a workout class day. Yoga. Since I still couldn't sleep directly through the night, I didn't sign up for a super early class. Still, the ones I did sign up for were early enough that I had to wake up and start my day before double digits hit the clock.

Even so, my class times were scheduled hours after Ox usually was up and out the door for the day. That way I could strategically hide from him until I too had to leave. So, that morning when I descended the stairs and headed toward the kitchen to grab a to-go tea, I hadn't expected to see Ox sitting at the breakfast table. He had a cup of coffee at his side and his computer in front of him. He was dressed in his usual blacks, but only in a simple shirt and slacks rather than his three-piece suit. The sight made me stop in my tracks.

Ox's eyes bounced up over the top of his laptop, his taps pausing as he noticed me. When he ran his gaze over my appearance—clad in long black leggings and a matching tank that reached mid-waist, my pale orange yoga mat rolled up and slung over one shoulder—his head cocked in speculation. A second later he opened his mouth to speak, but I took a big step backward and he snapped it shut, slicing me a disapproving stare as he tracked my movements.

When he realized I wasn't just putting distance between us, but actually leaving, he stood. "Clemen—"

But I was already spinning on my heels and racing out the door.

As the week unfurled, with me avoiding Ox and him staring me down while trying to catch my attention, I think it became known to him that I was busy. Or at least *busier*. And for the most part he left me alone. As alone as Oaxaca Fernandez could leave things, at least. Meaning he constantly asked where I was going, who'd I'd be seeing, if I had enough gas, and if my other keepers (my three brothers) knew where I'd be in case of an emergency.

It was clear he was immensely frustrated with what was going on between us. He constantly tried to slide in conversation about more than just the essentials, but I only entertained him enough to ensure he wouldn't spontaneously combust before shrugging off the rest of his interest and going about my days.

He hated it.

He *would* hate it, he was Ox. He liked control, and I was taking mine back. Still, regardless of his ever-souring mood, he never tried to stop me from doing anything.

Until the weekend rolled around.

Martina had apparently been speaking to her daughters about me and Ox's little tiff. On Saturday night, a night that Ox notoriously spent at home keeping me company while I baked and he worked on the couch,

Ceci, Alta, and even Melissa all showed up to my bedroom door carrying bags and clothes and heels.

Ceci led the ambush, charging into my room and calling over her shoulder. "We're going out, bitch."

"I'm not the bitch," I grumbled immediately in response. "Look in a mirror."

This garnered surprised looks from both Alta and Melissa who I remembered hadn't seen me talk back to Ceci and probably thought I had lost my mind. I sent sheepish looks their way and peeked out in the hall to see if Ox was around before shutting my door firmly.

Ceci snorted as she dumped all of her loot onto my bed and turned to face me with her hands on her hips. "You *so* are. You just don't know how to show it."

Everyone in the room turned their noses up at that. "What are you guys doing here?"

"We heard you're on an Ox rebellion mission and we happen to know a little something about that," Ceci said, a glint in her eye.

"And," Alta piped up. "We figured we could help you make him a little jealous."

I flicked my eyes over to Melissa expectantly. She was walking the outskirts of the room, quietly fingering the things I had slowly started to accumulate here. When she noticed we all paused, she flicked a gaze up. "I'm just here to watch."

Everything about Melissa seemed a little sad and reserved. From her head to toes, she was always so covered and polished and she only offered so much in every conversation. Almost like she was detached somehow. But I knew she wasn't. Those eyes were always watching and assessing. Much like Ox's in that regard.

Turning back to the two younger girls, I shook my head. "I'm not trying to make Ox jealous."

"You should be."

I worried my lip with my teeth and looked at Ceci. "I don't want to cause him any trouble. He doesn't deserve that."

"What, and you do?" she asked challengingly.

"Ceci," I sighed and looked at her, exasperation and exhaustion cutting past my usual banter with her.

She made her way over to me and grabbed me by the wrist, yanking me along with her. "Fine, fine. But you are over his shit, right? We're his sisters, so we've never wanted to use this tactic before. But since you're his wife... *You* should! And since you would never think to do it yourself, we're here to teach you how you drive men crazy... And maybe have fun watching Ox lose a power struggle once and for all."

"So really this is for your own entertainment?" I asked the gremlin in front of me. Clay was right to call her a half pint.

"*Come on*, Ferguson," she whined as she continued to pull. "Let's go to our spot."

"Our spot" turned out to be the closed toilet seat in the bathroom. They sat me down there and surrounded me as if they were a team of scientists studying something brand new. Pulling out makeup pouches and brushes and glitter cream and some brand-new foundation options in a multitude of dark brown colors, they got to work on my face.

Alta and Ceci were the main players in this project, taking turns painting me however they liked. Melissa hung back in the background, but quietly commented when she thought something was "too much" or "pretty".

Soon, I was all made up. Shiny glitter coated my eyes and a full set of makeup covered my face. Ceci had forced me to strip, then proceeded to rub this shimmering gold glitter lotion all over my body. When she was done, I was like a dark, shining star. And I liked it.

They flat ironed my brown curls down until they were bone straight and hanging down my back in a strikingly long brush of thick, dark hair. They dressed me in a short silky white dress that had no back, was held together with strings that were thinner than shoelaces and was shorter than any dress I'd ever worn before. It had slits running up both sides of the garment, putting the fullness of my bare hips on display. I didn't have any underwear that would go with that shape so the girls convinced me not to wear any at all. I was then given the shortest heels any of them owned. Short little white kitten heels that laced up the leg from the ankle and ended mid-shin in a cute little bow.

When they were all done and I looked in the mirror, I could only say the first thing that came to my mind. "I look slutty."

This was awarded with whoops and hollers that made me laugh nervously, but happily. I was going out. I'd never gone out with girls before in my life. These girls were essentially my sisters and I was going out with them. And I actually looked the part. I didn't look like a married woman, the role I'd been playing since I was nearly twenty. I looked young and *normal*.

The girls got ready as I marveled at this new, foreign Clementine. Together we picked out their outfits and did their hair and makeup, and pretty soon we headed downstairs on our way out the door. Melissa hadn't dressed up, but apparently as the oldest sister she was obligated to be our ride. She seemed okay with it, so I didn't protest.

Apparently though, getting ready and just leaving wasn't enough. No, we had to pregame too. Or at least do a couple of shots.

Into the kitchen we went, and into the liquor cabinet, then the shot glasses and then down the hatch. I gulped down the two shots of vodka they deemed the *minimum* for a night out and watched wobbly as they took a few more. Ceci played songs from her phone as she danced around with her sisters and poked fun at them in a way I hadn't seen her before. Alta turned a deep blush the more she drank and Melissa truly seemed content watching on, a small but true smile clearly noticeable in her eyes.

It was when we had put our mess away, by guidance of the sober Melissa, and were heading toward the front door, that the man who'd inspired this night finally appeared.

I was trailing behind the three sisters as they practically bounced to the doorway ahead of me when a large hand wrapped around my elbow and spun me carefully. Ox's tall frame filled every part of my vision as he stood *right there*, looking down at me with a dark, *dark* expression on his face. I watched as he looked me over with a tight jaw and tighter lips. But his eyes… His eyes were molten orbs of anger and *something else*. Something that twisted my belly in a way that wasn't actually all that bad.

"Clementine," he said tightly.

"Oaxaca," I mimicked unwisely. His eyes had been on my body but upon hearing my response, they snapped up to me hard and fast.

"What are you *wearing*?" he asked but then started to shake his head, thinking better of it. "No, wait. What I meant to say was, where do you think you're going wearing this?"

Just like that, my nervous jitters from that molten look were stomped out by reality. I pulled my arm out of his grasp and stepped away from him. I was making to turn away but Ox stepped into my path, knowing my only strategy by now. Running.

"We're going out," I said.

Ox stared for a few seconds too long at the slits in the sides of my dress before he lifted his eyes up past me and to his sisters who were congregating by the front door. Watching with metaphorical popcorn in hand.

"Where?" he asked. His eyes came back to me but still not to my eyes, to my dress.

"To bars and clubs and stuff." I was faltering. I had never seen him look at my body so much. Maybe I *was* dressed a little too slutty.

His jaw tightened even more and then he said something I don't think I ever imagined him saying. Even though he was a control freak-hardass-stubborn mule, I still never thought he'd say it.

"No," he murmured on a single shake of his head. Then he found his voice and said more authoritatively. "Absolutely not."

I took a step back, inclining my head so I could see his face clearly.

So he could see mine and see that I was serious. "Ox, you can't tell me what to do."

"Clem, you're barely fucking dressed and you're really shiny, and you're *not* going out like this," he said.

"*I'm sorry*," I said incredulously. Crossing my arms, I felt my boobs press together and almost spill out of the front of the dress. Ox's eyes slid down to them briefly before returning to mine. "On your list of things you'd '*love*' for me to do, I thought you said—ahem—'*leaving the goddamn house*'. I didn't know there was a dress code attached."

Okay, that was pretty sassy. Maybe I *was* a bitch like Ceci said. And go bitchy Clem, because in front of me Ox sucked his lips into his mouth and set his hands on his hips as he just looked at me. Not saying anything else. After what seemed like the longest moment in history, he blew out a breath and cursed.

Touchy.

"Come here." He ordered. I looked around myself dramatically as if he couldn't possibly be speaking to me. This grated him and I felt slightly guilty. Ox spoke next with immense control, but a gravely tone. "*You*, Clementine. Over here, *now*."

I obeyed.

When I stood directly in front of him, he reached for me, one of those big hands landing on my hip. I swallowed my gasp, because the tips of his fingers landed just underneath one of the slits in the dress and made contact with the bare skin hiding there.

"Fucking naked," he growled underneath his breath as he bowed his head to take one more long look at my body. Turning me slightly one way and then the other, he surveyed me from all angles, before raising his eyes to mine and giving me a miserable look. His fingers tightened slightly so he was *gripping* my hip now. "Clem—"

"They're waiting for me, Ox," I said breathlessly, deciding that I couldn't take the feeling of his fingers touching me there. But I also couldn't pull away.

"Don't go," he said, but this time it was less of a demand and more of a pleading request.

"Why?"

"I'm sorry," he said.

I shook my head, my hair spilling over my shoulders. "You meant it."

"I *didn't*," he ground out. "Don't. Go."

"I'm going, Ox," I said. I watched him for a second and felt myself melt a little to him, allowing some truth to slip out. I whispered my next words, and despite my better judgment, some excitement snuck into my tone. "I've never been before."

"Fuck," he murmured, his head bowing and that hand gripping me even tighter. I had the good sense not to moan right then, but I could have. After a few seconds of him breathing steadily, he lifted his head and removed his hand from my body. I felt the loss for all of a second before he was leaning down and grabbing my left hand.

He lifted it between us as if he was searching for something. Then he used his other hand to finger the diamond wedding band sitting there, scooting it up higher on my finger and patting it, as if confirming all was where it belonged.

Taking a deep breath, he wrapped his hand around mine as he looked at me again. "Got your phone?"

"Yes."

"Is it charged?" he asked.

"Mhmm."

"Got money?"

"Yep."

"Your ID?"

"I have *everything*, Ox," I breathed.

"Okay," he said but didn't move away. He lingered there as he looked down at me. My face this time, not my exposed body. He worried his mouth to the side, a troubled look on his face. "And you'll be okay?"

Gingerly, I removed myself from his grasp. If he wasn't going to let me go, I would have to do it myself. Taking a step back, I straightened my dress and then found Ox's eyes. He looked tortured, and I fought the surprisingly wicked smile I felt from pulling free.

Served him right.

But still something nagged at the back of my mind. Something that felt a lot like being abandoned and forgotten when it conveniently suited his mood and being remembered only when I was irking his nerves.

"It's none of your concern anyway," I said. "I'm done being—how did you put it? Such. A. *Burden.*"

And I was.

That night we danced and drank and partied our little hearts out. We hopped around from club to club and we rode in ride share cars and ate bad late-night food to sober up and we got hit on by guys and encountered mean girls and kicked out of places and let into other VIP places. We did it all, and it was so fun. As fun as it could be with the lingering feeling that after this was over, I'd have to go back to a place where I wasn't wanted.

Exactly a week later, a week of ducking and dodging and avoiding hurt feelings, I was heading out of the house *again*.

I had to admit, I was overdoing it.

I was a homebody on a good day, but a certified hermit most of the time. Being out and about constantly was, in some ways, doing me a lot of good and breaking me out of my shell. Before, I had a bad habit of sleeping most of the day and only finding something to do when I was super bored. Now that I had a schedule and actual things to do, I was kicking that habit. But in another way, even after experiencing the outside world, I would still much rather do a lot of those things from the safety of my own house.

Operation *'prove to Ox that I wasn't a freeloading lazy-ass'* was still in full swing though, so this weekend I had planned something low key. I was meeting one of my new acquaintances from French bread making class for dinner, so we could get to know each other better. But having been sluggish most of the day from overextending myself, I was running a little behind. My head was pounding from not having eaten yet and Ox had been on my ass lately, insisting that we needed to "talk".

As if I conjured up the man himself, I was just getting into the garage that was attached to the side of the house (Ox had made room for my car as soon as he realized I had one) when the loud self-closing door shut a second time behind me and the deliberate clicks of Ox's dress shoes followed me across the large space.

I turned around maybe a fraction to glance quickly back at Ox before unlocking my car door and ushering my bag into the passenger side.

"Ox, I'm late. Can we talk later?" I asked, having no intention of talking later.

"Late for what?" he asked, that false sense of calm leaking off him in puddles. He was frustrated, I knew he was. I didn't think he'd ever heard the word "no" so many times before in his life.

"I'm meeting a new friend from class," I said.

"Which one?"

"The bread one."

"Which *friend?*" He clarified as he settled himself in front of me and crossed his arms over his chest as if he was the bouncer of the garage.

I turned my nose up but otherwise said nothing about his weirdness. "His name is Marco. He sits next to me in class."

Ox stiffened right before my eyes. I jangled my keys between us impatiently, not liking that on top of being late already, I was now adding on minutes as Ox and I bickered. One of his eyebrows lifted and he looked as if I was the most absurd thing he'd ever seen.

"*His name?*" he asked, incredulousness dripping from his tone.

"Yes."

"And the two of you are getting dinner?" His stare was *wild*.

"Yes, Ox," I breathed out exasperatedly.

"So, you're going on a date then," he concluded rather than asked.

I stepped back, looking up at Ox's stony face. Was he serious?

"*No*," I said.

"*Yes*," he said back.

"No! Ox, stop, you know I would never do that," I said again, turning away from him and going around the driver's side of the car. I got as far as opening the door an inch before a hand slapped down on the black frame above my head, slamming it shut. I jumped and turned around to glare up at him, only, I was suddenly pinned between Ox's body at my front and the car at my back.

He leaned into me—his arm beside my head, his body hovering close to mine as he caged me against the vehicle. My body tingled, zinging electricity through every port. He was so close, and he was getting closer as his gaze locked on mine and refused to let go. Up and down, he trailed his eyes over the contours of my face. I wish I knew what he saw in my expression to make him shake his head in frustration.

His voice barely contained his anger as he spoke quietly—near silent. We shared so much of the same space he didn't need to raise it. "I know *you* wouldn't. But Marcus-whoever-the-fuck would," he said.

"You're wrong," I said, but my gusto was faltering. *Was* he wrong?

"Is he single?"

"I don't know, he could have a girlfriend." I shrugged.

"No, Clem." He held up his left hand, that black titanium ring he wore on his ring finger contrasting starkly with this tan skin. He wiggled that same finger. "Does he have one of these?"

"No," I said, and suddenly I realized from this close up I could breathe in his scent. All male and clean and sandalwood and *Ox*. I missed it.

"Then he's single," Ox said. Pushing away from the car and from me, having made his point clear.

Clem and a single man having dinner equaled date. *Damn*. I felt a pull of disappointment as I realized that I hadn't really made a friend, just someone who wanted to get in my pants. Then I realized something else. "Does that mean I have to cancel?"

The *'you must be insane'* look must run in the family, because Ox was looking at me like I was growing feet from my head.

"Do you have to cancel your date with another man?" he asked, all sarcasm and smartassery. A beat passed with us simply blinking at each other.

My head was hurting even more, so I looked away first saying, "I feel bad."

Ox simply let out a ragged breath and ran a frustrated hand through his hair before he turned on his heel and left the room.

It was that same night that things finally started to break. The hour was way past midnight, and I was having an especially hard time falling asleep.

I fell asleep prematurely with a headache immediately after dinner. Ox had warmed up spiced salmon from Maria's weekly meals and tossed it over a mixed green salad, adding in feta cheese, couscous, pickled radishes and tiny tomatoes. I'd offered my help, but he refused, telling me to sit down and drink some water because I was looking sick.

Him taking charge and taking care of me, again, put me on edge. I didn't understand why he was being so nice. Not after he'd already told me his entire truth. I got on his nerves, I got in his way, and I was cramping his style. He basically told me so to my face with multiple witnesses, and to punctuate the point, he had left the *country* to get away from me.

So why the hell was he making me dinner and asking me not to go out to clubs and cleaning the empty garage space for me and knocking on my door every night even when I kept saying no? Why was he acting so contradictory to what he'd *told me* he was feeling? And why did it matter so damn much to me?

The thought had been on my mind all throughout dinner. After, when I cleaned the dishes and wandered over to the couch, I found myself conking out before nine, having exhausted my brain with all my contemplative thinking. So on top of not being able to sleep at midnight like normal, I wasn't even sleepy to begin with. By the time two and then three in the morning rolled around, I was exhausted once again but my body refused to give in.

I was walking into the kitchen for my third round of tea past the midnight hour when I heard the pad of soft footsteps following close behind me.

"Clem, no more tea, c'mon," Ox said from behind me. I didn't look back at him, only continued my movements to the sink to rinse out my cup. Once I set the newly washed cup onto the counter beside the sink, I felt a hand on my shoulder nudging me to turn around. I did, leaning my butt backwards against the island as I faced him. Ox looked me over his eyes examining every inch of my face. "Come to bed with me."

"Why?" I asked.

My voice had stopped sounding authoritative and strong, like it did when I first started boycotting his advances. Now it was soft and hurt and held an emotion I didn't know was there until I heard it for myself. Ox seemed to register it too, because those dark eyes focused in on my own and he reached forward, taking my earlobe between his fingers and smoothing his gentle thumb over it. I shivered.

"You look exhausted," he said, his voice soft.

I hadn't heard *that* voice in a while. Lately it had been all out war between us. Him trying to keep control and me trying to break it. So hearing him speak in his Clementine voice, the one that I suddenly realized I freaking loved, I almost was the one to break right then.

269

He saw this and his eyebrows knit together in confusion. "What's wrong?"

Swiftly, I turned my head and averted my eyes as a sudden rush of emotion hit me square in the chest. Seeing the empty island right across the way brought up emotions I had tamped down the moment I realized how it was going to be between us. I tried not to think about it, but the fact of the matter was, I had stood there for hours and hours making that damn custard for him and he had left.

He had left.

He had left and hadn't talked to me and had told Sylvie instead of me and had come back and expected everything to be just fine? Just like before? Not for me, not when the longer I went with this newfound knowledge of what he really thought of me, the bigger the hole he'd torn in my chest grew.

"Nothing's wrong," I croaked.

"Something is obviously wrong. Something *has been* wrong. You aren't acting like yourself," he said, scrubbing a hand down the front of his face. I fought a scoff at this, but I think some of it escaped me anyway. "Is it because I yelled at you back at the station? I'm sorry I did that, but will you *please* come up to bed with me. *My* bed. I hate not knowing how you're sleeping. And you've hardly told me anything about all these new things you're doing. You've hardly said anything to me at all since I've been back."

No, no, no. I did not want to feel these things, not right now. Not the wrenching widening of that hole smack in the middle of my chest. Not the tingling feeling of my skin and all the nerve endings within. Not the burning sensation of my cheeks along with the stinging sensation of my eyes. I didn't know what was happening to me, but whatever it was, it was like a full body takeover of Ox. Ox caring was my kryptonite.

I couldn't handle it. So I tried to escape it. Seriously. Without another word, I ripped free of Ox's soft touches and tried to rush out of the kitchen. Only, two hands made it to either side of my waist first, pulling me back and rooting me in place. I tried to step away but the hands gently pulled me back, and when I tried again they did the same thing. Tired of my fleeing, he turned me around and pressed me backward against the island. Setting me there and holding until he was confident I wouldn't try to leave again.

The harder it was to get away from him, the more intense the stinging in my eyes became. I was going to cry, and I didn't want to cry in front of him. Because then he would know my entire hand. He would have me figured out. But he wouldn't let me leave, and each minute spent close to him was a minute closer to my breaking point.

I wrapped my arms around myself protectively and refused to look up at him. He had placed his hands down on either side of the counter beside me and was using his arms as a cage. He was so close that he was intoxicating. His scent, his body, the pressure of that stare all weighing down on me and bringing me closer to snapping.

But it was him who fractured first.

"Clem, *please*, would you just talk to me for God's sake?" He pleaded. His eyes seethed but they also begged me.

I swallowed the ball in my throat again and again and again. Crossing my arms around myself tighter, I whimpered. "Why? You *left*."

"I had business," he said. It sounded like an apology coming off his tongue.

"You. Didn't. Call," I said through my teeth because if any more air hit my throat, my dam of tears would break.

"I was mad," he said, another apology in the form of normal words.

"I apologized," I offered, that dam wobbling a little.

"I was still mad." He admitted.

"I—" I broke off, the memory of dumping the plate of expired sweets in the trash hitting me. I took a ragged breath. "I made you something."

His eyebrows knit together and he slid his hands from the table behind me up the entire length of my back and onto my shoulders. He kneaded the flesh there softly for a moment. I closed my eyes and took a breath trying to steady my emotions, but my head was swimming as his large hands rubbed slow, hard circles into my muscles. When he saw I had gained some composure he let his hands just rest there. Waiting.

"Tell me." His expression was the one he held when he was earnest, when he was listening. He wanted to know about the dessert, which meant he hadn't seen it. The fact didn't hurt any less.

The hurt was already done, the knife dug in deep. Maybe that's why as soon as I opened my mouth to speak, I felt slow tears start to roll out the side of my eyes.

"I just made you a treat, that's all. As another apology." I flicked my now wet eyes at him, his expression looked pained. "I guess you didn't want it."

"What kind of treat?" he asked, his voice gravelly.

My face crumpled because I didn't want to talk to him. But at the same time I wanted to soak all of him up right there while I still could. Too much emotion was clogging inside of me, all because of this stupid little custard. So instead of saying it, knowing I would probably just sob through the words like an idiot, I reached down with my free hand and grabbed my phone. Opening it to my most recent picture, I turned it over and showed it to him.

I saw the recognition in his eyes as they slid all over the bright screen. First it was confusion, then realization, and then tenderness. I clicked the phone shut and put it away and he blinked his eyes up to mine again.

"How'd you know I liked that?" he asked, confirming that he did.

"I asked around."

"Did you make your own recipe?" I nodded, then ducked my chin to my chest as he continued to stare at me. "How long did it take you?"

I sniffed, holding back another rushing sting in my nasal cavity. "All night."

"Clem?"

"Yes?"

"Those three dishes you make—for your brothers. Are they all their favorites?" he asked.

I raised my eyes to his. Another slow tear slipped down the front of my face. He'd figured me out. He'd always had me figured out.

I simply nodded once.

"And you made this because you found out it was mine?" he asked, even though I knew he knew.

"Yeah, Ox," I breathed out wobbly.

I didn't expect him to suddenly jerk away, letting me go and cursing as he turned his back and paced the kitchen. When he reached me again, he stood in front of me, placing his hands on his hips and surveying me.

I was in my newest set of cozy pajamas, the fuzzy material of them probably making me seem immature. I wasn't outright sob crying, but my built-up tears were freely falling now and I knew I was pouting. I couldn't help it. And he was seeing all of it. And not saying a word.

Until slowly he closed the distance between us, his hands going to either side of my face as they wiped away my tears and said, "Please don't cry."

This made me cry harder, my chest aching as tears tumbled down my face. Pouring out all the emotions I'd been bottling up for weeks.

"No, no, no," he murmured sweetly as he wiped at my falling tears. "Don't do this to me, alright? I'm sorry."

But I kept crying. So he kept apologizing. His mouth spewing out streams of curses and atonements, sounding something like— *Goddammit, I'm sorry. I'm so sorry. Fuck, Clem, I'm really sorry*—And on top of that, there was a smile that was forming on the side of his mouth.

"Why are you laughing at me?" I hiccupped and whined, fresh tears coming to the surface.

He shook his head and looked at me again, his eyes skating over my face. His thumbs rubbing at my tears. "You're just so fucking sweet."

"*Too sweet.*"

"And I don't deserve you."

"And I'm sorry." He went on. "I mean it. *I'm so sorry.* I was just mad, and I say stupid things when I'm mad. I wanted to protect you. But I found out I was doing a shitty job of it and I took it out on you. It was all about me, it had nothing to do with you."

More tears rushed out as my heart squeezed in remembrance of what he said. *You want to know what you can do for me?* The memory shook me and I wheezed. "It *sounded* like it was about me."

"I know, and I'm sorry. I didn't mean it. I won't do that to you again. *Never* again. I fucking promise, okay?"

"It sounded like you hated me." I went on, Ox's touch apparently acting like my truth serum.

"I have never hated you, Clem. I have never not liked a single hair on your head. I'm sorry I'm such an ass." He soothed.

My breaths were coming out as hitching hiccups as I tried to both speak and collect myself. "You…said I was…a burden."

"I'm an idiot, Lunita. *I'm sorry.*"

He was swiping at tears over and over because they were flowing like waterfalls now. I tried to stop, but all my frustration and guilt and sorrow about the situation had built up so high that I was a broken dam now. My pieces were falling apart one by one.

Ox ducked slightly, bringing his face down level with mine and finding my eyes. We were nose to nose—I could feel his breath mingling with mine as he spoke. Whispered. "Stop it, baby. Stop crying."

I didn't. I couldn't.

The tears kept coming. I held them back for three weeks. First, when Ox had left and then when I had something to prove. But now he knew all of that bravado was just a super-glued front, I couldn't hold the illusion of being any stronger than I actually was around him. He just *broke* something in me. Something that I strangely wanted only him to fix with his words and his touches and his promises. Which scared me even more.

So, I just cried and cried. Letting it all out. Letting myself crumble in front of him. Letting every emotion I'd been feeling leave me in the form of water. I could have cried all night, I think. Or I *thought I* could.

That was until Ox leaned forward and pressed full pink lips to my tear-stained ones. And my nervous system shut down. My brain short-circuited. My entire body *melted*.

He was soft as he gently caressed me with that one slow, closed-lip kiss. It was jarring yet comforting all the same. He *was* comforting me, right? There's no way he'd kiss me otherwise. Not when we spent nights together, snuggling close to each other and seeing each other in various states of undress, and we *still* did nothing beyond an innocent touch sometimes.

Yeah, he was just comforting me. And I could deal with that.

Ox moved ever so slightly to wrap both his lips around my upper one, effectively drinking the tears that pooled there. Then he did the same thing to my bottom lip, sucking it into his mouth. Still so soft, assuring me that this was nothing but comfort. Then, to solidify the point, he pressed me with one more featherlight peck before he pulled away.

Setting back on his heels, he held me just an inch away, looking right at me as he licked his lips. Those lips that were just on mine and were now wet from the tears he had tasted. My sobs had definitely stopped, but my excitement hadn't. My heart tried to beat right out of my chest. I shook from the force of the emotions. I shook from the force of *him* and what he could do to me.

"Will you make me another one?" he asked, his voice a hoarse whisper.

I shook my head, sucking my tingling lips into my mouth and holding them there.

"Why not?"

"Not ready yet," I admitted.

"The recipe? Or you?" he asked.

It seemed like his question was much more than just asking me to bake for him again. It seemed like it was about him and me and everything between us. If I was ready to forgive him. If I was ready to confront the (not agreed upon in the contract) types of feelings that had been stirring within me for a while now. If I was ready to admit things I didn't even understand to the world outside of myself. Maybe I could have been before this whole scrap, but seeing how quickly this man could break me had also grounded me.

I had been broken before, and I promised myself that I would never let anyone break me again.

That's why, with total resignation, I looked Ox in the eyes as my answer fell from my mouth.

"Me."

Chapter Twenty

OX

God damn Clementine Fernandez. She was sweet, she was sexy, and she knew how to rub salt into a wound.

I hadn't meant to turn tail and leave the country directly after my first fight with Clem, but business was business, and I had some urgent things to take care of. But she was right. She, along with my sisters, and my mother, and my brother, and my dad, and even Sylvie.

I should have called her.

The truth of it was, I hadn't known what to say, especially not over the phone where I couldn't gauge her reactions or comfort her. If I had known I was going to be punished for *weeks* after returning, however, maybe I would have said fuck it and called her anyway.

The immediate silent treatment was hard enough to stomach. That, following the mini heart attack she'd given me when she left family dinner without telling me was my limit. Or so I thought. Until she started running away from me and out of the house wearing those tight workout sets and that fucking yoga mat.

There was nothing inherently enticing about a yoga mat, but imagining her on it, bending and stretching and grunting with effort... *Yeah.*

And then there was the dress. Or should I say the napkin of a thing she had let my sisters dress her up in to go gallivanting around town. I tried to stay out of the girls' way when I realized they had come over to cheer Clem up. But then they started drinking and on top of that, they started to leave.

I only went down to see if they were okay. What I actually saw was a practically naked Clementine sauntering toward the door in a dress that was so short and open in so many places, I saw more of her deep brown skin than I had in any of her old nightgowns.

Blood had rushed south so quickly, I had no fighting chance of hiding the erection. But I didn't need to, because the girl was on a mission to not only make me hard but piss me off too. I nearly chained her up to stop her from leaving the house like that.

But she had to go and jerk my emotions around again with her excited little voice and tipsy little eyes. She was a young girl who had never gone out with her friends before. Sure, she didn't need to be dressed only in a napkin when she was going to be rubbing up against so many people in a crowded area. So many *men*... But I already made her mad, I didn't want to make her sad too.

So I backed down and instead resulted to following the group around in my black car, waiting outside clubs and stalking them down the street like a literal kidnapper.

Great.

I thought maybe the Great War of Ox and Clem had finally settled down after I'd successfully talked her out of going on a literal date with another man and she instead had dinner with me. But when I came to her room again that night and she ignored me as usual, I thought I might finally combust.

I didn't, of course, but I couldn't sleep worth shit and I couldn't focus on any work either. Instead, I just lay awake in bed listening to the sounds of the house and the autumn wind outside and the occasional click of Clem's bedroom door when she went to and from the kitchen.

On her third trip to refill her tea at nearly four in the morning, I decided enough was enough. She obviously couldn't sleep either and if we just talked it out, we could get back to whatever we'd had before.

That's all I intended to do. Talk, apologize, mend. I hadn't meant to make her cry. I never wanted to see that utterly broken look on her face. But I realized I had hurt her more than just a little and, in more ways than one. I'd ignored her, overlooked her efforts, and made her sad. And she wouldn't stop crying.

Because of me.

Those tears broke my heart. She hadn't even cried when Abuelo died, but there I was, making her cry. And I had to make it stop.

Kissing her in that moment was the only thing I did mean to do. Okay, maybe that hadn't exactly been the plan, but at the moment it was all I could think to do to make her stop crying. No, it was all my body screamed at me to do. Nothing sexual, nothing rough. Just enough to mend her worries and stop her pain. To soothe and to apologize and to beg her to stop breaking my soul with those little droplets.

After I stopped her crying, I scooped her under my arm and brought her to my room. I tucked her into the spot that had been empty since all of this started. *Her* spot, and I made her tell me all about the things she'd been experiencing lately. I watched her closely as the minutes went by and she burrowed deeper and deeper into the warm sheets. The words slowing but not stopping, never stopping until the last possible second when sleep finally overtook her.

When she was out, I leaned down and placed a kiss on her hair, breathing deeply as my heart fucking exploded in my chest because all was right again. *All was fucking right.* And I didn't realize how wrong it had been until it was finally fixed.

And that's how I realized there was something wrong with me.

There had to be, because I wasn't okay, unless she was.

The day before Thanksgiving Day, we packed up our weekend bags and headed to my family's house for the holiday. Usually, I would be there at least a few days earlier to help around the house and prepare for the immense gathering my mother planned—doing whatever I could between video meetings and emails—to ease stress off of my mother's plate. Since the time when I was young, I had always been her little helper and even though I was older, it was kind of a hard knack to kick.

But this year I had Clem, and I didn't want to throw her in the deep end of our family functions too soon. While she had been okay on our family boat for Labor Day (*mostly okay*), I didn't think she was quite ready for the entire extended weekend of a Fernandez family holiday.

For that reason, we were arriving late (the day before) and she was leaving early (after an early dinner on Thanksgiving Day) to avoid the crazy Fernandez clan and their yearly traditions. Especially because there may be an air of sadness about the day this year with Abuelo being gone. A fact that could end up being a source of anxiety and conflicting emotions for Clem.

The Ferguson boys had arranged for Clem to be picked up after dinner on Thanksgiving Day. We usually had dinner pretty early and apparently the Ferguson dinners started late. So, upon suggestion of the boys, Clem was going to try to join them for a couple of days. She hasn't spoken to her parents or her extended family in years and everyone seemed to think that maybe she'd face less scrutiny and awkwardness if they broke the ice in a group setting.

I protested, naturally, because they were throwing her into a situation that seemed stressful and daunting for her and they were leaving out an important component. Me. I was to stay behind while Clem faced her family alone. I wasn't too keen on the plan, but the thought of her rekindling something with her long estranged parents even sounded productive to me.

According to Clay, Arturo and Marsha Ferguson had lightened up in the years following their daughter's departure from their lives and they were even starting to show signs of remorse now that she was resurfacing with some obvious issues. The guys seemed to think that maybe now would be a good chance to try with them.

We were letting her go. *"We"*—myself, my siblings, and the Fergusons—all agreed that it *could* be good for her. But we were also aware that it could backfire. I was surprised and warmed at the added concern from my own family on Clem's account. I guess it turned out that the continued family dinners at the Fernandez homestead had endeared Clem to all of us, not just my mom and me.

Before any of that scary stuff, there was still the day before the holiday. Which meant preparations. We rarely made everything ourselves. The various tíos and tías and primos and primas that came over for the dinner brought their fair share of dishes for the occasion. And we catered some traditional American foods too. But since we were hosting, we also made a good number of dishes to contribute.

On preparation day, Clem and I were just settling into my renovated childhood room before we braved the tornado that was sure to meet us downstairs. I had always been a pretty simple person. The same clean lines and zero personality that haunted my current room, plagued me in my teen years as well. Consequently, the room had stayed exactly the same as I'd aged. The only renovation in the large black space, with its high ceilings and floor to ceiling windows, was the upgraded bed. What was once a high schoolers full sized bed with blue sheets and a gray checkered comforter, had been replaced with a California king bed and all black adornments. The headboard had changed too. What once was a simple iron thing was now a brown padded tuft of a board. Upgraded to fit the new bed and my adult body for when I came home to visit.

If my parents were surprised when I told them there was no need to make Clem up a separate room, they didn't let on. And if they wondered what we had done to become comfortable enough to sleep in the same bed, when we were often not even caught on the same side of the room, they didn't ask that either.

"Ox?" Clem asked from the middle of the room. When we first came in, she'd gone straight for the dresser, diligently putting away her small pack of clothes so she didn't make a mess. She hadn't even noticed me behind her, fussing with the bed.

Now, I suppose she did.

"Ox, there's an orange box on the bed."

"Hmm?" I hummed, flipping the light off in the ensuite bathroom as I emerged. I leaned against the doorframe as I watched her. She spun, trying to find me by my voice and her long ponytail whipped around her in a wisp. She had been straightening it on occasion lately and every time it made me almost as crazy as it did when she wore the napkin dress.

When she met my eyes, she seemed to know the box was for her and I smiled in response to her happy, stunned expression. The first gift I'd given her had been in an orange box. The box of tea in her namesake. This was not tea.

"Open it," I instructed, not moving from my spot by the bathroom.

"It's too early for Christmas. What'd you get me?" she asked, that slight dash of worry creeping into her voice. She did that so often. Started to worry that she'd done something wrong when she'd done nothing at all.

"Relax. It isn't anything crazy. Just open it for me, will you?" I prayed my voice came out nicely. I knew I could get irritable when she showed her insecurities like that. I just hated that they still kept surfacing anew. I wasn't sure if it was all Abuelo's doing, but something had made her this way. Otherwise, she would just be the sweet, shy, smart, and sometimes hellfire girl I knew her to be when she wasn't being so inhibited. But most of the time she was weighed down by fear.

It was hard to watch.

"Okay," she said with a single nod, as if readying herself.

Instead of pulling the box off the bed and opening it in her hands, she pulled the bottom of her mid-length dress up so it wouldn't get caught under her knees as she crawled across the black comforter. I watched her movements as the slightest bit of dark-skinned thigh showed before fabric covered it again.

The fantasies that thigh sent racing through my mind were so wanton I had to force them deep, deep down to get a hold of myself.

Clem was unaware, though, as she looked down at the box and raised her slender hands to it. They hovered slightly, but she didn't touch it. Instead, she stared at it for a long time before lifting her gaze up to me and smiling the cutest little grin.

"It's tea box orange!" she whispered.

The grin was infectious, and I couldn't fight it as one spread along my face too. Leaning forward on my shoulder, I caught her eyes and whispered back, half sarcastic. "*I know!*"

Happy, too happy for a girl who had yet to pull so much as the goddamn ribbon, Clem slipped the satin bow off the top of the box and peeled up the top. When she looked inside, her brow furrowed and for a moment I thought this was a terrible idea. But then recognition hit her features and nothing short of pure surprised happiness overtook her face. She scooped up the orange and white fabric from inside of the box and held it out in front of her to see it better.

"Ox!" she exclaimed. "It's cute!"

She sprung from the middle of the bed and scampered off the side. I turned my head, not thinking I could handle any more intimate glimpses of her smooth skin. *Damn*, what had I turned into? But I didn't have too long to think about that, because Clem was twirling around with her new orange apron, trying to wrap it around herself and tie it while simultaneously looking in the floor length black mirror near the corner of the room.

Blowing out a breath, I shook my head and pushed off the wall. In a few long strides, I crossed the room and stood right behind her. Using one hand, I slipped the long frilly ties from her grip and with the other, I stilled her shoulders. Facing us both toward the mirror.

When she stopped fidgeting and looked at me in the glass, I saw we were standing directly in line with each other and our reflections. Me standing a head over her and quite a few inches wider on both sides. We locked eyes and I held her hazelnut orbs for a long moment before letting my own eyes travel down the length of her slight frame to the pretty half apron I had noticed about a week ago when I was gathering groceries for the holiday. I had been shopping with my mom and she had even said how perfect the little orange apron would be for her "Clementina". So, I bought it. Not surprisingly, it looked perfect.

Behind her, I began to tie the straps around her waist, pulling at them softly as if not to hurt her.

"Tight enough?" I asked.

"A little tighter," she said. I obeyed, pulling at the strands more until I heard her quick, "That's enough."

I worked quietly at wrapping the strands around each other to create a neat and pretty bow. When I was done, I touched my fingertips not to my handiwork, but to the sliver of bare back that showed in the small cutout of her otherwise modest black dress.

In front of me, she sucked in a breath and I boldly let those fingers rise, tracing the deep line down the center of her spine. She damn near shivered. I took way too much pleasure in seeing that kind of reaction from her. But I took it no further, instead flattening my hand and leaning down toward her. My chest coming close to her shoulders.

"Will you make another one now?" I asked. Her eyes drifted over to mine and she stared at me for a long while.

I had yet to uncover how hard she'd actually worked to make me my favorite dessert the first time, but I did understand that it was connected to her heart somehow. That day she baked for me, she had been offering me a piece of that heart and stupidly—*so stupidly*—I had ignored it. Now, I just wanted to get it back.

As she took in the planes of my face, her eyes skating from one of mine to the other, a soft smile touched her lips. Still, she said, "Not yet, Ox." She flicked her gaze down at the apron and up to me again. Another unsure look crossed her face. "Okay?"

I gave her shoulder a reassuring squeeze. "Okay."

I wasn't surprised or disappointed. Actually, I was elated to see the little smile she'd given me. It was the most positive reaction I'd gotten to date.

The first time I'd asked for a redo, I bought all the ingredients for flan and laid them out on the kitchen counter. When she saw everything, her face had screwed up and I wasn't even able to ask before she turned around and left the room without another word. *Brutal.* Fast forward a new mixing bowl set, a fancy electric whisk, and a water bath oven later and the apron in the "Tea Box Orange" wrapping was what finally got a positive reaction out of her.

I was okay with a "not yet" because it didn't mean "never", and I could wait. But my family on Thanksgiving could not. And, if she wasn't going to make *me* anything, she might put her skills to good use for others. She had already agreed to make desserts for the dinner, her and my mom working out a schedule for kitchen time.

"However…" I started again, standing up straighter behind her and bringing her attention back to the mirror. "I thought maybe you could test this out this weekend. Put it to good use?"

Our eyes met again. She was looking at me with one of her old intense gazes. Like she was trying to figure out every cell that made up my brain.

She shook her head, her eyes fluttering downward to look at her feet. In the mirror, I watched as she toyed with the hem of her new apron. "Ox, I still can't promise you a do over. I don't think you can try it—"

"Hey," I said. Stopping her, because I knew exactly where her head was at. I couldn't touch anything made by her without her approval first. If she said she wasn't ready, she wasn't ready. I respected that even though it was just dessert, it meant something to her. I wouldn't ram through her emotions like that.

Reaching around her, I knocked a knuckle under her chin and raised her head parallel to the mirror so she could look at me there. My eyes were already waiting for hers. "*I know.* I won't take a single bite unless you tell me to, okay?"

"Okay," she said, her voice sounding husky as I ran a hand up and down her shoulder.

She breathed a ragged, shallow breath and I gazed down at her not mirror form in front of me. Her neck came into view. With her hair up and away from it like that, I could see the way it dipped and curved. Up to her hairline, around her ear, down to her shoulder. I bent a little and laid my chin on that shoulder, my hand leaving her face and falling to her other arm. She let out another little gasp and our eyes clashed in our reflection.

The way she was looking at me brought that feeling of wanton lust back with a force. I leaned in slightly, my nose angling toward the crook of her neck, my lips hovering just over her skin. "But maybe I can just lick—"

"Ox!" she yelped, looking scandalized. I let out a laugh that I felt in my fucking chest.

This girl. This fucking girl. The one who could walk outside in a dress that left less to the imagination than underwear, or could tell the cops with a straight face that she was on a sex schedule with her husband and had just married his grandson a few days after he died, but got squeamish at the mere mention of my touch. She baffled me. She excited me. She was becoming a part of my heart. And so, she scared me.

"I'm teasing, Clem," I said. She turned swiftly, breaking the cage of my embrace which left my hands to fall to her biceps as she faced me. I circled the muscles loosely to keep her close, rubbing my thumbs along the soft skin of her inner arm. She shivered again and I watched every minuscule movement. "Only teasing."

Looking up to me with her chin inclined to my face, she scowled playfully. "You tease too much."

"Not many people would agree."

"Not many people know you, then."

I raised my eyebrows. "And you do?"

"I know enough," she said and there was this look on her face that told me she was confident about this. Usually so shy and timid, this was something she didn't shrink away from. *Knowing* me.

"I ask you questions every night about yourself, and you never ask me anything back. But you think you know me?"

"I ask you stuff," she protested.

"You don't. You grumble and groan and fight sleep like a child." I smiled wider when she scrunched her nose at me. Leaning forward, I lowered my voice to a mocking whisper. "And you drool."

"Oaxaca!" She shoved playfully and I let her go with a chuckle. She flitted over to my bed and plopped down easily. "Sorry, not all of us can sleep like a corpse."

This made me snort, partly because it was true. But I'd never admit that. I followed her to the bed and sat behind her a good distance away on the opposite side. She may be more comfortable with me now, but she was still Clem. Jumpy and reserved. I'd give her space. Laying down flat on my back, I let my arms stretch high over my head.

She looked over her shoulder at me, and I caught her eyeing my torso before her eyes trailed up to my own. "No work?"

"Not yet. Maybe later, after I help my mom," I answered.

She nodded, her face thoughtful. Then she turned her head forward again, giving me a view of the back of her neck and her long swaying ponytail.

"Oaxaca Fernandez works every second of every day...*unless* his family needs him. Which tells me, he works so hard *because* of his family," she said aloud but to no one in particular. Then she flicked a glance over her shoulder again and smiled at whatever expression was on my face. "It's called *an observation*, Ox. Not everyone has the guts to just bulldoze answers out of people, so the rest of us humans have to get to know each other the regular way."

Scoffing, I rolled my eyes to the ceiling. "I do *not* bulldoze."

"You do. You bulldoze through *everything* you do. Clay Ferguson cannot even rival you in your directness," she said, laughing.

"Clay? Come on, I'm nothing like him." I countered, rolling onto my side and propping my head on my hand.

"You're not," she agreed. "But you're a little like me. I can tell you like him."

I scrunched my face in a way that she normally would. "No offense, but your brother is mean."

"No offense, but your *sister* is mean." She countered and as she did, we caught each other's eyes and both broke into slow, knowing smiles.

Laughing softly, she laid back too, her legs still dangling off the side of the bed, her head perpendicular to my chest. That ponytail swung back toward my stomach and I had no intention of moving the soft hair that landed there. I sort of liked when her things tangled with mine.

"Remember at the wedding, the way they kept looking at each other?" I asked.

She snorted. "*Glaring* at each other."

"Right." I laughed too. "I don't think they've acknowledged each other since."

"When they do, it's World War Three. I bet anything," she said.

"Oh, a gambler *and* a psychic? Aren't I a lucky man?" I hitched an eyebrow up. "Does that *observation* get me any points?"

She laughed, her face stretching wide in one of my favorite expressions of hers. Joy and contentment. "Smartass."

I was going to comment on how I didn't think I'd ever heard her say the word ass before, but as I opened my mouth to speak, a loud banging came from the other side of my door. I winced and grabbed a dark pillow to cover my face. "We've spoken the devil into existence."

"Who? Clay or Ceci?" she asked as she sprung up and did her graceful flitting thing to the door. Almost as soon as she swung it open, I heard my little sister's voice fill the space.

"Did I hear Ferguson talking about ass again?" Ceci said from the doorway. I heard Clem laugh sweetly and peeked at them from under my pillow shield. Ceci was peeking around Clem slightly and there was something about the look in her eye that had me rising to my feet to avoid any body slamming ideas before they were formed.

Being the oldest meant being the resident punching bag everyone tried to best. I thought it would get old the closer I got to thirty, but it seemed I thought wrong.

"Ceci, her name may start with the same letter, but I believe you meant to say *Fernandez*. Come on, it's the same as yours, even you can remember it," I said as I straightened out my slightly ruffled clothing.

"Right," she said in a long, drawn-out way as she eyed me strangely. "Mom wants you downstairs so you guys can get started on the sides."

Then she whipped her head back to Clem with an excited look in her eye. "Ferguson, can we do something fun?"

Clem chuckled and shook her head looking at Ceci with amused eyes. "Like what?"

"I don't know. You choose, you think of the best stuff." She shrugged but she was almost bouncing on her feet with excitement.

Clem seemed to notice this too and threw a look back at me that conveyed surprise and amusement. I bit back my smile.

"Celestia, I'm going to be helping with dinner. If you want to join, be our guest. If not, stay out of the way." Clem spoke with a familiarity that I had only heard her use with her brothers and recently with me. It warmed me to see.

Ceci screwed her face up, probably at the use of her full name, and crossed her arms over her chest. "Geez, Mom. You're no fun when you're with Dad."

"Ha!" Clem scoffed. "And you're even more of a brat when you know your brother is here to do everything for you. I'm actually glad you're here, I need a *little half pint helper* in the kitchen. Come on, show me where everything is and I'll show you how to make a pie."

Ceci still grumbled a little but surprisingly said, "I guess that could be kind of fun."

"It will be," Clem said and before another word could be spoken, she stepped forward and grabbed Ceci by the shoulders and started steering her toward the door.

She left me with a final look and a smile as she whispered, "Bye."

"Bye, Clem," I said softly as I watched her go.

The rest of the day passed in a weird series of familiar and unfamiliar events.

Familiar being that I had a list of side dishes I helped my mom prep and administer so they could be ready to serve for tomorrow's meal. Familiar was me sitting in the kitchen as Amá loaded the table up for me with ingredients and utensils while talking to me about anything and everything moms talked to their grown sons about (so, marriage and babies for the most part).

What was unfamiliar, however, was the sudden appearance of my brother and sisters in the kitchen, twirling their thumbs and asking what they could help with. Usually, they hung out and watched a movie together or played games or just scrolled through their phones, me only joining them when I was finished with Amá for the night. But curiously they all entered the kitchen and sat around the table with me, rolling up the sleeves of their sweaters and asking, "What can we do?"

Amá and I shared a stunned look before she jumped into action, bossing her children around like only she knew how. Ceci and Clem remained unseen. They were using the basement kitchenette to make desserts, but we could occasionally hear the bump of music or the padding of footsteps or even the clatter of something falling below us. Every so often Clem would float into the kitchen say something to Amá in her the soft slow voice she used when she spoke Spanish and leave with either more pans, or ingredients, or cleaning supplies.

At one point, she had left with both the vacuum and a mop. When she was out of sight, we all exchanged incredulous looks.

"What are they doing down there?" Melissa asked, her most telling trait slipping into her voice. She felt like she was missing out on something and she wanted to be a part of it. This made me laugh, because I truly believed the last thing tame, reserved, Melissa wanted to do was be a part of whatever weird bond was between Clem and Ceci.

"It sounds like fun," Alta said in a pouty Alta-like voice. She was pressing peppers into a bowl to make concentrated chili sauce. I reminded her for the millionth time not to touch her eyes as she was raising her hands to do just that.

"It sounds like a mess," I said with a shake of my head. But I also sort of wondered what they could possibly be doing down there. The last time they'd been alone in a kitchen they had gotten drunk and possibly into a fight. I doubted the fact that it was the holidays made this much different.

"You seem pretty chill about it," Mátti said, his hands working on slicing jalapeños, onions, tomatoes, and cilantro.

"Why wouldn't I be?" I asked.

They all just looked at me. I stilled my hands that were mixing a large bowl of ground meat with spices before they could go to Amá at the stove. "What?"

"Ox, you aren't chill about *anything*. Don't tell me your wife is making you soft." Mátti laughed. Something seemed to light up in his brain and he opened his mouth to correct himself.

I cut him off before he could say what I thought he would. "Sisters, Mateo. *Right here.*"

He grinned.

"Oh *please,*" Melissa said with an eye roll.

"What?" Alta piped up, not getting it. When none of us answered, it just made her want to know even more. "What? Guys, come on."

This brought on a laugh between the three of us which brought on a warm feeling throughout my chest. It was nice having these guys helping, even if I suspected they were guilted into it by a certain baker and her minion. It was nice to be around them with no other pretense than quality time.

Later, we got the idea of sneaking downstairs after hearing a loud clanging noise that jolted everyone. Even my dad had wandered into the kitchen and asked where the fire was. After we confirmed that there was no fire, we sent Alta in as a distraction while Mátti and I stole the pies that had already been made. Melissa ran them up and down the stairs, taking them to the main kitchen to hide.

We were almost undiscovered, until Mátti made a particularly hard step and Clem spotted him. Melissa and I promptly threw him under the bus and watched from the sidelines as Clem and Ceci chased him down and shook him for information on the whereabouts of their pie.

After Ceci, the enforcer, got Clem her pies back (by physically attacking Mateo until he confessed they were safe and sound upstairs), we made our way back to the kitchen to finish up our jobs before nighttime rolled around.

By nine, I dismissed my tired little brother and sisters, thanking them for the help and having to promise that Clem wouldn't be mad at them for bailing early. I told my mom to head upstairs too, sending her with some tea and the assurance that I would get everything put away for the night so she could go rest.

Not too long after, as I was wiping down the countertops, Mateo came in.

"Hey," he said hesitantly.

I looked up at the sound of his voice. "What's wrong?"

"Nothing," he said slowly. Cautiously. It was definitely something. Swiping the last of the dirt away, I folded the towel and placed it on the kitchen sink before turning toward my brother and leaning a hip against the cabinets. "It's just… She's asleep on the couch in there."

"Sleeping?" I asked, surprised. I looked down but remembered I took my watch off before the cooking started. "What time is it?"

"About ten." Ten? *Wow*. She must really be exhausted. Mátti scratched at the top of his head and looked at me awkwardly. "Hey, I know we were teasing you and everything but… If you want, the girls can just grab her—"

"No," I said quickly, moving off the counter and starting toward the living room. "I'll get her."

The living room was a room over, separated by a large wall of books and plants and picture frames. As soon as I entered the dimly lit room, I noticed her dark figure huddled to the side of the gray couch. It looked like she had fallen asleep sitting down, her socked feet still planted on the ground but her torso leaned to the right, smashed against the back couch cushion.

In front of the couch, a movie played on a low volume and my siblings littered around the room in different chairs or floor spots they had claimed since childhood. When they saw me in the doorway, they all seemed to look to Clem and then away, as if they were witnessing something they weren't supposed to.

I only looked at her, though. Sleeping before midnight always resulted in her staying up longer after she ultimately awoke. I didn't have the heart to get her up. She had worked her little heart out, and who knows, maybe it would be the day she actually fought that frantic call to be awake when the clock struck twelve. So right then, I just went to her.

Scooping an arm under her shoulders and another under her legs, I rose easily with her weight. When she wrapped her slender arms around my neck and brought her nose to my throat, nuzzling it, I chuckled.

"Ox?" she asked.

"You've reached Oxtopus," I said, my voice nothing louder than a soft murmur as I started to walk out of the room and toward the stairs. To my brother I flicked a quick glance at him and mouthed, "*thank you*". To me he mouthed, "*whipped*" and solidified it with a whipping motion. I shook my head.

"How many hands do you have today?" she asked. So tired. So cute.

"Not hands, Clementine. *Tentacles.*" I punctuated this with a hiss as she pinched the back of my neck. I laughed some more. She obviously wasn't *that* asleep.

"How many?" she asked again.

I breathed her in. The sweet and salty smell of her work in the kitchen and that lingering smell of honey that always accompanied her stirring up my senses. Letting out a short, contented sigh, I turned my head to nuzzle her hair—just a bit—and said, "Right now, just two. Both for you."

On Thanksgiving Day, I had every intention of doing what I always did. I usually woke up early to head downstairs and help mom with setting everything to cooking. But when I awoke this time, Clem was already out of bed, even though she hadn't gotten back to sleep until two in the morning after her little nap.

Thinking maybe she wanted to get a head start on topping off her desserts, I headed down as normal. When I arrived in the kitchen, I found Clementine dressed in dark jeans and a wine-colored sweater, her hair still straightened but braided back and her apron tied firmly around her waist. She was leaning down and pulling some non-dessert-like thing out of the oven while my mom directed her in Spanish. When she set the hot pan down on a potsticker, her attention grabbed onto me. And she smiled.

"What's all this?" I asked, edging into the kitchen.

"Aye!" My mom exclaimed and snapped her dish towel at my feet forcing me to step back. "Oaxaca! You are banned from the kitchen. Clementina will bring you breakfast when it's ready. Until then, go do something else."

"But Amá, don't you need help?" I asked, confused. I always helped.

"Mijo, your wife is taking your place today. Back, back. Go get some rest," she said, her voice airy. But as she turned to me, she gave me a look that said *'would you look at that'* as she gestured her head to Clementine who hadn't given me more than that one initial glance. She was too busy transferring prepped food into baking dishes.

As if sensing me, Clem whipped around to find me standing there watching her. When she saw me staring, she rushed forward and laid her hands on my shoulders and pushed. "Out of here, Ox. It's a holiday, remember? I only want to see two hands today."

"Tentacles."

"Keep talking and you'll only have one." She threatened and I laughed.

"What happened to my other seven?" I asked.

"Me," she said with a swift nod. She kicked me fully out of the kitchen and was blocking the path back in. "You deal with that one, and I'll take care of everything else."

"Everything?" I asked

"Everything."

And she did. In the morning she helped mom with cooking off the longer recipes and double checking that any catered food that was ordered was here or on its way.

Around lunch time, when I'd come around to check on her, she promptly turned me around and told me to find my dad in the living room and watch the game with him. She then appeared in the living room with two beers and a bottle opener, handing them off to me and Apá before opening both. Satisfied, she collected the hiding Mátti and left the room again.

Just before it was time we started getting ready for guests to arrive, I found her flitting around the dining room table, setting out mats and straightening chairs. She was buzzing as she moved around making sure everything was perfect. And she hadn't missed a single thing, expertly handling everything I usually did and more. Just like she said she would.

I know the whole point of it was to get me to relax, but the whole day I found myself trying to sneak peeks of her as she worked throughout the house. When so many hours passed and even Amá had handed the rest of the work off to the event staff who'd arrived in the middle of the day, I finally decided it was time to throw my weight around. All one tentacle of it.

She was making her way around the dining room, tweaking at different details on the table when I came up behind her and planted both hands on her waist.

"Ox! What are you doing?"

"Time to get ready, Lunita," I said, steering her away from the table and toward the doorway that led to the stairs.

"Already?" she asked, looking back at the table with worry on her face.

I leaned down and touched my nose to her nose. "Yes, already. Don't worry about the table anymore. It's perfect."

It must have slipped my mind that this was the first time the rest of my extended family was really meeting Clementine. Since the issuing of Abuelo's will, what transpired between me and Clem in result had become common knowledge. However, since Abuelo had basically kept Clementine locked away the entire duration of their marriage, the family had almost completely forgotten about her.

Seeing her caused a sort of swarming situation as my family started to arrive for dinner. One by one they began to realize the infamous young girl who had snared not only one, but *two* Fernandez men was at present and they all came right up to her from all directions in greeting. Asking questions, complimenting her, and *touching* her. Something I knew she didn't love.

It got so bad, that at one point I had to physically block Clem with an outstretched arm from the grabby hands of my Tío Ricardo who dove in for a hug. I'd never seen that man hug anyone with a Y chromosome; no way in hell he was laying a finger on Clementine.

Dinner, which had been completed by Clem and Amá hours before, was brought in by service staff, but they mostly hung back for the meal. The long table was set with elegant place settings and ample dinner utensils. We passed green beans and mashed potatoes along the line of bodies just like in movies and when the older relatives complained about not having enough native plates, we brought out the Mexican cuisine Amá had made as back up. It was a perfect occasion, gone off without a hitch.

Until dessert.

After the meal was finished and cleaned off the table, Clem disappeared to get her desserts while the staff got accompanying drinks. I was just standing up to follow and offer my help when the rush of voices vying for attention aimed themselves right at me.

"Oaxaca, how's it going Mijo?" Tío Ricardo asked.

"Oaxaca, I'm so sorry. I heard about Ronaldo's will and couldn't believe it!" This was Tía Diana.

"How have you been, Mijo?" Tío Monte inserted from way too far down the table to speak quietly. He leaned forward over the table and lowered his voice to a whisper that wasn't really all that low. "How is she?"

I had frozen midway to listen as I was rising out of my seat. But when the questions kept rolling in, I sighed heavily and lowered myself back down, smoothing my sweater flat to my chest as I sat. Even though they annoyed me, the majority of the people in the room were older than I was—and as bossy as I was, disrespectful I was not. So, I sat there and listened to my family's questions and apologies and curious inquiries. I gritted my teeth when they asked something a little too personal, like if we were trying to get pregnant or not. I smiled when my tías said things like, "Oaxaca she's gorgeous! Has she always looked like that?" But at the same time I found myself getting irritated when my tíos said things like, "Ox, she's a good looking one isn't she?"

They were terribly invasive questions, but questions from older relatives always tended to feel like that. I answered them appropriately and tried to lead the conversation away from Clem as much as possible. Of course, they were having none of it and continued to hound me with question after question. I threw looks of desperation around the table at my brother and sisters, but they all seemed to have disappeared or were suddenly quite interested in the shape of their drink glasses, leaving me out to dry. But even with the uncomfortable questioning, I should have known this dinner was going too well. I should have been prepared for the cut of Manny's voice through the throng of interested voices.

"Damn." Manny whistled from the far end of the table. Glancing down the length of it, I saw him lean back in his chair, a stemless glass of red wine in his hand. "Ox, you sure have a talent for getting your dick sucked everywhere you go. It's no wonder Abuelo left her to you."

"Yeah? Why is that, Manny?" I asked, setting my own glass on the table and leaning forward to hear his dumbass answer, whatever it was going to be.

He leaned forward, catching my eye and saying so much with that one look. I seethed, and an ugly smile spread across his face as he picked up on it. He made a wide 'O' shape with his mouth, his tongue moving in inappropriate motions that had me halfway to kicking his ass, but said. "*Obviously,* to keep you relaxed. What else, Ox?"

I'd already had enough of him, but it wasn't me who retaliated first. It was Ceci, who had been helping Clem gather the desserts from the kitchen to bring to the table. As she walked past Manny's seat, she kicked the leg of the chair, causing him to jerk and some of his wine to slosh just over the rim of his cup and into his lap.

To him she said, "Shut the fuck up, Manny. I don't even know what you're talking about and I know it's annoying."

To me she gave a hard glare, which honestly could have meant anything coming from Ceci, but I determined it as, *'if he's bothering you, let me know'*. I could have laughed at this, because I didn't doubt she'd put him promptly in his place. But I didn't laugh, because I had this sinking feeling Manny wasn't done yet, and Clementine would be coming back at any second. She didn't need to be hearing this.

As if on cue, she materialized to the right of me, balancing three pies between two hands. I jumped up to help her, but two of my tías beat me to it. I thought maybe she was done, but after she set down the apple pie, pumpkin pie and classic cheesecake, she turned and sauntered right back out of the room to go grab something else. I watched her pretty dress—that was green plaid and reached down to her calves—flow behind her as she left. That hair back to being the bouncy curls it usually was.

Almost as soon as she left the room, *another* annoying whistle came from Manny's side of the table. I'm not the only one who groaned at the mere sound of his breath. But for some reason we kept letting him speak. Mistake number two. Mistake number one was that he'd ever been born.

"Okay, okay. I take it back, Ox!" he started with a stupid, maybe even intoxicated smile on his face. "*Now* I see why he left her to you. Pretty little thing and she knows what a wife is for. Girls these days think they're supposed to be waited on, but they got it backwards."

I leaned back further into my chair, because if I didn't, I would be out of it and punching him. He was getting on my nerves, and from the other grumbles around the table, I wasn't the only one. I flicked a gaze at Mátti and then at Melissa, the only two of my siblings not helping Clem or Amá in the kitchen. They both wore stone faces of irritation as they stared straight ahead, probably fighting not to say something to our idiot cousin. My eyes caught on Clem who was entering the room once again. She flicked her eyes around the tension filled table and ducked her head as she set something down and quickly exited again. Dammit, she knew.

The third whistle was enough damn whistling. I turned abruptly in my seat and faced Manny before he could speak whatever foul thing that was bound to escape him this time. When I looked at him, I was caught off guard by the way he was looking at Clem—at *my* Clem. His eyes were glued to her back and were bouncing around every part of her like she was a piece of the pie she was laying out on the table. There was something in that gaze that I *really* did not like. Something lustrous and glutenous and wrong.

This got my jaw to hardening and my eyelid to twitching.

"What the hell do you think you're looking at, Manny?" I asked, deceptively calm. I was not calm. My insides felt like fire and my instincts wanted to rage. But this was a family dinner and I tried to hold it together for that sake.

I tried.

Manny stared at Clem until she completely left his line of sight and then he brought his slow appraising eyes over to me, a smirk on his face the whole time. "She's not hiding anything under that dress, man. *Damn.* Think you can share the family pet with the rest of—"

The chair Ceci had kicked earlier, I swiped completely, sending Manny flying backward in a tumble. He hit the ground in a hard crash, an actual yelp leaving him as he did. I imagined the hard wooden back of the chair hurt him as he landed unforgivingly on top of it. I didn't care. The only mercy was that he was no longer holding his glass of deep red wine. A shame, really. I would have loved to see him choke on it.

Bending swiftly, I grabbed him by the collar and the shoulder and hoisted his meaty frame up. He wriggled in my grasp, but I had him by the scruff of the neck. He had been halfway to drunk already, so it was easier than it normally would be to bully him around.

I brought him up to his full height, which was about four inches shorter than mine. So I brought him up the rest of the way, causing him to stretch hard on his tiptoes and choke a little.

"Manuel," I started, that calm still in my voice even though I was clearly anything but. "If you continue to talk about *my wife* like she's some kind of family heirloom, I'm going to beat the *shit* out of you."

He bucked at me, but I strained my arms to jerk him back into place.

"*And*, if you continue to put your beady little eyes on *any* part of her—especially parts of her you're not supposed to be looking at—I'll shut down your whole goddamn division, drain every cent of inheritance your ungrateful ass has ever received and *then*, I'll beat the shit out of you."

I gripped his collar tighter, my muscles screaming at me to deliver on my promises, but the hushed sound of my brother's voice whispering my name from close behind me brought me out of it. I let my cousin go with a hard shove and he shook me off like I was some sort of virus, swiping at his clothing to straighten himself out. When he looked up at me again, his red face said nothing but pure outrage. Not to mention the entitlement and arrogance that was always settled there.

Wiping his mouth, he laughed a bitter laugh. "Didn't think you brawled, man. Leave it to a *bitch* to knock strait-laced Ox off his high horse."

Yeah, I was going to kill him.

I had every intention of doing just that, my legs and my fists springing themselves into action, but two firm hands planted themselves on my chest before I could cross that threshold. My dad and my brother stood on either side of me, holding me back and reminding me this was a family affair.

Right.

If I wanted to kick his ass, I'd have to do it somewhere else. Still, once Mátti and Apá were sure I wasn't going to punch anyone out, they both moved for my cousin. My dad smacked Manny on the back of the head so hard his chin hit his chest and my brother grabbed his arm and yanked him toward the door.

"Get the hell out of here. Next time we won't hold him back you little piece of shit," Mateo said.

"Pinche cabrón," my dad muttered underneath his breath as he watched them go. When they disappeared past the foyer, he cut a glance to me. I cut a glance right back, *daring* him to reprimand me for my actions. I didn't care. If it had to do with Clem, I'd do it again. But instead of scolding, he gave me a curt nod before bending to pick up the fallen chair and returning to his seat.

When I spun around to return to mine, I caught sight of Clementine standing in the doorway to the dining room, staring at me. I couldn't place the exact expression on her face, but I could have sworn there was disapproval in that look. I narrowed my eyes at it, because even though disappointing her made me feel bad, I would never *ever* not stand up for her.

Not a chance.

Chapter Twenty-one

CLEMENTINE

For the most part, Thanksgiving went off without a hitch. The Fernandez Thanksgiving that is. From the time we'd walked through the doors of the large homestead on Wednesday, I'd had a good time. Ox was in a good mood, Ceci agreed to help me out with baking, and it seemed as if the rest of the family had finally warmed up to me being around. Even Ox's Dad, who for the most part can never look me in the eye or speak in direct sentences to me, offered for me to sit down and have a beer with him as he sat in front of the TV. I had been deep into preparation mode by then and politely declined, but the offer was still quite nice.

Guests started to arrive and realize I was present. When they put together who I was exactly, they either peppered me with questions or gave me strange looks. But people always did that, I was used to it. Besides, with Ox standing at my side scowling at everyone who dared look at me twice, I hardly noticed many of the curious glances. It was comforting to have someone there who I knew would stand up for me. I had always had that in my brothers of course, but they had their own lives, their sole purpose wasn't to protect Tiney and her delicate sensibilities. But with his family, Ox acted like it was his. He guarded me like a bodyguard, fielding questions he didn't like and turning away advances he found inappropriate.

Yes, I'm talking about Tío Ricardo.

But in the end, I was okay. Because Ox made sure of it.

I wish I had been able to do the same for him when his cousin started picking on him. I'm not sure what exactly had been said, I was so busy trying to impress all his relatives with the one thing I was sort of good at to hear, but I know Ox was madder than I'd ever seen him before. Maybe even more so than at the police station. Or maybe just in a different way. The way he was on his cousin, in his face, threatening him; it was so un-Ox like and I wasn't sure I liked him that way.

Not that I saw him differently because of it, I just...I didn't want him to have to fight like that. And I wondered what could have been said to bring him to that point.

I tried not to sour after seeing him so angry, but my mood definitely shifted as I began to worry.

What if it was about me? What if when I left the room they were discussing what to do with me after the three-year contract was up? What if they were trying to get rid of me sooner? What if I had offended someone and left Ox to clean up the mess?

My worries overtook my thoughts, so much so that when my brothers showed up at the front door ready to take me away, I was relieved. So relieved that I barely said bye to Ox and his family as I shot out of the door.

Being tucked away inside of a car with my brothers felt good... For all of three seconds. Then I realized where I was going. What I was doing. *Who* I was going to see.

My anxiety came back tenfold.

My head pounded the entire way to the other side of the sea. While the Fernandez's occupied the south of Seaside, my family resided up north. This only accounted for about an hour of distance, but it seemed as if it were totally different places.

Everything along the sea had a less businesslike atmosphere than the city did, but the separation from the north and the south were almost disassociated completely. While southern Seasiders wore t-shirts and strolled to lazy coffee huts and watched the sunset with their toes in the sand of their private expensive beaches, northern Seasiders were busy getting their tennis outfits tailored and taking organized tea and having dinner parties... On their private expensive beaches.

All of us kids lived somewhere in the middle where in some areas you could find a lot of the tourist beaches and in other areas (like ours) you could find the private Seaside manors or beach adjacent luxury apartments. It was also much closer to the city than the northern and southern houses and better for the working heirs to access their offices easily. If I had to choose a direction, I much preferred the lazy south to my family's uptight ways in the north.

I hadn't been back up north in five years. Granted, I hadn't been much of anywhere in the last five years, so it wasn't like I was really avoiding it. Still, I wasn't totally sure I even wanted to go back now.

It was the boys' idea to invite me home for Thanksgiving. They were still tightly ingrained in my family's web, not having the same history with our parents as I did. It hurt them to see me floating on the outskirts of a life that wasn't mine anymore but was still very much theirs. They proposed I try to work it out with my parents and start trying to build a relationship again. After all they continued to do for me, I could try this for them. I could try.

And try is exactly what I did. For exactly one hour and ten minutes.

When I first walked into my childhood home, I tried not to cry. Taking in the soft grays and blues of the shingled style house. Mom's hydrangeas, overgrown and blue (her favorite color) were still hanging in there even though the season was long over. The natural openness inside struck me because I never realized how much it resembled Ox's home. Light wooden floors, cream and beige furniture, soft natural wall colors and gold fixtures everywhere. The only truly noticeable difference being my mother's taste for large gaudy wall accessories and planting urns. And the sheer amount of space the mansion occupied.

I'm not sure what possessed our parents to buy properties the size of small museums, but it effectively made everything seem more clinical and detached rather than the homey closeness that Ox's or even my brothers' homes provided. The exception being the Fernandez homestead, however, I suspected the hominess there had less to do with the house decor and more to do with the people in it.

When I approached my mom and dad for the first time in so long, I tried not to hate them, even as they looked at me with a mix of surprise and detached emotion all over their face. They would never own up to what they did to me. They weren't those kinds of people, even if they felt bad about it, which I'm sure they didn't.

When I sat down for dinner and everyone kept asking me where I've been, I tried not to throw up at the prospect of having to tell them the truth about my first marriage and, subsequently, the truth about my second.

And when it all got too overwhelming; my parents basically still ignoring me even though I was right in front of their faces, my relatives bringing up my double Fernandez nuptials, my brothers doting on me like I was a wilting flower, and myself feeling less and less like a person and more like some alien thing that didn't belong anywhere and should just float away in space for ever and ever. When all that got to be way too much, I tried and I tried not to need Ox. Not to need to hear his voice or to see his scowling serious face or to need his arms around me. His hands touching me. His presence near me.

I tried, and ultimately, I failed.

I knew I failed when, after only forty minutes of dodging silent looks from my father and catching daggers from my mother, I escaped through the back patio doors and basically ran to the beach sitting beyond.

The sand and the water and the smells were somehow the same but not at all similar to the beach I walked frequently with Ox. It didn't matter. We were on the same coast, near the same waters, on the same sand. Although this beach was littered with cliffs and rocks and was cold as hell in the winter breeze, I could still feel him.

And I needed it.

"Tiney!" I heard from far behind me. I had been sitting down by the water, my toes just at the edge of the current, catching the icy tickle of moving waves every now and then. I whipped around, my hair blowing into my face, at the sound of the voice behind me. It was Connor. He was charging up to me, holding something dark in his hands, two dark figures following from further behind. When he reached me, he dropped what I realized was my coat around my shoulders and then used his strength to lift me to my feet.

Under his breath, he muttered, "This was so stupid," while he turned me around to face him.

"Con," I breathed, my voice hitching.

His face grew grimmer and he reached behind me to yank my hood over my head. "Come on. We're taking you back."

An almost panicked choke escaped me as I shook my head. "No, Con."

"*Yes*, Tine." He spoke through his teeth. Clay and Clinton were coming into view behind him and it made me wonder if Connor had stormed out trying to find me.

"I'm supposed to stay here for *two days, Connor*. I can't leave after an hour," I said, wrapping my arms around myself, suddenly feeling colder than I had when I was out here coatless.

"You came here happy and now look at you. You're fucking crying. Again, Tine. *Again*. It's easy to see what the problem is." Connor grabbed my arm and tried to pull me with him. I yanked back, standing my ground and he glared.

"Connor, the problem isn't you," I said, my voice going higher and breathier. "It's me, it's this place, it's all the questions and the memories. It's just a lot. And it's hard to handle it all without—"

I stopped myself, not wanting to say the words. Maybe not wanting them to be true. I had grown stronger in the last six months and I knew I couldn't equate all of that to a man I had only known in the same amount of time. I had done it for myself and was still doing it for myself. But there was no shame in admitting that I had some help. And that I still needed a little more. Regardless, I wasn't about to admit out loud that I needed someone I was only contractually obligated to.

Apparently, I didn't have to. Apparently, my brother had me all figured out.

"Without Ox," Connor finished. His eyes roved over me like he was trying to check for injuries or something. My eyes bore into him as he did, trying to figure out how I had been so obvious. And if he faulted me for being so weak and codependent. The hand he rested on my shoulder, gentle and big, told me he didn't. "Then let's go to him, Clementine. I'll take you there right now."

I shook my head, stepping backward just as my other two brothers came up behind Connor. They took one look at mine and Connor's faces and zipped their mouths. They all waited for me to explain.

I scrubbed my hands over my face and paced away and back to them frustratedly. "You guys don't understand, okay? You're the big guys of your big companies and you are so independent and *free*. And here I am, the little one who can never stand up for herself or fight her own battles or even be trusted to take care of herself. It's so freaking exhausting being the helpless one all the time. Especially in front of someone like him. I want to show my strength. For once in my goddamn life, I want to show that I can do something on my own. Okay? Do you get that?"

They were all quiet for a long time as they scrutinized me. All with different expressions on their faces. All mixed up and confusing and wrong.

Connor, usually controlled and logical about his emotions, was openly mad. Clay looked regretful and sort of *tame*. And Clinton looked like he wanted to keel over and throw up alongside me. He had never been good with processing emotions and I just threw a lot of them their way.

"Tine," Clint started shakily. "You're not helpless. And you're not weak. None of us think of you that way. And I doubt Ox does either."

I turned my head, forcing my gaze out to the ocean so I wouldn't have to look at my brothers' vulnerable faces.

"Clementine," Clay's voice growled at me. My eyes filled with water at the use of my full name from him. He'd been doing that a lot lately, and I didn't know what it meant. Not coming from him. "Are you ever going to stop fucking punishing yourself for who you are?"

He paced after me, coming up to me and getting in my face. "Sure, the last few years have been shit, but that's on us, Tiney. We could have done more. We *should* have done more. And I'm sorry.

"But nothing that's happened to you has happened because you're shy and quiet or 'cause you're boney as hell. You aren't the cause for the course that life takes. And it's okay to be who you are in both good and bad situations. Just because the you in the past endured terrible shit doesn't mean you were the problem, Tine."

"I should have fought," I said through my teeth. Through my tears.

"You should have," Clint said with a nod. "But not him, Tine. Not Ronaldo Fernandez. You should have fought *us*."

Blinking between the three of them, I watched with surprise as they all nodded their heads and agreed. And something in me broke inside.

The tears flowed freely down my cheeks, freezing as wind whipped at my face.

"I was nineteen," I croaked. "Why did you let them do it?"

"*Fuck, Tiney,*" Clinton hissed out, pained. Two things he didn't do all that often, curse and add the "Y" to the end of my nickname. I knew this hit him the hardest. While Clay and Connor had been pretty young themselves, both within a two to three-year age range of me, Clint had been old enough that he was out of college and well-integrated into the family businesses by that time. Well integrated into my family's circle. He could have said something, *done* something. But he was always too straight and narrow for his own good. He would have never stood up to our mother, not when he was that young. And I could tell it ate at him now that he knew what my life was like after. It ate at me too, to hold this resentment toward them and all these questions about past us, when I knew we were all different people now.

Grown or not, it still hurt.

"We just…" Connor started, but quickly trailed off, swallowing his words.

"We fucked up," Clay croaked. "We didn't think it would be like that."

"He was seventy!" I said incredulously. "What did you think it would be like?"

"I don't know. Some trophy wife type shit? We thought he just wanted something to show off on his arm while the companies merged. Not the damn opposite!" Clay said. He paused and shook his head, those curls of his moving just slightly. "Anyway, we were punks. Scared shitless of Mom and of disinheritance and too selfish to let ourselves believe that it was anything but good for you."

"Idiots," I grumbled with wet words. They all flinched, and I choked out a laugh-sob. "*All of us.*"

This brought my brothers' eyes back up to me, surveying me weakly. They looked beaten. And I kind of didn't care. They needed to know that I was not okay with being abandoned and used. And I never had been. But they also needed to know that I understood. We had all been young and just like I had been manipulated into "working" for my family's company, so had they. We were *all* young and helpless and we did the best we could when we could.

And I was doing my best now.

"How can I just be okay with being this girl who lets things happen to her?" I said, raking both hands through my hair in an irritated push. I turned away from them, their faces just making my eyes burn and my nose sting. "How can you say that's okay?"

"Because you're not that girl anymore, Tine," Clinton's voice said, closer than it had been before. "From the moment you asked the dispatcher to call us down, you started taking your life into your own hands."

"I married his *grandson*. He's still controlling me," I said with a whine.

"From what I understand, you two came up with your own agreement," Clay said. "Sounds to me like you took control back."

"That was all Ox," I said, my vision blurring again. That stinging present in my entire nasal cavity. If it hadn't been for him, I'd still be a shriveled up shell made up of tea and tears. His ever-patient persistence may be the only reason I made it out of those first few months without resulting back to my previous ways.

"You know he fought for you? From the very beginning. The cops wanted to take you away that first night." Clay laughed. "He threatened them all to hell and high water."

I laughed, but I also sobbed. "That's him. He'd fight for a sea turtle if he thought it needed him."

Connor, who had been quiet for a while, appeared in front of me. He grasped my shoulders and squeezed until I gazed at him. His face was soft again, that anger subsided. His voice was not soft though, it never was, but it had lowered back to that softer volume. "You could find worse men to love, Tine."

"I don't—" I started, my voice a weak plea of protest. I was cut off almost immediately.

"And it's okay to need someone you love when you've had a rough night. It doesn't make you needy, or helpless, or weak. It just means you're connected in a way that is different than with anyone else."

"I'm not in love with Ox, guys. Not like that."

"I only know one way to be in love with someone, Tiney," Clay retorted.

"Then I'm not it," I retorted back.

"Come on, Tiney," Connor drawled, his tone going almost mocking. So many sides of him I hadn't seen in a long time. "I've got two eyes and they work just fine. *And* I'm not a total idiot."

I couldn't help but blink at him in mock innocence. He sounded like *Clay*. I didn't think I'd seen this side of him *ever*. Come to think of it, I was shocked he'd been the one to storm out here after me first. Usually he'd fade into the background and then try to make it up to me afterward. This was a new Connor I was just now getting to know.

He took my sass as just that. And it earned me a thump on the forehead. "*Come on.* Anyone can tell that this is a bust. Dad is still too afraid to cross Mom and say anything substantial to you, and Mom is too stubborn to admit that she misses you, even though she asks about you all the time. This was never going to work, and we were stupid to force it all at once. I'm not saying we call it quits. We're a family. We need to stop all the bullshit and start trying to be a real one again, mistakes and all, but it's not going to happen overnight."

"*So many words, Connor,*" Clay mocked from the background. Con threw a look over his shoulder at him and he ducked away.

"Ox would never turn you away. Why are you fighting this?" he asked.

I bit my lip, my gaze flying from Connor to my other brothers and down to the sand. I twisted at my fingers, this feeling of failure washing over me as I thought about crawling back to Ox with my tail between my legs. Yet another situation I couldn't handle on my own.

"He'll be disappointed I didn't see it through to the end," I said in a weak voice.

A scoff sounded loud and amused through the air. Clay. "He almost fought me when I told him we wanted to bring you here. I guess he was right."

Ouch. That stung. I knew I was coddled and handled with kid gloves, but I didn't know quite how much. I guess Ox didn't trust me to do things alone. My face stung again.

"Not helping, Clay," Clint said quietly in his big brother voice.

"Want me to call him, then?" Clay asked, but as I shot my eyes up to him he was already pulling his phone out of the pocket of his dark jeans.

"Clay, no!" I shot forward in his direction. "He's probably busy and—"

Too late. He was calling, and worse, Ox was answering.

"I swear to God, Ferguson, if a hair is out of place on her fucking head, your ass is dead," Ox's voice vibrated through the receiver, all deep and masculine and *him*.

"Quite the poet, Oxy." Clay teased.

Ox retorted with some other cursed threat. But my ears were ringing, my blood pumping hard and fast at the sound of his voice. I could almost *feel* him through that sound. I could feel the warm safety of his bed. The quiet hum of his murmurs as I drifted further into sleep. The rumble of his laugh when I surprised him and said something funny. And I missed him. Not because of time apart but because of circumstance. I missed him and I wished he could have been here with me.

My mind came back down to the present as I heard my brother say, "Your wife wants to talk to you, man."

And then the phone was in my hands. I brought it up to my ear as I cradled it with both palms. I could hear him breathing on the other end, waiting for me to say something, but all the words I thought to say got stuck in my throat.

Would he really be disappointed in me? Would he be expecting me to call? Would he be upset with me for interrupting his family time? The questions raced around in my head, shriveling up my resolve and making me want to back out. I was just about to shove the phone away, not wanting to be the burden I knew I could be, when I heard it.

"Lunita?" Ox's voice filled my ears and by association, filled me. He was using *that* tone. The soft, patient one I knew for a fact he hadn't been using a second ago when he talked to my brother. The one that was meant for me.

Just for me.

The emotions I felt, that I *had been* feeling since the moment I left his side, they all hit me like a freight train right in the heart. I sucked in a hard breath trying to fight the sudden burst of tears that assaulted me. But I couldn't. The sobs that escaped me had been caged for too long. These tears were from scared me, and sad me, and lonely me, and the me that had been trying to be a fighter if only for the night.

They were so powerful they came out as a silent whine and then quick little gasps as I tried to catch my breath. They knocked me at the knees and sent me sinking into the sand. All while I held the phone close and listened to the frantic shushing and placating words from the other end.

"Fuuuck," Ox groaned from the other side of the sea. "Clem? Baby, talk to me."

I cried for a little while longer. But it was the distinct sound of jingling keys and the slamming of a car door that had me fighting to take deep breaths and wrangle control of myself.

"Ox?" I breathed out, my body shaking along with my voice. It was so small, broken down by tears and fear and exhaustion. "Can I come back?"

I heard his ragged breath hitch out of him for an entire second before he croaked out, "Always, Clementine. You don't even have to ask."

"Okay," I whispered, my voice lost to my sobs and emotion.

"Will you tell me what happened?" he asked, and I imagined him in his car, his head on the steering wheel as he held the phone up to his face trying to guess what I was going through. The image made me feel even worse for making him worry.

"Oh, you know me. I've got about ten sacks of old baggage I'm still lugging around." I sighed, wiping my eyes with the back of my hand. "It just gets hard to carry sometimes."

Ox fell silent and for a while I just listened to the sharp sound of his breathing and the rush of the ocean beside us.

"*Come home*, Clem," he growled softly at me. I whimpered a little, apologizing for bothering him so late. He answered again in a rumbling authoritative voice. "*Do not apologize to me*. Remember, I've got eight hands. Just come home, and I'll help you carry some of those bags."

My next sob was peppered with tearful laughter.

Later—after having a whole hour-long car ride to reflect on the fact that I had just ugly cried on the phone with Ox, *and* that my brothers thought I was in love with him, *and* that they apparently talked to him so often they had him on speed dial. After thinking over all of that, by the time we arrived back at the Fernandez family residence, I was about ready to disintegrate into dust.

Ox answered the door almost before I knocked. Our eyes connected and his face went grim. This got my feet moving immediately, pushing past him as I aimed for anywhere that wasn't right there. I got maybe a step by him before he swiped my arm up by the wrist and stopped me where I stood. I bounced nervously as I waited impatiently for him to say something, but he was facing my brothers.

"You've been gone for four hours. What the hell could've

happened?" he asked them. They all had grim faces too.

"Are you gonna let us in or what?" Clay asked, his tongue in his cheek.

"Are you the reason she was crying?" Ox asked in a tone that screamed he wasn't planning on letting them in.

"Ox!" I whispered a hiss at him.

He glared over his shoulder at me, surveying me up and down before redirecting his scowl back to my brothers. "Come in."

They entered, huddling close to Ox and saying things in hushed tones. Ox leaned an ear in and listened, his eyes occasionally blinking back toward me before he closed them and redirected them toward the group. The entire time he held onto my wrist, his grip warm, his thumb caressing the skin there periodically. After they had said what they needed, Ox thanked them and sent them downstairs where apparently the family was having game night. *Great*, I had interrupted yet again.

He waited until we were alone in the foyer before he used his grip on me to turn me around and face him. He held me out at arm's length as he ran his eyes over every inch of my skin. It burned under his scrutiny and under the possibility that my brothers had told him what they assumed I felt for him. On the bright side, at least I had stopped ugly crying. Now I was just sniffling and moping and I'm sure Ox was used to that by now.

When Ox took a step forward and pulled me in a step simultaneously, his head lowered toward me and for a second, I thought he was going to kiss me again. But then I felt his mouth land on my head and his arms wrap around me.

"I'm sorry I didn't go," he said into my hair.

Against my will, I burrowed my entire person deep into his embrace. Wrapping my arms around him and sucking in gulps of Ox filled air. I mistakenly didn't respond, and he pulled away so he could look at me. My eyes were dry but my soul was stripped and bare for him to see. I'm sure he could see right through me at that point.

"You're freezing," he said, voice soft.

I nodded. I hadn't been able to get warm enough in the car on the way back. But oddly enough, I felt like I was thawing now that I was with Ox.

"And you smell like the beach." He added.

I nodded some more, and he narrowed his eyes.

"You're not supposed to go there without me."

"Since when?" I croaked.

Ox used his long fingers to brush curly hair away from my face, tucking it behind my ears. "Since you almost clawed my eyes out both times I *dared* to step foot out there without you."

I laughed a laugh that gurgled out into a huffing sigh. Ox cupped my cheek and I exhaustedly melted into it, my eyes flickering shut briefly but opening slowly at the sound of his voice.

Ox swallowed, his expression decidedly pained. "I heard some concerning things, Clem."

"Did they tell on me?" I asked.

His mouth formed a grim line. "They're your brothers. They care."

"They didn't always," I let out in a whisper. I immediately felt bad. That was more than I'd ever let slip about my brothers. Probably more than I ever would again. I hated bad-mouthing them, even when I was mad.

He looked at me for a long time. His thumb rubbing at my swollen, puffy face. His other hand at the small of my back, keeping me close. In the softest voice I think I'd heard from him, he said, "Well, I do."

I felt the assault of emotion rush to me again, but I tamped it down, having cried enough for one night. Even though I knew on some level that Ox cared about me, it felt different to hear him say it.

It felt good. And right.

"Can you say it again?" I asked, almost pleading.

He furrowed his brow. "I care about you?"

I shook my head. "Not that."

He stared at me again, the same expression on his face as he tried to figure me out. I thought he wouldn't after a while until his features morphed into something soft. Something just for me.

He slid his hand underneath my chin and angled it toward him. And then he lowered his head the rest of the way so that we were eye to eye. Nose to nose. Inches apart as he gazed at me, eyes burning and serious.

"*I'm sorry* I wasn't there with you tonight. I know you said not to, but I should have been there anyway," he said to me. No mockery in his tone. No wavering in his voice. Every word he said, he meant. And he kept going. "Clem, I promise to be there for you when you need me. All the time, no matter what. I won't let you down again, sweetheart. Not ever. Okay?"

I held his stare the entire time he spoke. I knew he didn't need to apologize to me. I knew he hadn't done anything wrong. But I also knew that he *would*, if only I asked. Knowing that filled me up and up and up.

So, I stepped into his arms and savored every bit of him.

Chapter Twenty-two

CLEMENTINE

Q4 or quarter four really came down to the last month of the year here in Seaside, and thus Ox became super busy directly after Thanksgiving. And being the upstanding businessmen they were, so had my brothers. They had become single minded in their responsibilities as first, second, and third sons of a major corporation. Holing up in their offices or board meeting rooms or traveling to various locations where they rushed to tie up any outlying projects for the year.

It was all a mixture of very mundane business initiatives that piled and piled until it created one large, complicated end-of-year struggle. It wasn't new to me. It happened every year, no matter what family I was in, so subconsciously I had already been prepared for it.

Consciously though… Consciously, I hadn't thought about just how much of an integral part of my life Ox had become and how having him gone so frequently, even when I wasn't particularly used to seeing him all day every day anyway, would send me into an aching spiral of missing him.

I spent most of my time baking. I was trialing tons of new recipes for Christmas cookies and treats, getting myself ready for yet another stressful holiday. I had a feeling my brothers would want to try the whole "happy family" thing again and the only thing that really got my mind off the disaster that could potentially be, was diving into a new recipe. But not having my brothers around and not having Ox either, left me with little to no taste testers. Even though I still hadn't let Ox taste anything of mine, I had the sudden urge to have him here with me, telling me that what I was doing was good. Or telling me anything, really.

But he was busy and he would remain busy for weeks to come.

So instead, I recruited his DNA.

The Fernandez girls had become fast friends and surprisingly even faster family, since the whole *'War on Ox'* incident. They had surprised me by coming over to support my cause and they continued to surprise me with easy conversation, invitations to do things together and the inclusion in their tight sister dynamic.

I was so grateful for it.

It was one week into Q4 isolation and the start of December when the girls came over for dinner (made graciously by the only one with a homemaking bone in her body, Alta). Earlier that day I had made way too many cookies, getting a little carried away when I started breaking in the brand-new set of tools Ox had gotten me. I was maybe also trying to distract myself from the fact that he had been gone when I woke up every day that week, even when I made it a point to wake up earlier and earlier each day, hoping to see him.

I hadn't seen him at night either. He'd been coming back even after I got to bed. Each night I would fall asleep waiting for him in my room and wake up the next morning in his bed. I didn't have illusions of sleepwalking. I knew he had been carrying me into his room. And that made my heart both ache and want even more for him.

I missed him. And I had approximately three more weeks of this torture.

So yeah, I over baked cookies to distract myself and ended up having to invite over reinforcements to pawn them off before Ox came home and saw them.

"Wow, Clementine. This is…*a lot*," Alta said, clearly trying to keep her voice light. Her eyes gave away her wariness as she took in the extra-large platter of sweets I laid out in front of them after dinner was all eaten and cleaned up.

"What were you thinking making all this?" Ceci asked, even as she helped herself to several cookies and set aside several more on a paper towel beside her. I wonder what or who she was saving those for.

Wrinkling my nose, I said, "I got carried away in recipe trials. The boys are usually my taste testers but they're all busy."

"What about Ox?" Alta asked, primly picking the cutest white snowflake cookie on the entire platter and immediately starting to nibble the ends.

I suddenly found the corner of the countertop very interesting, my entire body from my toes to my forehead tingling with embarrassment. I couldn't *tell* them. If I told them that I was withholding my sweets from Ox for something he'd done over a month ago and unknowingly at that, I would feel silly. Because it *was* silly. But still…

It was important to me.

I thought after a moment of my silence and the murmured approval of the girls eating the cookies I was let off the hook. But apparently someone already had me all figured out. That someone was Melissa, who had been looking at me through narrowed eyes, cookie in hand but not eaten.

"Ox told me you haven't let him try any of your baked goods yet,"

Lis said, leaning forward on her elbows. "Why?"

"He told you that, huh?" I asked, my voice pitching up high.

"Mhmm," she said, her eyes not leaving me. "But if you make this much all the time, why hasn't he gotten to try?"

I found a spot on the wooden floor and I couldn't decipher if it was dirt or part of the design. I suddenly wanted to know very badly and busied myself grabbing a paper towel so that I could wipe at it and see. While I did, I asked "casually" over my shoulder. "What did he say the reason was?"

There were collective snorting sounds from above. Lis and Ceci. I guess I wasn't as casual as I thought I was.

"He just says it's not time yet," Lis said, her voice calculated. "In true ominous Ox fashion. Just thought you could give me a more concrete reason, no big deal."

"Is it some sort of metaphor?" Ceci asked. I popped up from my fake cleaning spot on the floor to give her a look.

"For what?" I asked.

"Your goodies," she said with an eyebrow waggle.

I immediately ducked back under the cover of the counter and to the floor, scrubbing at the spot that was most definitely a pattern in the wood. I stayed down and scrubbed anyway. They all giggled together at my expense.

"It is not!" I said, still hiding. "It's just—it's just private, okay?"

"It's definitely a sex thing." Ceci continued with a smirk on her face. I couldn't see it, but I knew it was there.

I popped up, discarding the useless napkin somewhere atop the island and pointing a finger in her direction. "Celestia Fernandez, it is not! Stop that."

This had Alta covering her mouth and snickering. I shot her a look too and she turned her face into her shoulder to hide her laugh. Looking to Melissa, I saw that she was curling her lips between her teeth to hide her own smile.

"She full-named you," Alta said, her eyes settling on Ceci.

"She did," Lis agreed, her voice quiet, like usual. She turned to me, her expression...*playful*. Something that was not usual. "It must really be weird."

"What?" I asked.

"The sex thing you're doing with our brother," she said. And then she did the cutest thing. She giggled.

Groaning, I tilted my head up to the ceiling and covered my eyes. But a giggle escaped me too.

"It's not a sex thing," I said through my own laughter. After a couple moments, I composed myself and brought my gaze down to the sisters. "It's a me and Ox thing, okay?"

They all looked at me for a long beat before they melted in a chorus of mocking, "Aw's".

I spent the next couple of weeks in similar fashion. Falling asleep and waking up alone. Not seeing Ox and visiting with his sisters. We went holiday shopping together, we decorated Ox's house in tasteful festive garb, and we watched movies together in the late hours of the night.

I think they could tell that I missed Ox and that it was making me a little sad to be with them. Lis wasn't always able to hang around, having to do some work herself, but for the most part, December was for the girls. Something I was definitely not opposed to. It made for a really fun month getting to know my three new quasi-sisters.

Not just for me either.

Some moments I could just tell that they were having a good time too. Like when I would glance over and catch Lis leaning back with her eyes closed, unaware and unalert, something I was realizing she almost never did. Or when Alta would hum a song and then pass the imaginary microphone to me to carry on for her. Even when I would turn to find

Ceci just staring at me, blank faced. I knew they all had been apprehensive about me at first and it was a relief to have them not be so cautious now that we had all gotten to know each other.

It honestly could have been one of the most fun holiday seasons I ever had, if it weren't for one particular meteor sized hole in the entire thing.

Or more accurately, a bull sized hole. His name was Ox and, God, *I. Missed. Him.*

It only got worse as one week turned into two and the days away at the office turned into multiple days away on business trips out of the state. I didn't think it could even get quieter and staler in the house. He had already been gone for most days and most nights, but somehow knowing he was out of the city and wouldn't be coming back, not even for a few hours at night, made it seem even more desolate.

It was the weekend before Christmas and Ox was away again. In Colorado, I think—or was it California? It could have been both, he often did multi-city tours—made a lot easier with his family's plane. Either way, he was gone and he was in a totally different time zone than me. That made it hard for communicating, though we didn't talk much when he was this deep into business anyway. He had work to do.

Which is why I was completely surprised when I received a call from him as I was lying in bed fighting a particularly hard sleepless night. I had been getting to bed easier and quicker since I began spending my nights with Ox. I was getting used to the magical sleeping aid of just being around him. So him being gone so often lately left me more and more sleepless each night.

It was gradually building up to a crescendo. My clocked sleeping hours became less and less while Ox's time away rose more and more. Tonight, I was having one of my hardest nights yet.

Earlier, I thought it would be a good idea to make Ox's flan—thinking a holiday twist, with a peppermint caramel topping and holiday sprinkles, would be fun. Only, once it was done, there was no Ox here to try it. Not even if I wanted him to.

After documenting the recipe and the dessert, I dumped it. The act of throwing away yet another flan brought back bad feelings and hence brought on another sleepless night of me obsessing over things Ox has said to me. Good things, bad things, sweet things, mean things. Everything.

I would've given anything to hear *anything* coming from him right about then. I couldn't sleep and it was damn near proven by now that the only sleep aid that worked for me was a tall, grumpy man with the name of a city.

Still, his unexpected call sent me into a rush of excitement and nerves. In a frenzy, I reached for the glass on my nightstand and gulped down the water there before relentlessly clearing my throat and finally answering on the second to last ring.

"Hello?" I asked groggily. Damn. That water had done nothing

"You sound tired," is the first thing he said to me. And if it hadn't been for the tingling sensation that hearing his voice for the first time in weeks spread over me, I would have wrinkled my nose at the non-greeting.

Instead, I sighed, sinking deep into my pillow and gulping twice to wrangle down the sudden emotion building inside me. *I missed him.*

"It's three in the morning, of course I sound tired," I breathed after I got myself under control.

"You also sound sad," he said in his curt, clipped voice that told me he was still in '*Work Ox*' mode. Was this a work call, then? Was he only calling because he was required to check on me every once in a while?

Pushing those thoughts out of my head, I breathed again before speaking, hoping to erase some of my too obvious melancholy. "What are you still doing up? Isn't it pretty late there too?"

"I'm working Clem, I'll be up for a while." He paused. "What about you?"

"What about me?"

"How are you?" he asked, his timbre going lower, *my* Ox beginning to appear. I closed my eyes and soaked it in.

"I'm fine," I answered.

"Just fine?" I could hear paper shuffling in the background and voices in the distance. "What have you been up to? I haven't seen you in a while, Lunita. Talk to me."

"Apparently, you've seen me every night." I teased, coaxing a chuckle out of him. "Why do you do that anyway?"

"What?"

"Carry me out of my room," I said, as if he didn't know what I was referring to. How could he not?

"You weren't where you were supposed to be."

"Oh really?" I asked. "And where is that, exactly? Last time I checked this is still my room?"

"With me, Clementine. You're supposed to be with me. Always." I hummed, not able to respond to that at all. So casually he held my heart and juggled it with words like that, having no idea what he did to me. "Tell me what you've been doing there without me."

I laughed. "How about you tell me? I know you already know somehow."

He laughed too. It fizzled out into a sigh and I imagined him settling back into whatever corporate chair he was sitting in, his top two shirt buttons undone, his Oaxaca Black suit perfect as ever on him. I imagined his eyes closing too, hopefully soaking in the conversation with me as much as I was with him. The image was a good one.

"Well," he started, "my sources tell me you've been Christmas shopping. And to dinners at my parent's often. They also tell me you put my Christmas tree in the wrong location, we'll have to talk about those decorating decisions later—" I laughed and he paused, listening to the whole thing. I could tell he was smiling when he spoke again. "And they've told me you have been absolutely annihilating my kitchen with your strange concoctions. I leave you alone for a few measly weeks and you become a mad scientist, Clem, really?"

He was joking and I was laughing and I had a suspicion this had been his goal from the start. I couldn't help the sunshiny glow I got when he talked to me. When he laughed with me. When he *was* with me. I just couldn't help it.

I also couldn't help feeling sad when I sobered. Because even though I could hear his voice, it wasn't the same as when he was here. I'm sure he could hear the dejection in my voice when I croaked out, "They don't seem all that measly to me."

My voice came out weaker and waterier than I thought it would, but I couldn't help it. Have I said that I missed him yet?

"Clem," he groaned painfully. I imagined him covering his eyes now, scrubbing at his face in frustration. "Please, tell me that you're alright."

"What do your sources say?"

I heard a sigh.

"They say that you've been strong. They say that you laugh often and you're generous with your sweets and that you're much different from what they thought you'd be," he said, his voice low. Husky.

"What do you think?" I asked. Not wanting to lie to him, because I was in fact alright, but not entirely.

"That you're doing just fine," he said but didn't sound particularly convinced. Like flipping a switch, his voice suddenly got all growly and authoritative as if he was speaking through gritted teeth. "So now, tell me why you're up so damn late and not tucked in my bed where you're supposed to be?"

"Those blabber mouths don't have an answer for that one?" I asked, my laugh a little strained.

"Actually, they have a theory," he admitted.

"Share," I said.

"They say that you might miss me," he said, his voice a low rumble now. Just like when he talked me to sleep.

In my own low voice I whispered, as if saying it too loud would scare him, "I do."

There was a soft curse on the other end of the line. I didn't mind it. I realized that I was just happy to hear his voice, no matter what mood he was in. And I don't know what that said about me or where that left my emotions, but I didn't have much time to think about it because Ox was back on the phone again, his voice harder and sounding a little strained.

"Clem, get in bed for me, okay?" Ox asked.

"I'm already in bed," I said, confusion leaking into my tone and sleepiness crawling its way into my eyes. It was like my body finally got what it needed by hearing Ox's voice and it was suddenly ready to tap out.

"Don't fall asleep yet, baby," he said. "I want you to get out of *your* bed, walk down the hall, and get into *ours*. I need you to do that for me."

"Why?" I asked, my sleepy pout coming out, which is how both Ox and I knew he was losing me.

"Just trust me okay. You trust me, right?" he asked, even though I had a feeling he already knew the answer.

A smile crept across my face even though he couldn't see it. "All eight hands."

A laugh escaped him and he sighed. "Damn, you're so weird. I love that about you."

"You do?"

"I do."

"What else do you love about me?" I asked, tiredness or distance or maybe even desperation making me bold.

"Get into bed and I'll tell you," he demanded softly.

I listened. Sleepily, I untangled myself from my blankets and exited my room. Padding down the hall in bare feet and a snug thermal Christmas onesie I approached Ox's room with my phone stuck close to my ear.

I hadn't been in his room for the entire few days he'd been out of town and I hadn't planned on doing so until he'd gotten back. I didn't miss the way he'd called it "our" bed, but it still made me nervous going into his room without him there. But weirdly, it also made me feel warm and safe and *wanted*.

The room was darker than normal. I was so used to entering when Ox was still engrossed in work. The dim light of his lamp usually warmed the space up. Seeing it now, all pitch black and abandoned gave me pause.

"Turn the lamp on, Clem," Ox's patient voice penetrated my thoughts before they got the chance to spiral even further.

I heeded him, walking over to the lamp on my side of the bed. It buzzed awake and illuminated the little bubble at the head of the room that I was so used to occupying. I was getting ready to wiggle into the dark covers when I noticed something on the other side of the bed.

Ox kept all of his things tidy and minimal. So, the little form that leaned up against the stacked pillows on his side was definitely out of the ordinary.

Leaning a knee on the edge of the mattress, I reached forward and grabbed for the little thing, even more surprised to see that it was a stuffed animal.

As if he was wise to what was happening in the silence, Ox cleared his throat on the other end of the line. "What have you found?"

Running a hand up and down the soft black fur of the stuffed creature, I felt a giggle tumble out of me. "An ox."

"Ah," he said, playing along. "I see. How convenient, you seem to be missing one of those. Now it can keep you company, and keep you in the *right* bed."

"Ox," I laughed out, my eyes roving all around the cute little creature. Black fur, black eyes, smooth dark hooves, and a little pink nose. I absolutely could not suppress my giggles as I took in the fact that Ox had gotten this cute little guy for me. I tried to picture him in the kid's aisle at the store trying to pick out the best stuffed animal with that serious look on his face. That warm glow I started to feel earlier spread throughout my entire body, illuminating me like a crackling fire in a hearth. "A replacement Ox."

"Woah, woah. Slow your road. No one said anything about *replacements*," he said, his voice deceivingly grumpy. I could tell he was still teasing me. It warmed me even more. "Are you in your spot?"

"Not yet."

"Get in there," he ordered. I obeyed. "In?"

"I'm in."

"Good. Now, flip little Ox Junior over," he instructed. I did, flipping the stuffed toy onto its stomach in my lap. A gasp puffed out of me when my eyes fell upon the thin white strip sticking out of the back of the toy. I couldn't make out all of them, but I could see that there were words written on the strip. Words that looked a lot like "three things..." Ox hummed. "Does he have something for you?"

"Ox, you didn't," I said through my smile. I pulled the paper out of the back of the toy. It came out like tissue from a tissue box and it did in fact read a prompt, asking me to tell Ox three things.

"I didn't. Oaxaca Junior did," he said.

"Oaxaca Junior, huh? Well, he takes after you then."

"What's he saying?"

Flattening out the little strip of paper, I held it up in front of me and read. "Tell me three things I don't know."

"Go on then," he coaxed. "Tell him."

"Did you do all this just so we could play our game before bed?" I asked.

He was quiet for a moment but eventually he cleared his throat, "I did it for you, Clem. To know that you're sleeping well. To know that you're not too lonely in that house this week. To know that, even when I'm not there, I can still take care of you."

"Ox," I breathed out, not knowing what else to say.

"*Wife*," he playfully growled. I warmed again, even if the false title made me a little bit queasy.

"I don't know what to say," I admitted.

"Nothing. Just settle in, close your eyes, and tell me three things I don't know, Lunita," he said, repeating what the paper had prompted a minute ago. "But I swear to God, if you tell me you've been on any more dates—"

"Oaxaca!" I hissed out in a laugh, surprised he would use that against me.

The laugh he let out warmed me up all over again.

Chapter Twenty-three

OX

God damn, my head hurt. I wasn't sure if it was because of the month-long work sprint I had finally just finished or because of…other reasons. Either way, I was more than glad to be walking up the front steps to my home just a couple of days before Christmas.

Words, thoughts, or expressions could not properly convey how off-kilter I had been the past weeks without Clementine. It was bearable when I was still in town—when I was able to come home at the end of a long day and find her curled up in a ball at the top of her bed, slumbering peacefully. I was at least able to hold her in my arms, to know she was okay, to have her in my bed, no matter how innocent or brief.

But being in another state, another time zone, it was different. It was like, for the first time I realized what my life had been like before she had come into it.

Pretty damn boring.

And cold.

Lonely.

Bitter.

Clementine was like a streak of sunlight splitting across a dark room. She couldn't help how starkly she contrasted against the bleakness. She didn't even notice it. She thought she was a part of that murk, but those of us around her knew.

She was light.

And she was mine.

Being away from her forced me to see the dependency I'd grown to her presence. Especially at night. Her sleeping demons had become my own, and they had followed me across borders and sunsets, keeping me up as if we were tied to some kind of lifeline. I could no longer go to sleep unless I knew she was sleeping first.

Phone calls and text messages held me over well enough, but the prospect of seeing her was making my nerve endings crackle to life, wired for the fix of *something* they knew they needed from Clem.

It was midday and unlike the last time I'd come home like this, I didn't know for sure if Clem would be home or not. Not with all the things going on lately. But I hoped she was. She had been spending a lot of her time split between my family, my sisters, and occasionally hanging out with a small group of acquaintances she was getting to know from her activities. But now it was only a couple of days until Christmas and unless she had rushed over to see her brothers upon their own return, I had a hunch she would be home.

That hunch was immediately satisfied when I walked into the opening between the kitchen and the foyer and spotted Clem standing right smack in the middle of the kitchen. She was wearing one of her tight little workout sets. The ones that drove me wild. This one was festive. The long-sleeved top and full-length leggings were a bright Christmas red. Her hair was wound into some kind of hairstyle I'd never seen before and was tied half back with a buffalo plaid scarf, the rest cascading down her back and multiple tiny braids.

Her back was to me as she leaned over the side of the island with her hands splayed on the countertop and her focus on something sitting there.

Padding as softly as I could, I snuck up behind her. The nearer I got the warmer I got, that glow she put off enveloping me the way it seemed to do. I resisted the very real urge to breathe her in and instead ran my hand down the length of her braids, picking a few up to test their weight.

She jerked heavily and I laid a stilling hand on her hip, squeezing it to let her know it was me. With a quick look over her shoulder, she breathed a heavy sigh of relief. I soaked in everything she was. Every little action somehow perfect and interesting to me.

"You scared the pants off me, Ox," she breathed.

"I wish," I muttered. I was tired and hence, my tongue was loose.

"*Oh.*" She sucked in a breath and turned her face to eye me over her shoulder. From her position, I doubted she could see much of me, not with my attention glued to this new hairstyle.

I flicked my gaze up to her eyes momentarily before returning it to her hair. Still holding her braids between my fingers, I said, "I like these."

She smiled a hesitant smile then she pointed her chin down to the counter in front of her. Her voice got breathy and emotion seemed to pull at her vocal cords. "I *love* this."

I laid my hand on the small of her back and leaned forward to look over her shoulder. Her braids were so long they blocked my hand from making contact with the skin there, but we both still breathed a little ragged as my front settled onto her back. It took me a couple of seconds to focus on what was in front of me.

When I did, I smiled, allowing myself to sink into her and relax. I laid the hand that wasn't on her on the counter beside her, trapping her in a cage of me. I didn't know why I was being so needy, but once I'd gotten my hands on her, I couldn't take them away.

"Did you see the inscription?" I asked. My chin lingered near her shoulder and neck, my face angled slightly so that it was damn near in her hair. I was addicted.

"No!" she said excitedly. Her hands shot out to the large item and turned it so that the side was facing us. The breath she let out was shaky at best. Peppered with surprise and disbelief and a sprinkle of laughter.

In front of us was Clementine's Christmas gift. One of them at least. It was a professional grade tabletop electric mixer. Special ordered in that pretty pale orange color that personified Clem and the warm glow she placed over everything she did. On the side, in large matte cursive lettering, it read: *Clementine's Kitchen.*

Topped with an oversized bow and a gift tag that I had written myself and express-mailed from the other side of the country, so she knew I wasn't just checking her off a list and buying the first thing I thought would sate her. I wanted her to know that I cared.

The gift itself wasn't anything especially extravagant, and it hadn't been hard to get. It had just taken a little bit of forethought. But by the way Clem's hands shook ever so slightly as she ran them along the glistening stainless steel of the appliance, I could tell I had made her happy. The glow I had been basking in intensified tenfold.

"Ox, I don't know what to say," she shook out.

"Say you'll make me something with it," I said into her neck. I was full on embracing her now. My chest pressed into her back, my arms caged around her shoulders, tucking her into me perfectly. I could feel the roundness of her bottom half curving perfectly into me. I had to swallow and breathe so I didn't make my approval of the touch very well known.

It didn't matter that I had never really touched her like this before. I was like a man starved and thus a man possessed.

"Maybe," she squeezed out.

I groaned. "*Clementina,* you're killing me."

"Why?" she asked. She had the nerve to actually sound confused.

I smiled, my face still half in her hair. Using my nose, I pushed the braids hanging past the crook of her neck away from her skin. She was smooth there, and soft and she smelled like sugar and honey. I knew because I'd trailed my nose slightly up the line of the area, taking in a long, steady breath.

"Ox?"

"I missed you," I admitted, squeezing her closer to me. Her scent was driving me crazy.

"Same," she said.

"You kind of smell like cookies, you know that?" I asked, and somehow my lips had found their way to her shoulder. Damn. What was I doing?

"Do you like cookies?" she asked.

"Fucking love them," I murmured, my attention being snagged by those damn braids again. The way they trailed down her spine and kissed the bottom of her waist where it met her…

She gasped as I fisted a handful of her hair. I was winding it loosely around my hand, transfixed by how many times it could wrap around my knuckles. And by the sound it elicited from her lips.

"Sorry, I was curious," I murmured, not stopping. And not really sorry at all. Instead, I tugged on the strands, pleased when Clem followed the movement by arching into me with a breathless whimper.

That sound went straight to my pants and with her so close, flush against my body, there was no hiding what she was doing to me. She squirmed, but not away, *closer.* I couldn't tamp down the hoarse rumble that escaped me then.

She was messing with the wiring in my head just by being her. And by not pulling away—not even a little bit—she was toying with my control.

"Lunita," I let out, rolling ever so slightly against her little body before forcing myself back.

"I think you have called me everything but my name today," she said.

"There's a reason for that."

"Why?"

"Because," I ground out. The hand that wasn't fisting her hair had moved and was pressed across her stomach, my fingertips inching under the fabric of her top just slightly. One of them had found the dip of her belly button as they trailed along her soft skin. "When I say your name, it makes me want to hear you say mine back."

"Ox," she whimpered, her hands bracing onto the counter. Her body sank completely against mine and she moved with purpose, her hips pushing backward, seeking me. Her head falling into the crook of my neck and shoulder.

"Do better than that, Clementine," I said. My hand sliding from her stomach down her front, landing on her thigh and squeezing. Opening.

Damn.

"Oaxaca." Her throaty voice sent more shots of static through my body, making every part of me stand on end. She groaned in her own approval.

It made me smile. A smile I brought down onto the side of her throat where I decided I wanted to taste her skin. I opened my mouth and sucked her into it.

"Oax—" she stopped and swallowed after taking a shuddering breath. "Oaxaca."

"Better," I purred against her throat. "Keep going."

"You first," she challenged.

I hummed against her throat, making her giggle. Biting gently in the same spot quickly turned her laughs into moans. Encouraging ones that had me nipping and sucking and kissing along the plains and hills of her neck. My hands were wandering. Well, my hand was. The other one I

337

refused to untangle from her hair. I wanted it right there, every so often tugging or pulling her head in the direction I needed it, giving me access to that delicious swell in her neck. I could feel her swallow every so often. Feel the pump of her pulse under my lips, under my tongue.

I wanted to possess her fully. I wanted her to be mine just as much as I was hers in that moment. As my mouth continued to basically devour her, my free hand explored—teasing, pinching, scratching. And her breaths started to pump out hard against my chest.

"Speak, Clementine." I ordered against her face. She had moved her head so that her chin was angled toward me, her eyes were closed and her lips were parted, lingering just an inch or two away from mine.

"Ox," she whispered. Her breath mingled with mine and she chased me for contact. I pulled away slightly.

I didn't want to kiss her now. Not like this.

Ten minutes earlier, I thought I just wanted her presence near me. This unexpected hunger had hit me out of nowhere, and although I had absolutely no intention of stopping unless she told me to, I didn't want to spoil her sweet kiss for the very first time on blinding need. I wanted to take my damn time.

"Again," I ordered, planting a kiss on her jaw.

"Ox," she said again. But her voice trailed off as I found my hand underneath the stretching material of her bottoms, slipping into somewhere warm and inviting. A biting suck of breath zipped between the both of us, and she shuddered at the same time I groaned.

"Fuuuck, Clem," I growled out.

"Ox," She whimpered again—Huskier, needier. I needed to slow down, to savor this, to take my time.

But I had no control left. I let go of her hair and filled both palms with handfuls of her instead. One high, one low. One wet, one full of soft, warm flesh. Both moving like this was a race, and I was making damn sure we were crossing the finish line. Or at least she would be.

Her moans were incredible, her writhing insatiable as I worked her over and over with my hands. With my mouth, between kisses—and nips and scrapes and licks—I told her exactly what it meant to have her in my arms like this.

"Si, cariña." *Kiss.*

"*Hermosa.*" *Bite.*

"Perfecta." My mouth just kind of latched onto her as we both groaned. Her, with shaking need and me, in response to the fire she was lighting within me.

"Oaxaca, I think I—" she puffed her breath, her chest heaving up and down, back arching wildly. "I'm going to—"

"My name, Clementine," I whispered directly into her ear. "Only say my name."

"Oaxaca, please. I can't—" she refused to make full sentences, instead cutting herself off with the wiggles and squirms of her searching body. I was steady in giving her what she wanted and needed, holding my own desire off. But when she followed my name with that begging "please", I couldn't help the groaning roll of my hips that escaped past my restraint.

And then she came apart.

Violently. Beautifully. *Noisily.* I held her closer to me as she rode the vast waves of pleasure that possessed her. When her body had finally slowed its quaking, I chuckled softly as we both came down off her high. Her plastered like literal glue to my front and me locking her to me like a treasure I had just discovered. We panted in unison, and I think the only possible atom in this entire house that wasn't satisfied was the one raging below my waist. But somehow, even that was okay because, *damn.*

"That sound—" I rasped into her hair. I was basically just hugging her now, my arm wrapped around her shoulders. I hadn't removed my other hand from her leggings, enjoying the little flinches of surprised pleasure my fingers brought out of her every so often.

"Don't say anything!" She tried to warn, but her tone was anything but stern. She was basically like jelly in my arms, all loose and moldable.

"—So *loud*." I laughed again because this was Clementine. Quiet, sweet, Clem. But she sounded…not quiet or sweet. I felt myself stiffen against her as I nuzzled, a groan escaping me. "So sexy."

"Ox," She laughed.

"Wife," I said softly. Contently.

"Welcome home."

"Damn right." I wouldn't let her go. I couldn't.

"Are you—" she trailed off, her hand fluttering backward and gripping my thigh. Searching.

Everything in me reacted to those soft fingers, but I just angled my hips so she couldn't quite reach what she was looking for. It created friction I wasn't ready for, and I had to clear my throat to mask a moan. "Perfectly content? Yes, Lunita, I am. Any man would be after—*that*."

"You didn't—"

"I *loved* it." I planted kisses along the curve of her shoulder. "I can leave and come in all over again if you want me to prove it."

She shook her head and smiled into her words. "You're unbelievable."

"I love those words coming out of your mouth." I cupped her involuntarily, remembering my hand was still touching her closely. She arched into me and whimpered. I watched her, amazed by this unexpected turn of events. With a nuzzle to her hair, I said, "I take it back. That sound—*that* is what I love."

"You're embarrassing me."

"Tough," I said. "Because you're killing me. You've *always* killed me. You know that don't you?"

"No," she said on a breathless whisper.

"How can I show you?"

She laughed. "You can start by looking at me. I haven't seen you in weeks."

She punctuated this by turning in my arms and gazing up at my face. She smiled a wide, beautiful grin, beaming at me. *For about a second.* I watched as her entire face fell, her eyes tracking across my person wildly.

She opened her mouth and breathed, no words coming out. She swallowed and tried again and when she opened her mouth the second time, she bit off the last thing I would have expected her to say.

"What the fuck!"

Chapter Twenty-four

CLEMENTINE

My entire body jerked, and not in the same way it had just minutes before, when Ox had moved his hands all over me. This was no less of a surprise, but instead of sending the same body wracking pleasure shooting through me, the sight of him caused me actual pain.

"What in the fuck happened to you?" I asked again.

"I think this is the first time I've heard you say the word fuck. And now you've said it twice," he said. He had leaned away from me, one hand going over the bottom of his chin, the other pointing at me. I noticed that his voice was neutral, as if there was nothing wrong.

"Oaxaca, your face!" I blurted. Not able to hold back anymore. Especially after what had just transpired between us.

When I came home from my last scheduled workout class of the year, I had not been expecting to be greeted by an early Christmas present on the kitchen counter. I saw the large white bow first. It stuck out as it sat high in the air on top of the *something* that was waiting for me on the island. A couple of steps into the kitchen and I quickly realized that something was a *really big something*.

It was a *KitchenShark 5000* electric stand mixer. The mother of all stand mixers and every baker's wet dream. And it was in a color I'm sure wasn't one of the five manufactured color options available in the catalog.

It was Tea Box Orange.

Maybe slightly paler. Even so, the appliance didn't come in *any* kind of orange and they definitely didn't come personalized with my name written on the side in pretty cursive script. Which could have only meant one thing. Ox had gotten it for me.

I was speechless. Surprised, elated, grateful. But it only made me miss him more.

Then he appeared. Standing behind me with my hair in his hand.

Another thing I hadn't been expecting Ox to do was wrap my braids around his fist and tease me seductively. But he had. And he'd done much more than tease. He'd touched, coaxed, and drawn a release out of me. I was reeling from the sudden occurrence. Shocked and stunned and maybe a little shy, but reeling. I had been excited to greet him and maybe see if he would also kiss me.

Until I saw his face.

He looked pretty normal. His short dark hair was swept back and to the side so it was out of his face. His creamy olive-brown skin was still clear and glowing, his deep brown eyes and accompanying full eyebrows were set on me. But when he turned his head, ever so slightly, I realized that his full chiseled jawline was marked with an angry purplish yellow bruise.

Quickly, I searched him for any other marring. The rest of his face was okay, but on the left side, where the bruise was, the coloring seemed to creep along the back of his jawline and onto his neck. Something had happened to him. Something that hurt. And he was standing here giving me presents and pleasure?

My body shook again, a shiver racking me hard.

"Clem?" Ox asked, noticing my tremble.

"Does it hurt?" I asked, staring up at the side of his face. I almost reached my fingers up toward it, but as soon as I had gotten as far as chest level, they had started to shake. I quickly folded them around each other.

"It's nothing Clem."

"Then why won't you tell me what happened?" I asked, crossing my arms to hide my shaking hands. "Accident? Fight? Did you fall?"

He eyed me like I was crazy for a second, then he turned away from me and began busying himself by pulling down two glasses and the water pitcher from the fridge.

"I definitely did *not* fall," he said with a scoff. Like he was above the human act of tripping sometimes.

I thought about his long, graceful legs which were decorated in dark denim and white long sleeves on top, and I sort of thought he was above tripping too. I mean, he was perfect in all other ways, I don't think I'd ever seen him so much as take a step out of place. The image of him slipping and falling onto his face did not compute for me.

He returned to me with a glass of water and when I didn't reach for it, he leaned past me and set it on the counter behind me. Before he ascended, he stopped near my shoulder and placed a soft kiss there.

"Don't worry yourself Clem, I'm fine," he said. He pecked another soft kiss onto the side of my neck, the same one I'm sure he must have marked with all his sucking just moments earlier.

Dueling warmth spread through me, both welcome and unwelcome. I loved these sweet touches he was showering me with. I wanted more, and I wanted to know why he was offering them all of a sudden. But I also hated that he was hiding something from me, something that had been potentially hurtful. Something that had *already* hurt him.

Both the anger and the fondness of it all warmed my skin. Ox noticed and picked the glass back up, offering it to me. I met his always steady gaze with my irritated one and held. This had become one of those few things I would not back down from with him. This had become personal.

"You're warm. Drink some water," he said, bossy as ever.

"I'm *angry*. I don't want any," I retorted.

"What's wrong?"

"What happened?"

"Is that what's got you upset?"

"That and the fact that you won't tell me what happened."

"Lunita—" he started to coax. I cut him off.

"Don't patronize me, Ox. Don't treat me like I'm too fragile to know what went down with you. I *need* to know what happened? And the fact that you're deflecting so much, leads me to believe that it was something bad."

He sighed, staring at me with a hard look. I think he was seeing how long I'd hold on for. So, I settled myself in and stared just as long back. After a while, he sighed even more heavily and gulped down both glasses of water before turning to the sink and walking them over to it.

"It wasn't an accident either," he said over his shoulder, his voice mumbling and unlike him.

I don't think I'd ever heard him mumble before. Still, I heard him well enough. He didn't fall, and it wasn't an accident, so—

"With who?" I asked, my voice going a little hoarse.

"My cousin." He was being vague, but when he glanced over his shoulder and saw that I was not amused by him withholding information, he added, "Manny."

Okay. He had gotten into a fight with his asshole cousin Manny. Which struck me as strange because I had never seen Ox so much as yell unless it had something to do with…

My mind chose that exact moment to flash back to Thanksgiving dinner, when I'd walked back into the dining room from the kitchen to see Ox entirely in one of his cousins' faces. He was speaking in one of his low controlled voices, but there was a bite to it. A vicious one that I had never heard before. He was too far away for me to make out what he was saying, but it didn't take a rocket scientist to know that it was my fault. I had somehow caught the attention of this cousin and all night he had been saying things that weren't exactly horrible, but just rude or invasive enough to make me uncomfortable. Ox had had enough and had sent him packing with barely restrained anger.

My breath stuck in my throat and my eyes continued their search along Ox's body. His face wasn't particularly bad, just a small bruise on the side, but… I caught sight of Ox's right hand, and I knew.

The purplish, almost red bruising along his knuckles, accompanied by scrapes that were just starting to heal proved it. Ox had gotten into a fight, sure, but he had done most of the fighting. Which means he was probably the aggressor. And it was all my fault.

"You fought him because of me, right?" I asked. My voice was this weird hoarse thing that was not of my control.

Ox peeked over his shoulder and looked at me. "It doesn't matter, Clem."

"It does matter!" I almost shouted. "It matters to me, Ox!"

I felt a shuddering breath leave my body and I pushed off the counter and started my way toward the front door. Ox was hot on my heels.

"Woah, woah," he said, his voice taking on one that you might use on a scared horse. "Where are you going?"

I walked faster. "I don't know. To find someone who will tell me what happened. To…to find that son of a bitch who hit you."

Ox jogged, getting in front of me and stopping me by my shoulders. He looked down on me seriously and I stared up at him with fire in my eyes. When twenty seconds, then thirty, then a minute passed with him saying nothing at all, I moved to try to get past him again.

He stepped with me, blocking me out. Then he whispered, "Lo

siento, Lunita. I didn't mean to scare you."

"It's not okay," I said on a whimper. I sniffled, my emotion showing past my anger for the first time. I crossed my arms to hide my clenching fists. "It's not okay that you're hurt because of me. Tell me what happened."

"It wasn't really anything, Clem. He's been saying all this stuff about you for months now and I don't know if it's just to get under my skin or because he really…wants you, but regardless, I'm done taking it." He moved his thumbs across the tops of my shoulders soothingly.

"You should have just walked away," I said, my head shaking. I hated, *hated*, that he was hurt because someone said something stupid and about me of all things.

"What, and let him get away with that shit?" he asked, anger slipping into his tone.

"*Of course*. He's your family," I said, even though I wasn't feeling the least bit familial toward the guy. On top of being a complete asshole, he had gone and bruised my Ox. "He's your family and I'm not worth you getting hurt over."

"You are worth something to me, Clem," he growled. His eyes were zeroed in on me, glaring laser-like daggers at my face.

My jaw felt as if it had locked, I was clenching it so hard. My throat burned along with the rest of my body, and I felt like a live wire about to detonate. "*You* are worth something to me, Oaxaca. You are worth something to a lot of people. And I am *not* okay with this," I said very carefully through clenched teeth.

I'm not embarrassed to admit that at this point I was on the verge of tears. It was like a curtain had come up off the veil of my feelings and now they were all out there on stage for anyone to witness.

Ox meant something to me. No, Ox meant *so much* to me, and he was still so hell bent on putting me first. Just moments ago in the kitchen he had done just that. I wasn't complaining, but I wanted him to understand that I could take care of him just as much as he took care of me. That I could give to him just as much, and that sometimes he could in fact expect something in return from others. Especially from me.

But he was as stubborn as a bull, and wouldn't accept anyone else stepping forward and taking care of him. And it killed me that he didn't trust me to lean on. Because I trusted him implicitly. I wouldn't have let him touch me like that earlier if I didn't.

Ox seemed to pick up on yet another switch in my emotions. He leaned back, inspecting my face diligently, then sighed. "Lunita."

"Ox," I squeezed out, my voice hitching and a tear slipping out the side of my eye. I turned my head to hide it, but there was no use.

He used his fingers to turn my face toward him. His mouth was pressed into a grim line and his eyes burned down to mine. But they also held a tenderness as he stared at me, trying to convey something with that look alone.

Slowly, he wiped the single tear I had lost with his thumb and then he smoothed some of my fly-always back into my ponytail. The smallest tick sent the corner of his mouth up in a fleeting smile.

"Always my sweet girl," he said in a soft voice.

"Always a *stubborn* Ox," I grumbled right back.

He chuckled. "What, no Oxtopus today?"

"No." I sniffed. "There's no reward for coming home with bruised hands."

That smile turned into a full-on grin. He took a step forward, bringing me into his personal space. His entire hand cupped my jaw as he leaned down close to my ear, so close that I could feel his breath inside of me.

"You seemed to like my hands earlier." He pulled back just far enough for me to see his smug raised eyebrows. I cleared my throat, my body heating all over. Damn this man, he was being… He was being so good yet bad all at the same time. And he was confusing my feelings which was making me crazy.

"You're not taking this seriously," I whispered, no longer trusting my betraying voice.

"I take everything you say seriously," he said back, and I believed him. "I'm sorry about the fight, Clem. I didn't know it would make you this upset to see a couple of scrapes."

I opened my mouth to protest with that insanity, but he cut me off quickly.

"And even though I hate that I upset you, I'm not sorry for standing up for you. I will never not stand up for you, you have got to understand that about me, Clementine."

I swallowed my words and rolled my lips in between my teeth. He stepped back and pulled me along with him. "Now, will you come and lay down with me? I'm tired."

I looked at him through the sides of my eyes. Relaxed, content, at ease. And yet, he was still *hurt*. And it was still because of me.

I couldn't let it go.

"Yeah," I said as I cleared my throat. "Yeah Ox, I'm sorry. Let's rest for a little while."

We spent the rest of the day napping, watching tv, catching up, and wrapping Christmas presents. It was positively catalog, the way we laughed and teased as we just spoke with each other. The way our lives had commingled so harmoniously and how we just fit.

And still, *still,* deep down I was pissed off.

Later, after Ox had fallen asleep for the second time that day out of pure exhaustion, I scrolled through my phone contacts and dialed the number I was looking for.

"What?" they answered.

"I need your help with something."

Chapter Twenty-five

CLEMENTINE

The night was cold and loud. Wind whooshed around us as we walked, and the only light that illuminated the downtown condo's rooftop parking garage was a single lamp post at the head of the structure.

I walked quickly, almost too fast for Ceci to keep up with my strides. She was positively bouncing beside me, the large stick she held in her hands swinging with each of her steps.

"Are you sure about this?" I asked, the first bit of nervousness shooting through me since I called her hours ago.

"You backing down on me now, Ferguson?" she asked, darting a disbelieving look over her shoulder at me before shaking her head. "No you're not. Remember what you said earlier?"

"That I wanted to hit something?" I asked.

"Exactly!" She bounced as she spoke. "So, we're going to hit some shit."

I swallowed and turned my gaze forward. The black sports car in front of us was the only one in the rooftop lot. We had needed to take a special elevator with a special code to get up there and, of course, Ceci knew all of this because it was her family's building.

We approached the car that was diagonally parked in the middle of the lot, because of course it was. The closer we got to it, the angrier I got. I felt my grip tighten around my own wooden weapon and my breaths started to come fast. Within another moment, we were standing in front of it.

We circled it, surveying the sleek doors, rounded hood and shiny dark paint. It was nice. Which just made me madder. I thrust my gaze upward, finding Ceci's from across the automobile.

"How do I do this?" I asked, my voice clipped and tight.

"Well, you raise the bat and—"

"Celestia!" I warned.

She had started speaking in that smartass tone that was native to her. But my adrenaline and fear were spiking through me with jagged, unsure edges and right then, I couldn't take her shit.

She shut up as soon as I cut her off. Eying me curiously, she must have found something in my expression that gave me away. The next thing I knew, she was coming around the hood of the car where I was standing and getting behind me. She stood close enough that I felt her there, but not close enough that she was in my swinging radius.

"Clementine." Ceci's voice was low, almost soft as if she was trying to fade into the blackness of my thoughts. "Why did you even come here?"

I felt a lump rise in my throat. "Because your cousin is an asshole."

"Yeah," Ceci agreed. "But *why*?"

I whipped around, my braids swinging around my shoulders. "He *hit* him, Ceci."

"So what are you going to do about it?" she asked, her voice still that soft, matter-of-fact tone.

An image of Ox's bruised face and even more bruised hands flashed through my mind and I expelled a breath that shook my entire chest. Turning back to the expensive hunk of steel, I raised my bat (gifted to me by the reckless Ceci Fernandez herself) to shoulder level.

I thought about that bruise, the one and only imperfection on him. And I tried to think of a single thing he had done to deserve it. Taken up for me? Take care of a girl he was left the right to in a will? Take care of a family that he loved? Take care of a business legacy that he devoted all his time to? He had given and given for the benefit of everyone else in his life, but when it came to himself, he'd take any amount of shit. No questions asked.

I wasn't exempt from the crimes either. The very first time we met, he had saved me while I... I hadn't even talked to him for weeks. And again, and again, and again the story continued. He was there for me while I was there falling apart. He made a career out of picking up my broken pieces, and in return, I just broke more of him.

My blood rushed through my face, roaring in my ears, but I didn't hear anything. The only thing I heard was Ox's voice in my head. His voice from that first night, calling out to me, trying to pull me out of my trance. *Clementine. Clem. Your brothers are here. Will you come with me to see them?* He'd asked. He'd asked it again and again until I'd answered.

He hadn't left. He hadn't yelled. He hadn't faltered. He'd been there. He continued to be there.

And I was ungrateful and bratty. Spoiled and difficult.

And still he was here.

So, what had he done to deserve this offense? And what had I done to deserve his protection?

I thought about all the apologies I could offer Ox for my neglect and exploitation and entitlement, and how he wouldn't accept a single one of them. He would simply tell me that I had done nothing wrong.

I thought about the consequences of doing nothing at all. About just letting this continue to happen and being the doormat for all others to walk on. About continuing to let Ox take the brunt of my punches. About being weak.

I decided that I wasn't going to do that anymore.

And then I took the first swing.

Right down onto the hood of the car. The bat made a hard banging noise as it slammed down onto the surface. Whizzing through the air, it ricocheted back at me hard and came swinging up at my face. I swept my head to the side, trying to dodge, but it nicked the edge of my hairline. The friction of the force scratching the skin there and stinging.

I hissed and jumped backward.

Another flash of the purple marks on Ox's body came to me. And then more sounds. The sounds of his laugh shaking me again. I could hear Ceci warning from somewhere far away. *Easy Ferguson. Hurt the car, not yourself.*

I paid her no mind. Instead, I brought the bat down again, this time *keeping it down* and causing a deep marring dent.

In my head, I saw Ox on the Labor Day boat with his family, laughing and playing around and enjoying himself. And then I saw those damn marks again.

I swung the bat harder, causing the dent to sink in further and eliciting a whining noise from the steel.

"Stay away from the engine, Ferg," Ceci said from somewhere beside me now. She had hitched her own bat up and was swinging at the side of the car, denting in the doors.

I followed suit. The cold, cold breeze that whipped across my cheeks reminded me of the windy beach Ox walked on with me every day he was able. And then I saw the scars again.

Swing.

Something flew from the car, swishing past my face. *Glass.*

I stopped. I hadn't even heard the window shatter. But my eyes seemed to clear of the raging haze I was in just in time to witness the flying glass shards as they flew past me in a buoyant rush before falling to the ground. The debris whipped around me in a tornado of movement, but I was wearing warm clothes, and for the most part I hadn't gotten hit. I could only feel a slight wetness on my face. Raising my hand to my cheek, I pulled it away and saw blood.

My breathing narrowed and I felt a sharp stab in my chest. The glass, the blood, the cold. It all reminded me of a familiar night. One during my marriage to Ronaldo, when I had taken a chance and tried to stand up for myself.

I trembled as my grip on the bat tightened to an almost painful degree. I didn't see Ox's face anymore. Instead, I saw my jailer's. I saw his face and blood and the glass of my teacups as they flew from their hutch and crashed onto the floor. The pain of my spine as I was bent backward at an unnatural angle. The fear in my chest as a harsh threatening whisper spoke directly into my ear.

A violent shudder racked through me and I breathed hard. Ceci called out to me in question, but I could only hear *his* voice. A voice that I had drowned out for months now. A voice that I had cowered from for so long.

Another tremor racked me, this one more violent than the rest. And then I was moving again... *Swinging* again.

Blood roared through me, but I still felt cold. Sweat nicked at the back of my neck and behind my eyes I saw another instance where Ron had made me sit and watch as he disposed of every single personal item I had brought with me from home. Effectively erasing my individuality.

Swing.

I saw how Ron watched my brothers for months on the security cameras. Knocking on the doors, leaving messages, trying to call in. All to get to me. And he never once allowed anyone to answer.

Swing.

I saw his face over and over and over again. So I swung the bat down over and over and over again. My senses were muddled. All I could clearly make out was Ron's face, Ron's smell, Ron's laugh; all of it. And all I could do was swing at it. I wanted to destroy it, to beat him until he was dead again. And this time not by accident, but because I finally took my control back.

Glass could have been flying or I could have beaten the car door right off its hinges and I wouldn't have noticed anymore. I was gone and nothing could bring me back.

Nothing, of course, except for the sound of Oaxaca's quick and gruff Spanish yelling at me to stop.

"Clementine!" he seethed.

He must have said it repeatedly, because by the time I realized it was him I was hearing, he had gotten so close that he was basically speaking into my ear. And I was airborne. A strong arm wrapped around my waist as he dragged me away from the car. His other hand was attempting to wrangle the bat from the vice grip I had on it.

"Clementine, calm down!" he rasped again at my ear. He was backing us away from the car, me slung against his front like a sack of potatoes.

We made it several feet away before he deposited me onto the ground in front of him and then angled his body so that he was between me and the vehicle, as if he thought I would charge for it. I honestly thought about it.

But then I saw Ox's face. His eyes were wild as he looked at me, his jaw set. He was in his thin, dark athletic joggers he usually wore around the house, a tight fitting long sleeve the only thing covering him on top. He must have rushed out of the house. I bet he was cold...

Or maybe not. Not while he looked at me with those burning pupils. He huffed out a breath that a foolish man would think sounded like a laugh. I knew better. I could hear the disbelief and shock and disapproval in his tone.

"Are you completely insane?" he asked me. I didn't know what he wanted me to say or what to say at all. I just watched him as I caught my breath, my chest rising and falling the only movement between us. His eyes narrowed at me and he raked a hand through his hair, messing up the dark locks. He raised his voice, anger booming from every chord. "Answer, Clementine! *What are you doing here?*"

"I think it's pretty obvious," I said between huffs of air. Ox damn near threw the bat down on the ground between us.

"*Clem.* Why are you out here on Christmas Eve, beating the shit out of my cousin's car?"

"Not Christmas Eve," I mumbled. I knew I was being petty, but I had no other defense in this situation, and I was pretty sure he was actually going to kill me.

He pinched the bridge of his nose, taking slow, measurable breaths as he visibly tried to calm down. When he spoke, the killing calm was back in his voice. "It *is* Christmas Eve. You want to know how I know it is? Because I went upstairs to collect my wife not too long ago, only to find that she was gone—*past* midnight, mind you—without a word of where the hell she was going."

"*And then,*" he continued before I could sneak a word in. "And then I find you on top of one of my garages *committing a crime.*"

I glanced sideways, eyeing the dented-up car. The black paint was scraped on both its sides. Just one window had broken, but it left an ugly gaping imperfection in the side of the pretty car. The rest of the metal was riddled with dings and dents, the biggest being the huge dent I had banged into the driver's side door.

Glancing further behind me I could see Ceci standing far away from the car, bat gone, her arms crossed over her chest as she talked to someone. *My brother.* Connor was over there lecturing Ceci, finger wagging and everything. *Weird.*

My eyes were wrenched away from them and so was my entire face as Ox used his fingers to pull my chin toward him. When he had gotten so close, I didn't know, but after only a few short seconds of looking down on my face, he was storming away again. His hands raking through his hair the whole time.

"You're hurt, Clementine," he said in a strangled voice I didn't recognize.

"I'm fine," I assured him, because I was. The look he gave me though made me feel like I was missing a tooth or something.

"You're obviously not fine," he spat. "You're bleeding! And for what? You put yourself in danger *for what*? A stupid fight?"

"Not for a stupid fight, Ox. For you!" I said, my anger returning in an all-consuming wave.

"Oh, for me?" He scoffed, raising his arms up at his sides before letting them drop again. "Oh, well, thank you very much, Clementine. Thanks for scaring the *shit* out of me."

He paced further away, his hands going to his hips and then to his head before he came charging back to me with heated steps. "You know, if this was anyone else's property, you'd be arrested by now."

"I don't care."

"*I care*," he groaned.

"And somehow that's more valid?" I spat out. "What's the difference between you taking up for me and me doing the same for you? I can't just go beat the guy up, Ox. I mean, Ceci said he wasn't home so—"

Ox looked at me disbelievingly. "*Tell me* you didn't try to—"

"No," I shook my head. "She talked me out of it."

He cursed on a hiss and paced away again. When he came back, he had exercised some deep breathing and was speaking in a semi-normal voice again. "Clem, sweetheart. Tell me what's going on. This isn't like you."

"No, this is exactly like me, Ox." It was my turn to advance. My turn to point at him menacingly and speak through my barely controlled anger. "I told you that this was not okay with me."

"Clem, I understand but—"

"No, you don't understand! You really, really don't. And sometimes, when you don't hear me like this, I start to feel just as silenced as before," I said, my voice going weak.

My stomach curled at the admission. Because of course, *of course*, Ox was no Ron. And I never wanted him to think I thought of him that way. But I needed him to understand that I wasn't just here to look pretty and be amenable. Not anymore. I wanted to stand *with* him, not in front and not behind. I'd used him as a human shield for my hardships from day one and I wanted to start pulling my weight.

But of course Ox couldn't read my thoughts. He could only hear my words and the bite of them made him hiss in a breath and stop his movements. He looked at me for a long second before he squared his shoulders with mine, folded his arms and looked me in the eye.

"Explain it to me then," he said. No more anger, no more judgment, no more reprimand. He was Ox again. My Ox, and he was as serious as a heart attack. He wanted me to explain myself. And considering the moment, it seemed like it was now or never. Stay the Clem I'd always been or become something different.

I took a deep breath that I felt all the way down to my gut. The cold air was brisk and it put pins and needles throughout my throat. I spoke anyway.

"I know all you can think of me as is 'sweet Clementine' or 'fragile Clementine' or 'so damaged she can't sleep through the night Clementine', but I'm not like that inside." I started. I was convinced I wasn't making any sense but kept trying anyway. "I'm not always sunshine and rainbows, Oaxaca. You know more than most by now that sometimes the dark in my mind gets to me and I sink. I sink so far down and I can't stop myself... And sometimes I don't want to.

"No. Actually, I refuse to. I fucking refuse to pretend like I'm some fragile, sweet little girl who will never fight back. I refuse to continue to let things that are important to me get trampled without me doing anything about it. Especially not when it comes to you, Ox."

"What do I have to do with any of that, Clem?" he asked, sounding, not angry, but sort of pained. "Have I really made you feel fragile and weak?"

"Sometimes?" I said. But his sincere confusion tripped me up. "Maybe. I don't know. I'm not explaining this well."

I ran my hand over the top of my head. It was shaking, and it was then I realized I was nervous. Not only nervous, but I was scared to admit all of this to him. Because what if after these thoughts and feelings finally left my body, nothing else happened? What if the world still didn't care and I was still in the same place as before? What if Ox didn't accept it?

I heaved in a breath.

"Clem." Ox's voice was soft, trying to coax my attention back. Instead of trying to placate me or coddle me, he gave me what I needed. Respect. "*I'm listening.*"

Another sharp breath, but this time a readying one.

"Ox, what I'm trying to say is, I've watched you go to war for your family *and* for me more times than I can count. And I can't stand that there's no one out there putting out the same effort for you." I squared my shoulders with him and straightened up.

"I'm not fragile, Ox. I can hold you and me both up. So just trust me to lean on sometimes." Leaning down, I picked up the bat and swung it over the top of my shoulder as if I was poised to strike again. But my voice was small, maybe even shy. "I'll be your backup too, okay?"

Ox laughed. I think more out of disbelief than actual amusement, but still the deep rumbling sound left him in surprised huffs. With his hands up, he edged closer to me as if he was trapping a stray cat. When he reached me, he first dislodged the bat from my grip. Then, he quickly replaced it with his hands, holding onto mine tightly.

"Clementine, listen to me," he started.

"Okay."

"Do you want to know why I call you Lunita? Why you are my moon?" he asked.

I blinked up to him, thrown off by his sudden switch in conversation. Slowly, I began to shake my head. "Because I stay up late?"

"No," he said. He pulled me closer, bringing both his hands up to cup my face. He ran his thumbs up and down my cheeks, stopping his fingers just short of the area that was bleeding. Looking at that spot, his eyes seemed to glass over with anger, but he swallowed it and continued. "No, Clem. I started calling you that in my head the first time you lit up my damn night. You came right in with all your shy looks and weird jokes and that sly little way you can be such a hardass while making it seem like you're being perfectly sweet."

My body began to pull away on its own. I always wondered why he'd started calling me that, but I hardly believed that it was because of something so…personal.

He held onto me, keeping me close to him. Keeping me looking at him as he continued. "No, listen Clem. You shine. In every room, at every turn, you've shined a light on me that I didn't know I needed. A light that's better than any amount of sunshine and rainbows in the entire world."

"The moon doesn't shine, Ox," I mumbled, my gaze hitting the ground. He used his hands to guide it back up.

"And yet," he started, kicking the bat away from me for good measure, "the moon still lights up the darkest nights."

"I don't get it," I said.

He lowered his head down to mine and lowered his voice down to a whisper. "I'm saying that I already lean on you, Clem. And I don't need you to run out and beat up my enemies in the middle of the night to prove it. The only thing I need you to do is keep lighting my way through the darkness."

Chapter Twenty-six

OX

It was Christmas and I was worried about Clem.

As soon as we got home from *the incident that should not be named*, she scampered off into the shower like she had a fire under her ass. She then tried to wait me out by staying in the shower for an obscene amount of time. Honestly, I should have known this wouldn't be easy by the quiet way she'd retreated in the car. Apparently, Ceci had driven the two of them to their little crime scene (probably so I wouldn't hear the garage door). So when we all parted ways, Clem had come with me and Connor had gone with Ceci.

I was lucky to have wrangled Connor out to help. The earlier realization that Clementine was gone had scared the shit out of me. She had been acting a little off ever since she saw my bruises, and when I woke up on the couch to a silent house, I just knew.

I called Clay right away, asking if he knew where his sister was. He said he had no idea, and he wasn't in town to help, but if I really needed backup to call Connor. I did. And he came with a plan, which was plenty more than I had. All I was able to do at that point was panic.

He quickly tracked the girls' phones to one of the Fernandez real estate buildings in downtown Seaside and when I realized it was a building that Manny occupied the penthouse of, I told Connor that we had to find them right away.

Which led me right to my bat swinging, expectation crushing wife.

I swear, the first thing I thought of when I saw her wreaking her havoc on top of that roof was how beautiful she was. Her dark skin glowed in the dim light and it was like she moved in slow motion. Each time she swung the bat down on my cousin's already dented car, her long hair flew around her like it was alive and angry too.

But that only lasted a second. And then I realized how afraid I was. There was glass everywhere, I had already noticed blood on her, and she was swinging that thing around so hard she could have knocked herself out with it. I had to get her.

And when I did, she got mad at me.

It was strange to have her mad at me again. But it was stranger to have her mad at me and for me to be mad right back. I couldn't understand why she was being like that, why she would go through so much trouble for probably the most anticlimactic fight of my life. Manny had hardly even put up resistance to begin with. I got about three good punches into his one before he was "apologizing" and scampering off to his planned vacation with his parents in Vail.

As a result, I now had a scarred and broken wife. After her whole spiel on the roof—where she basically admitted that she wasn't being understood and thus needed to assert herself (albeit by imploring the borderline insane method of trashing a man's car), she had barely spoken to me. On Christmas Eve, she spent most of the day pretending like she had things to prepare for the holiday. When before, I was sure that we'd planned to spend the whole day watching Christmas movies while she baked cookies, and I did '*whatever it was I usually did when I wasn't working*'.

Instead of movies, she left. Gone all day with her brothers to go shopping or something. At some point she was gone so long, I thought I wouldn't get to see her or have the chance to talk about what happened the night before. But later in the day I heard an almost banging entrance at the foyer followed by the sound of a huffing man.

"Stop running away, Tiney. Own up to your shit. You were actually pretty badass last night." It was Clay, apparently back from his own end-of-year work and having had possession of my wife all day. Rising off the couch, I walked just far enough into the foyer to see them. Clay was setting some bags down at her feet before stopping in front of her and looking down at her seriously. They exchanged a few more words, those more hushed, before I heard him say a retreating "alright" and ruffle her hair. His gaze flicked upward and a slow grin spread across his face. Something about that look let me know. I could just tell the bastard had rewarded her for her reckless behavior the night before.

With a dainty little finger wave he said, "*Hi, Oxy.* Your present's in the bag."

He blew me a playful kiss. One that I caught midair and patted to my heart with the seriousness of a surgeon. Laughing, he leaned down and kissed Clem on the cheek before saying he would see her tomorrow for Christmas dinner and to have a good night.

When the door shut behind him and Clementine turned to look at me, we held each other's eyes for one, two, three long beats before I made a move first. In the end, it was a move away from her. I assumed she needed space to think about the emotional discourse that had slipped from her while we were on the roof. And I needed time to think about— To just think. So, after raising my eyebrows at her in what I hoped was a look that said, '*I hope you're doing okay*', I turned my shoulders to head back into the living room.

I was stopped by a tentative call from behind me. "Um, Ox?"

Turning to look over my shoulder I waited for her to say something. She didn't. Instead, she looked at me with a look that resembled pain before she scampered off in the other direction.

Later, I panicked when I couldn't find her again. For a second I was afraid that she'd run away to her brother's or worse, to one of my sisters and we would have yet another rocky night. But on a whim, I decided to check the back mud hall and sure enough her beach shoes were gone.

I found her out there on the sand. Before I left the house, I made a split-second decision to bring two warm blankets and two thermoses full of her favorite tea. I also grabbed a hat in case she wasn't wearing one and some unused hand warmers that were sitting at the bottom of a junk drawer.

I was right to come so prepared. It was so cold, I was sure my eyelashes would freeze if I didn't keep blinking them. As to be expected for winter along the northern Atlantic coast on Christmas Eve.

Clementine was sitting outside in the sand facing the water. She wore her biggest puffer jacket; one I had gotten for her when she'd been persistent about her beloved walks. She was also clad in dark sweatpants that flowed around her legs in large rounds of fabric. They looked cozy. So did her matching sweatshirt and sherpa boots, her beach shoes in a pile beside her.

She didn't turn when I came up behind her, but I assumed she heard me. Although the crashing of the icy waves were loud in the mid-evening tide, the crunch of the brittle cold sand was quite obvious under my heavy steps. Walking right up to her, I stopped by her side. Sorting through the items in my hand, I leaned down to spread a warm sherpa blanket around her shoulders. As I did, I caught the smell of her honey scent and I couldn't resist kissing her hair before raising up and setting the other stuff on the sand beside her.

Within moments, I had lowered myself to the ground next to her. I opened the thermos to the netted filter top and placed the little cup-top into her hands. I noted that both of her hands and her head were ungloved. I would fix that later. But first, I poured the hot tea into her waiting cup. The smell wafted up the sweet floral notes and spicy holiday undertones that I knew she loved. She looked hungrily at the liquid, but when she looked up at me, her eyes held a different sort of expression. I met her gaze with one that I hoped conveyed my support for whatever it was she was going through, but it dropped swiftly in order to prevent the thermos from overspilling.

We sat in that sort of silence for long moments. Clementine sipped her tea, purring at the taste, and offered me some. I took a sip from her cup, just for an excuse to lean into her. Our eyes locked again and I could tell she wanted to say something, but was too shy to.

I didn't want to push her, but I sort of did. What she said the night before had excited me. The entire time I'd known Clem, I'd known her as a woman scorned. A woman who had been hurt badly before and who was still paying the price of the abuse from her past. I understood that side of her, but sometimes when I was with her, I got to see glimpses of who she had been before the worst happened. And I liked them.

If she was ready to start putting her pain away and moving forward with her life, I couldn't help but feel like it was a positive step toward our future.... *Her* future. I wasn't even sure there was an *us* in it. We only had a three-year contract after all.

Bumping my shoulder into hers gently, careful not to make her tea spill, I looked over at her. "Three things you're thinking about right now."

"We aren't in bed," she answered dryly.

"Would you like to be?"

"You're ridiculous."

"You're avoiding me. I don't like it." I gave her a grim look to show her I was serious. Her eyes were wide in return.

"I'm sorry," she whispered, her eyes fluttering down to her tea thermos miserably. I wanted to reach over to her but I had vowed to give her space. "That's the first thing I'm thinking about. I'm so sorry, Ox."

"Hey." I felt a lump in my throat at the sound of her sullen voice. "You better be sorry, that's *Oxtopus* to you."

She giggled weakly, but she didn't look at me. I bumped her shoulder again and she whipped her gaze to me after having to scramble to settle the sloshing liquid in her hands.

"Will you stop that, Oaxaca?" Her voice was just as quiet but it held that slight irritation that she sometimes let slip. There was fire under all that honey, and I wanted to see more.

"Don't 'Oaxaca' me, tell me what's wrong," I said, catching onto her mood.

With a grunt, she burrowed her head in her arms, covering her face. Reaching over, I slipped the tea out of her hands and set it down in the stiff sand. Her fingers were cold, even after holding the warm cup. I reached beside me into my bundle of supplies and found the hat and gloves I'd brought out for this very reason. I slipped each piece of clothing onto her extremities and when I was satisfied that she was sufficiently covered I leaned back to look at her fully.

She was looking back at me.

"What?" I asked.

"Why are you like this?" she asked.

"What? Overbearing and pushy? Nosey? Controlling? Stubborn? Set in my ways?"

"Ox, *no*…" she started, but she trailed off and just shook her head.

"I'm just naming all the things others have to say about me. Of course I don't think *all* of them are true. But some of them could be." I admitted.

"They're *all* true, Ox," she snorted. Her eyes flickering up to mine with a grin. "But *I* was going to say *perfect*."

Oh.

"Tell me what's wrong," I said again, needing to know.

"I feel a little silly, acting that way," she admitted, looking away from me again, this time out to the water in front of us. "I'm not sorry I did it, I'm just—I'm sorry it all came out like that."

"All?"

"All of *me*," she confessed. "I've been bottling it up for a while now. I could have told someone sooner how I was feeling, but when I saw you had gotten hurt and still all you wanted to do was take care of me… Something about it set me off."

We were silent for a little while. Her, I assumed, because she had said all she'd needed to say. And me because I felt sort of dumb. Once again, my attempts to take care of everything for everyone had somehow hurt her.

"I'm sorry, Clem," I said, meaning every single syllable of it. She looked at me once again, holding my gaze for a long while before leaning over and bumping her shoulder to mine. *It's okay*, the movement said. Instead of bumping her back I leaned my shoulder into hers and kept it there. "I meant every word I said to you last night, you know?"

"It's all kind of a blur," she said, a hitch in her voice. I knew she was lying by the way she turned her chin away from me, hiding her expression. The movement hurt in a way I never knew it could. Something in my gut twisted and that hard lump in my throat seemed to lodge itself there, getting comfortable. I didn't know entirely what I felt for Clementine, and sometimes that pull of emotions I didn't understand was frightening and all-encompassing.

But I was honest, and I knew this protectiveness and warmth I felt toward her, was more than just that of obligation and duty. I had a feeling she felt something more too, but we could go nowhere if she wasn't ready.

"Can I ask you something, Clem?" She hummed a little 'mhmm' in response. "Have you been back to that house? Abuelo's—*Yours*."

"Don't call it that," she said, her voice going hoarse and clipped. "That place wasn't my home."

"It isn't your home anymore, no," I said, keeping my voice even and non-threatening. "But it was. For a long time and you spent a lot of formative years there."

"What are you getting at, Oaxaca?" she asked, her shoulders caving in a little on themselves.

I felt a weight settle on my chest. She was definitely *not ready*. But damn, I wanted her to be. The time in the kitchen and all the times with us in my bed and every single time she laughed at me or looked at me like she wasn't hurting anymore, all made me want things. First, I just wanted her to be okay. But I also wanted her to be ready for an "*us*". Whatever "us" entailed and for however long.

"I'm just saying that it might benefit you to go there," I said.

"How could it possibly benefit me?"

"You carry a lot of your past around with you, and I think it's because you've never actually been allowed to properly shut the door on any of those chapters."

She was silent.

"I could go with you," I pushed. "I could—"

"Stop, Ox!" She cut me off with a miserable plea. "What is this, some kind of therapy session?"

"I thought about mentioning that, but I didn't want my car to be next on the chopping block—", I said. I was going for funny, but I felt a slight pang of bitter hurt slip into my chest. *She just wasn't ready.* "But no, Clem. This isn't therapy. We are just *talking*."

"It sounds like you're doing all the talking. *Again*," she said, voice hard, body language closed.

Not ready, not ready, not ready.

But I couldn't get myself to stop pushing. Overbearing was my middle name, after all. "Yeah? Well, it sounds like you're running away. *Again*."

She sucked in a breath and looked at me like I'd just struck her. I sighed. "I'm not trying to hurt you Clem, I just—"

"You're what? Just trying to manage everyone around you, like you always do? Have you ever thought that maybe I'm fine with things just the way they are?"

I pulled back too. Fine with things the way they are? As in, *fine with our contract ending in two years and six months?* Or fine as in, *fine with us hovering in this limbo of attraction and affection but never really committing to anything further?* I didn't like either option and I'm sure it showed on my face.

"Not so easy being picked apart?" she asked, sounding a little triumphant and gloaty.

"Not so easy to talk to you when you're like this," I corrected. I stopped looking at her then, feeling a little scathed by her heated mood.

"Am I supposed to be easy for you, Ox?"

I slid a glance to her and then back out to the water. "Why are you looking for a fight?"

"I'm not," she pouted. "I'm really not, I just feel so...open."

"And you don't like it?"

"I don't."

"Okay."

"Why do you say okay like that?"

"Like what, exactly?"

"Like you disapprove of me somehow."

I looked at her again. She'd drawn her arms around herself even tighter, effectively making herself more or less a ball. I sighed. "Have I been bad to you, Clem?"

She whipped her head around to me. "Ox, no!"

I flinched involuntarily at the answer. I wasn't trying to make her feel bad, that wasn't my intention. I just wanted to know where we both stood.

"Are you still afraid of me?" I asked. "Like you were at our wedding and before? Do I still scare you?"

"You know you don't Ox, don't say that," she said, sitting up and

369

turning toward me, her knees in the sand.

I shook my head and looked away from her. "Do you think I'm like him?"

"Ox—" she warned in a husky voice. "Stop."

"No, really. I'm his grandson, you never asked for any of this yet I still forced you into it. Do you think I'm him?" I asked again.

"Oaxaca, stop it." She breathed. "You know I don't think of you like that. You know this is different, so *stop*."

I looked at her pleading face, all pained and desperate and hurting. Squeezing my eyes shut, I tried to block out the image. Then I ducked my head into my arms. "Sorry, I just… I'm stuck, Clem."

"Stuck how?"

"Stuck between knowing what to do and not knowing anything at all. Stuck between feelings. Stuck in place by the reality that last night we both said things up on that roof and yet…" I paused and I took a breath. Looking up at her face, I let it out in a long, aggravated sigh. "Yet somehow I heard what you said to me—I heard every word and even the meaning *between* those words—but you still haven't heard me."

"You aren't hearing me."

"You aren't seeing what I'm trying to show you."

Water coated her eyes and suddenly I didn't want to be there anymore. I didn't want to make her cry, but in that moment, I couldn't take back what I'd said to her.

We had done a great job of not sacrificing who we were for the others' benefit. And it had worked up until then. Up until I'd gone and admitted something that was too big for her meter to hold. She was beginning to short circuit.

She was like a perennial flower. I'd seen her at all stages, I'd seen her beautifully full grown. I'd seen her wilting, and I'd seen her falling apart. It was sad to watch something so pretty lose all that it had. But the good thing was, that it would come back. Still, even as I watched her grow back from her wilted state into brand new flourishing petals, I realized that her pot was still too small to support a partner.

"Ox?" Clem's voice broke through my thoughts with a tentative whisper.

When my eyes cleared and I saw her again, I realized the toll my words had taken on her, and on myself.

So, I got up. It seemed abrupt, but really, I had been torturing myself ever since I'd asked about Abuelo's house. Torturing myself with hope that she would tackle something she just wasn't ready for. Hope that her willingness to fight for me meant that she was ready to fight other things as well. Hope that this was all going to play out the way I only wished for in my wildest dreams. I had suffocated myself with thoughtless hopes and watching her tear it away with every defensive word she spoke made my heart hurt. I had been wanting to leave ever since.

So, leaning down, I pressed a kiss to the top of her hatted head and said, "Come in soon so you don't catch a cold."

Then, I hightailed it out of there with my fucking heart in my ass.

It was coming to my attention that I was a hypocrite. As much as I wanted to know exactly what she wanted, I also didn't. Because, heaven help me, I had no idea what I'd do if what she wanted wasn't me.

Which brought me back to Christmas. I sat in my parents' home. It was long after presents had been opened and games had been played, candy and treats all consumed.

Clementine had left earlier that morning to spend time with her family, her brothers mostly and her parents maybe. Even though we'd made these Christmas arrangements ages ago, the space felt like some sort of rift separating us. Like our argument had wedged this insurmountable void in between us and we couldn't see past it.

Cold rippled through a spot on my neck as someone pressed something against it. I peeked up to my side and mustered up a half smile when I saw Lis standing there with a clear mug full of white milky liquid outstretched to me. I could see a light speckle of cinnamon floating throughout the drink, and a thick layer of whipped cream on top.

Spiced Horchata, a Fernandez holiday favorite.

Taking the cup Melissa offered, I raised it to my nose and peeked the other way, realizing all my siblings were filing in front of me.

"Who made it?" I asked.

"Not Alta," they all said at the same time. Alta's rendition was more a mockery of us than anything, hating that she still hadn't lived down something she'd done in childhood. I grinned and raised the cup to my mouth.

It was really good. Sweet, but not too much. The thought made me think that Clem would really like it and that thought had me slipping back into my own miserable thoughts.

"C'mon, Ox. What's wrong?" Mateo asked from in front of me.

I blinked down to him and I then realized that they were all sitting around me like some sort of campfire. *Or an intervention.*

I had been sitting down in the basement, where we did most of our family activities. As kids, we would play games or watch movies or have friends over down here. Or at least they would. Now, we usually did family game night, or as we got older, got drunk together.

At the thought, I pulled the drink up to my nose again, curious—and what did you know? I smelled tequila. I huffed out a small laugh and slid a look over to Lis, who was sitting on the arm of the large loveseat I was occupying. She slid me a conspiratorial smile and leaned a shoulder into mine. I shook my head, but took a large gulp, thankful for the addition.

"Oh my god, what do you think is wrong with him, idiot?" Ceci said, rolling her eyes. "Do you *see* Ferguson here anywhere?"

"No," Alta answered innocently.

"*Exactly*," Ceci growled, leaning back on her hands as she glared up at me. "He obviously did something. They're fighting."

"What?" Alta and Lis said at the same time, looking at me in surprise. When they realized they had both answered in the same way at the same time, they glared at each other.

"Why are you fighting, Ox?" Lis asked.

"What did you do?" Mátti asked.

"Ox, no!" Is all Alta could muster.

Ceci just glared at me. I glared back at her. She really was something else. She had been so largely against Clementine in the beginning and now instead of giving her dirty looks, she was giving me dirty looks on her behalf.

"You're irritating," I muttered to her.

"Back at ya," she said, sitting up and crossing her arms.

"You know something." I realized as she did the one thing she usually did when she believed she was justified in her actions as a ridiculously spoiled brat. She tucked her chin and scowled like a raging bull.

"I know enough," she huffed, tossing that chin over her shoulder and looking away from me in a harumph.

"Is she upset?" I asked, whatever fight I had building in me dissipating. Clem was telling her friends (my sister) about me. That couldn't be good.

Ceci turned her eyes to look at me and I swear I saw them soften a fraction. "She's scared, Ox. And you being pushy isn't helping things."

I cursed, sat back, and downed the rest of my drink. I knew I should have just kept my mouth shut.

"Is someone going to let us in on whatever is going on?" Mateo asked impatiently from the back of the group. Hums of agreement followed suit.

I looked at the lot of them, huddled around covered in blankets, wearing festive pajamas they hadn't changed out of all day, and drinking homemade sweets. I couldn't help that bittersweet feeling from hanging over me again. I wanted this; I'd always wanted this. But now, since I'd found Clem, I wanted it with her.

"This reminds me of when you guys were kids," I said almost wistfully as I remembered my little brother and sisters waddling around with wet diapers and stolen cookies.

"You know, Ox? Miraculously, when we were all kids, you happened to be one too," Lis said sarcastically, but she hadn't stopped leaning into my shoulder. I let her stay there.

"And you know, Lis. Miraculously, you guys have acted the same age ever since," I said back with the same amount of snark.

They laughed, and then they sobered, and then they were just looking at me, waiting.

I scrubbed my face and groaned painfully. "We did fight." I admitted. "Yesterday, about the roof."

"The—" Alta started.

"—Roof?" Lis finished.

"You did *not* get on her for getting back at that asshole for you? He doesn't even like that car, Ox. And he deserved it either way." Ceci said.

The others exchanged looks of confusion, and for a moment Ceci and I had to fill them in. After, they all stared between each other in shock. Until Mátti piped up, "That's it, you *have* to marry her."

"She's already my wife," I said dryly.

"Yeah, but you know what I mean." He waved me off. "You guys are married because you have to be. But will you stay married because you want to be?" I wanted to smack him, but only because he was right.

"That's sort of the problem," I said.

"That you love her?" Mátti asked. I visibly flinched.

"That I don't really know if I do," I admitted.

"You do," They all deadpanned. I looked around at their faces and they were all looking at me as if I was an idiot.

Still, I shook my head. "I don't know. I *can't* know. Not when we can't get past our hang-ups."

"You're an idiot," Ceci said.

"You're. *Irritating.*" I iterated again, throwing a cushion at her.

"No seriously," Ceci said as she caught the cushion easily. She hopped up to her feet and replaced it absently before she started pacing. "You're obviously off your shit for her. And what? You're upset because she's shy about it? You've known that about her this entire time, Ox. She's a shy person, of course she's going to be shy if you tell her you love her. Just tell her again, don't get butt hurt about it."

So irritating.

"If you *knew* the whole story, *why* did you even ask?" I said through my teeth.

Ceci stopped in the middle of her pacing and turned to me in an abrupt whirl. "You did *tell her* you loved her, right? In those words."

I averted my gaze.

"Ox!" All of my siblings groaned in differing levels of disbelief and outrage. I felt my jaw tighten and I swallowed, annoyed at their scrutiny and suddenly wanting out of this conversation. When it seemed like my silence wasn't getting rid of them, I sighed and said, "I don't know, okay?"

A mumbling chorus of "stupid", "you're an idiot", "so stubborn" serenaded my ears. I glared at them.

"Did you guys come down here to cheer me up or what?" I asked, annoyed.

They all looked at each other and communicated in a language I never inherited. One that younger siblings seemed to share with each other when silently discussing how dumb they thought their older brother was. I was inclined to get violent. But then, as if on some sort of cue, they all started shuffling around the room and taking their usual spots facing the TV. I guess we were watching a movie.

Ceci remained in front of me.

"Ceci, I swear to God." I started, exasperated by her attitude.

"Can I just say one more thing?" she asked, and I was surprised to hear her voice was low. Soft even. The unfamiliar sound alone had me nodding my head begrudgingly. She looked at me as if she was hoping to burn her words into my brain. "I know you think you can just do everything your way and bend everyone until they comply, but love isn't like that, Ox. You have to give a little and sometimes you have to give more than you get. And sure yeah, that sucks, but who the fuck cares? The only thing you'll care about when you're old and one of you is gone, are the things you got to say and the things you left unsaid. You love her, Ox. You need to let her know."

"And say it twice, will you? Our Fergy's a little dense. She won't get it unless you shove it down her throat."

Chapter Twenty-seven

CLEMENTINE

"So, you mean to tell me," Clay started as we walked up the driveway to our parents' house. "That Oaxaca Fernandez, who is crazy in love with you by the way, told you just how crazy in love with you he is and you somehow made the poor guy regret it?"

I glared at Clay. I couldn't help it. It was this place, what we were doing, the memory of last time. It was making me cranky.

"He isn't in love with me." I surmised as I eased up behind the boys on the front step. They all turned to look at me, dead serious expressions on their faces. I scowled, speaking slower. "He. Is. Not. In. Love."

Or at least he hadn't said as much. He'd merely said that he "needed" me. That I was his "light". That I was his moon… I shook my head as my eyes got starry. I hated the basket case I was being.

"He loves you. He definitely does. And you love him back. What is the problem? "He groaned dramatically like it was causing him pain just to waste precious air on this conversation. "For fuck's sake, just fuck already."

"Clay!" The rest of us groaned back. He held his hands up in surrender, turning back to the door. Clint and Connor were still turned my way.

"I guess we just don't get it, Tine. He's been great to you, great *with* you. Patient, kind, invested... From what we can tell." Unlike Clay, Clint was serious in his inquiry. It somehow made me feel sick. "What's the problem here?"

My face twisted. I didn't know how to answer that. The truth was, I had no idea what the problem was. One minute I was fine, basking in the glowing happiness of Ox finally returning home and the next I was spiraling down a tunnel of feelings that were too big for me to hold onto myself. It was like seeing Ox hurt had rushed everything to the surface. I had seen my own husband dead and had felt nothing, but seeing a scratch on Oaxaca made me want to scratch all my own skin off. I hated it, I hated what that might mean.

Because in truth, I didn't know how Ox felt. He was sweet, but he had always been sweet. He was caring, but he was a caring person. How did I know that what he felt for me was the same blood curling aching madness that I felt for him?

I was conflicted, yet I was also a little irritated. We'd argued and it was nothing like the heated match of raging emotions we'd come to a few months ago. That was all entitlement and hurt feelings and bravado. No. Ox and I were truly disagreeing now. Battling it out with soft words and long, painful looks and emotions that were clearly there but not expressed properly. And it was scary to think that we may never come to see eye to eye. Because then what would that mean?

Somehow, this was worse.

I felt terrible. The tortured look on his face was a thousand times worse than the bruise that had been there. And this time I was the one to put it there. With my insecurities and my defensiveness and my general aversion to facing anything hard. I'd boasted about not being fragile but I was the weakest where it mattered most.

Maybe I could work on changing that.

I chewed my lip as my brothers stalled at the door. It was cold out, so I knew they weren't waiting around to enjoy the fresh air. They were waiting to see if I was ready. Truthfully, I wasn't. But there was no progress without the first step.

"What, you guys forgot your keys or something? Let's go, I'm freezing my ass off out here," I said, tapping into my inner Clayton Ferguson. I always felt braver when I pretended I had the same nerve as him.

They shuffled forward, opened the door, and we pushed into the weirdest scene I'd seen all year. *My parents attempting to be civil.* A Christmas that was filled with less strife than I thought possible. A family coming together. It was awkward and strange, and we each had our bitter and angry moments, but we pushed onward and at least tried to get through dinner and presents and conversation without a blow up.

Surprise wasn't the right word for this feeling. I was stunned. So much so that I stopped thinking about Ox and I altogether, and instead found myself encapsulated by my family.

For Christmas, I got my parents a wine kit. It was equipped with fancy openers and stoppers and diffusers, perfect for lush people who liked to entertain. Even more perfect for when you had no worldly idea of what to get the parents who you stopped speaking to years ago. I only really signed off on the gift, but it was Ox who'd done all the heavy lifting. I wouldn't have even known what it was if it wasn't for him. But surprisingly my parents enjoyed it and didn't comment any further than a polite thank you.

I'd have to ask my brothers what they'd done to make them so agreeable for the day. To my surprise, I got presents from more than just my brothers. Further evidence they had prepped Mom and Dad for the gathering. Or so I thought until I opened them.

From my mom, I got a small box of teal blue paper hearts. They weren't hand cut, thank God, but they were the prettiest little things. They reminded me of butterflies or the hydrangeas she always grew that I secretly still thought about when I was sad. They made me smile the tiniest bit, because somewhere deep inside, I knew she knew this about me. Her gift was thoughtful. But when I'd thanked her and moved to sit the box aside, she chided me in her usual chastising tone.

"Do you honestly think I got my daughter a box of *paper*? Jesus, you've always been too accepting. There's *more* Clementine," she said.

I blinked uncertain gazes at my brothers, who returned it with just as much confusion. Instead of arguing, I picked up the box and dug my fingers inside. What I pulled out made my stomach swirl.

It was my mom's and my grandma's teardrop diamond pendant. Mom told me when I was younger that grandma had gotten it as a gift from her mother on her wedding day and she'd saved it to give to my mother on hers. On my first wedding day, my mother couldn't even look at me and on my second, she hadn't been allowed on the property. So, the jewelry had never been passed down to me.

I swallowed hard, and right then, I remembered something else Mom had told me. On her wedding day, there had been blue petals scattered down the aisle. Blue petals which looked a lot like the ones in the box. Mom was giving me my something borrowed and something blue about five and a half years too late. But, in her own way, I knew what it meant. She had been thinking of me. All this time she had been thinking of me and what I was going through, and by finally giving this up, she was acknowledging that she'd ripped away the sanctity of marriage from me way too young.

"Burn it, sell it, whatever you want. It's yours," she said with a flutter of her hand. She looked away from me with a sniff but eventually her eyes slid back to mine. I watched her dark features transform for only a second, into something sullen and regretful and tortured. I watched her body tell me sorry even if her mouth couldn't yet form the words.

Blinking back down at the shimmering pendant, I swallowed again and let out a quick whispering rasp. "Thanks."

My dad's gift was more straightforward. From an early age, I had a proclivity for bedtime stories. That's probably why I loved talking with Ox until I fell asleep so much. I loved the sound of a familiar voice lulling me away to good dreams. My brothers were usually the ones to read to me or just make something up. But if my dad ever missed an important date or event because of work, he'd come home with a new book and he'd read to me. Then right before I fell asleep, he'd say in his gruff accent, "I'm sorry, Mija. It might happen again, and if it does I will be even more sorry the next time."

When I opened Dad's gift and saw a book, I let myself release a long, ragged breath. I told myself that I would not cry, I would not shed tears for those who didn't deserve it. But did it count now that they were apologizing to me?

I flipped the leather-bound book over in my hands and soon realized it wasn't a regular book. Opening it, all I saw were blank pages, all a deep cream color with no lines. *A journal*. I felt my nose wrinkle in confusion, but as I found the first page, I kept it scrunched to contain the tears. It read:

Clementine,

I'm sorry. I've never stopped being sorry, and I will be even more sorry as more days go by.

I promise, it will never happen again.

Tell me, what did I miss?

I let a single tear escape the side of my eye as I looked up at my father and nodded. I didn't know when, or how, or if I'd ever be ready. But at some point, I was promising to fill him in on my story. And he was promising to listen.

The entire day came as a shock to me. Not just the fact that my parents had made a measurable effort, but the uncharted feeling of relief that washed over me because of it.

I had never spoken to my parents about what they had done to me, not even as it was happening. I'd never raised a hand of resistance or even a single word of rejection. So, in a sort of messed up way, my sudden disappearance must have seemed like a rebellion in their eyes. I'm sure they've been filled in since the boys came back into my life, but before. They'd probably just thought that I was angry and would someday get over it and come back to them. And when I never did, they suffered the loss of a daughter.

I had no desire to pass punishment on them myself. And I'd only realized it when this tiny olive branch was laid in my lap.

I didn't know if I loved them. I didn't know if I still could. But I knew I was done hating them and done blaming them for the rest of the things that had happened to me. And I was ready to try rebuilding that relationship I'd had when I did love them. On my terms.

And that felt good.

My terms felt good.

Maybe Ox had a point about Ronaldo's house. *My* house.

There was so much there that I hadn't yet confronted. And so much of who I was today, I'd become in that house.

I wanted to keep growing, and I wanted to grow toward Ox. *With* him. In order to do that, I needed to first cut off my wilted leaves.

I needed to face my past.

Ox and I were tense for a while after the holidays. He could never quite ignore me, but now when he looked at me, it was with a painful, fierce expression. I found myself wondering often if it was resentment or if it was just disappointment.

He still came to me at midnight and brought me to "our" bed. He still asked me questions about my day and listened with quiet intent when I answered. He still walked with me on the beach on sunnier days and brought me along to family dinners on the weekends. He was still my Ox, but some of his forward moving momentum, that I once barely thought I could maintain, had stopped. He was simply biding his time with me. Floating around me like I was a volatile bomb that he no longer wanted any part of defusing. I hated it.

Even so, I was still trying. At least two of my weekly classes had been swapped for a tentative appointment with a therapist. And I spent some afternoons when Ox was still out at work driving past the old estate.

The first time I'd only been able to make it to the road that led toward the long, winding driveway. I'd had to stop the car in the middle of the road and I damn near hyperventilated my way back home. The next few times I got closer and closer until, finally, I was standing at the front door. We never really used the front door. Or maybe *I* just hadn't used it because I never left. The thought of going *back there*—back into that old prison of mine—made me feel sick.

I realized then that, as much as it was home to me, it was also in fact a prison. Ox was right in thinking that I had grown into who I was in this place and letting it go was hard in a strange sort of way. But the thing was, I had grown even more now that I was out of there and losing what I had now would be much harder than anything else I'd ever done.

This place and that man had stunted me, abused me, caged me, and I knew it was strange, but somewhere in the back of my mind I felt like if I stepped back in there, I would never be able to break free of it again. Like if he could, Ron would continue to cage me until the day I died.

As I stood at the door, so close to finally stepping inside, I changed my mind and instead took a hearty step backward.

If I was going to do this, *and I was going to do this*, I would do it with Ox. I didn't need him to be here with me—this tremulous feeling in my stomach was one that I had faced alone before and survived—but I decided right then that I wanted him there. He had been the one beside me, always pulling me out from underneath the water for all these months. If I happened to slip again, there was no one else I trusted more than Oaxaca to pull me right back up.

It was mid-January when I worked up the nerve to tell him this. Or I tried to at least. But just like at the house, I got stuck whenever I got so far. Stalling in the doorway of his office or at the foot of the bed or when we watched each other from across the kitchen table. So many times, I worked myself up to asking him—*telling* him that I was ready. But I always pulled up short.

What would happen if I was ready and it turned out he wasn't? What happened if it turned out that I wasn't as ready as I thought, and we fell further behind than we already had? So many bad possibilities ran through my mind. So many opportunities for this scenario to go wrong. I was scared. I wasn't ready to lose Ox. I had just found him, and I didn't want to give him up. But if we continued down this road, I would lose him anyway.

It ended up slipping well past mid-January when my less than subtle brooding finally reached Ox. It reached him so much that one freezing afternoon he just up and dragged me out to the beach, leading me toward the water with a curiously exasperated expression on his face. By then, the winter had gotten brutal and there was a frigid feel to the air. Which only left me more confused as to why he was bringing me out to the ocean.

"What are you doing?"

"I'm taking you back there."

I froze, immediately thinking the "there" he was speaking of was back to the very place I was currently trying to gain the nerve to go myself. Somehow, him making that decision for me felt like a slight.

"Where?" I asked, pulling up short and slipping myself out of his grasp. He charged a few steps ahead as if his momentum didn't want to stop for me. Then, realizing I had escaped, he pivoted and reached back for me again, pulling me along once more.

"Back to where I broke everything. I'm going to fix it," he said.

Even from behind him I could see a hard set to his jaw, a stiffness in his shoulders, a pain in him I hadn't noticed before. Seeing this, my walls melted and then I just felt stupid.

Here was this man, giving me everything he had while I was too afraid to give him even a piece of me.

I stopped again and Ox sucked in a breath as he turned around to face me. "*Come on.* We're going back and we're going to talk this out. We never finished that conversation and—"

"And that was my fault," I piped up. He watched me, his mouth already open and ready to protest. "This is *all* my fault. I've been a baby. I've been acting the exact opposite of how I said I wanted to be treated." I took a deep, readying breath. "But I want to change, Ox. Will you help me?"

He questioned me with his eyes alone, his curious expression never truly relinquishing the slightly miserable quality it held.

I elaborated. "Will you come with me to your abuelo's house and help me pack up a few things? For good."

His dark searching eyes skittered to a stop. He breathed out an almost silent puff of air and then sucked in a sharp one. "Clem, you don't need to do this just for me. We can work something else out."

"I *have* to," I corrected. I wasn't going to let him keep bailing me out. He was strong, but he was a person too. Just because he was helping me, didn't mean I got to use him as my own personal stepping stool. Of all the things Ox had done for me, he had only asked me to do one thing. And I'd be damned if he took back that request.

Stepping forward, I re-captured his hands and brought them up to my lips. I puffed warm air from my mouth onto them and then rubbed them between my palms. With cold lips, I placed a kiss on the top of his knuckles. The ones he'd used to defend me when I wasn't even around. The ones that had started all this. I blinked up at him and gave him a weak smile before I whispered—promised, "*I will.*"

Chapter Twenty-eight

CLEMENTINE

I stood in the same spot as I had before, at the front door of my old home. Standing there, I felt the same heavy feelings of fear and rebuke and, in some ways, I wanted to turn right around like I did last time. But then I noticed the warm presence behind me. Ox was standing at my heels, hands laying gently on my shoulders while he stood silently with me as I worked up the courage to push forward.

I could do this. I could face this. This was nothing. All I had to do was go in, grab a few things, say thank you to the holy cosmos or whatever and then poof, closure! Right?

Well, that had better be the case, because I was not staying a moment longer than I needed to. As soon as I heard that metaphorical door close, I was out of there.

With that in mind, I found the strength to turn the knob and move forward.

Almost as soon as I stepped foot in the foyer I wanted to turn back. I *tried* to turn back, suddenly hit with the thought that maybe I *couldn't* do this. My stomach curled at details as small as the familiar Tuscan brown on the walls or as distinguishable as the famous fifty-five thousand dollar painting the size of a sheet of construction paper.

But my escape plan was short-lived. Ox was there, as he always was, to hold me up where I was falling down. He stopped my retreat and guided us another foot inside, letting the door shut behind us. I jumped at the noise, not loud, but startling regardless.

It must have taken me at least ten deep breaths before I was able to breathe smoothly again. And then I was opening my eyes, realizing for the first time that they had closed.

We were in the house. It was stale and stuffy from underuse. All the lights were off and since the foyer had little windows, a darkness cast about the room. But we were in the house, and we were okay.

I reached back and clutched Ox's shirt in the tight ball of my fist as I tugged him along with me. He had already been stepping with every one of my steps and breathing with every one of my breaths, but I wanted to grab onto every piece of him that I could. The squeeze of his hands on my shoulders said *'I'm here'*. I savored it, sucking up every bit of strength he had to lend me and using it to power every step of courage I took further into the home.

Step after step brought me closer and further away from my past.

As we exited the foyer, I remembered the first time I'd ever stepped foot into the house. Fresh with scars from the betrayal of my family, as my welcome home I was greeted by an immediate full body search right in the middle of the front foyer. I was stripped and poked and prodded. Doctors, dentists, optometrists, not to mention stylists, hairdressers and any other *groomers* he'd hired to pluck and pinch and shape me to his will.

He'd wanted me to look more "polished", almost fully erasing the Afro out of my Afro-Latina, even though I almost fully took after my mother in most regards. The memory made me realize that now, as I wore my frizz and curls out proudly, it had just been another way for him to strip my identity from me. I twisted a free hand around one of my new box braids and reveled in the small victory of taking that identity back.

That victory lapsed however when we rounded the foyer entrance to the formal dining room where he all but shoved a hand down my throat to force me to eat. It had only taken about a month in this place for me to be sick of food altogether, but he had made sure I'd eaten every single day. A perfect diet. Not too much sugar, not too much starch, just the right amount of everything to keep a fertile, sterile girl. I think the only reason I never got pregnant was because my period had disappeared. I was already skinny before arriving. The diet and stress alone had shrunk me from modelesque stature to need-a-sandwich-pronto status—As Clay would call it.

And now all I did was bake cake! And eat the cake at the small little breakfast table in Ox's house. So far removed from these formal, mechanical meals it was like night and day.

I guess, victory was mine again?

The walk through the house went much like that. I'd walk past something that triggered a bad memory and start to slip backward, and then I'd feel Ox next to me or touching me or watching me, and I'd remember that this wasn't the past anymore and I'd come a long way from where those memories still lay. Then I'd move on.

Coming here, I thought I would need to work through my complicated feelings with the past in order to leave it behind. But I was coming to realize, I'd already done it. Seeing this place was just confirming what my body and soul had already figured out. This had all died in my former life. *Died with Ron.*

It was like healing and breaking at the same time. Breaking open vulnerably every time I relived pieces of my history and healing up solidly every time I realized how far I'd come from it. It was almost seamless, this closure thing.

Almost.

Until we reached Ron's room. The room that made me feel dirty and ugly and used and degraded and I wasn't sure I was ever going to remedy that. I still couldn't sleep at night because of what happened in that room. I still couldn't close my eyes during that time of night without feeling like I was right back in that bed, squeezing my eyes shut and counting the minutes until it was over.

"I don't want to go in," I whispered to Ox who was still hovering right behind me like he had the entire hour we'd been in the mansion. I felt him breathe out onto my neck even though I couldn't hear him.

"You don't have to," he said, immediately understanding.

"I was doing so well," I whined.

"You still are," he said softly. "Even if you hadn't been able to step foot inside at all today, you're still doing well."

"You're too good to me," I said, trying for humor but letting it out in the same breathless way I'd confessed that I was scared.

"No such thing." He answered into my hair. His lips lay down onto the crown of my head, like he needed to be closer to hold me up. "What can I do?"

I took my time thinking about it for a second. As much as I didn't want to go in, I didn't want to quit either. I was almost on the other side of the whole damn nightmare, and I had become addicted to this triumphant feeling that came with every conquered memory. I *had* to do this, but...

I turned and looked up at him. At my everything. My Ox.

I loved him.

I knew it, he must know it (everyone else did), and I loved him even more for never leaving my side. Through both this instance and every other instance since he'd picked me up off the floor that fateful night.

But right then, I needed him to stand down.

If I was ever going to love Ox without also feeling like I owed him, I had to do this on my own. I had to break away on my own. Because I didn't want to give him all of me just because I felt like I had to. I wanted to give myself to Ox because it was him. Because he deserved *so* much. Way more than just my broken pieces.

He'd appreciate it one day. But today, he'd have to simply watch.

"Stay here?" I asked finally. My voice cracked unconvincingly and my eyes wavered with fear. But I didn't take the request back.

His eyes narrowed. "You want to go in alone?"

"I have to," I corrected. His eyes narrowed further, and I held a hand up to stop him before he even began. "Don't even start, Ox. Just trust me when I say, *I have to.*"

He regarded me for a few extra seconds before he sighed. "You're sure?"

I sighed too and turned back toward the door. "We're finally here. We might as well do this right."

As I stepped into the room, I caught a glimpse of Ox's face just before the door closed completely. I would have laughed if my stomach wasn't stuck in my throat. He was *glaring*. He didn't like this any more than I did.

And I *really* didn't like this.

The room felt colder than the rest of the house. None of the utilities had been shut off yet, so heat circulated the rooms the same as it would have with us occupying them. But Ron's room had more windows in a single space than any other room in the entire house. The entire back wall was made up of them, all facing out toward the beach. An addition he'd made solely for my torture. Or at least it felt like it.

I'd made it clear that I didn't enjoy public displays of our *relations*, so he'd sought to make them as public as they came.

I shuddered, my eyes moving to the bed. It had no sheets or blankets, having been cleaned and disposed of long ago. But I could still see them somehow. Crisp, white, and cotton. Fresh and new every time. So he could see the result of his attentions. How many tears, how much sweat, how much blood. He liked to see it all against the white sheets. Like they were his canvas, as well as my straitjacket.

Everything about the room was the same. The same lighting, the same furniture, the same smells. It all pulsed around me like I was in a bad dream, a dream where the last months of respite had been some kind of joke and the punch line was that I had to return to this horrible reality.

With shaky steps I moved forward, closer to the bed. I reached out to it, meaning to just touch it. If I could just touch it and be okay, I would have overcome it. But the closer I got, the shallower my breaths got. And when the one touch finally came, it pricked my skin like a sharp needle, sending ripples of hurt throughout my entire body. It painted a blinding red rage over my eyes.

One second, the very tips of my fingers had touched the edge of the fluffy white mattress pad. And the next, it was flying across the room.

Bone rattling rage seized my body. My limbs. My mind. And I suddenly only wanted to do one thing with it. Not touch, but break.

Destroy.

I tore across the room in a tornado of fury and spite. I pushed the mattress off the bed, which I kicked away from its perch at the center of the room. I ripped clothing from the racks of the closet and threw them around like they weren't more expensive than some people's rent. I ripped out the drawers from the dressers and dumped out the contents on the floor.

I tore apart the lasting imagery of that old wound, daring it to keep surfacing. Challenging it to keep messing with my life. And after enough ripping and shredding and breaking, it no longer did.

After what seemed like a while of undisturbed mayhem, I sat in the middle of the room, on the mattress that now lay on the floor, and I shook. This time not from fear. He was gone and he was not coming back. I was beginning to realize that as I sat on this bed where so much pain had once come, and nothing else ensued.

After several long moments, I began to feel my hands start to hurt, and then my feet, and then my head. I must have really thrown myself into this whole closure thing. After more long moments, my body began to settle and my nerves along with it. The bed was now just a bed, the room just a room, and this house was just a house.

A soft *tap, tap, tap* sounded from the other side of the door, causing me to flinch so hard you would have thought it was a gunshot. My pulse spiked and calmed dramatically all in the same few seconds as I realized it was just Ox. His voice was the next sound I heard.

"All done?" His soft voice carried from the doorway. He had turned the knob and cracked it open just a little.

"It's safe," I called out weakly.

The door opened and Ox stepped slowly inside, and I saw it then. As if the memory had been pushed down until I was ready to see and accept it.

That night, after I found Ron and called the police, I had curled up on the floor of my own room and waited. I didn't care what happened to me. I thought someone was in the house and I didn't care. Someone who could have come back for me and done God knows what, and I still didn't care.

It seemed like not even minutes later that there was someone banging on the front door. I wouldn't answer it. Instead, I stayed in my ball on the floor. The front door opened anyway, banging like someone had broken it down. Following all the noise was the sound of loud footsteps tromping up the stairs and down the hall. Ron's door opened and then it was quiet for several minutes. Then the footsteps sounded again, this time coming my way. I didn't even flinch. My heart started racing faster, but if this person had come to hurt us, at least they were finally going to end this nightmare.

My door opened and in came a dark figure, dressed in black from head to toe. Hair tousled from sleep, skin tan from heritage, and face beautiful, but grave. He entered the room with purpose, only faltering slightly when he saw me huddled alone on the ground. He crossed the room and scanned it as he walked. Tearing a blanket off the bed, he approached me and laid it over my body before pivoting and crossing to the opposite corner of the space. He slid down the wall, propped his arms against his bent knees and sat there, staring at me. He didn't say a word and he didn't move to do anything other than watch me.

Who was he? I thought I'd asked as much, but I couldn't be sure my voice was even working at the time. I'd never met Ron's grandchildren before and at the wedding my mind had been occupied with other things.

I must have made some kind of noise, because I caught his attention and he said, "Do you need anything, Clementine?"

I remember thinking that I needed this to end. At the time, I had been referring to the contradictory mixture of both fear and hope that was swimming throughout my body. I was tingling and burning and I didn't know what to do with the fact that, at that very moment, I wanted to both live and die more than I ever had in my entire life.

Ox had just sighed and leaned his head back against the wall. His voice was strong, I remember noticing that about him even before I knew who he was. *He* was strong, and when nothing else was registering to me, his words seemed like something I could trust. Especially when, of all things, he said, "Give me a few hours and I'll have this taken care of."

I felt hands on my face, bringing me back to the present, where the same man with dark features and sharp eyes watched me. He sighed long and hard and tried to hide his worry as he asked me, "Why is it that every time I leave you alone lately you end up breaking something?"

"Rebellious stage," I breathed out on a smile. I couldn't help it. From the very first moment, Ox had been the same. He'd promised me he'd take care of it. End it. I hadn't known that what I was really pleading for was for him to end this hurt that I felt so deep in my bones that I often couldn't sleep. To end my loneliness and to stop my belief that I deserved this feeling. I'd wanted someone to end my suffering. Now, looking into his beautiful black eyes and seeing everything I wanted to live for right in front of me, I realized that he already had.

He breathed out a humorless laugh at my little joke, but he was all serious when he spoke. "Can I take you away from here?"

I nodded and let him help me off the bed and out of the room. As I took one last look behind myself, I noticed Ron's bar cart tucked against the far side of the room, untouched. The top of his whiskey decanter was uncapped and an empty glass sat beside it on the cart. I smiled as the door shut and we walked away from the room for the last time in my life.

"You didn't want anything from your room?" he asked as we entered the kitchen.

I shook my head, "I'd rather burn everything in there."

"Alright, slugger, take it down a notch." he teased, but he eyed me warily. "You *were* kidding, right?"

"I was," I squeezed his shoulder as I passed him. I moved through the kitchen toward the one and only thing I'd missed about my old life. "There's really only one thing I'd consider taking with me. Everything else I'll just buy again."

He tracked me as I moved to stand in front of a tall floor to ceiling cabinet. In it sat shelves and shelves of all the teas I had collected over the years. There used to be an accompanying display for tea cups, but that had been collateral damage for one of Ron's tirades. Ox took in the fixture, eying it from floor to ceiling before bringing his eyes over to me. "Why is the top shelf empty?"

"It's not—" I peeked over my shoulder and caught a glimpse of the empty top shelf high above our heads. "Oh—*Oh*."

"What?"

"There used to be something up there. Ron's only apology, actually." I explained.

Ox stilled and looked at me like I'd grown another head. "*Apology*?"

I laughed out loud, because he'd said it like it was venom or something. I couldn't exactly blame him, Ron didn't really apologize.

"Yes." I looked up at the tall cabinet with fondness. "*This* is the only thing I'd ever take with me because it's the only thing I ever fought for while I was here."

Ox grunted his attention as he watched me finger the case of special tea sets and flavors.

"Ever since I started this collection, it irked the crap out of him. He couldn't stand that I had something of my own." I moved around Ox and pulled down a couple of mugs from the brown cabinets. When I glanced over my shoulder and raised the glass to Ox in question, he simply shook his head so I returned his mug and instead went to the stove to turn on the burner. With muscle memory, I moved around the kitchen, grabbing the kettle from the drawer underneath the stove and running water into it. I waited until I'd set it on the burner to warm before continuing. "So, he tried to get rid of it. And I sort of snapped."

"Did you break something else?" he asked immediately.

I gave him a look. "No, smartass. I ran away."

Ox sucked in a breath like he couldn't believe it. I didn't blame him. Nothing about me said I was a runner. Or a fighter. I was even surprised when I did it. It wasn't about the tea, though I really did love the collection. It was about enough being enough. I'd already submitted every other part of myself to him and he'd wiped them clean so that it no longer existed. I couldn't bear giving up this one last thing. The collection hadn't always been that large. It only grew after I'd fought, and I'd won. After that, I started to take pride in this thing that had emboldened me to fight for myself. And the collection grew.

I told Ox all of this as the water boiled in the kettle and he listened quietly, contemplating as he always did.

"He let me keep it, and I got kind of obsessed," I said. "It was the only thing I had, which was good for me. But it was also a weakness of mine and he knew it. So, whenever something happened that he didn't like, he threatened to get rid of it."

"That sounds like him," Ox said, probably thinking of his own memories with Ron.

"Toward the end, he started getting restless. He was angrier, more impatient, basically an overall menace. He threatened and threatened for what seemed like every little thing. And I don't know what had come over me, it had been years since I ran away that first time, but I started to get that same feeling of things getting to be too much, even with his threats at my back. He was making everything so hard. I mean *everything*, and I... I was gone. Not even the stupid tea cabinet was holding me together anymore. I didn't care if he hurt me, I hardly felt anything anymore. I was numb..."

I blinked at Ox. The kettle sang, but neither of us moved to get it. He was looking at me like he knew exactly what I was talking about. I had a feeling he was picturing a girl on the floor half-naked, silently begging a man she didn't know for his help. He *did know* what I was talking about. He'd seen it. He'd lived it. He had helped pull me out of it. And for some reason, the look on his face as he imagined, it was more pained than any I'd seen before.

"I couldn't *feel* anything anymore, Ox. All my pain and cries for help had fallen on deaf ears or blind eyes or people who just didn't care. Not enough. So, *I* stopped caring. And I started fighting back," I said, my voice lowering to a soft whisper. "Even when I knew there would be punishment for it."

Ox took a step toward me that I don't think he was aware of. "Did he hurt you?"

"You mean more than he was already hurting me?" A humorless smile tugged at my lips, but I lost it quickly and looked at Ox seriously. "At first no. He thought he could just wait me out. That I'd tire myself out and eventually go back to being everything that he wanted. When I didn't…"

I trailed off and Ox hovered closer to me again. I stepped back, needing space. I could see Ox's hands ball up and his fist strain as he fought the urge to come closer.

"One day he lost it and he *did* hurt me."

"Baby—" Ox reached forward, but I just wrapped my arms around myself and curled back, shaking my head.

"It wasn't… It wasn't bad. But it changed things. I could tell he'd lost control, and he hadn't meant to. But after, he was different." I took a shaky breath in and remembered how Ron had distanced himself from me. His eyes started to look almost as dead as my own. "He seemed paranoid, almost. Which was weird because he never showed remorse for anything he'd done before. He forbade me from telling anyone. Which was okay because, who was I going to tell? Plus, I was afraid to even try anything anyway, after *that*. And I guess when he realized he wasn't going to be outed, he apologized."

"With his mouth?" Ox asked.

"With a gift," I said. I turned away again and pulled open the cabinet I last used when I was here. It was lower than the large collection cabinet, for teas I regularly used that held no special value. Pulling out the red and green box, I turned to show Ox. It was some kind of Red Ginseng Tea. Supposedly, it promoted healing and good health. I didn't drink tea for health, but I saw the peace offering that it was. It was the first and only true gift Ron had given me. Everything else was essentially different collars he placed on his prize to remind himself and everyone else that I was his. So, I had put the tea on the top shelf, and I tucked my animosity for him aside. I tried to go about things differently. I didn't want to get hurt again, but I didn't want to keep hiding. I showed him I appreciated the gesture.

"He asked me every day if I was ever going to drink it. I caught him eying the top shelf sometimes and I think it was bothering him that I hadn't," I said.

Ox scrutinized the pretty little box of tea I'd handed to him before flicking his gaze up to me. "It's almost empty."

"Nothing gets by you," I teased, but moved forward and whisked the box from his hands, removing the tea bag and sniffing slightly. It never smelled like anything to me and I wondered if it was just old. I set the tea bag in the mug and pulled the hot kettle off the stove to pour the liquid in. "No. It was apparently pretty rare. There were only three bags in the box and I used two. I steeped it for a few weeks in Ron's favorite whiskey, as a surprise. That was just before—Well, just before he died. I thought we'd drink it together, as a kind of truce. But we never got the chance to. And I've never actually tasted it."

Setting the cup aside, I turned to Ox as I let it steep. He was watching me closely, hanging onto my every word with this look of anguish on his face. I felt bad. I'd unloaded a lot on him. Complicated truths about his family and about me. I didn't want to burden him with even more of my baggage than I already had, but for some reason, I didn't want to leave this house carrying those bags either. I didn't want to leave this place the same two people we'd walked in as. And definitely not the same couple.

"Ox, I want to talk to you about something," I said.

He flinched. "More bad news?"

"Bad news?" My brow furrowed.

"Yes, *bad news*. Everything you've said since we've gotten here has been bad. I'm so sorry—I never knew," he said.

My gut clenched, then expanded with butterfly movements. More apologizing for things he hadn't done.

I loved him. And I had to tell him. Even if he didn't feel the same.

Suddenly, the nervousness hit me. What was it I wanted to tell him? This absolutely perfect man with a perfect job and a perfect family who was perfectly thoughtful and caring and patient and kind. He was a little short sometimes and a little bossy at others, but perfect was still the way

I'd describe him, because if not truly perfect at least he was perfect for me. And he *was* perfect for me.

With a slow swallow, I leaned forward and grabbed my mug again. It was warm and the hot tingles that shot up my fingertips helped me come down from my thoughts and back to the room. Back to Ox.

"No bad news, Ox. I just need to tell you something," I said as I looked up into his face. His eyes roved over mine, his stern look holding both concern and intrigue, but he was unusually quiet today. Treading cautiously in unknown waters. I didn't blame him. I had been a basket case lately. Breathing carefully, I pivoted away from him. My voice hitched up high as I nervously asked, "Can we sit?"

I didn't wait for his answer as I shuffled away, tea in hand, toward the large French-style floor to ceiling windows that edged the end of the living room and spilled out onto the back deck. You couldn't quite see the light sand of the beach from the lower level of the house, but the ocean was visible just above the green bushes lining the backyard.

There were a couple of chairs tucked up against the windows for reading, but I stood between them and waited for Ox who sidled up beside me quietly. We stared out the window silently, standing shoulder to shoulder as we watched. The weather was overcast and dark, a couple of lightning streaks appearing, but no rain.

"You aren't sitting." Ox pointed out after some time standing in silence.

"I'm nervous," I admitted, my heart beating hard enough I could feel it in my throat. I took a few large gulps of warm tea, hoping to quill the funny feelings. It tasted strange, the aftertaste kind of chalky, but it didn't matter because it was wrestled from my fingers by Ox's long ones. He set my stolen cup on a console along the wall behind us. Then, back beside me, he turned me by my shoulders so that we were facing each other.

"You know I hate when you act jittery around me. It makes me feel like I'm doing something wrong," he said. And as if he was a conjuring force, suddenly I did feel jittery. Those nerves spiked high in my system, bringing my breaths out hard. Sweat beaded the back of my neck and my skin started to feel tingly. Ox ran his eyes along my features and frowned deeply. "And you're twitching. What's the bad news? Tell me."

I chuckled, despite my nervousness. "Ox, there's no bad news."

"Then tell me what's on your mind, Lu."

"A nickname for my nickname?" I asked.

Another frown. He eased a step closer to me and grasped the back of my neck in his palm. "I didn't think you liked the name, considering what happened after I told you about it. But it's a hard habit to shake."

"Hmm," I said sort of sluggishly. My mind had started to feel like it was underwater. The only thing I could think was '*I love him, I love him, I love him*'. And I had to tell him.

"I like it, Ox," I said, my mouth feeling like cotton. "...And I like *you*."

He just watched me, his jaw grinding slowly as it was set into a hard scrutinizing line. I felt a sharp pain shoot through my chest that felt less emotional and more physical than any I'd felt under Ox's hard stares. This was going to be harder than I thought.

I reached a hand toward him, needing to feel a part of him for strength. It shook visibly on the way there, so I pulled it back and cradled it to my chest.

"Clem?" Ox's brow furrowed deep, and I blinked slowly at his screwed-up features. Taking a step toward him, I staggered, and he caught me by the shoulders. Ducking his head down, he searched for my eyes with a new hint of panic in his own. "What's wrong with you?"

"Nothing. I'm just—"

"Nervous, yes you already said that." He snapped, his hands pushing me up as I began to slump a little. "But you're acting strange."

"It's because I wanted to tell you—" I coughed. My throat starting to burn at the worst possible time. I cleared it gruffly, or attempted to, but it wouldn't clear. I coughed again, reaching a hand out to motion for the tea. And I coughed *again*. But when I went to take in another breath, it didn't come in easily. Ox wrapped my fingers around the teacup and thrust it back toward me. I got it about halfway to myself before I felt it. "Ox—I can't—I don't feel—"

"Clementine?" He clipped, an edge of panic in his voice.

I coughed.

I breathed.

I gagged.

And then, I fell.

Everything moved slowly. Too slowly. The teacup clattered to the ground, the liquid splashing everywhere. Glass broke and skidded in different directions along the floor and Ox's chest was getting closer and closer to my face. He was screaming my name now, but my eyes were heavy and they were closing. My ears roared with blood and it felt like all the warmth in my body was being sucked out of me. Ox and I had hit the ground and I could faintly feel my body as it nestled against his. I liked it there, he was warm and I fit well against his chest. As my body got heavier and heavier, losing the fight against consciousness, there was a complete moment of clarity where everything felt jarringly normal, if only for that one second. Right then, I heard Ox's hysteric voice as he spoke urgently to *someone*.

"Hello—Hi.. Yes, my address is 1399 Waverly Lane. I need some help," he said.

What?

Oaxaca Fernandez needed help?

Shit.

This must really be bad.

Chapter Twenty-nine

OX

My fist was permanently pressed to my mouth as I watched the EMT gurney cart away my completely incapacitated wife. She was out, she couldn't breathe without an oxygen mask, and before she'd conked out for good, she'd coughed up blood. *Blood.*

"Would you like to ride in the ambulance, Mr. Fernandez?" The last EMT left in the room asked as she rushed out behind Clementine.

I waved her forward. "No. I'll follow right behind."

I didn't want to get in the way if something were to happen and they needed space to operate. The nice, short woman gave me a quick nod before she rushed out of the room. I was following right behind her when my eye caught on something in my peripheral vision. The teacup Clem had been holding was on the floor. The handle was snapped off and there was a large chip along the rim. I picked it up and stared at the pretty orange designs along the ceramic. They were little Clementine oranges scattered all around the surface.

A ghostly smile that felt more like a grimace skirted across my face when I saw it. It was just like her to leave behind a tea shaped stain on even the most inappropriate setting. I paused, something about that and the sight of the cup wiping the smile clean off my face.

Tea infused whiskey… Only three bags… Rare blend… Sudden body failure.

I looked at the cup in my hands and then at the pool of tea on the ground. As something Clem had said to me registered in my head, I felt all the warmth leave my body at once.

I've never actually tasted it. She had said.

Realization dawned on me in sudden, miserable waves. I felt hot and cold at the same time. I felt sick, like I would throw up, but I also felt like I was going to burst out of my skin right then and there. Cup in hand, I took the ceramic and chucked it against the nearest wall, shattering it into at least a hundred little pieces.

Then I bellowed out an angry, "Fuck!"

Residual tea leaked down the wall where the cup had landed and I felt myself scoff in actual astonishment. "*Healing and good health*" my ass. I screamed again, this time less of a coherent word and more of a whining release of anger aimed at the ground as I held onto the sides of my head. I could have been screaming at the world or at God or at who knew what else, but I knew for a fact that I was screaming at my abuelo.

Because this was without a doubt all his fault and if he wasn't already dead, his days would be numbered. Because the son of a bitch had tried to poison my wife.

Chapter Thirty

OX

The first day of thinking Clem might die…

I was okay. I was better than okay, really. My voice may have sounded a little strained from the constant dry swallowing I was doing, and I may have been checking in with the front desk of the hospital Clem was taken to every three minutes give or take. But overall, I was okay.

The fact that I couldn't speak in complete sentences or couldn't so much as replay her voice in my head without wanting to throw up, didn't mean anything. Nothing at all.

I sat in the hospital waiting room working, pacing, asking, researching. Rinse and repeat… *About a couple hundred times.*

And I was totally and completely okay.

Chapter Thirty-one

OX

The second day I thought my wife was going to die…

I couldn't think about anything else.

"Yoo-hoo, Oxy." Someone waved a hand in front of my face. I wasn't sure who. My head was locked in the same position it had been in for the past four hours. My chin in my palm, my hand covering my mouth, and my eyes set on the blue plastic chairs directly in front of me.

I was stuck. I couldn't lift my head or move my hand or any other part of my body for that matter. I couldn't even unlock my damn pupils from the spot in front of me. All I could do was run the same thought over in my head. Again, and again.

She was going to die.

Clementine was going to die.

My wife was going to die.

My *fucking world* was going to fucking die. And I had done nothing to stop it.

Chapter Thirty-two

OX

The third day I was sure my best friend was going to die...
I kind of felt like I would die too.

I had just come out of that dank little hospital room with her. Everyone had crowded around her in a way that she would hate. And worse, they were praying over her like she had one foot in the grave already. I hung back in the far corner, my arms and legs crossed as I leaned against the wall. I needed that wall. It was just about the only thing keeping me upright at that point.

I couldn't see her, there were too many bodies between us. But soon those bodies shifted and I caught a glimpse of her. My Clem.

She was laying down sleeping soundly. Those beeps on her machine not doing anything but going off in a steady, monotonous tone. She was okay, but it wasn't right. She was sleeping, but she wasn't taking those little panting breaths that she normally did or moving her shoulders ever so slightly until she inched her way over to me. She wasn't there. She was somewhere else entirely.

The sight of it brought this strangling feeling to my airways and this wobbling sensation to my knees. Before I knew what had happened, I was stumbling out of the crowded room and into the white walled hallway. There, I slapped my hands upward against the wall. Leaning forward with my head hanging between my shoulders, I tried to catch my breath. Nothing was coming. All I felt were rough, ragged spikes in my throat and all I could see was the memory of her.

Clem smiling, Clem laughing, Clem moaning. She was the movie that took up my every brain cell. I could see her, I could hear her, I could fucking smell her, but only in my goddamn memories. She was right there, but she wasn't. And I had reached my breaking point. She was supposed to be back by now. And if she wasn't, did that mean...

A shiver racked through me, and all of a sudden I was going down. I was going to fall face first on the weird blue-green tile of the floor, looking like a bumbling fucking idiot. And I couldn't give one shit.

Only, I was caught by two sets of large hands. Whose were they? I couldn't tell at that point. I could almost barely make out the sound of my little sister's voice. My little baby sister saying something that sounded like, "Get him the fuck out of this place."

If I could laugh, I would. It was Ceci, and she was growling again. I suppose I'd taught it to her, but she was better at it than me now.

"Make sure he eats," another calm voice said from the same direction. Melissa. Always practical, always under control.

"He likes soup when he's sad." That was Alta. Compassionate and soft as ever. If my ears still worked correctly, it sounded like she had been crying.

And all I wanted to do at that moment was lay down and cry a little too.

Chapter Thirty-three

OX

The fourth day I thought for sure the love of my life was going to die, maybe even soon…

I sort of lost it.

"Did you just fucking tell me I should pull the plug on my wife?" I asked the scrawny little blonde nurse who didn't even look old enough to be out of high school let alone be in charge of Clementine's care. I advanced her, but I kept my distance. Largely in part to the big hand laid on my chest, stopping me mid-charge. It was Clay. He and his brothers had been there a lot, just as much as me. I hadn't realized it before, when I was in a haze, but they'd been right there by my side freaking out in their own respective ways and holding me together in others. I ground my teeth down so hard, I thought I heard them break.

"Say that to me again and I'll make you regret—"

"Alright, Ox man. Let's go." Clay again. His voice was gruff and his hands were gruffer as he yanked me by my shoulders out of the trajectory of the nurse and down the hall of the hospital. We hit fresh air in the space just outside the sliding double doors and I winced at the light. I realized then that it was the first time that I'd left the hospital doors since I'd gotten there. I took a shower or two in the weird bathroom of Clem's room and I had my family bring my things, like my laptop or my planner or those fucking projections for next season's production. But I hadn't really worked. Just delegated like a tyrant and steadily gone insane.

When I realized Clay's hand was still clasping my shoulder, I swatted him off.

"You good man?" Clay asked and he must've really been shaken up because there were no expletives to be found in his question. "You're not having another panic thing, are you?"

"No, I'm not," I said, anger flaring up in me. While I was out losing my fucking shit the day before and being carted off to the hospital cafeteria by the fucking Ferguson brothers, something could have changed with Clem. And now I would never know. "No, I'm just…I'm just—"

"You're falling apart, Ox," he said, and for the first time, his voice sounded slow and cautious. *Gentle*. Like I was a wild animal, and he was the tame one.

I looked at him then, and I got mad. He looked like her. They had the same dark curly hair and the same shade of eyes. Both tall and lanky too. Looking at him and seeing her made me mad, but it also made me sad.

Rushing up to him, I felt like I wanted to hit him. But I didn't know why. Clay didn't flinch as I advanced him, only watched me curiously. Sadly. And that's what made me stop. He had the same damn eyes, and they were ripping me open.

411

Because she still hadn't opened hers.

"It feels like I'm being *ripped* apart, Clay," I gritted through clenched teeth. My voice choking over itself. "She won't fucking wake up."

"She will," Clay said, steel in his voice.

"You heard them. She won't Clay," I basically croaked. My eyes stung and I raised my chin to the sky to hold back the flood of emotions I was suddenly feeling. "She won't wake up and it's all my fault. What kind of a man just lets something like this happen to someone so good?"

"Ox, don't do that to yourself man."

"No." I held a hand out in his direction but kept my face on the sky. "No, really. What kind of man am I to have the whole fucking world standing right there in front of me, and not hold it tightly enough?"

"Ox," Clay said, grasping onto my shoulder once more. "You're one of the best guys I know. Tiney saw it first, but we all see it now. She's gonna wake up, you hear me, and she's gonna need her Ox back when she does. Her husband. So, you need to go get some rest and find him for her."

I looked down at his hand for the longest time. It stayed right there on my shoulder, gripping me tightly and holding what it could of me together. I huffed and finally said, "You're being nice."

A grin spread across his mouth, and he patted my shoulder *hard*. "One-time special, buddy. Don't get used to it."

It was six days post Clementine-coma, and I was entering my own home for the first time since it happened. I didn't want to do it. Not without Clementine with me, but according to my family, it was apparently time.

I made it as far as the middle of the foyer before I turned on my heels and headed back for the front door. I couldn't do this, not without her. I couldn't go back to an empty home like she had died or something.

Someone had prepared for this. My entire family was behind me, shuffling in groceries and scampering around the room to kick away evidence of Clementine. They were moving around me like a tornado on land and I couldn't find the strength in me to tell them to stop. Or to tell them not to dare touch that mug on the bottom shelf that Clem always used. Or to threaten if they dented her orange electric mixer I would dent their fucking skulls in.

I wanted to tell them all of this, but nothing would come out.

My head just continued to throb like it had for the past six days. And when I tried to focus on any one thing, shapes and colors and lights all blurred together. Pinching the bridge of my nose, I squeezed my eyes shut and tried to count down from ten, hoping it all would be over when I got to one.

"Let's go, Mijo." It was both my mom and dad who materialized by my sides. Their arms wrapped around my back and their hands rested at my elbow or my waist as they moved me. They lead me slowly, painstakingly, from the foyer and into the living room. I fought every step. But eventually, they got me into the beige space, sitting me down on Clem's favorite couch and clucking their tongues when they succeeded.

"Mijo, my baby, my first," My mom said as she stroked my hair. "What is so wrong? Clementina will be back soon."

"You don't know that." I croaked out, having been resigned to the fact that she wasn't doing all that much better. Pretty soon, we'd be pressed to make some "hard decisions" and because I was her husband, I'd be the one to have to make them. But in my heart and soul I knew I couldn't. And that weight of expectation pressed down on me, threatening to suffocate.

A hand came out to stroke my hair and my dad's hands had a tight hold on my knees. "We *know* Oaxaca. The doctor has been seeing small steady progress. You know Clementina has always been slow. She takes her time. But she is reliable. She will be back here."

413

Amá's gentle hands and Apá's rough ones stayed on me. Someone was in the kitchen rummaging in the fridge. Someone was opening the blinds and curtains and letting in light. Someone was upstairs doing God knows what, but I could hear the movements of their steps above us.

I felt my body stiffen as cold dread shot through me. I didn't want to do this. I *couldn't* do this. I said as much to my parents as I tried to rise from my seat. They both pushed me back down.

"Qué pasó, Mijo?"

"I—" I swallowed and shuddered a breath. "I can't do this right now, Amá. I can't be here."

"Why not, Oaxaca?" she asked.

I looked around the room again, but I still wasn't seeing anything. I couldn't tell my right from my left, all I knew was that my family was all there and they needed me to step up and come back to them. And I could do no such thing.

A frustrated sound came out of me and I yanked my limbs away from my parents. *Rude, Oaxaca.* But I didn't care.

"I'm sorry," I said. "But you guys can't be here. Or I can't be here. I just…can't."

"*Why?*" My mom asked again.

"Because I can't be what you guys need right now. I'm not… She's not… I just can't right now, Amá. I'm sorry."

"Mijo, Mijo, Mijo." Amá moved right up to me and crouched low in front of my knees so that her body was below mine. I could finally see her face. I could make out the lines that looked so much like my own. Make out the familiar way her deep skin wrinkled in certain places. "We don't need you to do anything right now. We don't always need you to do everything for us. Let your brother and sisters take care of something for a change. That's why we had a whole army of you kids in the first place."

"But—"

"But nothing," My dad spoke this time from beside me, low and deep. "Right now, Mátti and Lis are in your office working on your projects."

I felt a little ball of anxiety rise to my chest. "Are they okay?"

"They're happy to help," Amá said.

"And the girls?" I asked, feeling like a whining child as I spoke to my parents in this pleading, helpless tone.

"Alta's in the kitchen cleaning and making lunch," My mom said. "And Ceci is upstairs packing a new bag for your wife. She said if anyone else touched her stuff, she'd kill them."

A laugh escaped me as I sank deeper into my seat. "They're friends, I guess."

"Yes, they are and she cares about Clementina. We all do. Just like we care about you, okay Oaxaca?" She said, her hands had gone to either side of my head and she was rubbing soothing circles along my temples as she spoke. "We have it handled, so just relax for a while. Please, Mijo?"

They had it handled. They had all of my affairs covered for me. And they all cared. Got it. It took me a while, but I got it. And after a little more time getting used to that fact, I sat back, slumped into my couch, and let my family take care of things.

Late in the night, as I laid in my bed with no Clem lying beside me, I realized I couldn't sleep in there without her. Without knowing if there was even a *'her'* coming back to me.

So, when it was so late at night that even my watch dog little siblings had all fallen asleep, I left, and snuck back into the hospital to be with Clementine. Her beeping machine was the same, her sleeping face still calm and gentle, her hospital gown green today instead of the blue from yesterday.

Pulling up a chair beside her, I settled in up near her shoulders and leaned down to rest my head on the rail of her hospital bed.

"Lunita," I rasped. Swallowing a hard lump in my throat, I reached forward blindly to find her hand. Grasping it tightly, I said, "Why are

415

you doing this to me, huh?"

She, of course, didn't answer.

"I'm sorry, okay? I'm so fucking sorry. I shouldn't have pushed so hard for closure. It was so stupid to ask you to go back to that place. *So stupid*." I felt like I wanted to cry, but I was too exhausted and the only thing that came out of me was a strangled sigh.

"It's midnight, and you're finally asleep." I laughed humorlessly. "But now *I* can't sleep. Not without you."

I don't know how long I was quiet for. I sat and breathed softly as I waited for her to say something or make a sound or scrunch her nose. But she did none of that.

"Help me out, yeah? Help me sleep, Lu." I said, hoping I resembled some semblance of my normal self. Of *our* normal routine. Taking a deep breath, I brought her hand up to snuggle close to my lips. Closing my eyes, I began our ritual. "Three things I like about you. Your hair, your smile, and your beautiful skin. You're flawless."

She didn't move or respond, but that was alright.

"Three things I *love* about you," I continued. "Your loyalty, your big heart, and your goddamn obsession with tea."

A smile pulled at my lips and I slid closer to her, slipping the railing and laying my head onto her shoulder.

"Three places I want to go with you," I said. "Anywhere you want. If you come back, I'll take you anywhere you want to go."

I'd partly hoped that my bargaining and pleading would miraculously bring her back at that instant, and when nothing happened, I felt my determination falter a bit. I squeezed my eyes shut tighter and held onto her hand like it would float away. Dejected, I started another confession.

"Three things I regret not telling you," I croaked out in an almost whisper. I cleared my throat, but it was still raspy when I continued. "That I hated my abuelo. I always have. He's a dick, but I hate him more now that he's gone than I ever did when he was alive. That I think about you day and night, and I always have, since the second you were mine. And that I regret not telling you all the things I love about you, because there are so damn many."

"Three things I want to do with you." I could barely get this one out of my throat, because the truth was, I wanted to do anything with her again. So badly. Even if it was just lying in this hospital room with her by my side, *alive*, I'd do it. I took a breath, steadied my voice, and told her anyway. This was for her. "Clem, I want to kiss you for real, kiss you senseless and I never want you to think that I don't. I want to make you mine. I want to start a family with you. I want a million little you's running around and driving me nuts. And I want you to come back to me, baby. That's all I fucking want. If all you can ever give me is you by my side, I'd be the happiest man in the world, Lu."

"Please." It left my mouth like a breathless prayer. I didn't know who I was praying to exactly. Her, God, or whoever the hell else would answer this call. This *plea* to just please bring her back to me. I couldn't do this without her. Her sweetness had ruined the bitter taste of life for me, and without her to lighten it up, I didn't want it.

"Please, please, please," I whispered to nothing and no one.

I talked to her the whole night like this. Hope had slipped away from me, but determination had set in. This was my wife, and the love of my life. This was my whole world. And I'd be damned if she was going to leave this earth without even fucking knowing it.

Chapter Thirty-four

CLEMENTINE

I tried to peel my eyes open, but they wouldn't budge. I tried to move my arms to reach out to him, but they were so heavy I couldn't move them. I wanted to feel him. I needed to feel him. It had felt like hours since I'd gotten to run my fingers across that warm skin or feel the crush of his body around mine in an embrace. I wanted to feel his lips again. They'd only touched mine once, but that time had left me burning for more. I wanted so much more with him.

And it was the same for him too.

I want to kiss you for real, kiss you senseless...

Oaxaca's words shot through me again like a zap of electricity. I had heard him talking to me while I slept, but I couldn't figure out why he sounded so...wrong.

And I want you to come back to me, baby. That's all I fucking want. He'd said. *If all you can ever give me is you by my side…*

But I was right there with him, sleeping. I didn't understand. I didn't like the way his voice sounded or the constant beeping sound that was right next to my ear. I'd just have to get up soon so we could talk about this.

Because I wanted all those things with him too. And I wanted to give him so much more than just standing beside him. I wanted to give him everything he'd given me and then some.

Finally, after what seemed like forever, I felt myself waking up. But when I tried to open my eyes, they were borderline glued shut.

I tried to generate a yawn but the sharp feeling of dryness in my throat stopped me. I groaned, but the sound didn't feel right, and a weird sense of panic started to come over me. I suddenly felt like this wasn't right. This didn't feel like the warm cushion of Oaxaca's bed. And those incessant beeping sounds would have never lasted long when he was trying to work.

And I couldn't hear his voice anymore. I wasn't completely sure he was even still with me. Had my weakness finally weighed too much on him? Had he decided he didn't want those things after all? I whimpered and then I thrashed. *Dammit.* My limbs felt like lead and my eyes had started to gently peel apart with my constant effort, but the light streaming in seemed way too bright.

Where was I?

The distinct sensation of motion around me jolted me again. All of a sudden, my eyes were being opened for me, my body was being yanked around and moved, my mouth being pried open and my tongue being scraped. My arms and veins were poked and prodded all the while I sat there.

The people around me looked like medical professionals. *Weird.* The machines around me (still beeping) resembled ones that I'd seen in movies. And the smell. The smell was distinctly sterile. Impersonal and stale.

A hospital.

The doctors and nurses continued to check on me, saying things like "coma" and "uncommon" and "more tests". I had to grin and bear it because I couldn't find strength in me to do anything else. Then, like the parting sea, they all cleared out of the way to reveal three familiar bodies. But unfamiliar in their current states. They looked exhausted and stressed and downright bad.

"Hey, monsters," I choked out and coughed. I swallowed even though it burned. Standing there and making no move to come in were my big teddy bear brothers, looking absolutely shattered. They were definitely *not* okay. They looked so bad, it sort of made me wonder if I'd lost a limb or something. I had to say something, no matter how badly it hurt. "Last time I saw you three look like that is when Auntie Myla kissed you on the mouth."

"Tiney!" They all groan-laugh-whined at the same time and then shuffled into the room to fuss over me for the next few hours. I let them, mostly because they were looking a lot like the walking dead, but also because I knew they cared. They brought me water and snacks and found a way to fix my endlessly dry throat.

Even though I was happy to see them and feel their love as they reunited with me after who knows how long, I still couldn't help but wonder where the man who had whispered so many words in my ear had gone. I didn't want to ask, though. Not while my brothers were like this. Not when I'd already done my part to hurt them in ways I didn't think could quite be repaired.

"Where's Ox?" Clint whispered from the corner of the room, like my husband was some sort of secret. We were married for Christ's sake... But I guess it was still a secret that I was in love with him. And that he might...feel things for me too. He loves things *about* me. Three, at the very least. *I heard about them last night.*

"I saw him earlier. He looks better than before but—" someone turned slightly to look back at me, him and Clay were in a little huddle in the corner while Connor was at my side feeding me sips of water. I pretended like I wasn't listening, but both Connor and I knew that I was. "He's gonna need to sit down before we tell him she's awake. He might end up in here too at the rate he's going."

What?

As if conjuring him here, the door flew open and there stood Ox looking way too big for the small space. Looking way too tired for the man I knew to always look perfect. And looking so broken that it hurt me. But he was wearing my favorite Oaxaca Black from head to toe in dark jeans, a long-sleeved shirt, and walking sneakers. A sight for sore, tired eyes, but also a shot to my heart. Because the expression he was wearing was that of a blank abyss.

He'd stopped walking when he'd reached the door jamb. His eyes skating around from each of my brothers scattered about the room and finally landed on me. He bounced his gaze around every inch of my body before letting it reach my face.

Then he looked at me.

And then his face crumbled like I'd never seen it before. He looked as if he was holding back tears. But only for a second, because next he was turning his head to the side, tilting his chin up, and holding his temples between his index finger and thumb, shielding his eyes from the room. His strangled voice rasped in a way I had never heard it before. I knew then that he *was* crying. Instantly, my eyes stung too.

"Fuck," he spat out in a harsh whisper. Like he was trying to get it together, but it wasn't working. "*Fuuuck*, Clem."

Around us, the boys moved quicker than I'd ever seen them move before. Gathering their stuff and disappearing from the room. When the door shut behind Oaxaca, he was still standing in the same place. His eyes were cast back down to me, his hand over his jaw as he stood there and stared at me with wet eyes. I ached to know what he was thinking, and why he was looking at me like I was Jesus risen from the dead, but

I was patient as I waited for him.

Until I wasn't.

With effort, I held out my arms and opened them wide, gesturing for him to come over with greedy little *'gimme'* hands. He rasped out an unamused breath and shook his head, his fingers rising to pinch into the corners of his eyes.

"I can't." He kept shaking his head, his fingers still trying to hold in his tears.

"Please?" I asked quietly, but the sound of my voice still seemed to rock him backward a step. Those tears spilled over his fingertips and he breathed out the shakiest breath I'd ever heard him expel. My gut twisted. "What's wrong?"

"What's wrong, Clem?" He breathed exasperatedly. He looked at me with sharp eyes, tears-stained cheeks be damned. A spark of familiarity shone in those eyes. My Ox, my stern no nonsense man. But he was crumbling under the weight of something else, something new.

It became clear that he wasn't going to come to me. He wasn't going to touch me or hold me or kiss me or do anything but stand there and stare at me from the doorway. So, just like with my brothers, I would push my own feelings aside and do something for him for once, goddammit. Even if I had to physically pick up my own legs with my shaky hands to swing them over the side of the hospital bed (which I did), I would do it.

"Don't stand," he said in more of an Ox voice.

"Don't tell me what to do, Oaxaca," I said as I did exactly what he'd told me not to and almost fell flat on my ass. Ox lunged for me, but the bed caught me first. Before I could even cry out or dwell on the jelly-like feeling of my legs, I was using my forearms to push up again.

The second time, I held my ground.

"Clementine, don't," he said again. But he'd halted in the middle of the room, his hands extended out to me but his body stopped at some sort of barrier he couldn't push himself through.

I stood straighter, squared my shoulders to him and took a step. He reached out further, but otherwise didn't move. I took another step and his foot twitched in response. "Clem, stop it now. You need to sit."

"No." I shook my head and continued my torturous walk toward him. He was only a handful of feet away, but the distance seemed like the furthest we'd ever been from each other. "Ox, no. I'm not going to sit down on that bed without you. I woke up for you."

"You what?"

"I woke up because you told me you wanted to kiss me, and you wanted to go places with me, and you wanted to give me a million babies." I stepped and stepped and stepped as I said the words to him. Already breathless but not thinking about stopping. *Never.* "I woke up because you told me things that you loved about me and I wanted to find out if you—"

I was close, just barely under him. He looked down on me, fire in his eyes as he grit his teeth. "If I what?"

"If you loved *me* too. Like I love you, Ox." I was looking up to him, set under his large body like I had been a couple of times before. But still not touching him.

His breath came out ragged like before and then he was closing those arms around me. Crushing me to him in a painful, constricting way. Digging his face into my neck, he buried himself there and shook. *Violently* shook as he murmured both in English and in Spanish and found ways to hold on to me tighter. I made shushing sounds and used my fingertips to rub lines up and down his back as he continued to breathe harshly. Silently crying and audibly apologizing. He apologized for letting this happen to me; he apologized for being so bossy; he apologized for not telling me his feelings; he apologized that I didn't have my million babies yet. He said sorry for things like letting my tea get cold or working too late or not figuring out my sleeping problems. He apologized for every tear that had ever left my body and every bad feeling I'd ever felt. He apologized for it all even when he'd done none of it.

Finally, after a long, long time—So long that doctors had come in only to silently back away. Ox's family had shown up running and breathless, only to have kept their distance, watching from outside the window. And someone dropped off a pan of food for lunch, even though it had been breakfast time when my brothers first came—Ox finally let me go. Slowly, he unraveled himself from around me, his hands staying on my shoulders as he looked at me from an arm's length away.

"I love you, Clementine. I think I've loved you from the moment you first spoke to me. All these other little pieces of you that you've given me have just solidified your place in my heart. Forever. *So, stop trying to get out of the deal early.*" I felt my face burn, or was that my eyes? My nose definitely burned as tears of my own stung my airways. Ox laughed a tired sound, but his mouth pulled up in a reluctant smile. He sniffed a little then used his sleeve to wipe my eyes. "Don't cry. Save your strength for more important things."

"My million babies?" I asked in a squeak. And he laughed outright, the last of his tears slipping from the corners of his eyes.

"I don't remember saying a million."

"You did."

"Fine," he said. "We might need to renegotiate our contract, though."

"Fuck the contract," I said, and he smiled again. He liked it when I talked like him, I'd noticed it before.

He wiped my eyes as tears kept flowing. And then when I was done, he gathered my face up in his hands and held me there as I just looked at him.

Until kisses started landing all over my skin. On my eyelids, on my cheekbones, on the corners of my mouth, on my mouth, at my earlobes and my neck and my forehead... *Everywhere.* And then his forehead came down to mine, and he breathed one long, deep breath. A breath that seemed to hold the weight of centuries on its back. When he cleared his throat and opened his mouth again, he was the Ox I knew before this. But softer in some ways.

He shook his head on mine. "My sweet, funny, infuriating, surprising, talented wife. *I love you.* But if you ever do something like this to me again, I'm going to have to kill you myself."

CLEMENTINE

Three Years Later.

It had been exactly three years since Ox and I had gotten married. Now, as we pulled up to a tall building in the middle of the city, I found myself getting a little nervous.

Earlier we'd walked along the sandy beach behind the house like we often did, and Ox had brought me to a pretty table he set up for an anniversary breakfast. He'd kissed me and whispered happy three years onto my lips as we snuggled close on the sand. It had been perfect.

But for some reason as we pulled up along the curb of the posh glass building, I felt a little unsure. I'd never seen this development before. I hadn't heard Ox or my brothers talk about it either. It looked like upscale apartments, much like the ones some of his family kept out here. His *single* family.

I must have just been sitting there, staring up at the structure, because Ox came around the car and opened my door for me, ushering me out. As soon as I was on my feet before him, he crushed his mouth down to mine, holding my face in his hands like he loved to do and kissing me deeply right there on the sidewalk for everyone to see.

When a moan escaped me, he pulled up just a breath away from my mouth and I could feel his smile. "Not here, naughty wife."

Before I could answer, he was pulling me forward into the glass building (which he had the key to) and toward the back of a partially done lobby area. From the looks of it, there were still finishes to be made in the pretty white space. There was still plastic along the walls and support beams and ladders leaned up against surfaces. But Ox walked as if he knew where he was going as he pushed open two large swinging doors along the back wall.

My breath caught when we entered the space. I held it as my steps stopped following Ox's and started around the room on their own.

It was a large studio kitchen. The far back was outfitted with a pretty orange tile backsplash above white sinks and counters. There were large kitchen appliances on the back countertops, all with the trademark scrawl Ox had taken to engraving my gifts with, and all the pretty pale orange that Ox loved to see me in. Hanging from a rack along the side wall were pots and pans and baking utensils and in front of it all was a huge island table.

I spun. Across the room, on the opposite side was a mirror set up. But instead of the island being regular height, it had varying pedestals with adjusted heights—perfect for photographing sweets at any angle. Above each set up was an orange neon sign that read:

Clementine's Kitchen.

And finally, on the side wall—the one that wasn't a wall completely made up of windows that let in a ton of natural light—were door sized blow ups of the covers for my three published cookbooks.

After I'd gotten out of the hospital all that time ago, Ox and the rest of my family (including my parents) refused to let me do anything strenuous for a long time. So, bed ridden and bored, I found myself playing around with the recipes and photographs I created in the months prior. That had eventually resulted in a manuscript and portfolio, and then later, a book deal. I'd gone on to publish two dessert cookbooks and one book on homemade tea blends.

The book on tea blends, my baby, was in the middle and blown up slightly larger than the others.

I turned to find Ox and the second we locked eyes, him across the room staring at me as he leaned against the tall island, he started walking toward me.

I ran. Crashing into him and wrapping my arms and legs around his body.

"What did you do?" I asked in between raining kisses down all over his person. I squealed excitedly and kissed him some more. "Ox, *what?*"

He squeezed me tightly to him and caught my last kiss, that was aimed for his nose, with his mouth. It wasn't much of a kiss though, because I couldn't stop smiling. Ox smiled too.

"As much as I love you wrapped around me, Lu, I need you on your feet for this." His deep voice sent chills up my body as he spoke directly onto my skin.

He kissed my temple and then moved to set me on my feet. When I landed, I took another look around the beautiful orange-sickle looking room and broke out into another grin. When I met Ox's gaze again, his eyes were dancing.

He stepped forward and held his hands out to me, I placed mine in his and attempted to close in for more contact, but he held me at an arm's length.

"*Hold on,*" he chided gently.

My smile simmered to a closed mouth grin and I peeked around myself again jiggling and bouncing in excitement. "What is all this Ox? *Thank you*, but you know you didn't need to do any of it. I was fine with just using the rental kitchen."

"I did," he started. He was silent for a little while before taking a deep whooshing breath and squaring his shoulders, as if readying himself. My smile fell a little as I took in his stance.

"Ox?"

"Clem, it's finally been three years —"

"*Finally?*" I asked, immediately offended.

He cleared his throat, "And now that our agreement is over—"

Terms of Inheritance

"*Over!*" I ripped my hands away from his and took a step backward, looking at him like he had lost his mind.

Was he kidding? Sure, the allotted time for our arrangement was over, but our contract had been voided a long time ago. Three great years of '*I love you's*' and '*we belong together's*', and he was saying that this was over?

"*Clementine,*" Ox's stern, but soft voice snapped me out of my maddening thoughts and back to what was happening. He'd grabbed onto my shoulders to hold me in place. "*Listen.*"

I rolled my lips in between my teeth and bore my eyes into his letting him know I was listening, and whatever he had to say had better be good.

All of my angry thoughts immediately turned to mush as I watched him go from standing over me to kneeling before me, his hands taking mine once again. My eyes were wide as they took in his amused ones. He knew what he was doing to me, but I had no idea what was going on.

"Clementine, it's finally been three years and our agreement is over," he started again, glaring at me pointedly to let him continue this time. I was as quiet as a mouse looking at him in front of me down on one knee. "And now that it is, I can finally ask you to be my wife in truth."

Air left me in a harsh exhale. *Was he proposing?*

"I love you. I tell you every morning and every night and every chance I get in between and somehow, it's still not enough. I want to give you everything I can—everything I have, and while I know you'll cherish this space, like you do everything else I offer, it still isn't enough.

"I want to give myself to you, Clem. *Fully.* So, from today on, I am yours. No contracts, no wills, no one else involved. I know you're my wife and I've already asked you to marry me, but I never want to take a choice away from you again."

429

He cleared his throat and adjusted himself on his knee. He was nervous. I wanted to throw myself at him right then and there.

"You have my ring, you have my name, you have my heart. And I'm running out of things to give you." He blinked around us, looking at the space we were in before he looked up at me with flaming intensity. But there was vulnerability in his gaze too. It made me want to wrap my arms around him and tell him he didn't need to say any of this. But I was also loving it too much to stop him. "Will you have my life? Will you *share* my life, forever with yours?"

"Ox," I whispered. Bending down, I kneeled on both my knees, bringing us to the same level. Then I took his face in my hands. "You have my heart, you have my love, you have my *life*. Forever."

The smile that spread across his face was brilliant and bright and happy. He gazed at me with my favorite expression in his eyes. Love and mischief.

"Then can you do something for me?" he asked.

"What now?" I growled as I moved in closer to him, wrapping my arms around his neck and angling my lips just over his. I smiled, running my nose along his nose, brushing our lips along each other's.

"Can you *please* make me the goddamn flan already?" he growled back.

I laughed in full, and he brought his lips up to meet mine. I kissed him fiercely, pouring every ounce of emotion I had into our mouths as we kneeled together in each other's arms. The touch of his lips was just as electric as they were the first time we'd kissed. The touch of his tongue was even better as it tangled with mine, tasting like his favorite candy. *Orange cream.*

It only took my hands grazing once through his short, dark hair to get him groaning into my mouth. I couldn't help my smile. "How about here, naughty husband?"

He groaned again and pulled me close against his hard body.

And every kiss, every touch, every breath he gave me, was perfect.

Acknowledgements

To all my new friends—My beautiful, amazing, trusting new readers. Thank you for allowing me to take you on this journey. Thank you for taking a chance on my words. Welcome to my mind, it's a wild and inconsistent place.

To my family, my team—Thank you for listening to me obsess over details so small they became big again. Thank you for reading and re-reading and reading again. Thank you for your crazy ideas that sometimes miss but oftentimes hit. And thank you for your undying and never-ending support.

To my husband—Thank you for being hilarious and bringing light into some of the most frustrating times throughout this process. Thank you for sharing your culture with me and bringing me into your amazing family with no questions asked. Thank you for being you.

To my beta readers—Thank you for putting up with my million and one questions. Thank you for volunteering to meet my characters before anyone else would. And thank you so much for pointing out that one weird thing in that one weird scene. The book is better for it.

To Cindy—Thank you sooooo much for hyping me up. Your support and feedback have meant the world to me, and I cannot express how blown away I am by your kindness! You are the best.

To Kasryn—Thank you for being my VERY first reader. You

wouldn't believe how incredibly excited I was when you started the book. Yor feedback has been invaluable, and you'll always have that number one spot.

To my friends—Thank you for gasping loudly every time I mentioned I was writing a book, you guys would support me in anything. Thank you for being my ride or dies. Don't cringe too hard at the cheesy romance parts. *Love you.*

To my future—Thank you for continuing to excite me. I can't wait to see what you hold.

To God—Thank you for your plan. I trust it implicitly.

About the Author

Adorabol (Dori) is an avid lover of romance. She's a chronic binge watcher of TV dramas and loves curling up just about anywhere with a good book (preferably on the floor). The only thing she loves more than seeing a good love story, is creating one.

Dori has spent most of her life playing out stories in her head. She started writing in grade school, where she would pass her notebook around to her friends during lunch as they begged her for more chapters. Now, she hopes to pass her stories along to even more eager readers.

WANT MORE FROM THIS AUTHOR?

You can find more of this author and more on Seaside, Rhode Island in the next installment of the Seaside Mergers Series, Rules of Association.

Made in the USA
Coppell, TX
22 December 2024